Frantic in
Fiji...
and other ports of call

MIMZI
SCHRADI

Eagle Feather Press
2016

ISBN: 1537463616
ISBN 13: 9781537463612
Library of Congress Control Number: 2016914958
CreateSpace Independent Publishing Platform
North Charleston, South Carolina

"*Men at some time are masters of their fates:*
The fault, dear Brutus, is not in our stars,
But in ourselves, that we are underlings.
Brutus and Caesar: what should be in that 'Caesar'?
Why should that name be sounded more than yours?
Write them together, yours is as fair a name;
Sound them, it doth become the mouth as well;
Weigh them, it is as heavy; conjure with 'em,
Brutus will start a spirit as soon as Caesar.
Now, in the names of all the gods at once,
Upon what meat doth this our Caesar feed...?
...O, you and I have heard our fathers say,
There was a Brutus once that would have brook'd
The eternal devil to keep his state in Rome..."

Cassius—*Act I scene ii*—Julius Caesar *by William Shakespeare*

Other Works by Mimzi Schradi

PsyChic in Seattle: Volume I (Angelina Seraphina Series). Eagle Feather Press, Seattle, WA. 2012.

"Things I Forgot that I Loved", "I Knew You When", "A Spirit Song of Body and Soul" (Poetry) in *Tales for a Lazy Afternoon*, an anthology of the Skagit Valley Writers League, Armchair ePublishing. Anacortes, WA. 2014.

The "It" Girl in *Detective Ink*, a collection of detective adventures co-authored with Susan Wingate, Terry Persun, Michael Hiebert and Jeff Ayers. (e-book). Friday Harbor, WA. 2015.

Author's Note

Writing, for me, has always been about story. When I was young, I loved listening to stories told by my dad, the self-appointed storyteller in our family. He has passed many of his storytelling talents on to his children, grandchildren and great grandchildren.

From him, my humor springs forth and I infuse it into my writing whenever possible. Most of my novels are character-driven, but the story comes first. There must be a reason for writing. My stories speak from my heart—which drives the characters to come forth and take over. Then the characters come alive. They speak from their inner beings and let the readers know what makes them tick.

Stories also are universal. They are told in many places and many times by different people, yet they have connecting threads and designs, although they may be ages apart.

Perhaps George Balanchine said it best:

"You must go through tradition, absorb it, and become, in a way, a reincarnation of all the artistic periods that have come before you... We all live in the same time forever. There is no future and there is no past." (George Balanchine as quoted in "Balanchine Said" by Arlene Croce, *The New Yorker*. January 26, 2009.)

Acknowledgements and Thanks to...

The Sno-Island Writers, all experts in their chosen fields of writing, for helping me with revisions and for specifics on flying and sailing. Your knowledge of nature, people, places and things mechanical are indispensible. You are beacons in the darkness...

The Skagit Valley Writers League for always being a source of inspiration and spirit...

The Whidbey Writers who have been with me since day one...

My family and friends on the East Coast—you are loved. Distance does not keep us apart...

My brother, Ken, for sharing his time and his beautiful state with me, for taking me *safely* on the Cliff Walk and for showing me around Newport, Jamestown, Providence and Wickford. Also, for introducing me to boating on the coastal waters of Rhode Island—and for being just a phone call away...

My most precious GMBRS on the East Coast for editing tips and enduring friendships...

My friend and colleague, Elizabeth, for tackling the bulk of the editing—your dedication to the word and the intricacies of writing are treasured...

My Pacific Northwest family, Dara, Karl, Brett and Jared, Sean and Tany, and my many friends in the Pacific Northwest for their strength and encouragement—you are loved and always close to my heart and home...

Remember, artists everywhere, as you keep your feet on the ground, turn your eyes to the sky. Anything is possible if you can imagine it. Dream on, embrace the words of Emily Dickinson: *Hope is the thing with feathers...*

And fly away to that magic place in the sky, where you are your own creation.

Chapter One

"To be—*hedonistic*—or not to be, that is the question." Apologies to Shakespeare's *Hamlet*, but where I am now on Mamanucas Island, I want to stay forever. Yes, forever in Fiji, heaven in the South Pacific. Heck, Paul Gauguin basked in the sun in Tahiti, and look where it got him—famous artist. Good things happen here. Maybe Walter would want to live here. I want to live here.

Our bungalow at the Castaway Island Resort includes a private pool and sits above a secluded beach. Natural vegetation surrounds our habitat and shields us from any curious eyes. At poolside this morning, soft breezes, blue skies and warm sun greet me as they have every morning of our honeymoon. I hold my breath, not wanting to say goodbye to our island paradise. As I exhale, I think of the stars in the late evening saying goodnight to me, and Walter—always Walter, whose scent mingles with the delicious orchids surrounding our villa, whose lean muscular body makes me salivate, wanting more. How I love his body pressed against mine.

I remove my robe, shiver momentarily, naked before the world and test the water with my toe. I glance up at an orange dove, perched on a lone palm, cooing mournfully for his mate. I sigh and slip into the pool. The warm water, fresh and clean, heated by the morning sun, caresses my body. Ah, medicine for the soul. Holding my breath, I dive under the water.

Returning to the surface of my morning panacea, I notice the dove's mate, a dark-green female, swoop down to join her feathered friend. They nestle their yellow heads together in greeting and the bright orange male places a treat in his beloved's beak. I think of dinner with Walter, and how he shares his spring rolls with me. I can't help but grin.

The sun peeks out from behind a cloud, the first cloud to appear since we've been here. These wonderful days spent in this paradise just wet my appetite. I am not ready to return to civilization. Not yet. Maybe we could come back. Yes, I'll make Walter promise, on our anniversary. How weird is that? We've been married such a short time and I'm thinking anniversary. I've got to get back in the present, live in the moment. If I go anywhere else in time, I get in trouble. I definitely want to stay out of trouble. Had enough this past year to last a lifetime.

After swimming a few laps, I switch to the backstroke. I feel a familiar twinge and then hear a popping sound, the after-effects of a torn rotator cuff. Against all efforts to block two monsters from my memory, Sylvan Sargento and his brother, Adolphus reappear. I don't want to re-visit the past, not on my honeymoon.

I dive under the water to escape flashbacks of last winter's trauma and swim beneath the surface with ease, back and forth until I run out of air. Upon resurfacing, I breathe in the fresh air surrounding me and return to the present. I feel nothing but tremendous gratitude for my life and Walter. Yes, life is good and I plan to keep it that way. No more bad thoughts. No more nightmares, just the present.

I swim a few more laps, then climb the four steps out of the pool, put on my terry robe and shake out my tangerine sun-streaked hair. Yes, right now, life is excellent and I cannot wait another minute to feast my eyes on Walter.

I hasten up to the ten steps to the veranda, open the bedroom door and tiptoe into our boudoir. There lies Walter, his baby blues closed, his body reclining on one side, my friend and lover grasping a pillow and breathing softly. I touch his cheek. Before me lies a perfect specimen of man, his only cover being the downy soft black hair curling over his forehead and the matching hair covering his sinuous chest. In his dream state, he flashes a boyish smile, displaying his dimples, both on his face and...well, never mind. My libido aroused, I attempt to entice him into a compromising position. Walter starts to lean towards me and then falls back on the bed, like an iron weight is pressed on his chest. He is in a slumber so deep, so sound that I give up my advances. Poor Adonis needs his rest. He and I did keep each other up most of last night, and the nights before that...

My stomach growls and interrupts my intimate memories. After my "early bird" swim, I possess an irresistible craving for an espresso and some nourishment.

Opening my dresser drawer—my cleverly converted barista's supply closet—I pull out my portable espresso maker, which Walter bought for me in REI, in case we do some overnight hiking in the wilderness. No muss, no fuss. I spoon some Camano Island Roasters coffee into the top of my portable camp-style device. Then I pour the cold water in and heat it on the electric stovetop in our miniscule kitchen until it steams and drips down into my small espresso cup.

One luxury from Washington State that I cannot do without is my morning cappuccino. Although the local coffee in Fiji is strong and hearty, Papua New Guinea is my favorite blend and challenges the best coffee around the world. I'm not a snob, just honest. Walter and I discovered this organic blend in a quaint coffee house, while on an art tour on Camano Island located about two hours north of Seattle's Queen Anne neighborhood. That island also seems like stepping into another world, but not so far away. Peaceful. Calm. Quiet. No freeways. Needless to say I'm hooked, both on island living and coffee. Wouldn't mind vacationing there soon. Plus, it's much closer to our home and just across the water from Whidbey Island, where my mom now lives, with "her Charles".

Removing a small bottle from the tiny fridge, I pour some organic milk in a small pitcher and steam it until it foams. I add one cube of brown and molasses sugar and begin to salivate. How I love the smell of fresh-brewed coffee. After topping my prized beverage off with a Fiji sweet roll, I consider myself in business, another piece of heaven on earth. Doesn't get much better than this: Walter, Fiji and cappuccino.

I smell my black and white elixir and groan involuntarily, feeling refreshed by the little necessities of life. *"Thank You, God, for the coffee bean plant."* Sitting down on the bed next to Walter, I place my hand on his cheek and smile. As I contemplate what we might do today, perhaps take a final stroll on the beach and pick up a few more dozen shells for keepsakes, a phone rings—the resort phone.

Now who would be calling us at this hour? It's still kind of early. I look at the clock on the television screen. "Eight o'clock." Now that's way too early for the resort staff to be calling to remind us of our checkout tonight. They are undoubtedly all asleep. They are so laid back and they do like to party at night. I can hear their merriment, and all the music pulsating between our naps, between Walter and me...

"Ring...ring..."

The phone chimes in my ear like an annoying bug. Somewhere in the recesses of my mind a voice tells me to ignore it, that I don't want to answer this one. But being sleep deprived and knowing Walter needs to snooze a little longer, I ignore my intuition, stand up and grab the receiver. I sigh, not wanting to make contact with the outside world. I take a deep breath and make my voice as cheerful as possible despite my resentment over this unwelcome interruption of my morning meditation.

"Welcome to Fiji."

A gravelly voice responds, "I did it."

"Did what?"

"You know..."

"Who is this?" I ask as I stir my coffee and take a sip of the heavenly blend.

"You know, Babe. Don't get cute with me."

"Give me a clue."

"Steve. Your buddy."

"*Steve?* Sorry, I didn't recognize your voice." I sigh in relief, take another sip of my cappuccino, and a bite from my sweet roll, and think, *"So, there's nothing to worry about, after all."*

Then I add aloud, "You sound a little hoarse, good buddy."

"And you sound happy, for a change."

I smile and reminisce as the wonderful days and nights with Walter on our own special island return to my thoughts. "I'm always happy, Steve..."

"You could have fooled me, Sweetheart. But listen, this will grab you. I've been working late and I've been wading in the water, if you know what I mean..."

"No, I don't know what you mean."

Funny, Steve hasn't called me Sweetheart since he and Walter almost got into fisticuffs over his use of that word towards me.

I continue with a question of my own. "Steve, have you been to the ocean with Suzy?"

"Don't get cute, doll. You know where I've been."

"Boating? Did you go to the San Juans?"

"Listen, Sweetheart, I only did what you told me to do, and it didn't involve no Sam Juan."

"For Pete's sake, Steve, I only told you to give Suzy a chance. I thought you liked her."

"The boat's not named Suzy."

"Well, I wouldn't call Suzy a boat."

"That's because she's a yacht, and her name's Mercedes. You know that. You are the one who told me..."

"Oh, Steve, I don't know what you're talking about and I think I'm mixed up..."

"Isn't a little early there to be hitting the sauce, doll?"

Okay. Now I am beginning to get really confused. I stop speaking and think perhaps I am talking to an idiot, an idiot who sounds like Walter's cop buddy, best man at our wedding and whose name is also Steve. Perhaps I just presumed Steve is still dating Suzy, my bridesmaid, after noticing how lovey-dovey the two of them acted at our wedding.

I decide to set things straight. "Steve—you are *my Steve*, aren't you?"

"Now quit playing games, Evaline. Of course I'm your ol' buddy, Steve. And I've got really good news for you."

"You do?" I sit back down on the bed next to Walter and place my arm on my sleeping prince, in need of his support.

I am getting a really bad feeling about this whole conversation.

I start to shiver as I realize that this phantom on the phone is not Walter's buddy, Steve, and I'm no Evaline. This "Steve", although he sounds exactly like Walter's police buddy, New York accent and all, is a stranger to me—a wrong number.

With a burst of strength I stand up, ready to give the chump this bulletin. But before I can speak, he knocks my socks off.

"The guv'ner's on ice."

"What?" I gasp and sit back down on the bed. My hand shakes, violently this time and almost drops the phone.

5

"He's nadda—Missin'. But they'll find him soon—in the *Drink*. Soon to be washed ashore, along with his Mercedes."

I hear this strange Steve laughing, a sinister, high-pitched laugh, a ghoul in a horror film. My shoulders shudder and despite my cold hands, I begin to sweat.

"He'll be all wrapped up in sheets and the main sail—a real nice package for you, Eveline—dead as a doornail. You get?"

"Oh, *the governor*. Of course, I get." I pronounce like a puppet. Other body parts join my shoulders in shaking. A familiar icy chill, a chill that consumes me when I talk to creeps, starts invading my being.

"Watch the evening news, Eveline. You'll know for sure then."

"I'm in Fiji," I whisper, the only words that come out of my mouth.

"Oh, of course, my pet, you're on your little vacation. Good cover. I knew that. That's okay. I'll delay the revelation a couple of days. But hurry back to The States. I can't keep your prize in deep water forever. His good looks might fade."

I hear a chuckling, then a louder cackle—*Steve* finding amusement in his own sick joke.

My babbling begins. "Yeah, his good looks. Un huh. I guess...you're right."

The sweating resumes and my palms turn clammy.

"So, Eveline, when do I get my payoff?" Mystery Steve asks.

Gasping for air, I can hardly breathe. Time to end the call.

I whisper, "When I see the news."

I place the receiver on its cradle like it is a foreign object and wipe my hands on a nearby towel; I want to get the sweat and appalling message out of my body. Subconsciously thinking my hands are the carriers of the grim news, I walk into the bathroom and wash them, three times. Covering my face with a warm wet washcloth, I wonder how in the world I could answer this Steve, how I could speak to him at all.

I remove the washcloth and look at my reflection in the mirror and for a moment, I don't recognize myself. I see my own person on a different body of water, in a different place. I close my eyes. The vision begins to fade as my body starts to shake. In an attempt to come to grips with what's just happened, I splash water on myself again. Realizing that this strange conversation is the culmination of another one of my nightmares, I decide

I want no part in this unsolved mystery. But by just speaking with this Steve, I am already involved.

Why didn't I just hang up?

Leaving the bathroom in a daze, I return to the bedroom and sit down next to Walter. I lift my morning espresso to my lips and then place it on the bedside table. It is as cold as my fingertips. My interest in drinking my morning delight deteriorates, along with my desire to remain forever in Fiji. Standing up, my thoughts turn to fleeing to anywhere but "Almost Paradise", away from my ominous caller, away from another encounter with the seedy side of life. I don't want another Adolphus Sargento breathing down my neck. Murder is not my business.

My body trembles as I shake my love with what energy I have left. "Walter, please! Wake up! You have to get up. You have to listen to me."

"No more, Anglina," Walter mumbles, as he puts the pillow over his head and moans. "No more. A guy's gotta sleep. I'm so tired. Give me a break, love. Your bridegroom's exhausted."

"Walter, you don't understand. I need you…"

"I know, my sweet bride, my lovely Angelina. I need you too, but give me an hour…maybe two…maybe four. Yes, four. I'll be at peak performance then."

Walter takes the pillow off his head, rolls over on his back and smiles, eyes still closed, dead to the world. I kiss his cheek and, in spite of the rising bile in my throat and the grumbling in the pit of my stomach, my mouth forms a smile. My sweetheart's batteries need to recharge. In his exhausted state, there is no way he can perceive what I am trying to dump on him. Frantic or not, I've got no choice. I've got to take care of this mess myself.

Returning to the bathroom, I shower like a bird in a rainstorm, shivering the entire time, despite the hot water. I cannot get the chill out of my bones. After turning off the water and stepping out of the shower, I dry myself on one of the Turkish towels our first class resort provides. I scramble into the bedroom to throw some threads on my body, for the first time in three days. I slip on my Nike running shoes, kiss Walter goodbye, first on his upturned lips and then on his closed eyelids, and race out the door.

After climbing down the slope of our cottage hide-away, I jog full speed down the steep, sandy hill, hell-bent to visit the manager's office on the marina. As I zigzag along the winding path, the lingering scent of gardenias consumes me, momentarily. Cupid's flowers beg me to return to the sanctuary of our bungalow, our *Frangipani Bure*. I ignore their warning. Waiting is not on my list of skills. No patience. In my panic, only one thought captivates my mind—find out where this femme fatale, Evaline, is staying. What I will do with that information, I haven't got a clue.

Chapter Two

I jog at a steady pace until I spot the marina. Shifting into hyper mode, I begin running with all my might. My adrenalin kicks in and my body seems to fly down the wooden planks towards my destination. That is until I reach the cross section between the boardwalk and the dock. Fastening my sight on the manager's office, I neglect to spot a few beach walkers ambling up the walkway towards the resort lanai. The lanai is attached to the indoor dining room of Castaway Island Resort, and many vacationers eat lunch and dinner there. Not Walter and I. We spend most of the time together, hiding out in our own separate paradise.

A tall, well-endowed lady attempts, without success, to balance a Piña Colada, as she struts along in her elevated sandals. Her drink topples into the sand—mainly because I crash into her stomach—accidently of course. Two men rush to steady the woman and prevent her from tumbling into the sand along with the cocktail. The young men appear to be locals, dressed in canvas shoes, white shorts and floral shirts with white shell necklaces—just like me. *Hum, these guys could be my wardrobe twins.* They wear their thick black hair long, like I do, although the color of my hair is tangerine. One of the dudes wears his locks in a ponytail and he displays a distinguished air, oozing confidence and pride as he attends to the moaning damsel-in-distress. The other one picks up her belongings, that clumsy me knocked in the sand. He holds her arms as if protecting her from disaster.

I languish in a thorny wild berry patch nearby and lie there, helpless, listening to a lot of cursing and swearing flowing from a female voice, not mine. Little does this grating voice realize, that in an effort to avoid knocking her—the "delicate damsel"—down, I have sacrificed my own body to the thorns, my penance for running in the cross walk.

I open my mouth to apologize for not paying attention, but before I can get one word out, the "lady", while smoothing out her beauty salon coiffeur, continues hurling a barrage of insults directed at me, including some choice four-letter words. She concludes her tirade with a barking order to Mr. Ponytail. Under her slurred words, I detect a Northeastern U.S. accent. All the while the smell—a mixture of whiskey and expensive perfume—emanates from her personage and creeps over to my bed of thorns. This is no lady, but a vulture, someone who can eat her prey and spit it out.

The hair on my arms quiver when she flares her nostrils and shouts, "Kahani, if you can't control your help, please fire them. You don't need the likes of this tramp running around tormenting your guests!"

At this point I feel like the poor bull in the Seville Plaza del Toros. No mercy cast down to losers. In this woman's mind, I am the loser and she, the victor. I would not like to get into an arena with her. I can see her claws. Bright red long fingernails, certainly not as long as the fingernails of Adolphus Sargento, my old nemesis, but just as dangerous. Better to stay clear of this floozy, and the further away, the better. My nightmares of Adolphus serve their purpose, warning me to stay away from any psychopaths I may encounter in the future.

Kahani, whom I presume to be the manager at the resort, replies to the manic matador in a soothing voice, "Please, Madam, don't be upset. Mahani will get you another drink. I will talk to this girl."

Kahani nods towards me with his last spoken phrase and then focuses his attention back on "Madam". "Please, Madam, my staff will accompany you to your guest quarters. They will carry your shopping bags and other belongings. Not to worry. We will take care of things. And if you like, I will personally deliver our luncheon special to your villa, compliments of the resort."

"Hum. Well, all right, Kahani, but no raw fish. I don't want heartburn. Knock twice and I'll know it is you. I don't like to open the door for strangers. And make sure you speak to your help, and I mean speak to her."

"Madam" glares at me for a second, then secures her red and black flowered sarong around her torso, places her black straw hat on her head and struts up the stone path to a villa overlooking the beach and the resort's lanai. No doubt she likes being near instant room service. She carries a black woven Gucci beach bag and wears oversized silver and black designer sunglasses. Her crimson bikini peeking through the sarong matches the burnt red on her lips and nails. Her dyed jet-black hair flows freely around her face, hiding the rest of her features. However, I sense a partition of artificial body parts, which indicates lots of plastic surgery—nose job, boob job, probably a chin job. No doubt her plastic surgeon enjoyed a few tropical vacations thanks to her. Seems this senora likes to be in charge and if she doesn't like something or someone, she changes it or disposes of it, pronto.

I think I have become a person on her list of things to eradicate. Suddenly I feel a great deal of empathy for the support staff at Castaway Island Resort. If they have to put up with hotel guests like her on a daily basis, no wonder they get drunk and party all night. On the other hand, I feel complimented—My physically fit body, South Pacific tan and native outfit just happens to complement Kahani's—and this woman thinks me native to Fiji. The people here are so beautiful and pleasant I would not mind being native to this country, this paradise.

My mental wandering returns to my present mission as Kahani extends his arm to me, revealing his soothing, strong voice.

"*Bula.*"

Bula is the local greeting for hello. I echo his greeting as he helps me up out of the sticker bushes. I dust the sand and stickers off my shorts, and feel the manager's eyes, black and piercing, staring at me. Kahani raises his slightly bushy eyebrows and asks in perfect English, "Who are you, Miss? I don't recognize you."

I glance at the pathway that leads to the larger *Bures*, the private houses, set a little ways back from the main resort area, and wait for "Madam" to disappear into one of them. Only then do I answer. "Call me Tangie. That's short for Angelina. And I'm sorry, I am not part of your staff."

"That I surmised on my own."

"But you went along and let that woman insult you and your resort."

"It happens. I just let her vent. She'll be over it soon enough. Plus, if I *fire you*, she will be happy and all will be well again."

"So you know I am not staff."

"I know my staff."

11

"And you don't know me."

"I do now. Your name is Tangie. Like the fruit."

"Yeah, that's my nickname."

"I am assuming you are a guest that I have not yet met."

"I am. I am staying at the *Frangipani Bure* at the far end, the one with the private pool."

"Ah, our luxury hideaway."

"Yes. My husband has good taste, and we like the privacy."

"Ah, then you are newlyweds. But you, you are so young."

I smile. "Yes, newlyweds. This is our honeymoon."

"I am sorry for your fall. But tell me, why are you trying to break the speed limit out here? Is something wrong? Do you need anything?"

"Well, *yes* and *no*. I received an upsetting phone call. I was rushing to the marina office."

"I am sorry for that. Are you all right, Ms. Tangie?"

"Me, yes. Not so good for someone else."

"For that I am sorry."

"Speaking of sorry, would you mind telling me *Madam's* name? I'd like to send her an apology."

Kahani stares at me, studying my eyes and face, listening as I ramble. He sees through my storytelling, I'm sure. I'm not a very good liar. Certain people catch on right away, like Kahani. He senses something about me, and my story. Of that I'm certain. Kahani is one of those people. He may appear laid back and calm, but he emits an air of depth, an understanding of people, places and circumstances.

He flexes his muscles and gently takes my hand. I feel his strength through his soft strong grip and his hand makes mine seem like a doll's. He studies my palm for a while, then stares, questioning me with his eyes as he answers my question. "You ran into Evalina Carboni. Her husband is a rising politician in your country, so she says. She is what you call, a ladder climber. Is that what you want to know?"

"Evalina," I whisper as I ponder the name. *Not Evaline, but close enough.*

"Do you know her? Have you two met before?"

"No, I never met her." My voice trembles at first, betraying my motives. I feel my inner strength returning as my voice resumes its natural cadence.

"I do not know her. I never saw her before today but our names are similar. My full name is Angelina Seraphina-Cunningham. I think someone mistook me for her earlier today."

"Ah," Kahani's eyes twinkle as he begins to understand my distress. "That explains the disturbing telephone call." He smiles, displaying brilliant teeth. "Let me guess: Someone from the United States of America called her and complained about her temper, probably her husband or another gentleman, then began ranting."

I start fidgeting, unable to speak, struggling for an answer.

"And you, Tangie, got the call by mistake."

I exhale and nod, feeling somewhat dishonest, but relieved to find a way out of answering his questions. I bow my head and whisper, "Something like that."

I can't look Kahani straight in the eye. He understands me and I don't want to give too much away. It's bad enough I'm involved in this mess. No sense getting him mixed up in it. What could he do?

Kahani brushes a few leaves out of my hair. "It happens in the hospitality business every so often. I'm afraid one of my staff routed the call to you by mistake. I am truly sorry."

I nod, grateful for his explanation. "So, that is what happened to me." Close enough. His summary should suffice, and keep me out of trouble my last day at Castaway Island Resort.

I study Kahani's towering golden mocha body, a body so delicious I imagine his many girlfriends like to squeeze and caress his muscles. I smile at my innocent informant and begin a supplication in my "poor lil' ol' me" convincing way. "Say Kahani, could you please keep this conversation between us? I don't think...I don't want...to have another encounter with Ms. Eveline, er, Mrs. Evelina Carboni. She's liable to accuse me of interfering in her life or spying on her or something ridiculous like that. Heck, I don't even know the woman. And I don't want to know her."

"Nor do I want to incite her wrath upon me or the desk clerks. They have enough trouble as it is with all the intercontinental calls coming in at all hours. I say, let this one rest. My lips are sealed. Yes, I am thinking it would be better if you do not contact her."

"You are so right, Kahani. Thanks for your advice."

Kahani takes my hand. "No, let me say, *vinaka*, for you being so understanding and for being such a delightful guest. You are one spunky lady. I regret I did not get to meet you sooner. Hope the rest of your stay here is pleasurable."

"Unfortunately my husband and I will be leaving this evening. Our time on your beautiful island retreat is almost over."

"I hope you will return another day," Kahani answers with a voice as smooth as my favorite wine. Before he releases my hand, he caresses it ever so softly, like he is holding a rare jewel. I feel myself blushing.

"I hope so, too," I murmur, enchanted by his touch. I grin, intoxicated by his charm.

"Oh, one more thing, Tangie..." Kahani resumes his grip on my hand in a protective manner. "Mrs. Carboni is departing this evening as well. Perhaps you would be better to stay out of her way."

"You can count on it. I will keep a distance and make sure she doesn't recognize me. Thanks for clueing me in, Kahani."

"You are most welcome. *Ni sa moce*, Tangie, until we meet again."

"*Ni sa moce*, Kahani."

Kahani releases my hand and bows. Then he saunters back to the resort lanai to order lunch for Evalina Carboni. Some people are givers. Some people are takers. Kahani, without a doubt is a giver. Evaline, a taker, and from what I've discovered in the past hour, the last thing she probably took might be an innocent person's life. What I will do with this bit of information is a mystery to me, a mystery that without a doubt will get me into a whooping amount of trouble.

I peer at the manager's office on the marina. No sense heading that way anymore. Seems I have accumulated more information in this one chance encounter than I ever could from questioning resort security. If I visit them, they will no doubt detain me in Fiji, and give me the third degree. I need to get back to The States. I need to listen to the news. I need to contact someone I can trust with this story, someone like "our Steve" from the Seattle Police Department.

I'll talk to Walter first. He'll know what to do, for sure. And if he tells me to forget the whole thing, I am on my own. But knowing him, and knowing myself, we will be in this together, despite my desire to run like crazy the other way.

Chapter Three

As I walk back to our *bure*, our haven away from the world of crime and the unpleasantries of life, I feel the ocean breeze caress my face and evaporate the building anxiety stemming from my encounter with Evalina Carboni. I meditate on the beauty of the sea and take a deep breath. Relaxed and empowered, I exhale and recite to myself: "You cannot escape from the real world any more than you can escape from yourself, Tangie."

Sometimes I hate being a psychic. I know these things that I must do, and I just don't want to do them. Like go home. Look for Evaline's victim, "the guv'ner". I must check the newscasts and find out about the victim's family, how they are doing and how I can help. I know I'm now involved in this situation, and yet I don't want to be part of this sordid tale. Why can't I have a light airy homecoming? Like Walter and I, together as a couple, planning our future, enjoying my family's happiness for us. Why, for the love of all things sacred, do I have to be burdened with crime and the likes of Evalina Carboni?

Well, I know one thing. I am determined to stay as far away from Evalina/Evaline, "the bitch", Carboni as possible. If she can have a governor knocked off, just think what she could do with an ordinary citizen, like me. Careful is now my middle name. I must remember to proceed at a snail's pace and recognize when it is time to call in the professionals. "But," I ask myself, "Will the police believe me? And whom can I trust? In whom can I confide?" Walter, of course—for one—of course, I'll start with Walter."

17

Hate to burden him during our idyllic escape from the real world, but he's my man and he took that vow "for better or worse". Poor guy, he didn't think "the worse" would come the final day of our honeymoon.

On a whim I divert from the path to our cottage, kick off my canvas sneakers and climb down to the beach. Don't want to go and disturb Walter quite yet. I need to think. The waves start kicking up a bit and I can see a catamaran off shore, too far in the distance to notice me taking off my shell necklace, my flowered shirt, tank top, and dusty white shorts. I plunge into the water, cool and refreshing, and feel like a new person in one fell swoop.

Diving under the water, I wash the smell of Evalina's heavy lingering perfume off my body and when I come up for air, the waves obliterate her beady piercing eyes from my sight. I feel only the blue-green water on my skin and I smell only the salty sea—tonic for my soul. I swim out a little farther and decide to float. I can meditate here a long time and not be bored a bit. Just Mother Nature and me, communing with life. I lie on top of the water bobbing like a toy boat for about twenty minutes, taking in the serenity and beauty of Mamanucas Island, where Castaway Island Resort is situated. I look at the island in the distance and faintly hear a familiar voice shouting my name.

"Tangie! Are you all right? Be careful I'm coming to get you."

"Ah, Walter." What is he doing here? I thought he needed to sleep. But here he is on a surfboard paddling out to rescue me. Little does he know the water is not my enemy; I've got worse problems than a few white caps. I wave to him and smile, but I am sure he just sees my hand gesture and not my smile. I sense panic creeping into him and notice his intense movements. His gestures become more agitated so I smile as wide as I can to reassure him I am safe. I start swimming in his direction, feeling perfectly at peace in my little world in the sea. As I get closer, I see him point feverishly behind me. I turn around and catch a glimpse of a wave, gigantic and hovering. On instinct, I take a long deep breath and dive under the water just before the monstrous wave comes crashing down, yet still crushing me with all its force into the sea floor below. I roll over and over, tossed around like a wet noodle on a fork. Holding my breath and waiting endlessly for the thrashing to stop and for the wave to pass over me, I try to relax and flow with the current, knowing the undertow will go easier on me that way. The wave finishes its punishing force, quits whipping me about and leaves me alone on the beach like a broken seashell.

I crawl up to the dry sand so the next wave will not cart me away back into the sea. My eyes, slit and sandy, comb the beach for Walter. He is nowhere to be seen. A panicky feeling takes a hold of me. Surveying the following waves for my soul mate, I start screaming, "Walter! Walter, where are you?"

Pulling myself up, I hobble like a seagull with one leg and pace back and forth along the surf, hugging my shoulder, that by now is throbbing from the thrashing in the surf, and search for a sign of Walter. Nothing.

Turning from the shore I search the sea and spot a surfboard bobbing on the water, about 200 yards out, just a surfboard, no Walter. "My God! He killed himself trying to save me from a rogue wave! Somebody, help!"

There is no one in sight. My stomach constricts; I tumble to the sand and become a cast-off sea creature. My hair is matted with sand and my body is encrusted with tiny shells, hanging like earrings and a necklace, on my scraped-up skin. What a mess. I can't breathe. I can't cry.

The rogue wave's brothers form in the distance like an army of giant soldiers, each growing larger and more monstrous than the previous one. As if in a trance, I start counting them. Then the first one breaks and I see a head bobbing.

"Walter! You're alive! Thank God! Be careful—the other waves behind you are huge! My love. Careful! Please, come back to me. Duck—Walter—dive under!

Please, God. Please, let him get back in—back into shore—safely. Help him."

Walter's head submerges and does not resurface. The enormous wave crashes with its frothy turbulence and swirls at my feet. I stand like a statue not wanting to move or look at the sea anymore. I whisper, "Walter. Where is Walter?" I close my eyes, expecting the worst, but resume my prayer for my love to re-appear. I collapse and lie in the sandy darkness, not wanting to see anymore.

Then I hear a primeval groan, an "Ahw-wa".

Revived, I open my eyes a bit, cautiously, and catch sight of something moving in the distance near the shoreline. Dusting the sand out of my eyes, I squint and breathe a sigh of relief. A bare bottom emerges from a tide pool about 100 feet from me. I'd recognize that exquisite piece of art anywhere.

Tight. Suntanned. Delicious. "Walter. You're here. Alive!"

He gets up, stands erect and walks ever so slowly, towards me. Naked. Not limping. A piece of seaweed hangs on a strategic part of his anatomy resembling a fig leaf. I smile despite my panic. "Walter, you look like the new Adam."

I try to get up and run to him but my energy level registers zero and my breath fades to the blue zone. Falling back down in the sand, I will myself to breathe in and out slowly. I start counting my breaths to focus, and as I breathe in and out Walter takes a step to match each one. Each one of Walter's footsteps seems like an eternity to me, and then he starts to fade from my sight.

I force my eyes to stay open. I can visualize the curly black hair on his muscular chest glistening with water, salty from the sea. Without warning I feel his tan taunt body exciting me in the mist of my exhaustion. I gasp. He takes my breath away. Walter's body always has that effect on me. Sure we are best friends and love each other's brain, but our physical attraction to each other is a mixture of torture and ecstasy. When we are apart, total pain. When we are together, total bliss.

Walter reaches my refuge on the sand. I close my eyes and feel his warm hands wrap around me in the protective manner I've come to love. He kneels beside me, his body merging with mine. Unable to speak, I lean into my love and hug him with what strength remains in me.

We sit on the shore for a long time, hugging each other in silence. Wet, naked, sandy and windblown, we meditate on the surf, amazed that such a peaceful sea can turn so deadly in a matter of minutes. Having bargained with death before, we know how to be grateful. I say a prayer of thanksgiving for my Walter and he, I am sure, says one for me.

I shiver involuntarily. Walter takes my head in his hands, turns me toward him and brushes his lips against mine. Then he stands up, takes my hands and pulls me up alongside him. "Let's go back to our cottage, Angelina. We can talk there."

I nod and whisper, "I think I need a bath. I have sand in every crevice of my body."

Walter grins at me and kisses my nose. "I've lost my only swim trunks." He scoops me up and carries me back to our *bure*.

We shower together in the cottage's outdoor oversized combined bath and shower, just long enough to get warm, as our passion unfolds. We towel each other off, almost re-enacting our first time together, like young innocents not knowing what lies in the future. We hold on to each other for dear life, here in the present. But I know Walter and he knows me. And he knows something happened to me besides the thrashing in the surf, that being just foreplay. He doesn't ask me any questions. He trusts I will tell him in my own time. And I will. But right now I need him close beside me. I cannot wait any longer. I want to feel the heat of his body mingled with mine. I don't want to go into the dark. I want to remain here, in the light of the day, with Walter.

I throw my towel down, saunter onto the porch of our *bure* and proceed to our daybed and lie down. I pull the pillow-soft downy comforter over my body and beckon to my love. Walter comes up the steps, shuts the screen door and hooks the latch. He leans over and kisses me hard on my lips. He needs no more rest, nor do I. The leaves of the palm trees flap against the screened windows as a breeze kicks up. I hear the waves crashing upon the shore and the sea birds calling their mates, no doubt looking for morsels on the beach as they fly against the wind. The last of the sunlight glistens in through the doorway as Walter kisses my eyelids. I moan, whispering, "You are my love, you are all I want."

Walter answers me with his hand running gently down my spine and his lips pursuing my ear. "Ah," I groan, unable to speak. My skin turns to fire. My body trembles like the first time and I roll over to join Walter in our dance of love. The seedy side of this earth, including Eveline and her henchmen, will have to wait outside the door for a little while longer. I have my priorities.

Chapter Four

I awake from our "nap" around one p.m., starving. Looks like we slept through lunch. Don't think Walter even ate breakfast. I get up from lounging in our day bed on the porch and feel a chill in the air. I wrap the woven blanket around me as I look out and survey the horizon. The sun has disappeared and the palm trees are swaying like dancers. Seems a storm is brewing. If it is traveling in our direction, I hope we get airborne before it hits. I hate flying in bad weather. I just grip the arms of the seat and pray my Hail Mary's. I cannot relax one bit during turbulence. Walter can. He sleeps through anything. I look at my love, dreaming like a contented Cheshire cat. All he needs is a mouse. Sure, he has me as his main kitten, but I know he will be starving when he wakes up.

I pull myself up off the bed and stumble into the main room of our cottage and think, "Room Service. Yes. I will order lunch and Walter will wake to the smell of food. Hum, let's see, what has a strong odor? Thai food. That's the ticket."

Picking up the resort phone, I press one button, having the room service button down pat. I order Chicken Satay, Phad Thai with shrimp, steamed rice for two and Orange Beef. Walter likes the grilled beef, I like the seasoned vegetables and we love to share. I remember to order a pot of tea and of course, two desserts, coconut ice cream and black sticky rice. Memories of home and our neighborhood hangout on Mercer, *Bahn Thai*, consume me. We've been eating food native to Fiji all week. Time to break with tradition, order Thai and prepare for our homecoming.

I go outside and shower for the third time. I'm afraid the daybed is full of sand. Don't know what housekeeping will think. I guess they have handled worse. Washing my hair three times, I finally get all the sand out of my scalp. Barnacles and seaweed surround the shower drain, remnants of Walter's and my last shower together. I don't know what Walter could find appealing in my sand-encrusted body. We didn't even finish the showering before the fireworks started. Maybe today I resemble a mermaid, fulfilling one of his fantasies. Who knows? Maybe he feels the same way I do, grateful to be young, sexy and alive.

Ah, I wish I could stop the clock. Time with Walter is precious, like a leisurely swim in a calm sea. Without warning, our life together sometimes disappears into something unrecognizable and frightening when I am not looking, just like those rogue waves crashing down upon us.

I pick up the remote and turn on the television. Snow all over the screen, no reception at all, then, static. The reception returns, along with a pre-recorded advertisement for the resort. I flip the channels but nothing on but old movies and old news about Fiji. Nothing appears in the news about the good ol' U.S. of A., period. Not expecting to hear anything else, I push the "off" button, hunt in the cottage closet to find an outfit to lounge around in for a few hours, and decide packing will commence this evening. Our preparations will be a piece of cake. We'll just throw everything in our suitcases and while I sit on them, Walter will lock them. Doesn't matter if anything wrinkles. Just need to put the necessities in our carry-on luggage along with reading materials. Traveling is very simple on the return flight. Mostly I take home memories.

After buttoning up a jumpsuit, mellow yellow cotton, sleeveless and comfortable, I brush my hair and fasten it with a flower clip on one side. I study my face in the mirror and decide to apply some makeup to look charming for Walter, and the delivery person. Then, after searching the room for some tip money, I find some in my travel shoes. Great place to stash cash, as I only wear my hiking shoes when traveling or climbing up a volcano. I also hate standing in security lines in flip-flops or pumps. I don't believe in pain and could care less about the attention that comes with fashion. I smile, remembering Emily Dickinson's words, "How frightful to be admired all day, like a frog."

Strolling out to the porch, I hear signs of life—Walter waking up. He stretches, yawns then whispers my name, "Angelina."

I glance at my beloved.

Walter raises his head. "Where are you, Sweetheart?"

I tiptoe over to Walter and give him a kiss on the cheek. "Right here, Captain Neptune."

"Is that the best you can do, Mate?"

I move my lips from his cheek to his mouth and the dance begins again.

"Oh, no, Walter, I love you, but we have to stop. I called room service. Nourishment will be here soon, along with a waiter."

"Man does not live by bread alone, Angelina. Call them back. Tell them, no." Walter pulls me close to him.

I feel his heavy breathing and his intense desire. My body wants to succumb but my mind perseveres in my goal to nourish him. "Yes, my sweet, but you haven't eaten anything since last night."

"Oh, did we eat last night? I don't remember. I just remember..."

"You have a one-track mind. You've got to get up and take another shower."

"Says who?"

"Says me. Be presentable. Plus you smell like seaweed." I pull a large piece of green slimy weed dangling from his belly button.

"Angelina, you're no fun."

"Sure I am, Walter, but I take care of my man. A guy's gotta eat. Plus you have sand all over your..."

Walter grumbles a little more, gets up and drags himself to our indoor bathroom. I tidy up the porch as best I can, pulling the cover over the daybed to hide all the sand, and return inside to slip into my flip-flops. I hear the shower running and at the same time, I hear a knock at the door.

Kahani stands outside with our luncheon order. Gosh he's quick. Guess now I am getting the same service as Evalina Carboni.

"*Bula,* Kahani." I look at his hair. "You look a little windblown."

"*Bula*. It's good to see you again, Tangie. Yes, it is already very stormy, not very far from Mamanucas, on the islands west of us. I brought your order myself, as I wish to speak with you."

"Oh, bad news?"

25

"Yes. We are expecting a monster typhoon in forty-eight hours. The wind is kicking up and the surf is changing."

"I can verify that. The waves are huge. We almost got dragged out to sea this morning."

"I wish I could have warned you sooner, but we just received the latest weather bulletin."

"Not to worry. I survived, thanks to Walter."

"I am grateful for that good fortune." Kahani smiles, then his forehead wrinkles as his eyebrows furrow. "Tangie, I know you are catching our floatplane on route to the airport in Nadi this evening. Our resort is alerting all our travelers to be ready an hour earlier. If we can get everyone to the marina on time, the pilot will be sure to take off before the weather gets—how you say—*nasty*."

"Thanks for the warning, Kahani. I hate flying in nasty weather. Walter and I can get ready in a flash."

"Can you be at the dock by four p.m.?"

"Yes. Is there something else you wanted to tell me, Kahani?"

Kahani nods. "Mrs. Carboni is thinking of filing a complaint against you. Then everyone will know, you are not a staff member, and things will get bad for us all."

Studying his concerned face, I take his hand and pat it gently. "I think I know the perfect solution, Kahani. With your charm you can distract her. Offer to help her pack. Tell her she must get out early to avoid the weather. Keep her worried and grateful. Shower her with free samples. She'll let up on you and your staff. Drown her anger with alcohol. That seems to be her drug of choice."

"Good idea, Tangie. I wish you were staying longer. I enjoy talking with you."

"And me with you."

"You will return someday?"

"You can count on it. I love your island paradise."

Walter enters the room with a towel wrapped around his waist and I can sense unrest in him. I know he heard the last two sentences, that out of context sound suspicious, hence his radar on high alert. That's my Walter, so territorial.

I let go of Kahani's hand. "Sweetheart, this is Kahani, the manager at the resort. He brought us lunch."

"And?"

"*And*, to tell us we have to leave an hour early, due to the storm coming..."

Walter snaps out of his jealous husband bit rather quickly to my relief and extends his strong grip to Kahani. Kahani receives Walter's extended hand, giving him a vigorous handshake in return—two stallions confronting each other.

Kahani looks Walter straight in the eyes. "*La bula*. I met your wife earlier this morning. You are a lucky man."

"I know." Walter smiles with his lips, but his eyes study Kahani. He senses in him a loving, carefree nature—Kahani, a ladies' man. Walter continues to stare at him, searching further for Kahani's motives.

I know that look, *not a good one*. Seems it's time for me for me to intercede.

"Walter, this morning I plowed into one of the other guests and Kahani bailed me out. This particular guest threw a tantrum and got in a royal tizzy over the whole incident, to say nothing of her being three sheets to the wind and in a foul mood."

Walter raises one eyebrow and studies me as I start to stutter.

"I p...p...planned to tell you all about it, but those rogue waves came up and we...well...you know. I'll fill you in over lunch."

"If everything is all right, I will be leaving now," Kahani announces. "Your lunch is compliments of the resort. Also included are two passion fruit cocktails in addition to the pot of tea. *Ni sa moce*."

Our friendly manager smiles then turns to leave. This stallion knows when to pull a hasty retreat.

Touching his arm for a moment, I put a tip in his shirt pocket. "*Vinaka*, Kahani, for everything." I smile and shake his hand.

Kahani squeezes my hand, bows and smiles broadly, showing healthy white teeth.

Good clean living on this island.

"*Vinaka, Tangie. Ni sa moce*." On his way out the door he nods to my stern-faced husband then takes off jogging down the beach trail.

I watch as his arms move like a locomotive at full speed, a man on a mission. Probably warning more guests, or just trying to escape Walter's scrutiny.

Walter ordinarily is a pussycat, but he doesn't like other guys paying attention to me—his one flaw, jealousy. Don't know why. Don't know if it's a guy thing or if Walter's super-sensitive. I constantly reassure him that he is my one and only love, because he is. I know he trusts me but he's told me more than once that he's never sure about the swans that flock around me.

When I think of the terrible dates I went on in between my relationship with my ol' fiancé, Don, now Father Don, and my love and marriage to Walter, my soul mate forever, I can't say that I blame him. I know what's out there. I was out there for seven years before my beloved saved me from a life of "Dates from Hell". As I recall, before Walter came into my life, the slim pickin's almost made me give up on love or even a chance of romance in the future. To me, it's worth accommodating a few jealous outbursts every once in a while. Not a big price to pay for a soul mate.

We eat our Thai lunch in silence. As I lick the sticky rice off my fingers, enjoying our meal tremendously, Walter studies me. "You think I gave this guy, Kahani, too much static, don't you?"

I take a sip of Jasmine tea, garnished with a slice of lemon floating on the top, along with what looks and smells like an orange blossom, perched on the lemon like a crown. Sighing, I put my cup down and stroke Walter's cheek. "Well, just a tad. You didn't tip him. I had to do that. You are always a big tipper and you brushed him off. He's harmless. He's helpful and he's been a friend to me."

"A friend? I thought you just met him."

"I did. This morning. But he rescued me."

"Rescued you? How?"

I can see steam coming out of Walter's ears—his male ego interfering with his thought processes. Kahani is not the enemy here, but Walter cannot read this one clearly—all that testosterone in the way. All he can see at the moment is Kahani's bulging muscles. I have to plan what I will say next instead of babbling like I usually do.

"Walter, I need you to listen to me."

"I'm all ears." He crosses his arms and leans back on the wicker chair. I am thinking he will lean back and fall down like some of the teenage boys did when I was teaching high school. Passive-aggressive behavior. Show of dominance. I understand and I hope he will not freak out on me.

I finish my cup of tea and put it down. "Walter, I mean really listen to me, with a clear head. This is serious stuff and Kahani is the least of anyone's problem. You need to hear this story from the beginning."

Walter's blue irises glisten with tears as he straightens up, reaches over, and takes my hands in his. "I'm sorry, Angelina. I have this terrible habit of…well…you know…of thinking someone will come and take you away from me. I still have nightmares over your kidnapping—and me not being able to find you."

"Walter, Honey." Leaning over, I brush his lips with mine. *Yum.* He tastes like garlic and hot spicy red pepper. "That will never happen again. Not every male is a Sargento. You must know that."

"I do, but I worry about you all the time, even here on our honeymoon."

"I know you do, Sweetheart, and I love you for that. Please, hear me out. I need your advice, your counsel."

"So what happened before the rogue wave? What can be worse than losing you at sea?"

"Losing me in our own country to some gangster moll."

"Now you've got me stumped. What does Kahani have to do with all this?"

"Nothing, really, except he's promised not to reveal my identity to Evelina Carboni."

"Who's Evelina Car…"

"…boni. Evelina Carboni. She's a politican's wife and I almost knocked her over."

"Republican or Democrat?"

"Now how should I know?" I smile as Walter's sense of humor returns, making me feel better about going on with the story.

"Walter, I'm gonna start at the very beginning."

"Sounds good to me."

"You were sleeping."

"You wore me out last night."

"Uh huh. I did. And when I couldn't wake you up this morning, I went down to the marina."

"To run into Mrs. Carboni."

"Not intentionally."

"Then what?"

"Let me finish."

"My lips are sealed." Walter grins, making a motion to lock his lips. He is so charming he disarms me at times.

Focusing back on my latest dilemma, I begin my story in my *teacher* voice, quiet and serious. "I'll start over. I awoke early, made myself a cappuccino like I always do, then I sat down next to you. The house phone rang, suddenly at 8:30 a.m. and you slept through the ringing. I picked up the receiver, so as not to disturb you."

"And?"

"And Steve answered."

"Ah, Steve. How is my old buddy boy?"

"Don't really know. Not your Steve."

"Then, *Steve* who?"

"Walter, you don't wanna know this Steve."

"Why? Who's this Steve?"

"Evelina's Steve...*the hit man.*"

"Is he a musician?"

"Walter, I think you seriously flunked psychic school."

"Maybe I don't want to know this Steve."

"You don't. He thought I was Evaline."

"I thought you said, Evalina."

"I did. But *Steve* said *Evaline.*"

"Steve, the hit man?"

"Yes. It could be he's a paid assassin. And someone by the name of Eveline or Evelina hired him to kill someone...some *guv'ner*...in the United States."

"How do you know all this?" Walter rises from his wicker chair, goes over to the window and looks out towards the surf. He turns back, stares at the ceiling and then at me. "While I've been asleep for a couple of hours, you manage to get yourself involved in all of this?"

"Sweetheart, by the time I figured out this *Steve* could not possibly be our Steve, even though he did sound like our Steve, only a little hoarse, I tried to tell him he had the wrong number, but by then it was too late..."

"Too late for what?"

"Too late not to get involved. You see, before I could tell him, *Sorry, wrong number*, he spilled the beans."

"Like he was gonna kill someone..."

"Worse. Not the future. *The past*. He already killed some one. Eveline's designated patsy."

"Who is?"

"The *guv'ner*. Don't you understand? I only know what I told you. The governor of some state in the good ol' U.S.A. has been murdered! Eveline's *Steve* told me to watch the news—told me he'd keep the body on ice, hidden in the water."

"Where?"

"How should I know? He asked me for his payoff—wanted to know when he'd get compensated for his dirty deed."

"And you said?"

"I said, when I see the news on TV."

"Oh, great!"

"I didn't know what else to say. Call me dumbfounded, too scared to say anything else. I couldn't wake you up. You were sleeping like a zombie. And by then, I'm afraid, the damage was done."

"Oh, so now it's my fault because after two days I finally fell asleep! You're killing me, Angelina."

"No, Walter, please. I don't mean to hurt your feelings. The whole mix-up happened so fast. I got confused...and scared. I'm still scared. I'm afraid to bump into Evelina again. She may be *Eveline*—the hit man's *Eveline*..."

"Great. That's just great. I knew it! I could feel it. So now all my worrying about you, all my fears are justified. Only it's this crazy woman and some murderer, named *Steve*."

"You know what, Walter? When we first got here, I had this crazy dream. I can't remember exactly what it entailed but it took place on the

31

water—and there was a sailboat in it. You know sometimes I have these recurring dreams—So I might have this one again. I didn't pay any attention to it at the time, so I forgot most of it. Maybe it was a warning; I'm not sure. And...I don't have anything else to tell you..."

"So that's it?"

I nod. "Do you have any ideas as to what I should do?"

"I think maybe *we* should go to the police."

"Not here in Fiji. They'll think we're nuts. Worse—they'll take us seriously and not let us leave the country. We can't talk to anyone here. The officials will hold our passports."

Walter starts pacing. "That they would do."

"Yes, my love. We'll have to remain quiet until our feet are firmly planted in the United States—in Washington State. When we get home, we can watch the news. And we can contact *Our Steve* and the Seattle P.D. and..."

Walter gaze penetrates mine, as he pulls me towards him and strokes my hair. "And Theo. We can call Theo Lee with the FBI. But for now, you are right. We have no proof."

I sigh and my eyes begin to tear. "Yes, no proof—just my eavesdropping on a phone message—a message not intended for me. Maybe I misunderstood what I heard, but I don't think so."

"I don't think so either, Angelina. But how are you going to avoid Evelina on the plane? Isn't she flying out tonight with us? Isn't that what this guy, Kahani, told you?"

I straighten my posture, feeling stronger. "Yes, she is. I'm grateful he warned us..."

I can hear my heart doing the ol' pitter pat. I pull reluctantly away from Walter and start to pace in circles around the floor. *Think, think,* I say to myself. *Tangie, you've got to think.*

"Walter. I've got it! I'll figure out a costume. We still have a couple of hours. I can't let the perfumed lady recognize me. She might get suspicious. And if Eveline's Steve figures out that he talked to me, rather than her, I'm toast. It's better if she thinks the person who ran into her is one of Kahani's staff."

"Is that what she thinks now?"

"Yes. Kahani went along with her misunderstanding to avoid trouble."

"So he saved your skin. Remind me to thank him for that. Gee, I treated him like crap."

"I think Kahani understands how you feel, Walter. But we better keep him out of all this—for his own safety."

I shudder, thinking of a dear sweet man who tried to help me in my last adventure; he wound up in the hospital, beaten to a pulp. "I don't want another Mr. Benson on my conscience."

"Tangie, we won't let that happen. We know better now. But why do you think Eveline would suspect you?"

"I think she already does. She has this radar—this evil vibration—I can feel it through her made-up Hollywood eyes. Thank goodness I didn't touch her hand. I could have received a shocking sensation. I would have fainted."

"I'm sorry, Tangie." Walter takes me into his arms, comforting me with his warm embrace. "Honestly, Sweetheart, how do you get into these things?"

"Beats me." Sighing, I snuggle into his arms. "You know, Walter, this is not the way I want our honeymoon to end."

"Not to worry, Angelina," Walter whispers as he unbuttons my jumpsuit and caresses my breast. "Our honeymoon will never be over. Not if I have anything to do with it. We have an hour or so before we have to pack and play dress-up. Let's give Fiji a proper send off."

Walter has a way of putting things in perspective. Sure we have a crisis at hand, a dilemma we can't fix until we get back to Seattle, but we are still on our honeymoon for cryin' out loud. We are absolutely in agreement once more. We are going to squeeze the most out of our last final moments together here in our tropical paradise—before escaping the typhoon predicted to hit Fiji and before returning to face the firing squad waiting for us in the United States.

I slip out of the bottom half of my jumpsuit, kick off my sandals and tiptoe over to the bedside radio and tune in a mellow rock station. A romantic rock song sizzles. So do I. I love classic rock. So does Walter. So we *do a little dance, make a little love and*...okay, so our sixty minutes turns into two hours.

My eyes open suddenly as an alarm goes off in my head. I roll over and glance at the clock. "Walter! We have to be at the dock in forty-one minutes!"

"Walter lifts one eyelid. "Sure, Angelina. Whatever you say..." and then goes promptly back to sleep.

Chapter Five

I hop out of our soft downy king-size bed and stare out the window at the darkening sky. *Okay, Angelina, you can do this. You can gather all your stuff together and plan a disguise while you pack without any assistance. Sure. No sweat. Sure...*

I look at Walter and lose any semblance of calm. "Walter, get up! We've got to get out of here!"

"Tangie! Are you all right? What's happened?"

"Nothing Sweetie. We must vamoose—like leave. Help me pack. Help me get a costume ready. I can't do this by myself. I'm shaking..."

Walter leaps up out of bed in record time, gives me a tender teddy bear hug, kisses me gently on the mouth and then throws our suitcases on the bed and opens them up. I go over to the closet and start throwing things to Walter who stuffs them in, packing them tightly. Just as I predicted, my prince lifts me up and sits me on the suitcases—one at a time—while he snaps them closed. I rush into the bathroom to get our toiletries. I bring with me one outfit I left out to wear on our return trip, a floral jumpsuit I bought for my mother during our brief stay in Hawaii. It's a little matronly, purple, with large flowers all over it and ties in the back with a bow, just the right touch for my costume. I'll wear my hiking sneakers and large sunglasses, plus put my hair in a bun and don a scarf and hat to cover up the rest. Top everything with lots of costume jewelry and tons of makeup. That will do the trick.

I come out of the bathroom as Walter is buckling his belt and dusting off his chinos. I turn around and model my new outfit for him. He does a double take and blinks his eyes.

"Is this the same woman I married?"

"Good. You don't recognize me."

"Hardly. You look like your mother."

"The exact look I was fishing for."

"I'm going to look like a gigolo."

I hand him a good will package. "Not if you wear this straw fedora with the flowered band around it, these plaid shorts and your comfortable tennis shoes with black socks."

"I'm not a nerd or an old guy."

"Pretend. It's necessary."

"Do you want me to wear glasses with tape down the center?"

"No, that would be too extreme. Just act nerdy and carry a laptop."

"What kind of guy carries a laptop on his honeymoon?"

"You do."

"Okay. I'll carry it personally instead of storing it in my carry-on bag, but I refuse to put on the plaid shorts. You owe me for this one, Angelina."

"I promise, Walter. When we get home, I will make it up to you—if we get home..."

"You worry too much. The weather will calm down. By the time we reach Hawaii, it will be smooth sailing."

"You mean *flying* don't you? I don't want to go in the drink."

"Precisely. I'll race you out the door. We've ten minutes to get to the marina. I've already checked out on the Castaway channel."

"I love checking out in the twenty-first century, Walter. You lead, I'll follow."

Kahani, it seems, poured Evalina cocktails all afternoon. As we board the waiting floatplane at the Mamanucas Marina for the trip to the main airport in Nadi, I can smell the overwhelming mixture of pungent perfume and Jack Daniels. I notice my nemesis in the first row of seats with her head leaning against the window. She has her mouth open, snoring. Next to her sits a tall man who appears to be a bodyguard or escort. He has a look on his face that announces silently to the world: "Leave me alone. I've had enough of your crap." Come to think of it, if I had Evalina for my assignment, I wouldn't be a happy camper either. I tiptoe closer to Ms. Carboni and nudge Walter, pointing out the object of my anxiety. He nods discreetly, takes my hand and leads me to our seats in the second row. After we settle in our seats, he takes my hand, kisses it and whispers in my ear, "It would be better if we didn't talk until we have privacy."

I nod, kiss him on the cheek and squeeze his hand, thinking, *I can handle anything with Walter at my side.* I lean against his muscular body, close my eyes and wait for our journey home to begin.

Chapter Six

Walter taps me gently on the shoulder as the short flight to the main airport in Fiji ends in a splash. When the doors open the scent of sea air drifts into the cabin and I shake myself as if trying to get out of a trance. I need sleep! I stand up by my seat and sigh, as my main squeeze secures our bags. I will miss Fiji, its warm inviting beaches, its calm iridescent water, its gentle breezes—well, except for chatting with "Hit Man Steve" about murder, bumping into "Eveline the Bitch", lying about my identity, and nearly drowning at sea with the love of my life. Yes, I will miss our secluded hideaway.

Walter and I are the last of the passengers to depart from the float-plane—on purpose. No way do we want to encounter Eveline, A.K.A. Evelina Carboni. I can see her in the distance on the dock running ahead of us with her stacked heels and floral muumuu with her companion follow-ing, carrying all her matching luggage. Don't see any of his. He's prob-ably carrying his underwear and toothbrush in his suit pocket. I watch as a chauffeur greets the pair and leads them to a limo.

To anyone else, Eveline resembles any other snobby rich tourist leaving paradise. Sure she appears rich. She appears snobby. She doesn't appear to be a murderer. But I know better. This knowledge doesn't come entirely from being a psychic. I heard it first hand with my ears planted on a phone. Not a willing accomplice to this bit of knowledge. Not a willing keeper of secrets. Just not sure what to do at the moment, with the knowledge thrust upon me. So, I am doing what Walter suggested. Sitting on it for a while. Not an easy task for me. I am a woman of action. I hate to wait around and pace. Not my style. But he's right. Plunging head first into this one could be dangerous. And I don't do dangerous. *Now where have I heard those words before?*

Upon leaving the main island of Fiji in the dark, we begin our journey to the good ol' United States of America. After we board our 757, I look around discreetly for any sign of Evaline. Cannot make out her visage anywhere. Good thing. I can settle down for a long September's nap. After relaxing in my seat with Walter's arm around me, I succumb to my waiting dreams, not waking up until we reach O'ahu. The plane does a little bump and grind and I barely notice it. Guess being sleep deprived is a blessing when flying. No time to get stressed out. I open my eyes and observe Walter conversing on his i-Phone. I converted him from PC to Mac. Wasn't hard. He loves me so he will try anything. It didn't take him long to get hooked as he is a photo nut and the photography angle is superb. He turns and smiles at me.

"Tangie, I got us a quick return flight to the mainland straight to Seattle, leaving in about an hour. All we have to do is run..."

"What? No stopover in Hawaii? I thought I'd have time to shop in Honolulu. We didn't do much when we vacationed here on our way to Fiji."

Walter kisses my lips. I sigh. He whispers, "Sorry, my love. But Sweetheart, don't you remember? You want to get back to the mainland. Remember *the mission?*"

"Damn, I had such a good dream. I was in such a good place, I almost forgot."

"We'll come back to O'ahu. I promise."

"It's a deal." I put out my hand and Walter shakes it, all business-like. But then he takes me into his arms, leans me over and kisses me with lingering passion, reminding me we are still on our honeymoon.

After he releases me, my Adonis speaks in his Humphrey Bogart voice, "Come on, Sweetheart—let's hoof it. Glad you're wearing your Nikes."

We breeze through customs, as we have no fruits or vegetables to declare, and get to the Hawaiian Airlines gate right before they close the entrance to the airplane. We race down the connecting ramp and bumble our way into our first class seats. One of the things I love about Walter is he goes first class. Always. No more bargain, tight squeezing seats for me ever again. No more struggling private detective, just a lady of leisure. *Ha! That will be the day.* I'm still my ol' independent self but I vote *yes* on the first class tickets. *I can give in to a few things.*

I smile at my beloved as we settle into our seats, all roomy and cushy. "You are too good to me, Walter."

He squeezes me around the waist. "You are too good for me."

"I love it when you talk smooth."

"I know. That's why I do it."

Walter leans over and gives me a deliciously long wet kiss. Good things don't always last; our embrace is interrupted by a loud cackle and then, a barking sound. Not a dog, not a witch, but a close second—Eveline. She's come back to haunt me. Now how did she manage to get on this plane before us? No doubt her bodyguard pulled some strings and carried her here. I look at Walter. Fear reflects from my eyes to his.

He nods and put his finger on his lips and whispers, "Don't worry, Angelina. She hasn't spotted us."

I whisper back, "What if I have to go to the bathroom?"

"I'll do surveillance. When she's asleep, I'll tap your shoulder. "

"What if the bodyguard gets suspicious?"

"I'm dressed like a nerd and you—I don't want to say what you look like."

"Nice thing to say to a girl on her honeymoon."

"Shush, not so loud."

I grin, despite my trepidation. "My lips are sealed." I plant a kiss on Walter's lips, oh so gentle, but promising more later in safe territory.

After going through two time zones, I realize I have no concept of time, whether it is day or night. I remember eating a scrumptious first-class dinner complete with shrimp cocktail, Pinot Gris and Filet Mignon while our plane zooms over the Pacific on route to Seattle. I remember sleeping with my legs elevated and relaxing on a reclining seat with my head leaning on Walter's shoulder, and his hand holding mine as I drift off to sleep. I remember waking up as the lights flash on. I also hold on to a distant memory of a guy in a dream, a guy named "Buddy" and a boat. Then I hear the captain's voice, smooth and calm, on the intercom announcing we would be landing in twenty minutes. I look at Walter, still asleep. He is wearing his Bose earphones, that block out the noise of the jet engines. I remove his nerdy glasses and kiss him on each of his eyelids.

He opens his baby blues and smiles. "We're here?"

"Almost, my love."

Walter straightens up and moves his seat to an upright position. "Tangie, I think we need to follow your friends and see where they're headed."

"They aren't my friends..."

"Well, your *suspects*, then. We need to follow them..."

"Boy, you know how to jump into first gear."

"Practice, my dear Holmes, practice. You keep me on my toes."

"Walter, do you think that's wise, following them?"

"No, but it would be good to know if they are headed somewhere else after Seattle."

"Gotcha, Dr. Watson. When the plane stops, you grab the luggage and I'll hit the little girl's room."

"No time for that, Tangie."

"Walter, I'll die."

"All right, go. Ol' Ms. Nose in the Air will probably take a long time waking up. She's been snoring the entire flight."

"You had on earphones."

"Yes, I could hear her through the noise blockers."

The plane places down on the runway like a dove greeting its home turf. We have a good pilot. *I love smooth landings—makes me want to fly again.* I wait until the "Seatbelts Off" signal flashes, then dash to the restroom. After my brief stay in the sardine can, I open the door just as Walter passes by me with our luggage.

He turns and grabs my hand. "Let's go."

I follow Walter out the door after smiling at the steward, thanking him for a good flight. He raises his eyebrows at me and smiles a Colgate advertisement grin at me as I exit. "You're most welcome, Madam. Join us again on your next trip to Hawaii."

I nod to him. No one's ever called me "Madam" before. Then I remember how I am dressed.

Walter drags me out the door and down the ramp leading to the terminal. How Walter can run so fast carrying two pieces of carry-on luggage and his laptop is beyond me. I can barely keep up just carrying my tote bag. He tugs on my hand upon reaching the terminal and begins jogging to the escalator. I follow like a pull-toy. When we get to the lower level, the doors open to the mini-subway that travels to the baggage claim. We plow in with the rest of the travelers and I spot Eveline with her bodyguard in the far end of the tram. She is putting on fresh lipstick and fluffing her hair. Even from a distance I notice large bags forming under her eyes. Some people don't travel well. Can't say that I look that great myself, especially in my costume, but I don't age ten years after a flight on a plane. She does, and she isn't wearing a dress intended for her mother. Her bodyguard stands up allowing a young person to take the seat next to her. Seems to me Eveline resents others sitting near her. I notice her scrunching her body away, trying not to make any contact with the young teenager who happens to plop down beside her. The tram moves and the next stop is the main terminal.

When the doors open, Eveline gets up, assisted by her protector and departs from the tram. Walter and I follow from a safe distance. I grab one piece of luggage from under Walter's hand and smile. "I can pull my weight, Hercules."

Walter grins at me. "I know. That's why I love you. You are such a he-woman."

We follow Mrs. Carboni and her "Igor" to a Cinnabon pastry shop. She sits down and Igor goes to the counter. He gets her a black coffee and a Cinnabon—a luscious, warm roll oozing with butter, sugar and cinnamon.

Walter sees me salivating, pulls out a chair for me to sit down, a safe distance from Carboni and company, and departs to get us some nourishment.

He comes back with two cappuccinos and two warm over-sized cinnamon buns oozing with melted cream cheese frosting. "This may take awhile, my love. Hope you aren't in a hurry to get home."

"Nothing like doing surveillance our first day back. Don't worry about me, Walter. We gotta do what we gotta do." And what I have to do right now is enjoy this cinnamon delight. Thank you!"

As I consume my second bite of heavenly pastry, the Igor dude gets up. Walter's antennae rise with him. He leans over and whispers in my ear, "Stay put. Watch Eveline. I'll follow Mr. Bodyguard."

I smile at my charming nerd and nod like a dutiful bride. Then I chomp on the rest of the roll, take a sip of my cappuccino and whisper, "Be careful."

Walter walks off in a relaxed easy manner. No one would guess he is a man on a mission, a mission that will take the two of us to places we don't want to go. My body shivers as I glance at Eveline.

She continues eating her cinnamon bun with a fork. So dainty, she must have been a boarding school child. Miss Manners to the T, despite a tendency to stab anyone in the back who gets in her way. I must remember not to get in her way, ever. I see her fumbling for an extra napkin and fuming over sticky fingers. She probably would rather be caught dead than to lick her fingers in public. Funny how warped people become in their values. *What causes a person to be so caught up in appearances and to value things over people?* Maybe she experienced an unhappy childhood. Maybe no one ever taught her to be kind. Maybe she just developed a nasty streak over time—maybe, all three.

I put my head down and continue to peer at Eveline through my over-sized sunglasses. She wipes her hands on the seat next to her. I hope Igor doesn't decide to sit there. I feel a tap on my shoulder and I jump out of my seat, nearly spilling my cappuccino. A hand catches it. Not my own.

"Relax, Angelina," Walter whispers in my ear. "I found out they are headed to Boston. They'll be leaving in an hour if they can get back through security on time."

"So, may we go home now, my love?"

"*Mais oui*, my darling, unless you want to hang out around the airport. Or follow them to Boston."

"No, my love. Let's quit here. We can go home, watch the news and wait. We know now that Eveline Carboni is from New England. We can look her up on *Google* or have our buddy, Steve the Cop, do a search. A politician's wife shouldn't be too hard to find, and we know her name. That means a lot."

"My thoughts exactly. But let's wait till they leave. Then we can head over to Baggage Claim. I'll ring our Steve; he's on call to pick us up. We can explain everything to him on the way home."

I nod at Walter, touch his cheek with my hand and smile. *"Home..."*

Home—our sanctuary, our refuge from past fears, terrors and the world of crime—I feel it beckoning us. I love our quaint Dutch Colonial that is perched atop Queen Anne Hill. It is Walter's legacy from his grandfather and now our little nest overlooking the Puget Sound, the Columbia Towers and the Space Needle. The Cascades and Olympic Mountains serve as background for our neighborhood and give me a sense of peace and protection. I love our home on sunny days, when we can see everything for hundreds of miles. I love it in the fog, when only the top of the Space Needle is visible. I love it during holidays, when the city bedecks itself in lights and goodwill, and I especially love it on the Fourth of July, when the city puts on a spectacular fireworks display that can be seen for miles especially, if you live on one of the seven hills that encompasses Seattle, as Walter and I do. Yes, Queen Anne is an incredible place to live, and now, I too, call it home.

Chapter Seven

Our Steve picks us up in front of Baggage Claim. He insists on carrying my luggage and does not say a word about the outfits Walter and I are wearing. He must be tired. I notice he is not his usual robust self. Dark circles are visible under his eyes, a bandage covers his temple and a purple bruise encircles his left eye. He resembles a prizefighter that lost his last match.

Walter quizzes him in a jovial manner. "Did you have a rough night, my friend? Seattle P.D. working you too hard?"

"No, Walter, work's fine, except for maybe last night, bad ending to a bad situation. It's the usual crazy hectic place but I'm used to that. It's Suzy. She and I argued—and we didn't make up this time. I can't sleep. I've been pacing back and forth since the blow-up. I can't even bring myself to go to the station. Now that's never happened before. I don't know what to do. She's the first babe that's got to me this way."

"Man, you've got it bad." Walter relieves him of one of my suitcases trying to extend a little sympathy.

I study Steve. "How did you get the shiner? Picking on guys bigger than your self, as usual?"

"Not really." He frowns. " Yeah, the black eye's work related. But you should see the other guy. I took him down and he didn't go easy. Nasty drug dealer, selling candy laced with cocaine to school kids, no less. He's the worst kind, a real scumbag."

"I'm sorry, Steve."

"That's all right, Tangie. Right now I'm just down over Suzy and her leaving me."

FRANTIC IN FIJI...AND OTHER PORTS OF CALL

I nod. "Of course, Steve."

Don't know if anything will work to cheer our Steve up. He looks as miserable as he sounds. He ambles along with us into the parking garage, with his head bent over, as if carrying the weight of the world on his shoulders. I try to understand the depth of his heartache. I know something about misunderstandings. "What happened, Steve? Do you want to talk about it?"

"Well, you know Suzy. She likes to have her own way..."

"Well sure, that's Suzy. I always thought if anyone could go to battle with her, it would be you."

"That's just it. I don't like to fight with her. It depresses me. At work I can fight. At home it's a different ballgame."

Walter nods. "You've got it bad, Steve. And, don't tell me. She moved in with you while we were in Fiji."

"Yep, she did..."

Walter lets out a sigh. "Man, maybe you're acting too quickly on that one."

"Yeah, I know, but it just sort of happened. One night we're going out clubbing and dancing till dawn and the next day, we're living together."

I know my impulsive bridesmaid. She's not exactly good at thinking things through. "Let me guess, Steve: Suzy thinks you two should have a bigger place. Am I right?

"Bingo. You see, Tangie, I like my condo. It's close to work. I can see the skyline and the ferries crossing the sound. I like Belltown. It's near the market and the police station..."

"And she wants you to move to her place on Magnolia, so she has room for her shoes."

"Worse. Bellevue. In a gated-community, if you can believe it. Commute to work, in rush hour traffic, over the bridge, and tolls! I'll never get to the station on time."

I shake my head, knowing how Steve operates. He feels trapped. "Sounds like you need to compromise, Steve."

"Compromise? You know, Tangie, with Suzy that's like asking a lioness to share her meat."

Walter smiles a wee bit, looks at me and then at his best man. "Tangie's right, Steve. You've got to figure out an arrangement the two of you can agree on or split up."

"I can't break up with her. Suzy's got me, hook, line and sinker."

Walter places the suitcases on the concrete as we stop by Steve's car and pats his friend's shoulder. "Listen Steve, this is important. "Find a new place, special, just for the two of you. Work on it. It will turn out. This is the least of your worries. But if you don't get this one right, other stuff will fall apart."

Steve opens the rear of his car and relinquishes my suitcases to the trunk area. "I guess that's what's bothering me. I don't wanna lose Suzy but I don't know how to get this one fixed. You're right. I'll make a date with her to talk this out."

I smile. "Make a date? I thought you were living together?"

"Yeah, well, we were, till this morning. She packed her bags and went back to her luxury apartment."

"I know Suzy, Steve. I bet she's just sitting on her suitcases waiting for you to call her. You'll see. I think she'll be ripe for a discussion. No doubt she's as miserable as you are."

"Gee thanks, Tangie. You and Walter are right. And you are the best, to help me sort this out."

Walter raises his left eyebrow, and smiles. "Hey, good buddy, that's what friends do." He shakes Steve's hand. "Thanks for picking us up."

"Yes, Steve, and thanks for carrying my luggage," I add.

"No problem. How was your honeymoon? Or do I need to ask?" Steve mumbles as he surveys our apparel, noticing our costumes for the first time.

Walter winks at me then smiles at Steve. He waits for my signal.

I nod at my Adonis and give him the lead to talk. *Let him break the news.*

"How much time do you have, Steve?" Walter asks, as he loads the rest of our gear into Steve's brand-new Ford Edge. "Nice choice of vehicles."

Seems Steve's old Mustang met an unfortunate end while we were gone. Poor Steve. He goes through a lot of cars, one of the casualties of his job.

Steve stares at me, knowing I'm always an easy target for information, but questions Walter. "What do you mean, good buddy? How much time do I have?"

Then he turns back to me. "What's going on, Tangie?"

"My speech becomes stilted. I don't know how to begin. "Steve, don't get the wrong idea, we loved our honeymoon. We loved Fiji, until the last day…"

49

Steve takes my hand and guides me into the back seat. "Uh oh, what did you get yourselves into this time?"

Walter looks around the parking garage before he hops into the Edge. "Maybe we should wait until we get home to fill you in, Steve. You have to drive through traffic."

"That bad, huh?"

We nod in unison like a pair of Mariner bobble-head dolls as our police escort shuts the door for us and then climbs into the driver's seat. As Steve drives his midnight black Edge down the ramp from rooftop parking, I take Walter's hand, relax in the heated leather seat and start humming the jazz tune that flows from the car radio.

After traveling I'm always grateful to be back home in Washington State. I'm in awe, always, whenever I return. I take in the sights and sounds along the Puget Sound as if noticing them for the first time and marvel at the tall evergreens, strong and stately. To me, they are my long lost brothers. I'm coming home to the rest of my family.

The clouds start moving swiftly over the horizon and I can hear rumbling. Not a good sign. Thunder seldom roars in Seattle.

Chapter Eight

When we arrive at our home, I can see the sun closing its eyes over the Olympic Mountains. I watch as the lights of the city glow and twinkle in rhythm with the stardust melody in my head. I love twilight time, especially on Queen Anne. The Space Needle still shines with red, white and blue lights, in observance of Labor Day and *911*. The ferries, wearing their lighted hats, cross the Puget Sound as if in harmony with one another. Peace and calm surround us at present in our city beside the bay.

The car crunches to a stop. Steve gets out and helps Walter with the luggage. I trot up the stone steps leading to the entrance of our home that is freshly painted mellow yellow. I notice new-sprung yellow and white mums lining the walkway. The jasmine still blooms by the doorway; its scent cures my jetlag. I take a deep breath and smile as I push our new fancy code lock that opens the massive wooden front door. I notice lights on inside through the beveled windows on the upper portion of the door. Quite a different entrance from my first home in Ballard, where I struggled with the key all the time. Sometimes I couldn't even get into my own home. I left it unlocked most of the time, which in hindsight turned out to be a very bad idea. My brother, Bryan, his wife, Andee, and their two twin sons live there now. Bryan, always the handy man, took care of the lock first thing and managed to make the rest of the house resemble Craftman's homes pictured in *Northwest Homes Magazine*.

I am so proud of my brother and I adore his wife and children. Jason and Jeffrey, the twin terrors, hang out with us sometimes on weekends and Walter is determined to be their favorite uncle. Actually, he's their only uncle, so they haunt him whenever they come to visit. They still love me to pieces, and I them, but Walter is their idol, probably because he's still a kid at heart. He loves hanging out with them and wrestling in the grass, playing soccer at Kinnear Park and rollerblading around Queen Anne. Sometimes we all hop on bikes, cruise around Green Lake and take side trips to the Woodland Park Zoo along the way.

Walter startles me as he grabs my hand, put his arms under me and lifts me up in the air. "Hum, you seem a little lighter, Angelina. Good! I can still sweep you off your feet." He laughs as he carries me across the threshold into the foyer.

I lean into Walter and give him one of my extra-special kisses, that always promises more, later. I forget about Steve standing next to us, until I open my eyes and notice him standing there with his head turned away, not wanting to spy on us.

Shrugging his shoulders, Steve blurts out, "Uh, I think I better be going. We can talk later."

"Nonsense, good buddy." Walter releases his hold on me, giving me a wink and a smile as he places me upright in the foyer. "Stay. Angelina and I will control our selves. We're just happy to be home, that's all. I'll open a bottle of wine and we can talk a bit."

"Yes. Please, Steve, stay. I'll go fix some sandwiches. Walter and I just spent two weeks in paradise, Hawaii and Fiji. Doesn't get much better than that and you're not intruding. I expect our entire life to be a honeymoon."

Walter grins. "Ditto."

"Oh, all right you two but if I drink, I may wind up sleeping on the couch."

"No problemo, my good man." Walter smiles. "We've got lots of wine, lots of room and lots of time."

We talk into the wee hours of the morning, polish off a good number of bottles of *vino* and strategize on two plans of action, one for Steve and one for us.

Steve's task involves patching things up with Suzy, his new love, first thing in the morning, so he can snap out of his depressed state and return to the living, in this case, with Suzy. Our next adventure calls for us to travel again, this time to Newport, Rhode Island to visit Walter's Aunt Hattie. We decide to leave as soon as we hear something on the news about any governor in New England found dead, under questionable circumstances.

Around three a.m., Steve falls asleep on the couch and Walter and I succumb to sleeping upstairs in our four-poster ultra-comfortable bed. I sleep like a log for four hours but at seven a.m. my eyes open and just for a while, I forget all about Evelina Carboni. I glimpse at my sleeping prince and grin. I love being married to Walter. *Love, love, love him.* I lean over and kiss his soft, warm lips, hoping for a response. But Adonis remains comatose. I think he drank a lot more wine than me, and I think Steve drank more than Walter. *Guess that leaves me to fix breakfast.*

I swirl my legs around the side of the bed and try to get up. *Uh oh, dizzy.* Guess I too, over-indulged on the vineyard's good fortune. I limp my way to the adjoining bath and turn on the shower. I love our shower. A body can just walk in. No curtains and there is a seat built into the wall that makes it useful in times like this. I allow the warm water to cascade over my head and shoulders. I close my eyes and dream of the waterfalls in Fiji. I pour a few ounces of coconut-scented shampoo over my head, washing my hair. With my soapy giant sponge I soak all the remnants of travel from my person. When I emerge from the shower and towel myself off, I feel refreshed and ready for a new day. *Hum…what I need more than anything right now is Tangie's Special Cappuccino.* That's the ticket to starting the day.

I take my ice-blue terry robe off the hook on the door, slip it on and tip-toe down the stairs, like a cat hiding from mice, and at the bottom almost trip over a sleeping Hildie, Walter's faithful Maine Coon Kitty. So, she's finally making an appearance. Last night we couldn't find her anywhere. I think she hid because she got mad at us for leaving her and going on our honeymoon. Or maybe she misses our dog Pebbles, who has spent the last fortnight at my mom and Charles's home on Whidbey Island.

Pebbles—Wonder when we'll pick up Wonder Dog? Probably won't have to. Mom will hop in her Mini-Cooper with him the moment I call her up. I miss my West Highland Terrier, but I'll put off phoning my mom for a bit. I've got to get my act together before facing Marianna. She'll know something's up. She's not expecting us home until tomorrow.

Hildie starts meowing, hunger taking over her desire to hide and sleep. I tiptoe to the cupboard and find her favorite crunchies and her trusty trout morsels and mix them together in her ceramic dish, shaped like a fish. She meows one last time, and rubs against my leg to thank me as I put her dish on the kitty placemat. I know Walter's housekeeper takes good care of her when we're gone, but Hildie missed us and that's what she's telling me.

I figure I won't disturb Steve, who lies sleeping on our couch in front of the marble fireplace. He looks dead to the world, like the ashes from our blazing fire, remnants of last night's heat. Don't know why Steve didn't retire to our guest room. Probably wanted to sneak out first thing in the morning, but got himself plastered instead, poor guy. I understand his heartache. Your first romantic fight sucks all the life out of your resolve to be true to yourself. Being a twosome takes some adjustment and he and Suzy need to find that out for themselves. Suzy is not big on compromise. Hopefully she loves Steve as much as he loves her and they can work things out. Maybe I will call her. No, let them work this one out on their own. I don't like anyone interfering in my personal affairs, even though I only had two real loves in my life. I think the first one doesn't count as it ended with one of us becoming a priest and it wasn't me. Have to hand it to my former love, Don, now Father Don, officiating at the marriage of Walter and me. It's funny how life has a sense of humor.

I spoon out some Camano Island Roasters coffee, which I ground last night, just in case. I remember now, I didn't want to make any unnecessary noise this morning. I add water to the water tray in my Italian cappuccino machine and secure the ground coffee beans in place to drip. After the water drains through the granules and magically turns a delicious shade of dark brown, I steam the milk as quiet as I can, pour my special sugar blend in my favorite Coffee Roasters mug, add the foam and last, the coffee. I sip the warm creamy mixture and sigh, indulging in its fragrance and its heavenly taste. I gaze over at Hildie, who stares at me, anticipating another treat. I lean down and pour some leftover steamed milk into her empty bowl. She sighs along with me and begins purring. *Great minds think alike.* I'm beginning to like this cat. Really like her. At first, I appreciated her as Walter dotted on her. However, since living in this house, I've become attached to the little furry beast. Well, not so little. She out weighs Pebbles by about ten pounds and yet can still outrun him. I love to watch them race around the house, like a tiger and a polar bear cub. The two of them keep me in good humor. It's hard to get depressed with two ecstatic fur balls running through the halls.

I pick up my steaming hot cappuccino and head back up the stairs to our combination office and den. I miss Pebbles following my heels. On my way up I glance at Hildie settling herself on the couch, at Steve's feet. She loves to sleep with our guests. She feels she is honoring them.

In the den, there's a high-definition television set up. As I don't want to disturb either Walter or Steve, I shut the door and turn on the morning news. I recline on the couch, sip my coffee and wait for the inevitable.

A double tall espresso and I fall asleep. Must be jet lag. I open my eyes to a screen blinking color and a husky voice saying, "There's been some breaking news out of the Northeast." My antennae buzz up and my body stiffens. I open my eyes wide and stare at the television. I sit there, mesmerized, wishing Pebbles was on my lap for support as I concentrate on every word spoken by the news reporter on location in Newport, Rhode Island.

"This morning at approximately nine a.m., a body floated ashore off the coast of Narragansett Bay, a few miles north of Newport, Rhode Island. The body is believed to be the body of Governor Peter Van Beek. His daughter, Sarah and his son, Peter Van Beek, Junior, left their respective colleges this morning and are on route to make a positive identification. An assistant to Governor Van Beek, Graham Gotthree, has given the police a preliminary identification. Authorities also discovered Governor Van Beek's sailboat, the *Mercedes,* on its side, nestled between the rocks and shore, a vessel without a captain."

Oh no! This is not what I want to hear. Now I have to act. *Rats.* No more procrastinating. Have to let our Steve know. Walter probably knows already. He always knows stuff before me…

Speak of the devil. I hear the doorknob turn and Walter pokes his head through the opened door. "Hey Tangie, guess what I just heard on the television..."

I frown. "The governor of Rhode Island is dead."

"So you heard."

"Yup, just now. Curses."

"So, my love, what do you want to do?"

"You don't want my real answer." I shrug my shoulders and sigh. "Does Steve know?"

"Yes, we have the news turned on downstairs. We didn't want to disturb you. I thought you were conked out."

"Well, I got up early, made an espresso, but fell back asleep while watching the news. I just woke up, again, in time to hear the grim tidings. I came in here because I didn't want to disturb you two..."

"Oh, I thought it was to get out of making breakfast."

"Breakfast! I'm starved..."

"You are in luck, my sweet." Walter sits down next to me and starts rubbing my feet.

"Ah," I groan. *Nothing better than a foot massage.* "Mr. Cunningham, you are the answer to my prayers."

Walter smiles. "Today, *Mrs. Cunningham*, I am your chef. You will be served your favorite breakfast very shortly. But today I cannot bring you breakfast in bed because we have a guest."

"That's fine, my love. Who needs breakfast in bed? My short order cook is back!" I wrap my arms around Walter and hug him tight. "Um..."

Walter grins. "Well, for this morning, anyway."

Walter continues massaging my feet, and then lingers with his hand on my thigh. I nuzzled up to him, feeling content, secure.

My love whispers, "Later...I promise." He kisses my thigh and continues to move his lips up my body, ending at my mouth.

Before I close my eyes to return his kiss, I capture his steel blue eyes penetrating mine. I know *later* will be delectable. *Yum...*

Walter releases my lips reluctantly, takes my hands in his, pulls me up and leads me down the stairs. "Come on, Angelina. We can talk over bacon and blueberry crepes. You, Steve and I need to discuss strategy."

"I thought we did that last night."

"Yes, Tangie, over wine, and we spent most of the time singing and reminiscing about our wedding."

"We're in a jam."

"Affirmative, Sweetheart, but this is one jam we're going to solve, and not get hurt in the process."

"Is that a promise or a hope, Walter?"

"Maybe a little of both. Come on. I'm hungry, and so is Steve." He takes my hand and leads me downstairs into our cheery kitchen and over to the breakfast booth, where we can look out at into the garden. I notice our gardener mowed and edged the lawn before our homecoming. All the fall flowers I planted are blooming to perfection. Mums, Gerber daisies and purple asters stand at attention and seem to smile at me through the window.

Walter, holding my hand, kisses it like a French courtier and escorts me to the window seat behind the over-sized table. He lets go of my hand, smiles and pushes in the table. He grins at Steve, who sits like a gargoyle eyeing the feast. "Let's eat, Steve. I always think better on a full stomach."

Steve comes to life, grabs his fork and while grunting, starts woofing down six slices of thick Fletcher's Canadian Maple Bacon along with three ultra-light, ultra-large berry crepes topped off with organic butter, Vermont maple syrup and local dairy whipped cream. I blink and his plate is empty. Walter hands him the platter of ultra-thin pancakes and bacon and our fearless friend fills up his plate again. He pauses only to chug down a large glass of orange juice.

I, being more concerned about my weight, eat only three crepes. After all, they are my all-time favorite breakfast food, but I leave off the syrup. So, maybe I spooned a little more whipped cream and berries inside the crepes. I only took three slices of bacon. *Well, it's also my favorite and you know, a girl's gotta eat, a girl's gotta think.* I chuckle, remembering Walter's maxim.

After we stuff ourselves silly, and drink two cappuccinos each, Walter and I roll over to the couch in the living room and Steve crawls into the Lazy Boy chair. I need a nap. So much for carbs, caffeine, protein and fat pepping you up. Jet lag looms above my energy level. My eyes start to close. Walter looks at me and touches my shoulders in an attempt to revive me. "Oh no, you don't, Tangie. You've got us into this; you've got to stay awake until we have a game plan."

I yawn and stretch my arms. "Yes, my love. It's just that I'm so tired..."

"I know, Angelina, but Steve can't stay here forever."

"Sure he can. Maybe if I drink some wine..."

Walter sighs. "We drank it all last night."

"I thought we have a wine cellar."

"Curses, Steve. She's on to me." Walter croons out of the side of his mouth.

Steve covers his mouth, burps and says, "Excuse me. I think I need a drink too."

Okay, now I'm surrounded by the Marx Brothers and I'm the silent one with the harp. All I need is a squeaky horn. I nod as if reassuring myself. "Let's talk. I'll be fine. If the two of you can do it, I can do it. I flex my arms over my shoulders, shake my hands up and down, then sit up straight and stifle another yawn.

Steve notices my attempt to revive myself. "Thanks, Tangie, and I'll just stick to water."

Walter stands up, goes to the kitchen and returns with three tall glasses with lemon slices inside and a pitcher of sparkling water. He pours Steve a glass, hands it to him and watches him as he chugs it, suppressing a burp.

"Thanks, buddy. I needed that."

Walter nods.

I smile. "Steve, thanks for helping us. Any ideas you can throw our way?"

"Well, I wonder if we should contact the FBI—and Theo Lee?"

I feel all wound up, like a spinning top not ready to be released. "I don't know, Steve. What could we tell them? Would they believe me?"

"Beats me, Tangie. They may think we're all nuts. What do you think, Walter?"

"I think maybe we—you, Tangie and I—should fly to Rhode Island and check things out. You talk to the cops in Providence, as if you're following the story for the Seattle Police—make up a connection. Tangie and I will snoop around a bit in the area and we could all stay with my Aunt Hattie."

Steve shakes his head. "I don't know, Walter. The timing is not so good for me. I can't get away from the force right now without telling my boss what's going on. You know Barry. He might think it strange, me taking time off suddenly. I'm wrapping things up on an important case."

"So it's Tangie and me…"

"Unless you want to involve Barry."

Now, Barry Cardoso, Steve's boss, is a good guy, and someone you can trust, but he plays by the rules. We don't have a lot to go on except for my phone conversation with a thug. I decide to throw in my two cents. "Steve, how about if Walter and I fly to the East Coast and do a little research around Newport and Providence. If we get any more tangible information, we'll call in the troops, like you. And you can decide when Barry and the FBI should join us in Rhode Island."

"That sounds feasible, Tangie. My work here should be finished in a week, probably no more than ten days. Then I will be clear to help you on the East Coast. You two head out there first. Get some more *Tangie-able* information." Steve smiles, then laughs at his pun.

Walter chuckles.

I groan.

Steve continues. "Sorry guys. You know, I feel like I am leaving you holding the bag. I'm not being very supportive right now."

I reassure our best man. "Steve, you worry too much. Stop. We know we can count on you when things get tough. You know we won't hesitate to call you."

Steve relents with a sigh. "All right. So, you'll fly to Rhode Island to *visit* Aunt Hattie and the two of you will do some *research—just research—* while you are there. And you will call me everyday."

Walter acquiesces. "Sounds like a plan, good buddy. We can do that. I'll get the tickets and square things with Aunt Hattie."

I squeeze Walter's arm as an alarm buzzes off in my brain. "Wait on the tickets for a bit. I have to speak to my mom before we leave, Walter."

"Sure, but don't tell her anything, Tangie."

"Yeah, Walter, like I'd tell her I'm looking for a murderer. Do you know how she would freak out? I'm not crazy, you know. Well, maybe a little."

"That's why I love you, Angelina," Walter whispers and kisses me on my ear. I start thinking about things that have nothing to do with Rhode Island.

"Okay, you two." Steve rises from the overstuffed chair. He stretches his arms above his head and then puts them down at his side. He extends his hand to Walter. "I really gotta get going, guys. I'm four hours late to work and I haven't even called Suzy. Now I'm gonna have to explain my whereabouts to multiple people. Geez, I get tired just thinkin' about it. But thanks for breakfast, and the wine, the couch and good company."

I hug the big lug. "Sorry we kept you from work, Steve, but thank you...a lot." "You are my favorite policeman, and a good one at that." I kiss him on the cheek and he grins. "Tell Barry, *Hi*, for us, and I'll call Suzy before we leave. But I won't mention anything to her about what we talked about..."

"Sounds good, but wait until later to buzz Suzy. I want to talk to her first."

"Sure, Steve. No problem. Good luck. I have a feeling you two will be back together before we leave for the East Coast."

"I hope so." Steve wipes his brow with his sleeve, walks to the hall and opens the door. "You two behave yourselves."

"Now, Steve, really." I lean against the staircase and laugh. "We're married. Respectable. Homebodies. Pet owners. Gourmet cooks. What kind of trouble could we possible get into?"

Steve groans, shakes his head and closes the door.

I look at Walter. He stares at me with that look of love in his eyes, his eyes now fiery, the blue like the hot part of a flame, undressing me in his mind. I know that look. *I love that look.* I groan involuntarily and place my arms around his neck as he comes towards me.

"Hum...Walter, dessert is waiting, upstairs."

Walter literally sweeps me off my feet, caresses my cheek and despite his own jet lag, manages to carry me up the staircase into our bedroom. He tosses me into the middle of our four-poster bed. I feel him devouring me with his eyes. When he touches me, I quiver.

"Ravish me," I command, giving in to Walter's passion, my own matching his. I tear off my few remaining pieces of clothing as Walter strips himself of everything except his St. Christopher's Medal, a wedding present from Don. He considers that to be his good luck charm. And who am I to argue, especially at this time? My husband, my lover, my soul mate gazes into my eyes. I feel the fire consuming me. At this moment, a primeval urgency grasps our beings, as if our lives will be interrupted forever by terror or turmoil if we stop for one moment. The truth of that thought keeps haunting me and remains in the back of my mind, however hard I try to dismiss it. It remains there, locked in a part of my being, no matter how fast and furious our love fest continues into the late afternoon.

Chapter Nine

Sure enough—in the evening after both of us lay exhausted in our love nest, at last consumed with one another, and after drifting off into a much-needed nap—Terror comes knocking on our door, and close behind, Turmoil, rearing its ugly head, strikes us when our defenses are down.

Through my pleasant dreams I hear banging and a dog barking. *Nonsense.* Pebbles—our Westie—is at Mom's. I relax and place my arm around Walter's chest. I hear the grandfather clock in the hall chiming eight times, and in the distance a doorbell—ringing again and again. I open my eyes and sit up.

"Walter, our doorbell's ringing; someone's here. Who would be calling this late?"

"Your mother."

"My mother? Maybe you're right. I do hear a dog. Wait a minute. Listen. That is Pebbles barking."

"I told you." Walter yawns and places a pillow over his head.

"What if it isn't my mother?"

"Trust me, Tang. It is." Walter removes the pillow and pulls the covers off his body.

I stare at my Adonis and start salivating all over again. "Maybe we should just ignore the bell."

"Ignore your mother?"

"Well, we are on our honeymoon. We're not supposed to be home until tomorrow." I lean over and brush his lips.

Walter kisses me back, but with restraint. I can feel him pulling away, but not from choice. Something's coming between us. He senses it and sighs. "Honey, I'm sorry. Life is getting complicated again." He crawls slowly out of bed as if getting ready for a funeral, puts on his jeans that are resting on a nearby chair and announces like a porter on a train, "Time to get up."

He hands me the yellow fluffy robe that he gave to me when I first came to his home, when I needed a safe house. "Sweetheart, I think we better go downstairs and answer the door. Your mom wouldn't be here at this moment without a good reason. She doesn't just pop in. Maybe someone's sick..."

A sinking feeling creeps into my limbs. Shaking involuntarily, I slink out of our warm comfy bed, slip on my robe and sigh. I look at my designer jeans lying in a heap on the floor. I toss my robe aside, slip on my jeans, grab a long-sleeved studded tee shirt and slip it over my head, like a soldier getting up in the middle of the night to fight a battle. I need to get dressed to face my mom. After brushing my hair, I slip into fleece-lined clogs waiting at the side of the dresser and peek in the mirror. Inspecting myself, I decide I look presentable enough. Walter adds a Hawaiian shirt and sandals to his outfit and we face each other. I brush his hair down and off to the side with my fingers. God, I love his dark curly locks.

I kiss him gently on his lips and look into his eyes, seeing sadness and disappointment mixed with a touch of anxiety. We hug one another and walk down the stairs. Walter wraps his arm around my waist, giving me strength. I look at the old chestnut door adorned with beveled glass that reflects both the light from the sun and the moon outside our home. I know when it opens our honeymoon will certainly be over. There will be no more escaping back into our selves. The outside world with all its challenges and disturbances awaits us. I want to flee, to run up to our bedroom and hide. Instead, I open the door.

"Hi Mom. It's good to see you."

And I mean what I say. Marianna means the world to me. Next to her sits Pebbles. He begins whining and dancing in circles like he just discovered his favorite bone. Laughing, I pick him up, scratch his head and hug my furry beast. I hand him to Walter so I can embrace my mother and invite her into our home. For a minute all my worries and fears disappear. That is until I look in her eyes and see the terror reflected in them.

"Mom, what's wrong? Is everything all right? How's Charles? You look good and Pebbles looks healthy but…"

"I'm fine, Angelina. Charles is fine. Pebbles is doing great. It's not me. It's…"

That's as far as she gets in her explanation. She stumbles into the living room and collapses on the Lazy Boy club chair, the same chair that Steve sprawled upon earlier in the day. I call it our comfort chair but Marianna looks far from comfortable. She starts pulling on her hair and rubbing her temple, first the right and then the left. Then she starts sighing. Bad sign when Marianna sighs. When I worry I bite my nails but Marianna sighs.

Tears form in her eyes and begin falling down her cheeks smudging her mascara, giving her the wide-eyed appearance of a raccoon. Her shoulders shake and she grasps the arms of the chair like she's sitting in a boat sinking, a raccoon in a lifeboat with nowhere to go.

"Oh, Tangie, I don't know what I'm going to do! And Andee. She's just beside herself with the boys and just moving into *that Ballard house*. I just don't know what to do…"

My mom has taken to calling my former residence, now Bryan and Andee's home, "that Ballard house", ever since Bryan began fixing it up. Just last month, he completed all the necessities like new plumbing and lighting and this month he started refinishing the basement before Walter and I embarked on our honeymoon.

"Bryan," I whisper. "Something has happened to Bryan. That's it, isn't it?" My voice starts to crack. "Mom, tell me."

"We don't know where he is. He never came home…"

My eyes widen and I feel myself fully awake. "He never came home from where?"

Walter takes my hand, kisses it and begins to press my mom for more information. "Where did he go?"

"The other side of the Cascades. He took a job in Leavenworth, trying to make some extra cash. He and Andee want to buy a bedroom set. You know they just have a mattress on their bedroom floor and cardboard boxes for dressers. They spend all their spare money on the twins."

"I know, Mom."

Tears form in my eyes. I start to cough a little. I need a drink. Walter senses my distress and my need. He goes over to one of his stowaway drawers, one that is not visible from the front of the cabinet, takes out a bottle, opens it and pours each of us some brandy. He hands me the first glass. I give him a nod of appreciation.

At least now I am onto his hiding places.

The brandy is warm and relaxes me. I straighten up and become serious. "Mom, where exactly did he go? Do you know?"

"Yes. I told you. He went to Leavenworth. His old boss asked him to help on a carpentry job setting up for Oktoberfest. You know, putting up platforms, building some shelters, temporary structures. It was supposed to be a weekend job, no more than three days. It's been four days and no one has heard from him. He doesn't answer his cell phone. The police won't look for him. They keep saying we haven't waited long enough, but Tangie, I'm worried. I'm sick with worry."

"Mom, listen. We'll help you. It's a good thing we came home a day early. We'll start looking in the morning at the crack of dawn."

Walter looks at Marianna and nods. "Yes. First things first." He speaks directly to my mother, but I know the exact meaning of his words. Our plans to fly to New England are now on hold. The likes of Eveline Carboni can wait.

I decide one of us will call Steve in the morning and let him know of our delay. He won't mind, as he's busy anyway. As far as my chat with Suzy, well, that will just have to wait until things get less crazy around here.

I look at my mom and nod. A look of relief appears on her face, her body relaxes and she almost falls out of the chair. Walter notices and steadies her.

I kneel down in front of her and take her hands. "Stay with us tonight, Mom. I don't want you driving back to Whidbey."

"Oh no, please don't worry about me, Angelina. I'm not driving back to Whidbey. My Charles secured a room at the Elliot Bay Hotel on the waterfront, after he realized how distressed I've become. You can contact us there. We'll be there until you find Bryan. I just know you will."

I smile at her, thinking my mom has more confidence in me than she should. "Your Charles certainly is a peach, Mom. I'm glad you married him. You still sound like a newlywed."

"Well, I am, Tangie…"

I give her a hug and grin, thinking about how Mom always refers to her new husband as "my Charles".

"Angelina, I stopped here hoping you'd be home and I could drop off Pebbles. I love the pooch, but I am such a mess. With all this uncertainty, I think he is getting ignored and they don't take pets at the hotel. I didn't find that out until after we registered. I didn't want to board him somewhere else, so I..."

"Woof." Pebbles immediately makes his presence known as his feline friend, Hildie, saunters around the corner. In a flash the two of them are running up and down the stairs, around the kitchen and living room, jumping on and off the furniture. Pebbles stops, sniffs the air, smelling the leftover bacon from breakfast, and begins whining.

I laugh. "You are such a beggar, Pebbles. Come on, I'll get you a treat."

I get up and look at Marianna. "Mom, have you eaten?"

"Tangie, I can't eat."

"You've got to take care of yourself. What about your blood pressure? You can't afford to get light-headed."

Walter takes her hand and helps her up off the chair. "Come on into the kitchen, Marianna. I'll fix you a cheese omelet, with peppers." Walter's voice is soothing and charming, but insistent.

Walter can be such a sweetheart. *That's my love.*

Marianna nods. "Thanks, Walter." With his assistance she stands straight with more determination. Arm in arm, they walk into the kitchen, as she murmurs, "I can't remember the last time I ate."

"Mom, want some toast?" I pop four slices of seeded rye bread in the over-sized toaster.

"How about you two? Will you eat with me?"

"Of course, Mom. Walter's cooking three omelets." I turn to my husband. "Hey Honey, do we have any mushrooms?"

Walter nods and smiles. *"Certes—aussi les oignons."*

I smile back despite my worry about my brother. I drop some leftover bacon in Pebbles' bowl. Pebbles gobbles it up and then retreats into the living room to resume chasing Hildie. I butter the toast and bring it to Marianna. "Mom, did Bryan go anywhere else besides Leavenworth?"

She picks up a piece of toast and crunches on it like it is a delicacy. "Well Tangie, on route to his job halfway over Steven's Pass, he called Andee and told her he would stop for lunch somewhere. He did get to Leavenworth in the afternoon and started work. He called her twice the next two days and then again, just before he left Leavenworth." Marianna stops to take a sip of coffee and sighs. "That's the last time Andee heard his voice. Bryan never came home. After he finished his job, he headed towards Seattle, but never got there."

Marianna puts down her cup and looks at me, searching for an answer. "What's happened to him, Angelina?"

I take her hand and try to reassure her. "I'm not sure, Mom, but we'll find out. Please don't worry. Walter and I will start out before dawn."

I study my chef who's hard at work over the stove. "Hey Honey, how about we get up about 4 a.m. and get an early start? We can get to the pass by daybreak."

"We can do that, Tang. I'll set an alarm. We'll have to dress warm." Walter turns off the stove and dishes out our cheese omelets, two with peppers and one with mushrooms and onions. He places the condiments on the tablet beside the rye toast with butter and my mother's favorite bacon.

My mother takes a bite of her omelet and sighs. *Walter's cooking has the same effect on her.* She grins for the first time since she came in the house, and accepts two pieces of bacon that Walter places on her plate. "I love it when a man cooks. Thank you, Walter."

Marianna inhales her supper and seems determined to get her strength back. She winks at our chef, then turns to me and speaks in a somber voice, a voice I only hear her use in hospitals, churches or in the past, in the principal's office, whenever I was summoned there in my youth. "I think, Tangie, if you would take a look at things, maybe something would trigger an idea, or something in your subconscious..."

Her voice lingers on the word, *something.* I know she hopes I can visualize Bryan and his whereabouts. I hope for the same thing. In my line of work nothing is certain. I cannot conjure up visions. I have to wait for them to come to me.

"Mom, I'll do my best. So will Walter. Perhaps an idea will come to me while we're traveling up to the pass. Please try not to worry. We'll find him."

I wish I could be as confident as I sound, but I have to give my mother some hope to keep her positive and steady. God knows Andee doesn't need my mother being a basket case. Bryan's wife needs all the support we can give her. I study my mother. Her voice shakes when she speaks and her eyes appear sunken in their sockets, like she hasn't slept in two days. *She probably hasn't.*

"Mom, you shouldn't drive to the hotel. Walter will take you. I'll follow in your car, and leave it at Elliot Bay Parking for you. After you finish Walter's famous omelet and your Canadian bacon, we'll take you back to *your Charles* at the hotel. You need a good night's sleep."

Bacon, Fletcher's Canadian Maple-Flavored Bacon, twice in one day—I'm gonna roll over Steven's Pass tomorrow morning—but a girl's gotta eat. A girl's gotta find her brother, and soon. Time is running out.

Chapter Ten

Snow. Haven't seen snow since our last trip to Alaska, but I don't have time to think about that now. It's not even October and it's snowing in the passes. Walter insists we take his Porsche Cayenne. It's faster than my Escape. Four-wheel drive territory, here we come.

Once the sun comes up, I enjoy our ride. The two of us relish the first snowfall in the mountains. Only catch is this time I look at the snow with different eyes. Searching eyes, wondering eyes, worried eyes...*Bryan is stranded out here somewhere, but where?*

Walter and I decide to drive the entire way to Leavenworth via Route 2 and then backtrack. We plan to stop along the way at restaurants and rest areas and try to visualize where Bryan may have stopped or where he could have gotten into a jam. This is the first snowfall, so we can rule out an avalanche.

I look out the window, admire the scenery and enjoy our first glimpse of winter wonderland for the season. Walter grips the steering wheel.

"Tangie, the roads are slick even for four-wheel drive."

"Do you think we need to chain up?"

"Not yet. So far the snow tires and four-wheel drive are doing the job okay."

"That's a relief. There's a diner up ahead. Do you think we could stop?"

"I don't think they serve cappuccinos, Angelina."

"Hey, I'll settle for hot coffee, a trip to the ladies room, and maybe a sweet roll, but no bacon."

Walter smiles as he expertly accelerates the SUV up the steep hill. "I love that diner. Always makes me feel like I'm back in the fifties."

"Walter, you weren't alive in the fifties."

"I know, but I have a good imagination and a hankering for some more bacon." He smiles, braces the car and swerves to avoid hitting a snowdrift.

"You can eat bacon, but I have to start my diet. Starting with a sweet roll."

At the second mention of the word, *bacon*, I can hear Pebbles rustling in the back seat. There are certain words I have to learn to not say in his presence. Words like, *bacon*, *walk* and *beach*. These are triggers that make him go absolutely bonkers. Good thing he's tired now or he'd be chewing on the upholstery. I take out a few doggie treats I keep stored in my pocket and pass them to him in the back seat. "Good dog, Pebbles. We're almost there."

Pebbles usually comes everywhere with us, except on our honeymoon, date nights and dangerous missions. I don't know where this mission will lead us, but I think Bryan is the only one in danger and I know we have to find him soon. Just a feeling, but I can't shake it.

I cannot believe they have espresso at the Fifty-Niners' Diner. We order two grande cappuccinos with extra foam. Combine that with two enormous cinnamon rolls, two buttered biscuits and bacon for Walter and Pebbles. I grin at Walter. You never saw such happy campers walking out the door with takeout bags in hand. After our short stop for caffeine and nourishment, we take a few minutes to sip our coffee and walk Pebbles around the icy, freezing parking lot, where our furry beast christens every snowdrift with a sprinkle of yellow. We hop back in the SUV. Walter cranks up the heat and defroster as we head up towards the mountain pass. Upon reaching the summit and Stevens Pass Ski Resort, we plan to follow the road straight down leading us right into the Bavarian-themed village of Leavenworth.

I notice a sign signaling that we are near Deception Falls Park, a little respite near the summit for weary travelers to pause, take pictures and hike around a scenic trail with winding paths and waterfalls. After dwelling on this place of comfort and peace, I start to choke on my sweet roll and anything but peace creeps into my being. I get a sinking feeling in my stomach and realize it isn't indigestion. Something grabs me inside my chest and says: "Tangie, pay attention." After the choking stops, I cough for a bit and take a sip of my cappuccino.

Walter glances at me. "Are you all right, Angelina?"

Nodding, I whisper, "Sorry. Didn't mean to scare you."

I close my eyes and concentrate on a vision beginning to form inside my mind. *I see Bryan, with his eyes closed. Lying in the snow. Still. Not moving.*

Gasping, I open my eyes, focus on the road and notice we are passing the entrance to the park. "Walter! Turn around!"

"Sweetheart, we just stopped. "

"It's important…"

"Did you drink too much coffee?"

"Walter, quit clowning around. Just do it. Turn around. Head back to Deception Falls…the Park…"

Walter glances at me and our eyes meet. My urgency registers with him. He does not wait for a lookout or turnaround area. He looks behind us and then in front of us and does a U-turn on the steep mountain road, spinning the car a bit as he does. I hold my breath. *Be careful of what you wish for.* I don't breathe again until he straightens out the car and we reach the park entrance.

As we drive slowly down the narrow snow-covered road to the parking lot, I exhale and take a deep breath. "Walter—believe me—Bryan's here. *I know it.* We don't have much time."

Walter pulls into an area near the entrance to the main hiking path, made practically invisible by the snow. He comes around to help me out of my side of the car. Good thing. My knees will not stop shaking. I cannot control my movements. I feel like a fragile elderly lady on an ice skating rink. Good thing I am wearing boots, even if they are designer ones with little traction.

"Can you walk, Angelina?" Frantic becomes Walter's middle name.

"Just help steady me, Honey. I'm sure it will pass."

I close my eyes as I lean against him. Good thing Walter understands my eccentricities—probably because he has them himself.

I dig my hands into his side. "Walter, we've got to find him. He's in pain. I can visual him in the snow, covered up. He's not moving; he's gonna freeze to death!"

"Angelina, he won't die. Trust me. We'll find him." Walter hugs me tight and gives me much-needed strength. "Come on, Sweetheart, let's search the trail."

Walter wraps my hands in his and steadies me. I release myself from his grasp for a moment and put on my gloves. Taking a few more deep breaths, I grab his hand once more, take a few steps beside him and feel better. I wipe the tears from my eyes and search my pockets for Pebbles' leash. Walter opens the back door, releases our bouncing Pebbles from the SUV and secures him with the leash I hand him.

"I'm better, now, Walter. I can walk. Let's go down toward the stream."

We hike on the boardwalk and cross the bridge that borders the rushing stream running under the Highway 2 overpass. Our hiking path leads to a large waterfall. After we pass the flowing water that is slowly turning into one gigantic icicle, I feel a constant tugging on my chest. My heart starts beating faster and I stop to rest for a moment. Walter joins me, puts his arm around my shoulder and picks up Pebbles.

I look up at Walter. "Bryan is nearby, but not visible. Let's go to the end of the boardwalk and see if there are any places to climb down."

"Angelina, we should call Andee. She might know something about this place. Maybe there's a connection between this park and Bryan and her."

I ponder Walter's idea. "Yes. You're right. That's it! I'll call her. But do we have phone reception out here in the wilderness?"

Walter puts his hand into his chest pocket and pulls out a cell phone I have never seen before.

"Satellite. I asked Steve to order us a set before we left on our honeymoon. I planned to surprise you when we got home. They just arrived, but..."

"Bryan went missing..."

"Yes."

Walter presses Andee's number and hands the phone to me.

She picks up immediately. I stutter from the cold. "A..An..Andee? Thank God, you're home."

"Tangie?"

"Yes. Listen, Andee. This is important. Walter and I are at Deception Falls Park."

74

"Oh, that's where Bryan proposed to me…"

"Andee, that's helpful. Where about did he propose to you, exactly?"

"Just beyond the waterfall, you know, the big one at the end of the path to the right. We even have a picture of it and…and when Bryan leaned over to place the ring on my finger, it fell into the water. We never recovered it. We searched but never found it. I guess the moving water carried it away. I never told anyone because…because it embarrassed Bryan so much. Why do you ask?"

"I'll tell you later. Walter and I are right there now, looking for Bryan."

"Oh Tangie, thank you! Your mom called me early this morning and told me you were heading over the pass to Leavenworth. Your helping us means so much to me and…"

"Andee, this information is key to our search. Thanks. I'll call you back as soon as I know anything. Hug the boys for me."

"I will. Please, Tangie, find him for me…and for Jason and Jeffrey…"

I hear her sobbing between her words and then her voice breaks down entirely. She cannot speak.

I speak softly to her, trying to comfort her. "Andee, listen. Be strong. We will find him. I promise."

I disconnect the phone and look at Walter. "I know where he is. He jumped off this bridge."

"Bryan isn't suicidal."

"Of course not. He came to this spot to find Andee's engagement ring. That's why he jumped off the bridge—to look for it. He couldn't afford to buy her another one."

"What?"

"Walter, we have to climb down off this bridge and get Bryan. He's down there somewhere and we don't have much time."

Walter looks down at the rocks and rushing water and sighs. "Okay, Tangie. I'll climb down there for you. You stay put. I don't want both of us getting trapped. You cannot risk messing up your shoulder again. It's finally healed. Use the satellite. Call 911. Ask for the mountain rescue team. Tell them someone is stuck under the bridge beyond the rocks and large waterfall at Deception Falls. It won't be a lie. Once I jump down under the bridge, I won't be able to get back up, same as Bryan. I'll find him, Angelina. He can't be too far away."

"Be careful, my love..."

"Aren't you glad you married me?"

"Everyday of my life."

I hold Walter in a death grip, not wanting to let him go. He kisses me gently, then extracts himself from my embrace. I wipe the tears falling from my eyes and push 9-1-1 on the phone.

"911. How can I help you? What is the nature of your emergency?"

"Hi. I am at Deception Falls Park. My husband and brother are lost beyond the bridge, by the waterfall. They need help. One of them is hurt..."

"Where are you now, exactly?"

"I am by the bridge, on the boardwalk."

"Take shelter and stay there. A search and rescue team will be with you as soon as possible. Keep your line open, so I can call you back if I need any more information."

"Please hurry! It's a matter of life and death. My brother has been out in the snow for over twenty-four hours. I am sure he has frostbite, and now my husband has gone after him."

"They will be there as soon as possible. For now, stay put, stay warm and keep your line open."

"Yes, Ma'am. I'll stay open for you."

"Good. Signing off for now. Keep the faith and keep warm."

I hear a click and she is gone. I put the phone in my pocket and take Pebbles' leash from Walter who nods and gives me one last kiss before he swings one leg over the thick wooden guardrail. He swings his other leg over and jumps off the bridge toward the stream. He lands softly in the snow and gives me a thumbs-up before I watch him disappear into the castle of snow-covered cedars. The towering cedars bring back a vision of the magnificent churches I visited in Europe during college with my choir and orchestra. So majestic, but with the snow icing over their branches, they leave me feeling cold, blocking out my hope. I shiver as loneliness overtakes me. The whiteness of the snow, that begins falling and drifting all about, encompasses my body. I slink down against the rail and pet Pebbles. "Good dog. You stay with me until Walter comes back."

I take a paper bag out of my pocket and place it under my body, so I won't get the seat of my pants encrusted with snow. Opening my jacket,

I stuff Pebbles inside. Pebbles licks my face and I smile at him, feeling somewhat warmer. I pet his head, close my eyes and wait.

I can still visualize my brother, Bryan, lying in the snow, this time with his right leg at an unnatural angle. He wears a fleece jacket, his working boots, and a baseball hat with a hood over it. At least his clothes cover his body parts. Maybe he won't suffer hypothermia. Maybe Bryan will be okay, if Walter finds him in time. He's got to find him. The twins need their father. Andee needs her husband. I need him. He's my only brother, my only sibling. And my mother, Marianna…Oh Lord, what will become of her if anything happens to her baby boy? *Please, God. Help Walter find Bryan. Walter, please find him…find him…*

Chapter Eleven

I don't know how long I've been sitting on the wooden bridge, leaning against the rail, with Pebbles on my chest keeping me warm. My eyes remain closed. My mouth incessantly forms the words of the prayers I learned in my childhood. My body is frozen in place, unable to move.

"Are you all right, Miss?" A voice speaks as if from a distant far-away land, because of the fog forming in my mind.

I open my eyes and see not one but three rescue workers surrounded by the white cloud encircling me.

"You're here," I try to say. I speak, but no words come out of my mouth.

The man speaks again. "Yes, Miss. I'm an EMT and we're here to help you." He wraps a blanket around me as another person takes Pebbles out of my jacket, removes his doggie vest and wraps him in another blanket.

"Thanks." I speak again, but I don't think they hear me. I start to cry and feel tears stinging my face.

"What seems to be the problem?" The second rescue worker, a woman, asks.

A fine time to lose my voice—I cannot speak—I can only imagine how Bryan must feel. I start to sob. "My brother..."

I cannot go on. I can only see the fog coming again. The man and woman disappear, but I can hear their voices.

"She's going into shock. Quick! Lift her and take her to the van."

"No." I manage to get out a raspy whisper. "First, help Walter. He's down there."

Blindly, I point with my left hand towards the embankment below. I manage to squeak out the words that are excruciating to form. "He went to get my brother, Bryan. Help them, please..."

"Okay, Miss. We understand. We already have a support staff en route. If there are people down there, we'll find them. Don't worry. We're going to take you back to the van and get you warm, and your little dog too. Hold on."

I feel strong arms picking me up and carrying me, and then I feel those same arms lifting me onto a cot and covering me. Another one gives me a warm beverage. Tastes like cocoa, but I cannot swallow it. I feel Pebbles by my side. I pet him and he is cold to my touch. *Poor dog.* Then, I cannot feel him anymore and I cannot hear anything. But I can sense a wonderful warm light as I drift peacefully into the unknown.

Chapter Twelve

My shoulder aches. My knees hurt. Darkness surrounds me. *What's going on? Where am I?* I struggle to open my eyes but cannot. Someone has put fishing weights on them. As I attempt to lift my arm, the heaviness continues and I soon give up.

Maybe it's better I don't know. I drift off again into my recurring dream. *Walter, me...on the water...in a boat...sailing around a bay...looking for something...Just Walter and me...and someone else on the salt water. I can taste it, I can smell it, but I can't feel it. I can't feel anything.*

The second time I wake up, I am able to open my eyes, but I can only squint. Daylight. Bright sun. I stare at the wall—white, no color, not the ceiling in my home. But, it looks familiar. Seems I've been here before. Putting my arm down at my side I try to push myself up. This time I succeed, but the effort is exhausting. I look around at my surroundings. No people. Just me, the bed, some machine and ah, yes, the IV—dead give away. *How did I wind up here?* Last thing I remember, Walter jumping off the bridge, looking for Bryan, and me sitting down with Pebbles at my side. Freezing and not caring, just waiting for Walter to return, but wait, *Walter! Where is Walter? Where is Bryan?*

I don't realize that I am screaming. I think no one hears me as I continue to scream, "Help! Somebody help!"

Swinging my legs around to get up turns out to be a challenge. Seems my legs don't move like they used to. Panic takes over. I can't breathe. My feet—I can feel them, slightly—they tingle. I look down and see bandages and padding...

"Oh, no!" I shout again. "My legs!"

Hysteria sets in. "Help! Please! Somebody help me!"

Apparently somebody finally hears me yelling. A nurse in a pink-striped shirt comes running in. She looks familiar.

"Oh, good! You're awake, Tangie. Remember me?"

"Well, oh yes, *Grace*? Are you Grace?"

"Yes. *Grace Chen*. I was one of your nurses the last time you were here, but I'm surprised you remember me."

"I remember you being kind to me. "When did I come in?"

"You came in yesterday."

"Did I come in alone?"

"No. The medics brought you. I will buzz the doctor." Grace takes out a cell phone and taps it once. "He will explain everything. It's good to see you awake."

"How long have I been asleep?"

"Many hours, but not to worry. Sleep is the great healer."

"Grace, there's something wrong with my legs."

"Don't stress. The doctor will explain."

I give her a helpless stare and my eyes begin to tear up. She takes my hand and sits next to me on the bed.

"I'll sit with you until the doctor gets here. He's in the hospital so he should be here any minute. He wanted to see you when you woke up."

I nod, put my head back on the pillow and close my eyes. I try to hold back the tears and not think of Walter and Bryan. I whisper over and over, "The doctor will know. The doctor will tell me..."

I relax as Grace holds my hand and hums a soothing chant that lulls me into a light sleep. The humming stops and I hear a door opening, then footsteps. I open my eyes and stare into the familiar face of Doctor Gibbs.

He grins. "I told you I didn't want to see you again, except as a visitor."

Dr. Gibbs refers to my last stay at Swedish, a rather lengthy stay, when I was in a coma.

I try to smile, but give up the effort. "Sorry, Dr. Gibbs, I don't know what happened. Could you please tell me?" Tears start to form in my eyes.

He places his hand on my shoulder and smiles. "Well, for starters, you are going to be okay. Not a long recovery, just a day or two. Things could have been much worse. You have a mild case of frostbite. You are lucky the search team found you when they did. He pats my bandages. No permanent damage to your legs. You just need some rest."

"Oh thank you. I am grateful, truly, and can deal with the frostbite. But I am so worried. Dr. Gibbs, tell me about Walter and Bryan."

"Sure, but maybe you would like to talk to Walter yourself. He came in with you."

"Where is he? Is he all right?"

"Well, yes. He's in much better shape than you. He's been here at your bedside all night. He just stepped out to get some espresso. He thought you'd like a latte when you woke up. I gave you a rather powerful sedative last night. You needed to sleep. You kept thrashing around and were a wee bit incoherent."

"So you drugged me."

"Well, just a little."

"At least I had pleasant dreams, I think."

I hear more footsteps. Walter appears like a bright shining light to wipe out my earlier depression. Tears stream down my face, "Walter…"

"Yes, I love you too, Angelina." He puts two grand cappuccinos on the nearby cart and kisses me gently. "Glad you are awake. Thought you'd need one of these about now."

I put my arms around him and let out a sob. "Thanks, Sweetheart. How can you be so chipper?"

"I didn't get frostbite, and I have some good news. Well, some good news and some bad news."

Dr. Gibbs clears his throat. "Tangie, I'll leave you in Walter's care and I'll check on you later. Don't get out of bed alone quite yet."

"No chance of that, Doc. I already tried that and my feet would not cooperate."

"Yes, they're a little numb right now but you should have some feeling in them soon. Frostbite takes time to go away."

"Thanks, Doctor Gibbs, for everything."

I turn to Nurse Cheerful. "And you, too, Grace..."

Grace nods her head.

Doctor Gibbs smiles. "You're welcome, Tangie. Get well. Follow orders, you hear?"

"I hear and I promise."

Dr. Gibbs shakes Walter's hand. "Good going, son."

Walter grins and nods. Dr. Gibbs grins back and heads out the door to continue his morning rounds, with Grace at his heels.

My Adonis gives me his full attention. "Angelina, now for the news."

"Bryan, did you find Bryan?"

"Yes. He's alive, but unfortunately he'll be at Swedish for a while. Frostbite, like you. He also broke his leg in two places. He slipped and fell while trying to retrieve that ring which, incidentally, he discovered next to a rock in the water. How it got wedged in there is anyone's guess. But he found it—Andee's engagement ring—a rather big price to pay for a near-death experience. Dr. Gibbs expects him to make a full recovery but says Bryan will be here for at least ten days."

"I guess that's about the best possible scenario under the circumstances. When can I see him?"

"When you can walk."

Now the floodgates open. Not a little whimpering but loud, cantankerous wails.

Walter sits down next to me on my cranked-up hospital bed. He takes me in his arms, kisses my eyes as if to stop the tears and speaks to me in a soothing tone, not too soft, but reassuring and firm. "Sweetheart, please. Take it easy. You will be able to walk, probably tomorrow. Don't cry. Look, I'll talk to Grace. Maybe she could rustle up a wheelchair for you, okay?" Walter looks into my eyes, and hugs me tighter. "Don't cry. Bryan just came out of surgery. They set his leg. He's asleep now. He will be for a while. But sure, you can go see him. Your mom is with him now and Andee, of course."

"And the boys? How are they doing?"

Walter smiles. "They're fine. Andee sent them to stay with Charles at the Edgewater. She didn't want them getting upset, watching their dad just lying there, not talking. When Bryan is a little more lucid, they'll be in to visit him."

"Jeffrey and Jason are gonna know something's up. They're smart kids. You know they miss their dad. He's as much a kid as they are. They all love horsing around."

"Don't worry. Charles is a great gramps. He's keeping them occupied. He's taking them around Seattle. They've been to the zoo, the aquarium and ferry hopping all over Puget Sound. They're delighted to have a holiday from school. They don't totally understand what's happened."

I look at Walter, giving him a smile filled with gratitude and love. "You're wonderful, Walter. Do you know that?"

Walter squeezes my hand. "I'm just glad I found Bryan. He was hidden in bushes and under the snow. He made a shelter for himself and I think that is what saved him. However, we're lucky we found him when we did."

"How did you avoid frostbite?"

"Well, Tangie, for one thing, I kept moving. When I found Bryan, I couldn't drag him out by myself, so I adapted the shelter to fit the two of us. I stayed calm. Together, we waited for the medics. I knew you called them. It didn't seem that long to me, once I found him. But I'm sorry I left you out in the cold.

"Walter, don't ever be sorry."

"Well, I am. I didn't realize you stayed out in the open. I thought you'd gone to the car. I was focused on searching for Bryan."

"Walter, It's my own fault. I wasn't thinking clearly. My brain got fuzzy and I didn't want to leave the bridge. I wanted to stay close to you. I thought you'd be back any minute. Then I zoned out and didn't care about myself anymore. Thank goodness for Pebbles. He saved me from turning into a Popsicle. Pebbles! Oh my goodness! Is he all right, Walter?"

"Yes, Angelina, he's fine. He started sneezing, so your mom convinced the vet to keep an eye on him. He's doing well. According to Dr. Kate, he should be home in time to greet you."

"Poor little pooch. I didn't think."

"Promise me, Angelina, that you'll always care about yourself. Think of me. I need you. We all need you."

"I promise, my love." Tears begin to flow freely down my face, tears of happiness and relief. "And Walter..."

"Yes, Sweetheart?"

I touch Walter's cheek and smile. "Thanks for staying with me all night. I could sense your presence in my dreams."

"Probably because I climbed in the bed with you. Don't tell anyone. They thought I slept in the recliner by the window."

"My lips are sealed. Now, Honey, could you please call Grace? I need her help. I have to go to the little girls' room. I can't drink the rest of my cappuccino until I do!"

Walter chuckles, takes a hold of the red chord and pulls it. "Your wish is my command."

Chapter Thirteen

Sometimes if you say to yourself, "Life is good", it is. I am now in the second day of my recovery. I can stand a little on my own and move around. So right now, I think life is great. I am ready to do the happy dance.

After I finish breakfast, Grace comes in and pushes me in a wheelchair to Bryan's room. Hospital rules. They don't like patients falling on their boney behinds in the hallway. Walter walks beside my wheelchair and caresses my neck when we arrive at the door. I smile up at him. I can feel my body coming back to life. My toes tingle, and I feel a warm glow encompassing my body.

Grace tells Walter he can now maneuver my chair and that she'll return to push me back to my suite. He nods and wheels me over to Bryan.

"Tangie!" My brother grins like a Cheshire cat.

"Bryan! You're sitting up. You're awake!"

"Yeah, and I'm alive, thanks to you and Walter..."

Andee comes over and gives me a hug. She starts blubbering then turns away, unable to stop crying. Walter touches her shoulder. "Come here, Andee." He opens up his sinuous arms and she buries herself in his embrace.

I grasp my brother's hand. "Seems like I'm not the only one who gets emotional. Good to see you, Bryan. I've missed you."

I notice my mother sighing in her seat by the window. She puts on a smile, gets up and walks over to me. We hug and join Andee in her wailing, allowing the tears to flow freely. We sound like the Anvil Chorus.

"Cut it out, you three. You're liable to set off an alarm." My brother smiles and hands me an oversized blue magic marker.

I place my hand on his cast leg, my hand touching it like a feather, afraid of hurting him. I smile through my tears. "So, am I the first to sign your cast?"

"Be my guest."

I sign both of my names, my baptismal name and the name, *Tangie*, given to me by Bryan. "You know I have a split-personality because of you."

"Of course, Tangie, Angelina, Sis."

"Still, you are my favorite brother and I don't ever want to get that close to losing you again."

"Yeah, I'm your only brother. I promise, no more taking chances with my life, unless it's to preserve one."

"Uh, oh. Are you trying to tell me a good news, bad news scenerio?"

Andee, after wiping the tears off her cheek with Walter's fresh supply of handkerchiefs, says, "He hasn't told you yet, has he, Tangie?"

"Told me what?"

"He's been thinking about joining the force."

"The Air Force?"

"No. The police force."

I look at Andee, who instantly becomes stoic. Then Bryan, who despite frostbite and a broken leg displays a brilliant toothy grin. My mother stumbles back to her chair, like an abandoned puppy, with zero expression on her face. Marianna, I fear, has just heard this news for the first time, like me. She is still suffering from our family's trauma last spring, caused mainly by my over-active detective brain and my amateur crime-fighting ways. Now, the thought of her baby boy, joining the police force, battling the evil forces on a daily basis, has pushed all the wrong buttons. Her reaction remains a blank stare, as if she does not want to listen to the announcement. If she doesn't take it in, it won't happen and it won't be real.

"What about your leg, Bryan?" I ask. "How can you be a cop with a broken leg?"

"Well, Sis, I'll have to wait until it heals. My frostbite is not permanent. I will recover completely. At least that's what Dr. Gibbs tells me."

"Good ol' Dr. Gibbs." I wish the Doc would downplay the speedy recovery bit.

Walter, during all our blubbering, remains silent. Now it seems he decides it's time to speak up. "Okay, ladies. I know you are all worried about Bryan. Especially since he's in the hospital and has given all of us a bad scare."

"A really bad scare," my mother says, regaining her voice and composure.

"Yes," Walter continues. "But he is a grown man. He has a right to make his own decisions."

Andee begins to cry again. "Even if it hurts his family?"

"Andee," Walter answers. "Bryan doesn't want to hurt you. He just wants to be a policeman. There are worse things."

As I stare at Walter, I quip, "Yeah, like bomb detonating and mining for coal." I cast my eyes down. *Oh why can't I bite my tongue?*

Andee nods and whispers through her sobs, "Walter, I am so worried about him now. Just think how frantic I'll be when he's on the force."

"Andee," Walter lowers his voice, in an effort to soothe her fears. "You'll cope. It takes time."

I sigh and think of four officers in Lakewood recently gunned down in a coffee house by a violent felon let out of jail before he completed his sentence. There are a lot of crazies roaming around and they aren't always visible to officers or ordinary citizens. Walter and I encountered a couple of these scumbags this past year. Not a pretty world, the world of crime.

"You know," I speak softy, looking at Walter and my entire family. "I don't think you get used to bad things happening in this world. You just learn to accept life as it is, and try to make the most of the time you have here on earth."

Bryan locks eyes with Andee and motions her to sit by him on the bed. She rushes to him and buries her head on his chest and resumes crying quietly as he brushes her hair with his partially bandaged calloused hands. He pulls her head up to his and kisses her lips. "We'll be okay, Andee. I won't leave you again. I promise. I am learning to be careful. That will help me as a police officer."

"What are you going to do for now?" Walter asks.

"I've enrolled in classes in Criminal Justice and Psychology. I've already spoken to the dean at North Seattle Community College. I can start right away. Tuition is cheap and they have grants. I'll work on an Associate Degree and then continue my studies at the university, which is right next door to Ballard. When my leg is healed, I'll work part-time in the criminal justice system and go to school full-time. There are all kinds of scholarships available for careers in law enforcement. We can get some help for our family also. There is free childcare at the college and other discount stuff for students. Funny, college didn't appeal to me after high school, but now I want to achieve something, get a profession and make my sons proud of me."

"You don't have to be Spider-Man to get the twins' respect." *There I go, putting down my brother's dreams, when he speaks with such sincerity about his career choice.*

Walter frowns. I immediately become penitent.

"I'm sorry, Bryan. I don't know why I said that." I take his hand and groan like a sheep that strayed from his master.

He pats my hand. "Apology accepted. I kind of expected this reaction from the rest of the family, but somehow, Tangie, I thought maybe you'd understand. Understand that I am meant to do this work."

I look at Andee and our eyes lock. Sisterhood. Instant. We're in this together. I turn to my brother. "Bryan. I'm your sister and I love you. If we support each other, we'll be okay. So let's make a pact that we will be there for each other. That's about all we can do. None of us knows what the future will hold."

Now that is sort of a half-truth, because to tell the truth, I sometimes know what is going to happen. And Walter, well, Walter, he sometimes gets premonitions of things that could happen and the future is always a gray area for the two of us. When we know stuff, it is usually scary. I, for one, am not thrilled that my baby brother is about to descend into that foggy world of crime. It's wicked out there. And I don't mean wicked good.

My mother pushes herself off the chair with more vigor than she has displayed all morning. She comes over and hugs me. "Thank you, Angelina." Then she looks at Walter. "And you, too, Walter, for my son." With tears swelling up in her eyes, she smiles bravely and walks towards the door. "I think it is time I went home to my Charles. And I think it's time we leave Andee and Bryan alone."

Walter nods, grabs the handles to my chair and turns me around. My mother goes into the hall where I hear her talking to Grace. As Walter wheels me towards the door, I catch my brother winking at me. I notice a gem sparkling in the sunlight and observe Bryan slipping the ring onto his wife's finger. Andee pulls her head up from Bryan's chest and gazes at it. She sinks into his embrace, squeezing tighter, not wanting to let him go. I feel like an intruder in an intimate moment, but I can't help but treasure the love that encompasses them.

Bryan and Andee are going to be all right. They will stand up to anything fate dishes out. Their bond is deep, deeper than anything in this physical world. And, they have everything that matters in this universe.

Chapter Fourteen

By the next morning, my legs move with no tingles, no weakness. Well, maybe a little bit, but they feel almost normal. I awake refreshed and relieved, knowing I'll be going home today. My room is devoid of people. Just as well. I want to take a shower and get myself in order. Today, I will wash my hair and walk unassisted. I swing my legs around the bed and carefully exit my nest. All body parts working. *Yay!* I take one step and then another. *Yes! I can walk. No problemo!* I amble into the bathroom and my heart leaps for joy. *Independence is highly underrated. To me it is everything.*

When I finish taking a shower, and toweling myself off, I unfasten my robe from the hook on the bathroom door, then hear footsteps in my boudoir. Must be Walter with our cappuccinos and breakfast. I know him. He's a breakfast kind of guy.

I step out of the bathroom and smile at my sweetheart, who stands in front of me with an armload of goodies, not all food.

"Hi honey," he says. "You smell delicious."

"Hospital shampoo."

"You're standing firm on your own two feet."

"Yes, my love. I missed our vertical embraces, so I decided to give real walking a chance." I lean into him and give him my special morning kiss.

Walter puts down his packages, overwhelms me with a powerful embrace and lifts me off my feet. "Ah, it's so good to have you back!"

"Ditto. I missed myself."

"So, Angelina, what are we going to do today?"

"Well, go home for starters, as soon as Dr. Gibbs signs me out. After that, who cares?"

"Well, I have a little welcoming home ceremony planned for you and me."

"Oh, good. I love those ceremonies."

"And after our special homecoming, we'll get Pebbles from the vet. I called Dr. Kate. He is getting so frisky her staff is begging us to pick him up."

"Speak kindly of Pebbles. He's my faithful pooch."

Walter grins. "And, I need to make reservations to fly to the East Coast. We can get a direct flight from Seattle to Boston and then, ground transportation to Newport, Rhode Island."

"Oh, I almost forgot about those plans. I suppose we better act on that one soon. Did you call your Aunt Hattie?"

"I did and she can't wait to see us."

"What about Pebbles? I don't want to leave him again. Can we bring him with us?"

"No problem. Aunt Hattie loves him. She even suggested we pack the pooch."

"My love, thanks for everything."

"You're welcome, my sweet." Walter scoops me up and gently places me back on my bed. "Rest for a bit. Time to eat breakfast. I'm starved. I brought us some croissants and flowers for your breakfast in bed tray!"

"Yum! Sounds wonderful. Ah, yellow roses. Like you, they intoxicate me with their scent."

Walter smiles at me, fills a vase with water and arranges the bouquet on my breakfast tray. I lean over and smile back as I sip my espresso from a ceramic mug decorated with a picture of a Westie. "Thanks for the mug, my love." I caress his cheek. "You're a keeper."

Walter grins back at me. "So are you."

Sometimes life doesn't get better than a warm cappuccino, my sweet Walter and a bed of yellow roses.

Chapter Fifteen

I push the button and allow my seat to recline after our 757 Boeing Jet enters the clouds. The "Fasten Your Seatbelt" sign disappears, but I leave my seatbelt on for insurance. I'm sort of a chicken when it comes to flying. I'm getting better, but I still imagine all sorts of terrible things happening. Sometimes having a vivid imagination is a curse. Walter, on the other hand, is Mister Calm. Nothing much bothers him when we are airborne, probably because he's flown places far and wide since his youth. His late parents were jet-setter musicians flying from one concert to another, country to country.

I lean over and kiss my sleeping prince's eyes. Poor guy didn't get much sleep our last night at home. My fault. We survived the wilderness and frostbite, saved my brother from a near-death experience and spent a few hours planning our next adventure to the East Coast. I, being ecstatic over our survival, kept Walter up till the wee hours of the morning reminding him over and over again that we are still newlyweds. Walter didn't seem to mind a bit. He amazes me. But how he can go from alert to conked out in ten seconds flat is a mystery. I push his seat button and mine to raise our footrests and get into a reclining position. Love that position and love first class. I lean over and nuzzle myself into my lover's shoulder. I can use some shut-eye as well. Chances are we'll be keeping late hours when we get to Newport. We'll need our beauty sleep to track the bad guys and one nasty broad, Evelina Carboni.

Before I close my eyes and fall into a deep sleep, I think of Bryan and Andee and their sons, my adorable nephews, Jeffrey and Jason, A.K.A. the

Twin Terrors. I will miss them. Bryan and Andee are so right for each other. They give each other strength and bring out the best in each other, just like Walter and I. Bryan works so hard; he'll make a good policeman. And his entire family, including me, will support him in his endeavor, no matter what our reservations may be about his career choice. He's his own man, and I don't think I'd want him any other way.

After five hours of snoozing, I hear the wheels on our aircraft drop. Time to get ready for landing. I open my eyes, put my footrest down and turn to Walter.

I catch him staring at me. "I thought you'd never wake up, Angelina. Have sweet dreams?"

"Well, probably. I don't remember but I do feel great. Rested. Ready to face the music."

"Come on, Tangie, I thought you like my Aunt Hattie."

"Oh, Walter, I don't mean her. I love your aunt. I mean, well, you know. I don't want to mention it here."

"I get it. We'll talk later. Aunt Hattie arranged to have a limo service pick us up in Boston. We can chat while we're waiting for the chauffeur to appear."

"Ruff, ruff."

Pebbles. Gosh, I almost forgot him. First time he's been in an airplane and he's been quiet as a mouse until now.

"The royal pooch is awake, Angelina. He slept the entire trip, like you did. You missed your snack and lunch."

"That's why I am starved. Bet Pebbles is too."

"I'll get you something in the airport, but I know Aunt Hattie will have dinner waiting for us."

"If I can get some caffeine and protein, I'll be fine for the ride to Newport."

"No problem. Oh, look, Angelina, Boston Harbor. I always love landing in Boston. It's like landing on the water."

I look down and see sailboats that look like toy boats floating in a bathtub. Only this tub resembles a harbor and the edges of it consist of stones and more stones, and charming houses all around the water's edge. Boston from the air reminds me of Seattle somewhat, but more water, more dense housing, and no mountains. But what a waterfront, no place like Boston Harbor. The skies began to darken and soon the sun will be setting, perhaps before we leave the airport.

We chose not to fly into the Newport area via Providence Airport, because direct flights don't exist between Providence and Seattle. Flying into Boston means a quicker flight, but more time with ground transportation. With the limo service, that should be not unpleasant.

Did I say, *not unpleasant*? Wrong—unpleasant, for sure. We sit in rush hour traffic trying to get out of the city of Boston until way after suppertime. Forty-five minutes turns into two hours. Next time, we'll take plane changes over this traffic. Pebbles starts to whine, poor dog.

"Walter, when we get out of this traffic jam, do you think we could stop somewhere? We have to get a hamburger for Pebbles. He's starving."

"Just Pebbles?"

"Well, maybe me, too."

"Tangie, the pooch is psychic. Seems he's not the only starving creature here. There's a Ruby Tuesday's around here somewhere. We're almost through this tie-up and out of the city. I'll ask the driver to make a pit stop. He's probably anxious to get out of the car as well. They have great burgers at Ruby's. I used to stop there in my college days, on my way home from Boston. I'll give Aunt Hattie a call and let her know we are stopping for a bite after getting stuck in traffic. I hope she didn't plan a big dinner."

Chapter Sixteen

Well, it seems Aunt Hattie did plan a feast. Walter and I offer our profuse apologies for spoiling our appetites and not eating the meal she prepared for us.

She laughs, "Not to worry my dears, we will all eat leftovers tomorrow and I won't have to cook."

Walter hugs her and stares into her tear-filled eyes. "Thanks, for allowing us stay with you."

I give Aunt Hattie a kiss on the cheek and smile. "And thanks for welcoming Pebbles. Not many people like guest dogs, Aunt Hattie."

She leans down and scratches behind Pebbles' ears. "Nonsense, Angelina. Pebbles and you are family. This old house needs some company for a change. I'm beginning to get too set in my ways as a spinster."

Walter grins. "Nonsense, Aunt Hattie. You could never be a spinster and you know it."

"You are so right, my dear nephew. Just call me an independent woman, who never found her soul mate."

I smile at Walter's aunt, who is wiping away her tears with an embroidered handkerchief. She looks extremely happy despite the tears.

"Your soul mate's probably out there somewhere, Aunt Hattie, waiting for you." I take Walter's arm. "I never thought I would find the love of my life."

"I suppose there's always hope, but at my age..."

"Aunt Hattie!" Walter exclaims. "Why you are as young as ever. You have a timeless beauty that goes on and on..."

"And you, my dear nephew, are as smooth as ever. But that is why I love you."

I laugh, agreeing with Aunt Hattie. "Yes, that's one of his endearing qualities."

"Now, what have you two newlyweds been up to, or should I ask?"

I avert Aunt Hattie's eyes. "Oh, not much." I sense that Walter's aunt has a knack for perceiving things out of kilter.

Walter steps in and presents a good cover story. "Aunt Hattie. Well, first we came to see you. Then, I want to show Tangie around Rhode Island. You know, explore the sights in Newport, visit Providence and Brown—my Alma Mater. I thought we'd begin with Newport Harbor. Are you up for a day sail tomorrow?"

"Sounds wonderful. Let's just make sure we are home for supper. I can't save this dinner indefinitely!"

I hug the dear sweet lady. "That's a promise."

Aunt Hattie reminds me of my mother and grandmother combined. She's peppy like my mother and perceptive like my grandmother. She shares the same steel blue eyes that I admire in Walter. Analytical. Methinks Walter gets some of his gift from her. *How are we going to keep our investigation plans a secret from Aunt Hattie?* We will have to tell her something.

As if reading my mind, Aunt Hattie begins questioning us about the news. "Angelina, Walter, did you hear our governor died, under mysterious circumstances?"

I clear my throat. "We heard something before we left."

"A boating accident, I believe. Poor guy." Walter interjects as he sits down on the piano bench and crosses his legs.

My goodness, that guy can do innocent so well.

Aunt Hattie sits down on the couch and Pebbles leaps up to join her. She does not shoo him away, but pets him on his back. "Well, my dear nephew, good sailors don't get tangled up in their masts. Peter Van Beek excelled at sailing. Before he became governor, he taught sailing at the Newport Center for Wooden Boats. If he had his way, every person in Rhode Island would be a sailor. I can't see him dying the way the newspapers reported it. It just doesn't fit."

I sit down in an overstuffed rocking chair by the front bay window. "Perhaps something else happened before he got wrapped in the mast?"

Walter gives me a quick glance.

Aunt Hattie picks up on that and nods. "Well it's food for thought. I certainly will be following this story closely. The governor's older sisters, Jenny and Clarissa are friends of mine. We belong to the same garden club. They are heart-broken. They had such high hopes for Peter. He knew how to govern. He had an appeal with both political parties. He devoted his life to public service. What a loss for our state. And I think of his poor children. They must be devastated."

I nod, remembering the two college students mentioned in the news. In the back of my mind, I start thinking...*we could let Aunt Hattie help us in a round about way with our investigation. She could introduce us to his family and friends. Heck, she's a family friend of the governor.*

I glance at Walter. Chances are he's thinking the same thing. That pensive look appears on his face—the one I recognize—the one he gets before a brainstorm.

Walter stands up. "Aunt Hattie, are you going to the funeral?"

"Of course. I don't know all the details, but it will probably at St. Mary's in Newport or at the Cathedral of Saints Peter and Paul in Providence. We won't know until after the body is released to the family."

"Perhaps Angelina and I could escort you."

"Why thank you, Walter. That would be very kind of you both."

I look at Walter as he walks over and hugs his aunt and on the sly, winks at me. I wink back at him.

Then, without warning, that familiar queasy feeling hits me in the pit of my stomach. I hate funerals. I hate wakes. Stems from my father dying when I was only seven, after I dreamt about his passing. Not knowing how to deal with my premonitions, I sunk into a depression and spent a lot of time in the counselor's office at school. I didn't fully recover until my teen years. I spent many years feeling out of sorts, not fitting in socially. Luckily, I have a loving, supportive family. That helped a lot. Maybe I will not feel faint; maybe I will be strong. Maybe I will finally learn to deal with these flashbacks. *Yes, Tangie. Get real. You're in love. You're married. You're safe. No one's going to get hurt because of you.*

I start reciting my mantra, beginning with: *Take the joy in today. Don't live in the past hurts of yesterday.* And I feel better, almost.

After chatting with Aunt Hattie for two hours, and telling her all about our family in the Pacific Northwest and our trip to Hawai'i and Fiji, minus the part about Eveline, Walter and I decide to take an evening stroll around Newport. I put the leash on Pebbles. It isn't easy as the pooch tiptoes circles around us. He starts his dance routine when I mutter the word "walk" and does not quit until we stroll out the door. We skip down the porch steps at a rapid pace. I turn, look back and see Aunt Hattie sitting in her chair by the front bay window, gazing out at the harbor in the twilight and intermittently reading the evening paper. I think of the old saying, "I wish I had a penny for your thoughts."

Pebbles being his usual male-dominant self, christens every signpost, bush and fire hydrant we pass. The neighborhood seems unusually quiet, hardly a soul venturing out. No doubt, in the summer, it's an entirely different scene. Aunt Hattie's home, a comfortable New England Saltbox, looks like it has perched on its hill forever. No doubt it has. Most of the houses on Wedgewood Hill possess a unified classic design, that settled in, well-preserved appearance that takes lots of work, tender-loving care and a certain amount of money to maintain. We stroll down the alternating cobblestone and brick sidewalk, careful not to trip over the bumps along the way. As we near the bottom of the hill, Pebbles sniffs the salt air and starts pulling on his leash like a thoroughbred at the starting gate. My canine loves the beach and senses the water nearby.

I hand Pebbles' leash to Walter, as Walter has a firmer grip with our feisty pooch. Pebbles doesn't pull his "I can get away with anything because I'm so cute" routine with Walter. Walter doesn't even have to raise his voice. Pebbles simply obeys him, viewing Walter as the Alpha Male. Me—it's a different story. The pooch knows I'm a pushover.

We arrive at the waterfront, which is about three and a half blocks down from Aunt Hattie's home. I admire the sailboats secured to their docks, lined up and elegant, like proud racehorses awaiting their masters.

I hear the lines clanging together with the masts, as if in chorus with one another. The air smells fresh and clean. A few errant seagulls caw as they fly away to join their mates for the evening. The surroundings remind me of Shilshole Bay Marina in Seattle. However, this marina is much older. One can feel the ghosts of sailors and their phantom ships along Newport Harbor. True, the harbor doesn't have a view of the Olympic Mountains rising up in the distance past the water like in Seattle, but Newport possesses a special charm and long history dating back to before the Revolutionary War, before we were a country.

Walter takes my hand and pulls me to the left. "Let's check out Aunt Hattie's gallery. It's over here, next to the excursion boat docks."

"I bet she gets a lot of tourist trade."

"Yes, she does. But the locals also appreciate her talent for finding great art and frequent her shop on a regular basis."

"Your aunt is the neatest lady. If it weren't for our mission to uncover this *Seedy Steve* guy, we could have a great time with her."

"Don't sell her short. She won't mind snooping around with us. She'll have fun no matter what we are doing. You know it's possible to work and enjoy ourselves at the same time, don't you?"

"Walter, I need to adopt your attitude. I always get caught in the drama of the situation. I need to develop your laid-back style. If Aunt Hattie is as laid-back as you, maybe some of her resilience will rub off on me. I'm tired of being so intense about our detecting."

"I like you intense, Angelina."

"Yes, Walter, I know." I kiss him lightly on the cheek as we approach a cluster of shops and casual dining places, all closed for the evening. "You like me intense in bed."

"Elsewhere too. On the beach, in the car, on the…"

"Okay, I get the point." I smile as we approach one shop in particular with a sign hanging over the door. It reads: The Crow's Nest.

"Is this your aunt's gallery?"

"Yes, it is. I used to hang out here in the summer when I came to stay with Aunt Hattie. Sometimes I'd help her with the customers. Some days, she'd drop me off at Beach One at the end of town and pick me up after closing time. I have great memories of this shop, the harbor and the beach. As a kid, I used to pretend I pirated all the ships that came and went along

Newport Harbor. Sometimes, Aunt Hattie and I would pack a picnic supper and take an evening sail after closing time. You know, the three of us could do that—a picnic and a sail—for old times' sake."

"Sounds wonderful, my sweet. We could locate the governor's home, that is, the late governor's. It's on the waterfront, isn't it?"

"Not too far. Aunt Hattie would know."

I peer into the display window of the Crow's Nest and admire the variety of art from oil paintings to Scrimshaw, a few wooden carvings of sea fowl, metal sculptures of fish attached to granite bases and stained glass with nautical themes. Must be what sells around here. "We aren't taking advantage of Aunt Hattie, are we?"

"Of course not."

"Walter, maybe we should level with her."

"Angelina, I think she may already know something is up. She doesn't know what, but she's curious. Maybe you're right. Let's sleep on it and maybe in the morning, tell her. Everything is clearer in the morning. Plus, Aunt Hattie is probably asleep by now."

As we turn, I notice a raven perched upon the Crow's Nest sign. *Fitting*, I muse. Or perhaps he is sending a warning that something is in the air, and this something or someone is about to envelop the two of us.

I shudder. Walter takes my arm, caresses it and leads me to the docks where we check out sailing vessels and day cruisers. We decide on one or two of them to venture on tomorrow, depending on availability.

"Yes, Mrs. Cunningham. Tomorrow, we'll pack a lunch and take a cruise around Newport Harbor and Narragansett Bay. Maybe you could get an insight into what happened if we pass the governor's home."

I begin to shiver. Don't know if it's from the night air, or the thought of going into the dark world of crime again. Life's been so good to us for the past few months, our wonderful summer in Seattle, our wedding on Whidbey Island, our honeymoon...well, until the last day. Then add Bryan's disappearance when we came home. Seems like life cannot stay on an even keel forever.

Pebbles starts whining, as if sensing my mood.

Walter responds to my distress by taking me into his arms and crushing me in a warm embrace. "Everything will be all right, Angelina. I won't let anything happen to you."

I start to tear up. I'm a sucker for tenderness. I gaze into Walter's eyes and sigh. "I know, Walter. You keep me grounded. Life is so good with you. I just get scared sometimes."

"Me too." Walter pushes the hair out of my eyes, fastens the loose strands behind my ears and kisses my cheek.

God, I love it when he does that, my wonderful, caring soul mate. *Who says good guys aren't sexy?*

Walter tightens his grip on me. "For your information, my love, we are not going to go around chasing anyone. We are just gathering information. Then we call our Steve. Got it, Angelina?"

"Yes—Our Steve. I wonder how he's doing with Suzy?"

"No doubt, back in the saddle. I'm sure they made up and are making each other crazy, again. That's what lovers do." I hear Walter chuckle.

"I always love the making-up part."

"My favorite too. You know, Angelina, we rarely fight."

"It's early yet. Wait until we're married a year. We're bound to have one knock-down drag-out fight before the year's over."

"You're no Suzy. I can't stay mad at you for long. I can't even remember being really angry at you."

"And you're no Steve. Come on, Walter. I'm getting chilled and hungry. Maybe we can raid Aunt Hattie's icebox when we get home."

"My thoughts exactly." Walter takes Pebbles' leash from me, grabs my hand and leads us off the pier toward the hill to Aunt Hattie's. After we cross the main intersection, I let go of Walter's hand and race him up the incline. He beats me. He has an advantage, Pebbles pulling him all the way home. The dog understands the word "hungry". Seems we all have worked up an appetite.

Chapter Seventeen

When we open the front door, I smell roasted chicken and gravy, and fresh bread baking. Aunt Hattie, with an apron tied around her waist, meets us at the door. "I thought you two weary travelers might be up for a late supper, so I reheated your dinner and baked some fresh rolls."

Walter hugs his aunt and gives her his famous grin. "You are a mind-reader, Aunt Hattie."

I join in the hug, but no one can compete with Walter's priceless grin. "Thank you, Aunt Hattie," I whisper, out of breath. "Believe it or not, we're starved…"

"I am kind of hungry myself, children, and I just took a chance you'd be also by now, with the time difference and all. You know, if you want a snack, there's no place open this late on the waterfront, in the off-season. Come into the kitchen. I've got a fire going there. Sit down."

Aunt Hattie pushes us gently into her gourmet hideout. "Have some supper. I even placed a bowl of chicken and kibbles out for Pebbles."

I smile. "Thank you, Aunt Hattie. You're wonderful."

"Well, reserve your compliments until after you've eaten the feast I've prepared. One never knows…"

To me, the meal is as wonderful as Aunt Hattie. Roast Chicken, with glazed carrots, mashed potatoes and gravy. A Chicory salad, with vegetables from her backyard garden and for dessert, strawberry-rhubarb pie—my favorite comfort foods. My grandmother used to make this meal, but her dessert consisted of *Icebox Cake*—chocolate pudding and graham crackers and whipped cream. Hum, maybe I can make that while we are here. Simple enough. Aunt Hattie probably makes it also—same generation as my mother and grandmother. She probably ate it as a child like my family did.

After we stuff ourselves silly, Walter and I help Aunt Hattie clear the table, store the leftovers, and load the dishwasher. Then we stroll into the living room where Walter starts a fire in the old massive fireplace to take off the chill in the living room. The fire in the kitchen kept us toasty while we ate.

"Thank you, Walter," Aunt Hattie sighs and sits down in the chair by the front window, which appears to be her favorite spot. "I love a roaring fire, especially with the fall chill in the air. We've had such a warm summer, that fireplace has set unused for months. It's so peaceful watching the flames coming up and capturing the wood."

"I love it too, Aunt Hattie. Reminds me of old times. Speaking of old times, Angelina and I would like you to come with us on our sail tomorrow afternoon. Can you get away from the gallery?"

"That's not a problem, Walter. Louisa can watch the counter—and Pebbles. She loves all animals, especially furry adorable ones. But are you sure you want me to go with you? I would think you'd want to be alone—together."

I take Walter's hand in mine. "Aunt Hattie, we've had a lot of alone time on our honeymoon—and there's something we want you to help us with, if you don't mind."

"If I can be of any assistance, of course. You just let me know, dear."

I look at Walter, and he nods. Seems like our confiding in Walter's aunt cannot wait until morning. I take a deep breath and unburden all my suspicions and conjectures upon Aunt Hattie, who sits composed in her bright yellow-plaid overstuffed Queen Anne chair, enjoying the crackling fire, with a calm and caring look in her bright eyes and her mouth wide-open.

Chapter Eighteen

The noon sun shines down upon us as we board the *Misty Morn*, a forty-foot sailboat. A gentleman, tall, tan and seemingly a little older than my mother's Charles, greets us in an inviting and invigorating voice as he introduces himself as Captain Jack. "Sit anywhere you'd like topside."

Aunt Hattie smiles at him, giving him an extended handshake, like they are old friends. They probably know each other from years gone by. A lot I have to learn about Aunt Hattie. I am thinking, *definitely not the prime and proper New England maiden.*

The crew loosens the lines and lifts the bumpers from the side of the sailboat. I enjoy watching the rhythm of their work and their contented faces. Must be wonderful to work on the waterfront, and sail out to sea on a daily basis. Walter takes my hand and pulls me up from my comfortable perch. "Let's go out to the bow. That way we can get an expansive view of everything along the shore while watching the ships pass by."

With enthusiasm in my toes, I hop up and follow. Aunt Hattie possesses no fear of sailing vessels and joins us as we venture forward. We find a few cushions and huddle together, ready for our journey.

The crew casts off, with Captain Jack at the helm. Gazing around the harbor I zero in on the people we left ashore at the marina—leftover stragglers from the summertime, trying to hold onto vacation time. In a few short weeks, Mother Nature will consume all tourist weekends. Wind, snow, ice and rain will replace the guests on this festive port of call.

As we leave the safety of the harbor, our captain instructs us to view the former home of Jacqueline Kennedy Onassis, a beautiful mansion, situated not far from the shoreline. He points out her extravagant childhood playhouse by the water's edge, a scaled-down replica of the main house. Afterwards, he shares a story about an elegant waterfront home built by an ambitious American entrepreneur who, with a partner in the 1880's, made his fortune developing Worcestershire Sauce.

We sail past a famous historic fort—Fort Adams. Next comes the War College. While I am contemplating that Newport is a virtual history book, Captain Jack steers the boat into the open water of Narragansett Bay. Before we reach a less-crowded area of the bay, I admire a home at rest on its own small island.

Aunt Hattie points to it. "They call that Fox Island."

A peaceful feeling consumes me as I sigh.

Walter notices. "Having a good time, Tangie?"

I lean against Walter's shoulder. "I love being on the water. I could get used to this life. It is so relaxing."

"We could do this more often. My grandfather and I used to sail around Puget Sound. He taught me the fundamentals of sailing. So, when I stayed with Aunt Hattie, hardly a day went by that I wasn't on the water."

Aunt Hattie nods. "Yes, Tangie. He took to sailing like he was born with a tiller in his hands."

"*Walter the Sailor*. Why didn't I know that?"

"My love, we've been too busy chasing the bad guys."

I chuckle, and kiss Walter's cheek. "Sweetheart, as usual, you've been holding out on me. Another one of your surprises."

Aunt Hattie smiles and can't help bragging. "Walter won a lot of races. You should see his trophies. I think they are still in my attic. I loved watching him compete."

Walter hugs his aunt. "You love me because I'm your favorite nephew, Aunt Hattie."

"Yes, child, and my only nephew, it seems."

"So, you're stuck with me."

"I'm afraid so. And I do love you. You are like the son I wished for when I was a young woman.

110

I smile. "He kind of grows on you, doesn't he, Aunt Hattie?"

Aunt Hattie answers with a smile as the wind comes up and blows my hat off. Walter catches it and hands it to me before it becomes a balloon at sea. Aunt Hattie laughs. "Walter has a way of making himself indispensible."

"Tell me about it! Did you know, when we first met, he passed himself off as my secretary, working for his rent?"

"No! Aunt Hattie pats his cheek. "Walter, you are such a fox. What other shenanigans did he pull on you, Tangie?"

"Well, for starters, he kept his entire identity a secret from me."

"He didn't!"

"Yes. He pretended to be a starving teacher."

Walter interrupts my banter. "Now, you know, Tangie, I did teach..."

"Yeah, but not at a crummy junior high, like you led me to believe. You rubbed elbows with the likes of Bill Gates at Lakeside School."

"Yes m' love, but I quit my job for you..."

"I know, and I love you for that. You haven't regretted it, have you?"

"Of course not. But I never did complete that book I planned to write. It seems you kept distracting me with your dilemmas. No time to write. So I'm thinking, maybe I'm not really a writer. I would have found the time. Now I'm thinking, perhaps I'll pursue music. That never leaves me, no matter what I do."

Aunt Hattie, enjoying our exchange, is surprised by my latest remarks. "Walter, you never told me you wrote."

"Well, Aunt Hattie, I did write a few articles for *Jazz Magazine*—and started a manuscript, but I never finished it. Somehow I became engrossed in Tangie's detective business."

"Oh there's a time and place for everything. You'll make time for writing someday. Maybe this winter, when there's nothing to do. You could try composing music. Remember you used to share your compositions with me, when you were in college?"

"Um hum. You're right. I've been thinking of getting back into my music. Next to Angelina, that is probably where my heart is. I do miss hanging out with my jazz buddies. When we return to Seattle, I'll call them. We can invite them over for dinner. Okay with you, Angelina?"

"Yes, Maestro, I'd like to meet them." Another sudden burst of strong wind blows our way. I snuggle up to my honey, content in the protection of his arms.

Walter kisses my cheek and grins. "And they, my sweet, will love you. Did I tell you the leader of my old band called recently? Said he was sorry the group couldn't come to our wedding. He and his combo are still on tour. Seems those guys are in demand all over the place these days. Seems their next stop is Europe."

Aunt Hattie smiles. "Oh, Walter, I just know one of these days, I'm going to see your name on the jazz circuit. I bet by Christmas time, you'll have your first gig. I'm delighted you are keeping in practice. You could make a living playing the piano. I love listening to you and your music."

I love this woman. She's so positive. Seems she thinks we'll be done with this case before the Christmas holidays. Makes me feel content right now, knowing there will be an end to things and then new beginnings. Walter the Jazz Musician—has a good ring to it...

Aunt Hattie points, while viewing through her binoculars. "Oh look, there's Rose Island."

I squint and spot an island, small and desolate with a lone lighthouse upon it.

Walter smiles. "Oh yes, Aunt Hattie. Remember, you told me that the first lighthouse keeper named the island after his wife."

I squeeze Walter's hand. "How romantic. Some sailors name their boats after their loved ones. Rose got an island. Lucky gal."

While we chat, whitecaps appear in the distance and another strong gust catches the sail. The *Misty Morn* heels over as the waves splash down upon us. We hang on and ride up and down as the white caps increase in size and turn our smooth sail into a rollercoaster ride, which alternates between thrilling me down to my toes and scaring me to half to death. I take deep breaths and crunch Walter's hand. Then an old familiar churning starts in my stomach, and it's not seasickness. A picture emerges, suddenly. Something sinister. Closing my eyes, I visualize a shape and a place. I listen, hearing the voices seeking me out, calling me, and then they are gone. On board our vessel, another voice, loud and clear takes prominence. I open up my eyes and in the distance notice an estate peeking out from the trees on shore.

Captain Jack announces to the passengers, "Fellow seamen and ladies, hope you are enjoying the excitement. Perhaps the wind will calm down soon. If you will look over there on the starboard side, you will see our former governor's retreat. He used to sail on the bay every weekend. Poor guy. I miss him already. Newport has lost a favorite son."

I close my eyes and hear other voices emerging from my dream, speaking more clearly...*First, the governor, and then Buddy. Who is Buddy? Buddy. I remember that name. I remember. That dream, that dream—I remember now—in Fiji, before the phone call or was it after? Everything is all mixed up. The dead man—Peter—the governor...I see him—the murder happening near here—and his death. And Buddy, Buddy, he knows...He...*

I feel slight pressure on my shoulders and other voices, filled with concern, calling to me...

"Angelina, are you all right? Honey, what's going on?"

"Oh my! Walter, what's come over her? Is she sick? Should I call the captain?"

Opening my eyes, I stare into the frightened faces of Walter and Aunt Hattie. My face feels flushed. Embarrassed and a little faint, I put my hand on the lifeline and straighten up. "Oh, I'm sorry to have scared you. I get that way, sometimes, when I experience a—a flashback. Don't worry, please. I'll be all right."

Aunt Hattie studies me and then glances at Walter. Walter remains stoic. He doesn't want to give anything away, leaving me to decide what to tell Aunt Hattie.

I look at Walter and then at his aunt. "Aunt Hattie, this place, on the bay—seeing it triggered a dream. Well, more like a nightmare, like one I had on our honeymoon. It involves...well, I'll tell you later. It's a bit distressing."

Aunt Hattie nods. "I can see that my dear." She takes my hand, squeezes it gently and says no more. She doesn't push me. *I like that in her.* Not one to pry.

I close my eyes and imagine myself in Fiji and try to relax. I really don't know what to expect next. Our vacation in Fiji does not appear to me, but what does tears my heart out. *I see the helpless face of Governor Peter Van Beek, and his mouth open, crying for his children, trying to say good-bye to them. Then, someone else, sinister, laughing as he pulls a rope, tighter and tighter*

113

around the Governor's neck to ensure his death. I cannot see this someone's face, but I can smell him, he reeks of an unpleasant odor. Sweaty and foul...

The sun starts to descend and with its inevitable setting, our sail comes to an end. Walter shakes Captain Jack's hand as we prepare to depart at the same place our journey started, telling him we how much we enjoyed sailing with him, and that we hope to return another day. Then he assists Aunt Hattie and I as we step off the sailboat and together we walk down the dock onto the main concourse. I motion to a bench and collapse. Walter sits next to me, after scooting over to make room for his aunt. Aunt Hattie stares at my face, her eyes wide with wonder. Walter waits patiently for me to speak.

I glance up, furtively, waiting until there are no people mulling around before I speak. "I know what happened."

"What, Tangie?" Walter takes my hand in his and kisses it in a attempt to keep me calm.

"I know about Peter Van Beek."

Aunt Hattie pulls her sweater close to her chest. "How could you know that?"

"I saw it happen, in my dream."

But my dear, you have been awake. You closed your eyes for a few minutes, but you weren't exactly in a deep sleep."

"Aunt Hattie, this dream is a dream I had in Fiji. I didn't remember it or anything about it until just now, aboard the sailing yacht. I try to put unpleasant dreams out of my mind but sometimes they recur. This one came back to me on the water, in pieces. I saw the governor die."

Aunt Hattie puts one hand on her mouth and with the other grabs Walter's arm as she speaks my name in disbelief. "Tangie, I cannot, I don't know…"

Walter reassures his aunt. "Aunt Hattie, please don't get upset. Angelina gets this way sometimes. And she's usually right on."

Aunt Hattie sighs as she quits leaning on Walter and gently hugs me. "You poor dear, you must be exhausted. Let forget stopping at the Crow's

Nest. Let's just pick up Pebbles from Louisa's supervision and go back home. I'll make us some nice hot tea."

"I think I'd rather have a glass of wine."

"That too, but first the tea. You need to warm up. Your hands are freezing." She dictates her orders as she rubs my palms. "Come on, Walter. Let's get her up to the house. Poor dear needs some attention."

I don't really like being the center of attention, but Aunt Hattie's concern seems like a tonic to me. Walter kisses my cheek and puts his arm around me until we stop at the Crow's Nest. He lets me go, dashes inside and returns in a nano second with my Westie at his side. He holds Pebbles' lead in one hand and puts his other hand in mine. "Lead the way, Aunt Hattie. We can have a early supper, a quick chat and an early bedtime."

I smile, liking the idea of bedtime. I always like the idea of bedtime with Walter. Soothes my soul. But sometimes it wears me out. I didn't sleep much last night—by the time we got to Snoozeville, it was almost morning. Yawning, I grin. "Yes, an early supper and bed sound great. I'm exhausted."

Chapter Nineteen

I tell Walter and his aunt about my dream over three cups of Darjeeling and three glasses of Pinot Grigio. For nourishment, we have Aunt Hattie's wonderful cucumber and chicken sandwiches made out of the leftovers and served with some homemade New England clam chowder prepared the previous day. Aunt Hattie excels at East Coast cooking.

I relate everything I can remember about my dream to her and Walter. Everything that is, except for mentioning the name of *Buddy*. For some reason, I feel the need to keep that bit of information to myself. Don't know why. I will probably live to regret that, but something causes me to hush up over that detail. Maybe it's my protective instincts coming to play. Maybe I don't want them to get hurt. If they meet up with *Buddy*, they may get reckless, unlike me. I never get reckless. Scared, maybe. Frantic. Impulsive. Impatient. Not reckless. Then again, there's always a first time. I can honestly say, I wish I never remembered this dream or talked to Hit Man Steve. Life would be so much simpler. But I have a job to do. Why else do these thoughts and visions appear? Why else did this Steve call me by mistake? Seems I've got to get involved whether I want to or not.

That evening, the phone rings in Aunt Hattie's kitchen, while Walter is playing musical selections from *An American in Paris* on Aunt Hattie's slightly out of tune piano. Aunt Hattie, so enthralled in Walter's playing, lets it ring. I get up and answer it, knowing it will be important. I take a message. Seems the governor's family wants Aunt Hattie to attend the funeral and leaves me all the details to give to her. When Walter finishes his piece, I hand Aunt Hattie the message and watch her reaction as she reads it.

She glances over all the words, and dries a few tears flowing down her sun-tanned cheeks. A sob breaks in her throat making it difficult for her to speak. Her words flow like her tears, if tears have a sound. "So, my dears, we are to go to the funeral, morning after tomorrow at the Cathedral of Saints Peter and Paul in Providence. It's the biggest church in the area. Peter Van Beek has—*had*—many friends and family members. You are coming with me, aren't you?"

"Of course, Aunt Hattie." Walter gets up from the piano bench, leans down and hugs his aunt. "Of course. We'll be your escorts. You don't have to go alone."

She melts in his arms and sobs for about three minutes, after which she straightens up, brushes her blouse and smoothes her slacks. "Thank you, dears. I am so grateful you came to visit at this time. Regardless of why you two are here, I am glad you made the effort so soon after your honeymoon. I hate to be alone at a time like this. You are both a blessing to me."

Now that is about one of the nicest things anyone has ever said to me and my tears start flowing. Walter hastens to the bathroom, returns with a box of tissues and puts it on the maple coffee table. Aunt Hattie and I both reach out at the same time, bump hands and laugh.

"Misery loves company." Aunt Hattie smiles and dabs her eyes. "Crying does terrible things to these old eyes of mine."

"It does terrible things to my eyes too, Aunt Hattie and I'm a blushing bride."

Walter starts pacing. "When you two are done weeping, we need to talk about tomorrow. Like, what are we going to do?"

"Well, my dear nephew, I am going to rest. Today wore me out. I will just have enough energy to send flowers to the Van Beek family and pick out my outfit for the next day. Plus I must do some work in the Crow's Nest. Two big orders are coming in and several going out. So tomorrow, you are free go your merry way."

"Sure, Aunt Hattie. Maybe I'll take Tangie to see my old Alma Mater and we can have lunch in Providence. We'll also check out the cathedral, so we don't get lost the next day."

"Oh, don't worry about going to the church. I know where it is. I can show you the way. The streets have changed a bit. One way and all that..."

"Okay, dear aunt. Tangie and I will do the town. Maybe take in a concert or a play in the evening."

I perk up. "And shopping. Walter, I've got to do some shopping. A girl's got to be well dressed for a state affair, even if it is a funeral. I don't think I brought a suit."

"They have a Nordstrom's in Providence."

"Walter, I'm in heaven."

"Okay, but I'm imposing a time limit on you. I cannot do shopping all day."

"Me neither. Just a suit, I promise."

Chapter Twenty

Well, promises are meant to be broken. After breakfast the next day, I insist we go shopping early, as I may need to have the suit, that I will purchase, altered, pressed and ready by the end of the day. Turns out, Walter didn't bring a suit either, so he has to get one as well. Talk about being prepared.

Some women hate shopping with their man. Not me. In the Brass Plum Department, I pick out a suit, a basic black silk and wool. It compliments my curves and adds visual height to my not-so-tall frame. Walter winks at me, stressing his approval. It just needs a little hemming. So we send it to alterations and hustle over to Menswear. Walter picks out a charcoal grey pinstripe suit. It doesn't need much in the way of alterations, just the pants legs to be hemmed and pressed. Not fancy, but very stylish. After our necessary purchases, we shop for accessories: shoes, stockings, blouses, shirts, and some jewelry—well, that's for me. I also add a scarf, an extra skirt and dress, just in case. I insist Walter purchase an extra tie. We leave with assorted bags and boxes after being asked to return in the evening when our alterations will be finished. Our basic shopping is finished in record time.

"Thanks, Walter. Great fun. We should go shopping together more often."

"Angelina, I don't mind in a pinch, but this is not my regular idea of fun."

"Oh come on, you enjoyed it. Say it."

"Well, I enjoyed looking at you trying on stuff, but that's about it." Walter flops down on a bench near the door. "You know my feet hurt? My feet never hurt!"

Grinning at my shopping buddy, I pull him up from his perch. "I'm famished! And you know I'm *never* hungry! Why don't we eat at Nordstrom's Café? I have the menu memorized and service is always speedy. We'll have lots of time to do the town."

"Anything you want, Angelina. I'm beat. A little R&R would be fantastic."

Except for the exclusion of beer and wine on the menu, Walter likes every item I recite to him as we ride the escalator to the second floor.

"Relax, Sweetheart. We can stop in a bar while we stroll through the city. I'd love to go to the old section of town. You can take me to all your old hangouts."

"If they're still there. This city has morphed into something I don't recognize. I haven't been away that long, but that hometown feeling is gone. It's become your typical urban sprawl."

"Well, you know the old saying: *Everything is in motion. Nothing stands still.*"

"Einstein?"

"He's da man, Sweetie." I squeeze Walter's arm and smile. "Let's eat. Then we can store the bags in the trunk and play tourist."

"Well, you play tourist and I'll be your guide."

"I love playing with you."

"Me too, with you." Walter caresses my thigh under the table.

"Easy, Walter. You're tempting me in a public place. I might embarrass you."

"Never." He leans into my body and kisses me, real friendly-like on the lips, as our waitress comes up and places our salads on the table.

"Will there be anything else?" the young girl says, with a hint of embarrassment, as she put her hands behind her back.

"No, thank you, Miss." Walter displays his pearly whites while he resumes grabbing my thigh under the table.

"Walter. Not only are you an irresistible hunk, you are a flirt."

"Angelina, *I only have eyes for you.*" He starts caressing the inside of my leg.

"Don't get musical on me. Eat your crab salad," I say in my fake stern voice. I can feel my body surrendering to his passion and mine. My knees began shaking.

Walter sighs as he stabs his crabmeat with a fork and places it in his mouth. "Yes, dear."

"God! We sound like an old married couple."

"Yes, about a month as a married couple. Sounds ancient." Walter chuckles, then chomps on a warm roll oozing with butter.

"That short?" I sigh. "Seems longer." Then I smile and plant a long wet kiss on him. I can taste the butter on his lips. "Yum. You taste marvelous. How do you like that kiss for an old married woman? The heck with appearances, I always say."

"Maybe we should check into a hotel?" Walter groans as he licks my neck. "You are much more appealing than these crab legs."

"Uh hum. Eat your lunch first, Sweetie. You'll need your nourishment. And Walter, as far as I'm concerned, the historical streets of old Providence can wait. Just show me the inside architecture."

I chow down my grilled shrimp cilantro and lime salad and chug my lemon water. Walter practically chokes on his artistically displayed crab legs, veggies and baby bud lettuce. I hand him a glass of ice water and he gulps the liquid. Somehow we finish our meal, get some protein in our bodies and stand up, revived and ready for action, deep passionate action. Walter throws a large tip on the table and together we pick up our packages, race out the restaurant, down the escalator and out Nordstrom's revolving door to the nearest hotel. The Four Seasons appears within walking distance. Ah, I just love the Four Seasons, always there when needed. Being the desperate lovers that we are, there is no measure to our gratitude.

We bounce through the hotel entrance, laughing, overloaded with shopping bags, but no luggage. The desk clerk does not raise an eyebrow when Walter requests the honeymoon suite. I am thinking he might say to us, *Sorry, sir, but we don't rent by the hour.*

But no, my Walter secures our room in record time and I distinctly hear him ordering champagne as the concierge interrupts him, whispering, "It's already there, sir, waiting for you. Will there be anything else?"

My love answers him, "Not now, we'll order dinner later."

I cannot stop grinning at Walter, the Smoothie. His charm works everywhere. I have a suspicion he planned this getaway. He knows we need a little vacation. I love the way my sweetie anticipates our desires and makes delayed gratification a thing of the past.

While the two of us ride the glass elevator up to the top floor, my body heats up. My knees start shaking. I put my packages down. Walter reacts spontaneously and does the same. We lock into an embrace, in full view of any onlookers outside the glass, until the elevator doors open at our floor. Walter grabs my packages, lifts me up in the air, and gets as far as the door to our suite before he groans, "Ah, Angelina, you'll be the death of me, you wee lass. I cannot, alas, carry you any longer."

I laugh till my sides hurt. "If you put all these packages down, my charming Scot, you can lift me. I don't weigh that much, Mr. Muscle."

Walter sighs, puts down the bundles and crushes me in an embrace.

"I love it when you get serious, Sweetheart," I gasp.

"I am serious." Walter kisses me hard on the mouth. "I miss our love life. All we did was sleep last night."

"Me too. Open the door."

"I'm trying. The card seems to be stuck."

"I'm going crazy."

"Me too." Walter wipes his sweating brow and takes off his sweater. Then he takes out his cell phone, presses for Siri, and says, "Get me the Four Seasons phone number, pronto."

I start giggling. Imagine searching for a hotel's phone number when you're inside the place.

Well, good intentions are always bound to screw things up. A bellboy shows up, almost immediately, although to us he seems to take an eternity. He opens the door to our suite and I'm certain, after looking at Walter, he doesn't expect a tip. My spouse looks rather red under the collar. Soon steam will be coming out of his nose, and he'll be pushing his feet back. I smile at the bellboy, thank him and press some bills into his hand. He rushes out the door before Walter can complain about the hotel needing major reconstruction.

"You know, I wouldn't mind, Tangie, but this is the Four Seasons, the big buckos hotel. They should give you the correct card to open the door."

I kick off my shoes, remover my jacket and toss it on the brocade-covered chair near the doorway. "Don't get so wound up, Honey." I kiss his cheek and then his ear, adding my tongue for effect. "Save your passion for me." I start breathing heavy, my body out of control. "We have lots of time. We can be here more than an hour. This doesn't have to be a quickie. Heck, we can stay here all night."

"Now that's the best idea I've heard all day." Walter takes my hands in his and kisses them. "How do you stay so positive?" He nibbles on my ear. "Always looking at the good. I'm sorry I get so moody. It's just that I've missed you and our nights together."

"We've been together."

"Yes, in my aunt's home. I love Aunt Hattie, but…"

"Ah hum, it's hard to run around her home naked, especially when we share her bathroom."

"I guess I'm not so good at sharing."

"Sure you are. You share your body with me." I unbuttoned Walter's shirt and put my fingers on his chest, getting excited by the feel of his hair, soft and curly. I reach down to his waist and unbuckle his belt and then unzip his jeans. I can feel the warmth of his body and his rising action as I caressed his Abs. "And oh, how I love your body."

Walter groans and slips out of his trousers and shoes.

"Adonis, you need to take off the rest of your clothes," I command, peeling off his shirt.

He does as I wish. "You next, Venus."

"I guess we don't need to play strip poker."

"I am not in the mood for games."

"Just action?"

"Yes, no more talking." He lifts my cashmere sweater off my head and kisses the top of my breasts and then strips off my new *Victoria Secret* sweet nothings, while all the time not removing his lips from mine. I moan and my knees buckle, unable to support my weight any longer.

Walter grabs me and I hang on for dear life. We cling to each other and stumble over to the bed, . Walter tears off the bedspread with one hand, and uses his other arm to roll me onto the expansive king-size bed. I urge him on with my body, finding it hard to breathe, wanting him so much.

Tears form in my eyes. I whisper, "No need to slow down, my love. I need you as much as you need me."

Walter abandons his gentleness and tears off my remaining undergarments. Good thing I've got some new ones in my shopping bag. Nothing but threads left of my black lace panties. No wonder I like to shop, always replenishing my passion wardrobe.

The rest of the hour is private with a capital P. Walter's secret passionate ways can be described as fire meeting fire, ocean meeting ocean and, well, you get the picture.

After two hours, I sit up in bed and admire the view of Providence from the air. In this penthouse, we are floating in a cloud, Cloud Nine, you might say. After a few minutes of total relaxation, I stretch, get up as if walking on air, and announce, "I think it's time for champagne."

Walter lifts his head from the down pillow, leans back and smiles. His eyes flame with pleasure. He nods. "Make mine a double."

I grin, go over to the bottle of bubbly and return to Walter. He opens the bottle of St. Michelle Domaine and expertly pours the dreamy liquid into two tall flute glasses. We entwine our arms and sip the drink of Bacchus.

"Are you hungry, Angelina? I can order us some food."

"Not a bit. Maybe later. Right now, I just want you." I brush his lips, slink out of our fabulous round bed and stroll over to the nearby Jacuzzi, that bubbles and gurgles at the switch of a button. "Care to join me for a soak?"

"I thought you'd never ask," Walter murmurs, as he follows me to the soaking tub. So the dance continues. I can hear romantic music playing in the background. Walter must have flipped another switch. Ah, a Rachmaninoff Concerto. Our dance intensifies. Walter and I, the music and the water, warm, inviting, intoxicating. And the dance becomes fast and furious until neither one of us can move or speak.

The drums begin again and a primal urge consumes us. We return, naked and wet with warmth, to our nest in the clouds and enter our own blue heaven. No cares, no panic, no crime. No bad guys, just us, living in the moment. Ah, how I love being in love.

After a blissful three hours, Walter sits up, "I think it's time for a massage. Let's relax your muscles."

"I am relaxed," I groan, not wanting to move.

"Ah, my love, you are delectable." Walter kisses my back and then pours oil over his fingers. "Trust me, I bought some special massage oil just for you."

"A girl never refuses a massage."

"Nor a guy."

Walter taps muscles I didn't know exist, awaking feelings of pain, pleasure and excitement all twisted together. Each day I find something new to love about my husband. I grin, "I'm glad I married you, Walter Cunningham." I sigh and sit up. "Come on, now it's your turn."

"With pleasure, my love, but first…" Walter picks up another champagne bottle stashed under the bed. This one reads: Dom Pérignon. My eyes widen as he purrs, "I need to make another toast, Angelina."

"Please do."

"To us."

"To us," I chirp, parroting Walter.

"And to Dom Pérignon, the Benedictine Monk from Hautvillers, who made this all possible."

"Cheers, to Don Pérignon, our champion of French wine."

Walter refills our champagne glasses and raises his glass. "And to the rest of our lives. May we never lose our zest or our stamina."

I click my glass to his, stare into his eyes and start to quiver. "I will love you, forever, Walter."

That does it for Walter. He takes a long sip of champagne and then places the glass on the hearth of the fireplace, which glows golden in the dim of the late afternoon. He puts mine, half-full, alongside his and lifts me into his arms.

"Remind me how you love me," Walter whispers, as he crushes my upper torso in a heated embrace. It's the kind of crushing I love, the kind that turns my whole body on fire. I can feel the flame of passion rising up, consuming me, as if it will never stop. And I never want it to stop.

I remind Walter how much I love him, how I can *count the ways*, but not in words. Sometimes words are highly overrated. I am a woman of action and Walter loves action. Neither one of us speaks for a long time, but I can hear music playing in the background, "Nights in White Satin". I happen to love white satin, and Walter, in the cool crisp night.

I don't know how long I slept, but I remember the dreams. *Walter and I back in Fiji, swimming in the surf, lounging on the sand, loving each other. Then, a familiar face from last year, on the streets of Seattle appears, menacing, threatening me with his eyes and fingernails. And then Walter is smashing him to bits, until he melts into the pavement. Next, Walter and I are floating in a sailboat bound for a place we never expected. I can see the rooftops of beach homes in the distance, on the shore, calling us.*

I wake up to a knocking on the door.

I open one eye and squint at the bedside lamp that seems enormously bright in the darkened room. I open the other eye and focus as Walter puts on a Four Seasons terry bathrobe and shuffles over to the door. He peeks in the viewing hole and opens the door.

"Thank you for delivering these. Here is something for your trouble."

I heard a strange high-pitched male voice saying, "Thank you, sir. Anytime. Have a good evening."

The door closes and Walter walks a little more erect and carries our suits on hangers to the closet. He comes over to the bed and sits down next to me. He leans over and kisses me on the shoulder. "I love you, Angelina."

I sit up slowly and murmur, "I'm awake, Walter, and starved."

"Me too." He hands me a menu from the bedside table. "Order something for us, anything you want, while I call Aunt Hattie. I cannot visualize driving to Newport now, when we are so comfortable here. My aunt will understand. I'll order a limo to pick all of us up tomorrow. No sense taking the car. There will be no place to park at the funeral."

"Oh Walter, I love room service, and I love you."

I order medium rare filet mignon for two, the house salad and another bottle of champagne. I can't resist the *Crème Brulee* with raspberries. Might as well celebrate. Who knows when we'll have another *tête à tête?*

Walter's aunt approves our plan. She tells Walter she will love limousine service. Informs him she'll meet us with the limo in front of the hotel and not to worry about Pebbles. Louisa offered to dog sit. Seems the two of them have bonded.

I get up from the bed and smile. "I like your style, Walter." I stroll into the bathroom, wash my face and notice a glow, warm and rosy, either from the champagne or lovemaking. Either way, my mood matches my coloring. I take a robe off the hook on the door and put it on as I hear a knock on the door. Love room service. Love my man. Sometimes life doesn't get much better than this. I want to relish each moment we have this evening, even if it means staying up all night.

Walter answers the door, signs for the dinner, then takes the tray and champagne and places both on the bistro table near the skyline window. He takes me by the hand, leads me to my seat overlooking the city and kisses my hand. "Dinner is served, madam."

I giggle like a schoolgirl.

"You know, Angelina, I've always wanted to say that, and now you are a madam."

I laugh. "Yes, call me madam. I don't know if you know, how much I appreciate you."

"I do, Angelina and I love you for it. Let's eat! I'm starved."

"Yes, and after we eat, drink and are merry, we can continue our dance of love." I smile with half-slit eyes at my lover and brush his lips gently with mine. Then I take my fork, slice my filet mignon and chomp down my steak. I look at Walter who is content to woof down his food like it is his last supper. I hear him sigh when his body signals an energy boost. After eating the last of the Crème Brulee and berries, I get up from the table, untie my robe, and let it drop to the floor. Picking up my last glass of champagne for the evening, I raise it in the air. "To us, always and forever." I clank Walter's glass, and he, mine.

Walter takes one last long sip of the drink of Dionysus, then comes over to me and lifts me up in the air like a present he has been waiting for all his life. I understand how much I mean to him. I nuzzle myself into his neck and kiss his earlobe. He carries me over to our white satin nest overlooking the clouds and twinkling lights of the city, and places me in the middle of the bed. He looks at me for a few minutes and says nothing. I can see his eyes penetrating mine and I feel his passion before his touch. I realize at this moment that he loves me more than I think is possible. He consumes my body with his gaze, feasting on my breasts and my contours. My need for him increases with his desire. I open my arms as he throws off his robe and comes to me. At this moment, perfection is no longer just a word. It is the force that consumes us.

I block out thoughts that creep into my mind without permission. I know tomorrow will be the beginning of a dangerous journey, a journey in which I want no part. My unwilling footsteps will take me there anyway, where I don't want to go. But those nightmares are reserved for tomorrow. Tonight, tonight is for lovers.

Chapter Twenty-One

Walter arises with the sun. He always does. Sometimes he comes back to bed; sometimes he goes for a walk. This morning he takes a shower and then calls room service. As I open my eyes and stretch my arms, I smell the aroma of bacon and waffles. Hunger entices me to leave our love nest.

I swing my legs around the bed in a circular motion like a bird landing on a branch and sing, "I love breakfast."

"Me too. I ordered some of your favorites, Angelina."

"Yum!" I tiptoe over to the bistro table, sans robe. "Sorry, I didn't dress for breakfast."

"You look marvelous, Angel. Are you ready for a Mimosa cocktail? I squeezed the oranges myself."

"You lie so well."

"I love the way you lie, also, Angelina."

"Maybe we should lie down together after breakfast."

"Maybe. Depends on how fast you eat. Remember we have places to go, people to meet."

"Maybe we should just opt out." I caress his cheek with my hand.

"Sounds like a plan."

"No, we can't, my love." I sigh. "Your aunt is depending on us. What time is it?"

"Eight o'clock."

"Great! We've got plenty of time. Ten minutes to eat. Ten minutes for me to shower and get dressed, and in between..."

"We'll have to set a timer. We are liable to fall asleep."

"Walter, call the desk. Have them give us a call at 9:30, just in case."

"Done deal. I like your style."

"And I, yours. Let's eat fast, drink fast, and be merry, as long as we are able."

We only keep Aunt Hattie waiting ten minutes. I feel somewhat guilty and apologize profusely. The dear sweet woman reassures me with a hug. "Now Angelina, don't you fret. I used the extra time to put on some powder and rouge. We are going to a funeral, but I want to look alive."

I grin as I hand my packages to our driver. "Thanks again, Aunt Hattie, for your understanding."

"I am just glad you two got to spend a little time on the town together. After all, you are newlyweds."

"And I hope that never changes," Walter interjects as he climbs into the limo and sits down next to Aunt Hattie and me.

I blush like a schoolgirl. Seems the lack of sleep tears down my defenses.

Aunt Hattie grins and pats Walter on his hand, which looks like a bear paw next to her delicate, tan fingers. I smile at the thought. *Come to think of it, Walter is my teddy bear.* I ask Aunt Hattie, "How far is the cathedral?"

"Oh, just a few minutes away, but there's always traffic in the city."

It is after rush hour, but the traffic moves at a snail's pace through the streets of Providence. Construction doesn't help either. Still, we get to the front of the cathedral with ten minutes to spare, a minor miracle considering our lack of progress in the limo. The driver tells us he will keep our things safe and pick us up when we call him. To Walter, he reiterates, "I won't be far away, sir."

"Thanks, er, Edward." Walter responds after he checks out the chauffeur's nametag. "We will do that."

Aunt Hattie and I follow Walter away from the comfort of the limo and toward the Cathedral of Saints Peter and Paul.

I bless myself as I enter the church. As the only Cradle Catholic in the group, I lead the way into the cathedral and together we follow an usher to our seats. We come to a pew halfway to the altar. Aunt Hattie makes eye contact with a few faces familiar to her and waves discreetly to her friends.

Although I alternate between being spiritual and a fallen-away Catholic, I appreciate the solemn ritual of the Mass, and look forward to the beginning of the service. When the organ swells to *Amazing Grace* during the prelude music, my heart swells with it. The melody mesmerized me. I close my eyes and feel Walter taking my hand in his.

The organist shifts to another classical hymn, "There is a Balm in Gilead" and I open my eyes. The late governor's son and daughter walk down the isle painfully slow, leaning on one another, broken-hearted. Empathy consumes me. My thoughts shift to my father's funeral and I start to tear up, thinking of Bryan and me that day. I look at Aunt Hattie, whose moist eyes match mine. Walter remains stoic. Seems men can hide their emotions better than women. Don't know if that is a good thing or not, just a case of being wired differently.

I try not to stare at the people in attendance at the funeral service. I recognize some celebrities as they walk down the center isle and are escorted to their seats. Politicians, entertainers, CEO's, bankers, people constantly in the public eye, people that previous to this morning, I only viewed in the media.

I catch a glimpse of Evelina Carboni—Creepy Steve's Eveline—and don my sunglasses. Don't want her to study me or recognize anything about me. If she looks closely, she might catch on. She's a sharp cookie but not very sweet. At present she wears fake eyelashes and a fake expression of sorrow. Her eyes dart around. I visualize a crazed hawk hunting for prey. Her dyed-red hair seems especially bright and out of character in this solemn place. I imagine horns popping out of her head. She carries a large red purse that matches her hair and crimson-stacked heels. Her black v-neck dress, cut low in the front, clings to her body and is accented by a red and black shawl that hugs her shoulders.

Eveline moves like a tiger in heat. I can see a number of men's heads turn as she struts down the isle. One man does not seem captured by her charms and appears rather reflective and respectful. He is about six feet tall and in his late forties, with coal black hair, streaked with silver at the temples. He appears to be a rather rugged, but handsome man with a concerned look on his face. His eyes appear to water as he glances around the church. He takes a handkerchief out of his pocket and dabs at his eyes. He escorts Evelina Carboni into a front pew, sits down next to her and hands her a program. I can see her grasping his hand. Must be Mr. Carboni. I don't notice anything phony about him, but I could be wrong. His actions certainly show kindness and concern. He continues to dab at his eyes as the Mass begins and while the priest delivers his homily. I do sense something unpleasant about him. Perhaps it could be fear. As a politician, he may be concerned about his ability to keep up with the late governor's popularity; perhaps he is unwilling to let the public down, or something else. I wonder how he ever hooked up with Eveline. No doubt she pursued him. I bet he resisted her at first and then gave in to her for any number of reasons, one of which could be her wealth. She does dress like she has money, lots of it. Eveline doesn't seem the type to give up on anything or anybody she targets. I must remind myself to stay out of her sightline. Keep a safe distance at all times. My new motto: Avoid Eveline at all cost.

Eveline stifles a yawn and closes her eyes. When she re-opens them, she glances around the people assembled for the funeral, as if looking for someone in particular. She centers her gaze on a younger man, seated in front of her and smiles. She taps him on the shoulder and says something to him, a phrase I cannot decipher. Other people in front of her turn around to see who is speaking during one of the quiet times in the Mass. When they notice who is chatting, they frown, turn back around and resume praying. Seems Eveline is not as respected as her husband. Typical spider lady—she is intent on setting traps for people and doesn't care who gets hurt. People sense those kinds of things. Eveline recognizes their distrust and disgust, but could care less. There goes my psychic mind, kicking in again. I wonder what Walter is thinking. I study his face. He remains motionless and stares straight ahead. If he feels anything, he doesn't show it, part of his defense mechanism. He doesn't let on to many people about his intuition and his heightened sense of what is going on or what could be going on. Heck, most of the time, I'm not privy to these thoughts of his. He likes to protect me.

A few more hymns are sung and played by the musicians, communion commences and lines of people walk ever so slowly to the altar. After the liturgy of the Eucharist, the church becomes filled with incense, then thoughts and reminiscences of friends and family. The booming bagpipes begin to play outside the cathedral's massive wood doors, signaling the end of the Peter Van Beek's Funeral Mass. I start to tear up. Bagpipes always do that to me.

"A beautiful service, wasn't it, dears?" Aunt Hattie dabs her eyes with a fresh handkerchief Walter places in her hand.

"Yes, Aunt Hattie." I wipe the tears from my cheek with my sleeve and take her arm. "I'm just grateful that my stomach isn't bouncing up and down, like it usually does at funerals." Walter hands me a handkerchief. He must have an endless supply. I look at him in appreciation and become pensive. Maybe I am cured of anxiety during funerals. At funerals, memorial services and wakes, I usually feel like I am about to faint at any minute.

Walter studies me for a minute, as we wait for the limo. "You did great, kid. I know these events are hard for you."

"Maybe I am getting better. Perhaps it was the mimosas we drank at breakfast."

Walter smiles. "I'll have to remember that—*The Mimosa Cure.*"

"The limo is here," Aunt Hattie announces. "The reception is at the Newport Yacht Club. It may take a while to get there, with this traffic."

Walter takes his aunt's arm. "Aunt Hattie, suppose we have the driver drop us off at our hotel. You can stay in the limo and head over to Newport. We'll pick up your car and drive it back to Newport. We'll see who gets to the yacht club first. And we won't have to come back to Providence later to pick it up."

"I wouldn't mind that a bit. I love the challenge of a race, but I know I will win. I'll have a head start. Why don't you park the car at my home and walk to the yacht club. It's only about four blocks from my house and parking will be difficult at the Yacht Club. You can't miss it. It's right on the waterfront, two blocks north of the Crow's Nest."

Walter nods. "I know the place. Tangie and I will unload our packages and then head to the club."

To no one's surprise, Hattie arrives first. As we enter, looking like the successful young married couple we are, she waves, comes over and grasps our hands. "So glad you made it. Come with me. I'd like you to meet my friends."

Aunt Hattie escorts us to a small open area in the cocktail lounge and introduces us to Peter Van Beek's two older sisters, members of Aunt Hattie's garden club. They politely shake our hands and welcome us to Newport.

I answer their kind words. "We are so sorry for the loss of your brother. Walter and I were so distressed by the news."

Their eyes begin to swell and tears fall upon their cheeks. From the redness of their faces, I can tell grieving extracts a toll on them. The pain in their hearts is evident.

"It's just that Peter had so much to live for," the elder sister, Jenny, blurts out. "He was in the prime of his life. How he ever got tangled in those lines on his sailboat is a mystery to me, not like him at all."

Aunt Hattie nods in agreement. "Those are my thoughts, exactly, Jenny. Peter was an excellent sailor."

The other sister pats Jenny's arm. "Jenny, we have to accept God's will, that it was Peter's time."

"I know Clarissa, but it is hard. I miss our dear brother so much."

Walter steps away for a minute, and promptly returns with four glasses of white wine. How he balances them in his hands is beyond me.

"Have some spirits to soothe your souls." Walter hands each of us a glass.

"Why thank you, dear boy." Clarissa smiles. "You are very kind. You and your lovely wife must visit us while you are in Newport."

Walter squeezes my hand and nods. "We will try to do that."

I study the geography of the room as Walter continues to chat with his aunt and the sisters. I get an urge to do some canvassing of the surroundings. I excuse myself, saying I have to use the little girl's room, which is partially true. The ladies room is a good place to hear gossip and also a good place to check out people. A lot of information gets exchanged in that little retreat.

After using the facilities, I sit on a soft-cushioned seat by the mirror and stare at my face. I decide it needs some cleaning up after all the tears and a little more makeup. I take out some lipstick and mascara and go to work on my coloring. As I do so, Eveline strolls in. I can see her face reflected in the mirror and she looks like a crow whose crumbs were stolen by a seagull.

"I hate these affairs," she retorts to a young woman following her like a faithful puppy. She appears to be Eveline's assistant. She lugs an over-stuffed red purse on her shoulder.

"Try to relax, Mrs. Carboni. We won't be here long. Just dinner. Not many speeches."

"Everyone around me is either sad or snooty. If I don't get high, I won't be able to stand it another minute."

With a certain degree of tolerance in her eyes, the assistant stares at Eveline. "Now Mrs. Carboni, you know you can't get drunk. Governor Carboni will have a fit. But you can have a glass of wine to take the edge off. We are all upset today."

"Thank you, Lacey. You're sweet. I know you are looking out for me, but I just don't care. I don't know how I am going to get through today."

"Think of it in small steps. You made it through the funeral, didn't you?"

"Only because I took two Valium before I left the house."

"Well, take it easy. They will be serving lunch soon. You will feel better after that."

"I'd feel much better after a double martini to cut the pain."

"Gee, Mrs. Carboni, I didn't know you cared so much for Governor Van Beek."

"More than you know, Lacey. He was like a brother to me. A brother I never had..."

I continue to look in the mirror and almost say out loud, *"What a crock of..."* Instead I put powder on my face. I never wear powder but I have to think of a stalling device to stay in my spot undetected. Eveline doesn't notice me. She continues her blabbering to Lacey and then uses the facilities, taking an unseemly amount of time in her stall. I decide now would be a good time for my exit. She seems to have everyone fooled. Everyone that is, but me and of course, Walter. Add Aunt Hattie, now in our confidence. Maybe in time, others will see through her. One can hope. Walter and I have to get some proof of her evil intentions, whatever they are, and decipher her role in the death of Peter Van Beek. Now that's a tall order for anyone, and I'm just an ordinary citizen. I don't even live here. How am I going to make that happen?

I close my makeup case and shove it back in my patent leather purse. I get up, straighten my silk jet-black suit, and nod to Lacey who nods back at me as she dabs her eyes. I brace myself and walk out into the crowd of politicians and their families milling around the cocktail area waiting for lunch to be served.

I don't have a clue how all the people gathering in the lounge area will fit into the yacht club for a sit-down luncheon. Apparently Newport is equipped for such events, having hosted the World Cup's sailing luncheons and numerous famous weddings in the past. I hear the hum of a motor. As quick as an eagle flaps his wings, sliding walls move, doors open up and space for everyone appears out of nowhere. I'm impressed—so much for my detecting skills—didn't see that one coming.

Walter and I sit with Aunt Hattie at a round table with two of Peter Van Beek's sailing buddies, their wives, and a thirty-something blond dude who introduces himself as Graham Gotthree. Graham makes a point of telling us he used to be Peter Van Beek's right-hand man, but is now assisting Governor Carboni during his transfer to power. He appears to be the only politician, or quasi-politician at the table. Good thing. He's about all I can handle. The yachtsmen entertain us with nautical tales centering around Peter Van Beek, and give us insight into the late governor's character. I formulate a striking image of him as a charismatic, strong and courageous individual that adored his family. I begin to wish I knew him before his demise. His sailing buddies share some off-color sailing jokes that Peter Van Beek told them. While Aunt Hattie and the wives laugh with glee, I listen intently to the other conversations in hope of gaining some insight into Van Beek's death. I glance at Graham Gotthree seated next to Aunt Hattie. He appears unmoved by the laughter and focuses his eyes on the ceiling, as if searching for flies. Strange fellow. He looks uncomfortable as he pulls on the neck of his shirt and straightens his tie. His eyes lock with mine for a moment and I think I detect a look of distress. The distress instantly turns to arrogance as we break eye contact. He stares at the others seated around the table as if they are paupers sitting at the head table by mistake. Well, perhaps in the political world, they are, but there are other worlds existing outside of politics. Maybe the guy misses the governor and the adrenaline rush. Maybe his job is in jeopardy. Maybe Eveline is making his life miserable. I remember now. He's the guy Eveline was poking in the pew, at the funeral. Hum, maybe he just doesn't want to be here. Come to think of it, he would be a good one to talk to after lunch. I don't think I could tolerate him on an empty stomach. I smile at him with a demure grin on my face and hold up my glass. He gets my signal and leans over and picks up a bottle of wine. I pass my glass to Aunt Hattie and she gets the hint to pass it to Graham.

Graham fills my glass to the top and some of the Chardonnay spills as Aunt Hattie hands it to me.

"Not to worry," Graham says in a forced low-pitched voice, "The wine flows freely around here."

"I can see that." I raise my glass to him before I take a sip. "Thank you, Graham."

"My pleasure, sweet lady."

Well, I certainly am not feeling sweet toward him, but I smile back, pretending to be grateful and impressed by his charm. I feel a thigh bumping mine under the table—Walter, reminding me of his presence. *Walter. When will he realize I am just fishing for information?* I have no desire to make time with another man, especially with the likes of Graham Gotthree— definitely not now or ever my type. God knows, before Walter, I met many men like Graham, self-centered boors who love to talk about themselves.

In due haste, the meal appears at our table. Four waiters place Peter Van Beek's favorite foods in front of us. The entrees are served family-style. We can take our pick of lobster, crab, clam cakes, chowder, corn on the cob and three kinds of salad. Throw in some baked potatoes and sour cream and the feast begins. Peter Van Beek, poor soul, is not here to enjoy the feast. *Did he have time for a last supper?* Perhaps not, but today he is going out in style.

I content myself with a little of everything, except for the Maine lobster, my favorite seafood. That is, my favorite seafood on the East Coast. On the

West, it's Copper River salmon or Dungeness crab. Anyway, I chow down a humongous portion of Maine lobster, which I consume whole-heartedly until I feel the waist on my new suit cutting into my skin.

As I let out a burp that I am sure everyone at the table hears, I observe the waiters getting the dessert trays ready.

I've got to get out of here while I can still walk. I stand up and move away from the table.

"I need some fresh air," I whisper to Walter.

"I'll come with you, Babe."

"No, Walter. I'm okay. Stay with Aunt Hattie. I won't be long. I just need to take a little walk."

Walter grasps my hand and kisses it. "I'll be waiting for your return. Be back in time for dessert."

"You devil, I can hardly breathe, let alone eat dessert." I smile at him, take a sip of wine, stifle another burp and buss his cheek. I hear Walter chuckling under his breath. He knows me so well.

I stroll past the other tables by the window and climb up a few short steps to the landing and open the door to the outside deck. The salt air soothes my senses and for a moment I forget why I have come to this haven on the water. I understand why Peter Van Beek loved it so. I walk to the end of the deck, open the latch to the gate and stroll onto the pier. When I get to the far end, I can see the houses that dot the hills above Newport across Newport Harbor and along Narragansett Bay. For hundreds of years people have lived and dined along these shores. There is so much history, such beauty to digest all at once, a humbling and exhilarating experience.

I inhale the sea air and smile. I love being near the water. The wind picks up and I see white caps forming. Suddenly I become homesick for Seattle and my own body of water, the Puget Sound. Perhaps I'll call Mom tonight and see how things are in the Pacific Northwest.

"So, how are you related to Peter?"

I turn around and can see nothing due to the glare from the sun blocking my vision. "I beg your pardon?"

"It's Graham, Graham Gottree. How soon you forget."

"Oh, Graham, I'm sorry. I can hardly see you; the sun is in my eyes."

Graham hands me a pair of sunglasses. "Perhaps these will help."

"Thanks. Yes, it is you! I didn't forget. You are kind of unforgettable."

"Just like the song."

"So you like jazz?"

"Some." Graham sighs and leans over the rail. "Where are you from? I don't detect an accent."

"Seattle, the land of no accents, green hills and great coffee. I didn't know Peter Van Beek, but my husband's aunt is a family friend. So we are her escorts to the funeral. We came here, to Newport, for a visit...and when...when this terrible thing happened to the governor...we decided to stay a while longer."

"Well, I must say, it's convenient you arrived to attend the services with her."

"Well you might say that, but I am not a fan of funerals."

"Neither am I. All that pomp and circumstance."

"I like tradition, and caring for others and their families. It's just that I usually faint at funerals."

"Not so bad if you have someone to catch you. I could offer my services."

"Thanks, but that job is taken."

"Oh, that's right. The Walter dude."

"Yes. The Walter dude, my husband."

"Well, I've been known to not let a husband get in the way of fun."

"Yes, but I don't play that way."

"Pity. I can see that you would be a lot of fun."

"Not exactly bereavement conversation, Graham."

"I thought you hate funerals, uh mm..."

"Tangie. Call me, Tangie."

"Now that's cute. I like your name."

"So does my husband. And I don't hate funerals. I just faint at them."

"You know, you are really cute. Especially when you are difficult."

"I'm not difficult. I'm honest."

But to tell the truth, I have been known to lie a bit when necessary. I may start lying to this dude.

"Are you implying that I am not?" Graham begins to squirm.

Bingo! He is hiding something. I can tell by his blinking eyes and his beady stare, like he is trying too hard to stop the blinking.

I smile. "I am not implying anything. I just told you I am honest."

"I appreciate you being candid, Tangie. And to demonstrate my appreciation, I would like to invite you to a get-together for a few friends."

"Where?"

"I'll call you. Where are you staying?"

"At Aunt Hattie's home, here in Newport."

"Will you come?"

"I'll think about it."

"I could show you around."

"Been there, done that."

"Not with me."

"That's true."

I hear footsteps on the pier. *Walter.* Just in the nick of time. I can't keep up this façade forever.

"Oh, hi Walter. Graham and I have been chatting."

"I can see that, Angelina."

Graham frowns. "Hey, I thought your name is Tangie."

Walter answers for me. "Yes, Graham, that's her professional name. For me, it's Angelina."

Graham looks like he doesn't like the game Walter is starting to play. "What profession are you in, Tangie?"

I lie. "I am in public relations."

"Never heard of you before. Do you have a website?"

"I work out of the Northwest, small business, my own. And no, no website yet. I'm just starting out. You know, for Easterners, anything northwest of Chicago is the end of the world. How would you have heard of me?"

"*Touche.* Now I understand."

"Glad you do, my man. We'll see you around." Walter grabs my hand, rushes me off the pier and steers me into the direction of the nearby boathouse.

"Walter, what's gotten into you? I've just been on a fishing expedition. You have nothing to worry about."

"I don't trust that guy, Angelina. I think he's dirty. Fishing with him could be dangerous."

"Probably. But he's interesting. And he may know something we don't, consciously or unconsciously."

"I wouldn't mind seeing him unconscious. He's a real pain. I would enjoy punching him. Are you forgetting, my love, that someone has committed murder?"

"Yeah, a guy named Steve, and Graham doesn't sound anything like that Steve."

"No, but what if he knows him? He could be dangerous."

"Oh, please. Graham? He reeks of being a spoiled-rich playboy."

"Angelina, he may be a snob and a skirt-chaser, but he could be something else too. I think he's a phony."

"Oh Walter, you are bothered by the skirt-chasing part. Don't you think you are blowing up his role in all of this, this terrible mess?"

"Maybe, but I don't like him chasing your skirt and I don't trust him. He is too smug and too proper. I think it's a cover. The only thing that is true about him is his sleeze."

"Ya think?"

"I'm positive. You know I have good instincts. You know I'm telling you the truth, as I see it."

"You're not blinded by jealousy?"

"Come on, Angelina, you know me better than that."

"I know you can be jealous, a tad bit overly-jealous at times."

"Please, Angelina, you're killin' me. What's a guy got to do to convince you?"

"Okay, Walter. To prove your genuine concern, let me meet him. He has invited me to a gathering of friends. I could pump him for information, or get some kind of intuition from hanging around him a little longer. It's worth a try."

"Tangie, I'm not that desperate to reassure you, or for you to reassure me."

"I am. You should know by now I have this compulsion to solve mysteries, especially mysteries that entangle you and me."

"We don't have to be involved. We can just go home to Seattle."

"Now Honey, I never knew you to walk away from a challenge."

Walter takes me in his arms and kisses me on my cheek and then my lips. I squirm and get short of breath, as he whispers, "Angelina, I am not walking away. I am protecting my wife."

"Yum. You taste good. What a tempting offer."

I think for a moment about the pleasure I feel in Walter's company. Then my business head takes over. I stand up straight and clear my throat. "My love, how about this: I accept his invitation and you follow us, wherever we go. Heck, I'll even wear a wire if you want. We can call our Steve and get one from him. Let's tell him to take the Red Eye to Boston. I can plan to meet up with Graham after Steve gets here..."

"Angelina, slow down. I don't like putting you in harm's way."

"Walter, my love, I don't want anyone else to get hurt. For everyone's sake, I feel we have to do this. So far, this smug bastard, and what he might know, is our only lead. We need to take it, wherever it goes."

Walter shakes his head. "I don't like it."

"I'm not crazy about seeing him again, but what else can we do? He's our only link to this whole political situation. After all he was Peter Van Beek's assistant."

"I feel like I'm sending my wife into the lion's den. I just don't like it."

"So that is why we call Steve. Agreed?"

I detect a note of resignation in his voice as he takes my hands in his. "I agree to call Steve. After he arrives in Providence, I will think about you meeting this Graham Gotthree fellow, but I will never like it."

"I promise you, Walter, I'm not crazy about spending another minute with him. But really, do we have any other choice?"

Walter takes me into his arms and embraces me as tight as he can without crushing me. I feel his heart pounding as his body quivers. He whispers, "You know, Angelina, sometimes I hate our work."

"Me too," I whisper back.

"Why can't we be normal and just have simple jobs. We could play in a band. Sell newspapers. Wait tables."

"Ah," I whisper, relishing his embrace. I can scarcely breathe, but manage to speak up in my wisecracking way. "It may come to that, Walter. We might wind up in the Witness Protection Program if we are found out. I wouldn't mind playing in a band, but the waitress part—been there, done that."

Walter laughs out loud and releases me from his Kodiak bear hug. "I love you, Sweetheart. Especially when you show no fear."

"Oh, Walter, I have fear alright. I just hate these smug pseudo-politicians and their henchmen, perhaps more than my fear. Let's go get them."

"That's my girl. I will do the surveillance, and Steve will be our back up. You are not going into this one alone."

"I would not think of it."

Now to tell the truth, I might, out of stupidity. I did that once before and had near-disastrous results. My gratitude for Walter in the past year has increased tri-fold. I reach up, pull his head toward mine, bend his six-foot four-inch frame towards my five-foot-five inch frame, and give him one of my extra-special kisses, one that I have never given to anyone else before him. He reciprocates in kind. *Ah, how I love true love.* Good thing the boathouse blocks anyone from viewing our public display. We would shock the neighbors and onlookers. And Graham Gotthree would never believe the crock of *you know what* I am about to deliver to him.

Chapter Twenty-Two

Except for my encounter on the pier with Graham, no more leads surface at the funeral reception. After Walter and I return to our table, we say our goodbyes and tell Aunt Hattie we'll see her later at home. I take Graham's extended hand and tell him how much I enjoyed chatting with him. I figure he can take that any way he pleases. I notice his fingernails are manicured and even have a touch of polish on them. His handshake is limp when he grasps my right hand a little longer than is necessary. *So what if he's not the macho type. He can still be a villain.* What you see on the surface is not always the real thing. I sense one thing when I touch his hand, and that is enough for me. Graham Gotthree is not an honest man, nor can he be trusted.

Pebbles bounces around, whines and cries when we open the door to Aunt Hattie's front hallway. You would think we were gone a week from all the dancing he does. I pick him up and hug him as he licks my face and continues to act like a deserted pooch. The dog really knows how to plaster on the guilt. He's only been home alone a couple of hours, as Louisa watched him until she went to the shop, but you think he was stranded for days.

"Walter, for some reason, I'm not in the least bit tired. I'm going to stroll down the hill and take Pebbles for his *W-A-L-K*." I always spell the word "walk" as Pebbles becomes insane at the mention of it. Plus he's already acting as if he's on steroids. I need a fighting chance and a modicum of control over him if I take him on a leash.

Walter yawns. "Do you want me to go with you?"

"No, Sweetie. I know you're exhausted. Why don't you take a nap or relax? Play the piano. I won't be long. I just want to spend a little time with the pooch."

"Rather than me?"

"No, silly. I just need some think time. Maybe I'll go meditate by the sea."

"I get it. Go." Walter smiles as he yawns again. "I think I'll settle down on the couch. No, wait a minute. Aunt Hattie might return home with the Van Beek sisters. I'll head up to our room and crash an hour or two. Somebody kept me up all night, and a guy needs his sleep."

I give Walter one of my Cheshire cat grins. "Yes, it's about time to play catch-up. And I will catch you later."

"I'll be waiting, love. Stay out of trouble, Sweet Thing."

"I'll have Pebbles to protect me."

"Dang dog will only get you tangled up in something."

"Not today. Today I am in charge." I laugh as Pebbles pulls me out the door before I can open it all the way. "So far so good."

I hear Walter chuckling as he closes the door behind me. At least I make him laugh. I pull my naughty dog close to me with his leash. "Sit down, Pebbles, now!"

The pooch listens and does so, while staring at me.

"Okay, good dog. Let's go."

Once again we head down the hill off to the races. The way I figure it, I need a good run after eating that lobster, corn on the cob and two hard rolls, all dipped in butter. Good thing I skipped dessert. Otherwise, I would be rolling down the hill instead of jogging. I laugh out loud and shift to top speed. For once, it's me, not Pebbles, who leads the way.

When we reach the waterfront, the salty air greets woman and dog like an old friend. I don't think I could ever live far from the water. It revives me every time I am near it. And after the funeral and little sleep, I need lots of reviving. Pebbles starts pulling on his leash, wanting to go in the direction of the Crow's Nest. Seems he recognizes his new territory. Together we stroll over to Aunt Hattie's shop. Pebbles stops and takes a long drink from the dog bowl waiting for such occasions. I notice Louisa inside waiting on a customer.

I wave to her as I stroll in with my pooch. "Hi Louisa. Just browsing around the waterfront. Thanks for watching Pebbles earlier."

Louisa pokes her head up from waiting on her customer and smiles. "You're welcome, Tangie. Hold on, I'll be with you in a minute. So glad to see you and Pebbles again."

Her customer, a gentleman about sixty-five with windblown white hair, looks like he just came in from a day sail. He wears a yellow windbreaker, Dockers and boating shoes that look a little wet. I can see a puddle forming on the wooden plank floor.

I smile back at Louisa and the gentleman. "Thanks. Don't mind me. I'll just look around."

Everyone is so friendly around here. Well, almost everyone, thinking of Eveline for a split second. I glance at the shelves on the wall. A few souvenirs capture my attention. I can purchase some gifts for Marianna and Bryan, Andee and the twins. I can't forget Charles; he's part of the family now. For Marianna, I pick out a silk scarf imprinted with a nautical theme, and for Charles, a leather keychain with a sailor's bowknot attached. Bryan, I think would like that also. For Andee, I select a Scrimshaw charm with two bear cubs carved upon it. For the twins, I grab two kites, one in the shape of a dragon and one in the shape of a flying fish. Bryan and Andee often take Jason and Jeffrey to Gasworks Park and sometimes to Long Beach Peninsula, both havens for kite flying in Washington State. I am beginning to miss Seattle. I always do when I think of my loved ones back home. For sure, I'll call Marianna tonight. I know she's wondering about me.

The gentleman shopper pays for his purchase, a clock/barometer combo made of glass, polished wood and brass. He smiles as I stand nearby waiting my turn. "Good day, ladies." He tips his Greek fisherman's cap to us before he leaves the gallery. I grin. He would make a great sailing companion for someone. Perhaps, Aunt Hattie, if she is free. I smile. *Too bad she's not in the shop today.*

Louisa interrupts my thoughts. "Oh, Tangie, don't feel obligated to purchase anything."

"Oh no, Louisa, I really want these. They are presents for my family back in Seattle."

"In that case I will give you the family discount. Hattie would insist."
I grin. "No argument from me. Thank you."

"How are you enjoying your visit so far?"

"I love Rhode Island. It's like a jewel in the middle of all the hustle and bustle on the East Coast."

"I agree. I moved to Newport after I graduated college in New York. Never went back."

"It's a good place to live. Aunt Hattie loves it. She's lucky to have you working for her."

"Well, I enjoy the customers and working in retail pays the bills. In the winter months, when everything slows down, I have more time to do my painting. My work is on display around the corner, in the rear of the shop, near the back door."

I stroll over to the knotty pine wall that is lit up by small track lighting and study her work. Abstracts and impressionist paintings of sailing and the seacoast fill the surface. "You're good, Louisa. I bet these paintings disappear quickly. They capture the beauty of Newport and the thrill of sailing."

"Thanks. Luckily, they are selling, even in these tough economic times. Lots of art lovers around here, as well as wealthy mariners."

"That's a plus. I'll plan to come back with Walter and let him pick out some of your art for our home in Seattle. I love them all. Whatever he chooses will be fine with me. The two of us will get great satisfaction supporting your career. Today I can only handle these few purchases while I finish my walk with Pebbles."

"Sure. Sounds great. Thanks. Glad you like the paintings. I look forward to seeing you and Walter again."

I smile at Louisa, pay for my loot and saunter out the door with Pebbles. I love walking with my pooch. Gives me an excuse to just cruise around without any direction. I head over to the pier with the leash in one hand, and a clumsy shopping bag in the other. *Hum, maybe I should have stashed my purchases in the shop.* As I think about returning to the Crow's Nest, I notice Louisa putting a "Closed" sign on the door.

Guess I'll carry my treasures, but no running up the hill on the last leg of our journey. Maybe I should get a cart for Pebbles to pull. Make him work for his supper. That would expend his boundless energy. I smile at that picture in my mind and don't focus on the people in front of me coming the other way. I look up as I hear someone breathing heavily and find myself staring into the sweaty face of Graham Gotthree.

"So, Tangie, we meet again."

"Now how did that happen?" I groan, inwardly, not expecting to see him for a few days. I don't like to be caught off guard.

Graham speaks in a wheezing voice as if he just ran a marathon and lost. "I wasn't expecting to bump into you again today. What a pleasant surprise."

Now why do I feel like this dude's been watching me? Maybe it's the tone in his voice. Maybe he's a bad actor. Maybe it's his heavy breathing. Maybe it's his sweaty appearance or maybe, all of the above. He's just weird, and makes me uncomfortable. It's a feeling I cannot shake. No wonder Walter hates the guy.

Graham is no longer wearing his beige funeral suit, nor his brown and green pinstriped tie nor his polished cordovans. He sports a green golfing shirt soaked in sweat, tan-colored shorts and beige New Balance running shoes. The guy must have a thing for earth tones.

After scrutinizing him, I remark, "On your way to the golf course?"

"No."

I detect a hint of briskness in his voice.

"For your information, I'm taking a stroll around the harbor after the funeral, like you appear to be doing." He looks down. Is this your dog?"

I am tempted to say, *No, I just rent him,* but think twice. "He's my guard dog."

"He doesn't look like a guard dog. He's cute." Graham bends down to pet him.

Pebbles growls at him and when Graham attempts to touch my pooch's head, Pebbles attempts to bite his hand off. Good thing Graham goes into retreat mode and jumps back in a flash. No telling what my attack dog would have done to Graham if he got a hold of him.

"I can see you aren't kidding." Graham winces and his blazing eyes show intense displeasure. They reveal to me a picture of hidden pent-up anger that seeps out through his stare.

"Sorry. Can't say I didn't warn you." I speak with a fake hint of apology in my voice. "I hope he didn't hurt you."

"No harm done. He didn't draw blood."

He grunts as he wipes his hand on his shorts, as if Pebbles contaminated him. Guy probably never had a dog.

"Well, that's a relief."

While I am glad the creep will not sue me, I have to hand it to Pebbles. He knows how to read people, whether they can be trusted or not. I think in this case, I'll side with Pebbles.

I decide to start fishing; I bait the hook. "So, Graham, do you live around here?"

"Well, not on the waterfront, but not far away."

"Closer to Providence?"

"I commute to Providence like all the other politicians."

Well, so much for finding out the location of the lion's lair. I give myself points for trying, and one point to Graham for being elusive.

"I didn't realize you're a politician, Graham."

"I never ran for office, but I work in politics. I run the campaigns and do behind the scenes work when we're not running."

I want to say, *a necessary evil*, but instead, I reply, "Sounds like you keep busy."

"Yes I do, but never too busy to have a good time. How about you? Do you like to have a good time?"

"That depends. What is your definition of a good time?"

"For starters, I like the company of beautiful women. You, Tangie, just happen to be the most beautiful woman on the waterfront."

I can't help myself. I blush. Not from embarrassment, but from anger. This guy bugs me big time. Still, I play along. Don't know why, but probably to get more insight into his character.

"Graham, I've heard that line before, but thanks. A compliment is a compliment." That's about as grateful as I can get. "Tell me, Mr. Campaign Manager, what else do you do for fun?"

"Well, I like to take my beautiful women out to dinner, go dancing and cap the evening off with a midnight sail on my boat."

"I guess if you live around Newport, you must have a boat."

"It comes in handy."

"With the ladies?"

"Yes, but I'm still looking for the right one."

"So I surmise."

"How about a dinner date?"

"Graham, I'm married."

"I know that. You could still have dinner with me. Tell your husband you're going to the beauty parlor."

"I never go to the beauty parlor. A friend cuts my hair."

Well, that's a lie, but I enjoy seeing Graham squirm. He probably sees through me but I just can't help myself.

"I have a thought, Tangie. You could tell your husband you need to go shopping. Every woman loves to shop. We could have lunch."

"That might work. Walter hates to shop. We could just happen to meet in a public place."

"I like the way you think, Tangie."

If you only knew, Graham, that I don't trust you for a second. I give Mr. Creep my most endearing smile. Gosh, I should have majored in Drama. I'm good.

I shake Graham's sweaty palm, bid him *adieu* and turn with Pebbles to head back to Aunt Hattie's. The fog is starting to settle into the harbor and a chill is in the air. Rain tomorrow, no doubt. It will suit my mood. I take a roundabout way despite the heavy packages that cramp my shoulders. For some reason, I don't want Graham to know what direction I am heading. Don't know why. Graham works for the gov'nor. No doubt he can find Aunt Hattie's home in a flash, if he so desires. I have a sneaking suspicious he wants to do just that. I just don't know why. I may be a tad bit vain, but I don't think he's interested in me solely for my looks.

One of my shoulders aches sharply as Pebbles pulls me up the hill. My old battle wound is acting up again, reminding me I am the walking wounded. No matter how much I try to put traumatic memories out of my mind, Adolphus Sargento still resurfaces in my waking hours, as well as in my dreams. My therapist tells me forgetting my old nemesis will take time. I should not be alarmed by recurring flashbacks. *Yeah, good luck with that one, Tangie. Good try, Doc.* If it weren't for Walter, I would be a nut case.

I don't know why meeting Graham at the pier triggers memories of Adolphus. I just know it does. And I know I will have nightmares tonight.

"Honey, I'm home!" I announce, as I walk in the front door, doing that ol' Desi Arnaz imitation.

However, instead of Walter greeting me, I hear, "Hello Dear," in unison, from Peter Van Beek's sisters, Jenny and Clarissa.

I smile sweetly to cover my embarrassment. "Oh, I'm sorry, I thought Walter would be here."

"No need to apologize, dear. We love your imitation. It's a good one," Jenny chuckles. "It's from our generation and you do it so well."

Clarissa nods. "Walter is upstairs, Tangie. I think he has a bit of a headache."

I don't want to reveal to the ladies he is replenishing the sleep he lost last night, so I nod in acquiescence.

Aunt Hattie enters the living room with a tray of teacups and scones, like a grand lady of merry ol' England. She places them next to a pot of steaming tea and looks at me. "My, it looks like you've been shopping." Then she eyes the logo on the bag and continues, "Oh, you've been to the Crow's Nest, Tangie. How lovely. Glad you found a few remembrances. Thanks for giving us your business."

"My thanks to you, Aunt Hattie. I love your shop. Great stuff there and Louisa is so helpful."

Clarissa smiles broadly, showing her dimples. "Tangie, did you know that the Crow's Nest has been in business for over twenty years? Before that Hattie had her own art studio."

"No, I didn't. But I surmise she has multiple talents. Walter told me he used to stay here as a teenager and hang out at the gallery as well as the beach."

Aunt Hattie's eyes twinkle as she hands me a teacup and saucer. "Yes. Those were great summers. I loved having Walter stay with me when he was a youth—such fond memories. His visit was always the highlight of my summer. She sighs and pours me some tea. "Tangie, please sit down and join us."

What I really want to do is to wake up Walter, but instead, I acquiesce. "Of course, I'd love to visit with you." I plop down on the overstuffed sofa, sandwiching myself between Jenny and Clarissa.

I have three servings of Twinings English Breakfast tea and two scones with lemon curd while listening to the sisters chatting amicably with Aunt Hattie. Seems my appetite has returned. I find myself licking the lemon curd off my fingers. The sisters relate stories about Peter Van Beek and Aunt Hattie, and they relive the times spent together in their youth, at clambakes, and sailing in regattas. Then the conversation drifts to the present.

Jenny turns toward me with her eyes wide open, staring like an owl on the hunt. "How long will you be staying in Newport, my dear?"

"I'm not sure, Miss Van Beek. It depends on Walter. He hasn't been here for a visit in quite some time and there are many things we would like to do and see."

Well, that is a half-truth, but I cannot open up completely to these sisters. The truth would only upset them, and I am sure our true intentions would become known from Newport to Providence in a flash bulletin. Better to stay silent as long as possible.

I stifle an uncontrollable yawn, chug my fourth cup of tea and lean on the back of the sofa to get up out of my hammock position, my body being stuck in the middle of the couch.

"I think I need to lie down for a bit, if you ladies don't mind. It's been a long day. I think Pebbles will be all right for a little while, Aunt Hattie." I point to my Westie lying by the hearth, feet up in the air, dead to the world. "The pooch is lights out for the next few hours. Thank you so much for the tea and scones." I smile at the visiting Van Beek sisters as I extend my hand to each of them. "It's been a pleasure to meet you today."

"You, too, Tangie." Clarissa speaks for the two of them. "Do come visit us if you have time."

Aunt Hattie nods and points to the hallway. "You go right upstairs and rest. I will call you when dinner is ready."

"Oh, don't bother to cook, Aunt Hattie. We had such a wonderful meal this afternoon and the tea and scones filled me up."

"I just have some leftovers. Trust me; we all will be hungry later this evening, especially Walter. But don't you worry; I will not fuss at all."

155

I sigh. "Thank you, Aunt Hattie." I can no longer stifle a yawn. "Feel free to call me in a couple of hours. I just need to lie down for a bit." At this point, I can hardly stand up, but I turn to the sisters before leaving. "Walter and I will definitely visit before we leave. Bye for now."

"Bye, dear. I'm sure we'll run into each other again," chirps Jenny Van Beek.

I smile at the two sisters, then climb my way up the creaking stairs, holding on to the rail like a faltering drunk, and head towards the bedroom at the end of the hall, envisioning a soft bed and downy pillow to soothe my body and soul.

I open the door to the guest bedroom and notice Walter lying sound asleep on his side of the bed, as if waiting for my presence. I smile and brush his lips with mine, sit down and take off my Nikes. Fully dressed, I crawl into bed with him, too tired to remove my clothes or contemplate anything else.

Chapter Twenty-Three

I wake up screaming. No Walter. Darkness. *Where am I?* In a minute, the door opens and a light flashes. I can make out Walter standing in the shadow of the room behind Aunt Hattie. She gazes at me with a wide-eye stare.

"My goodness dear," she exclaims. You gave us such a fright! Whatever is happening to you?"

"A dream, a horrible dream."

"A loud one at that," Aunt Hattie murmurs.

Walter comes close, sits down on the bed and encompasses me in his arms. I can feel myself trembling as I cling to him.

"Your forehead is sweaty, Tangie," Walter observes, as he wipes my brow with his shirtsleeve. "How are you feeling?"

"Not well right now. But I'll be okay. Give me a minute or two."

"Maybe I should take your temperature, dear." Aunt Hattie suggests.

"No. Really, I'm all right."

"I'll get a cold washcloth for your head." I hear the door open and close. Aunt Hattie is gone momentarily.

It was a bad one, Walter." I sob into my love's shirt. Then I tense up again, grab his arm and cling to his shoulder.

Aunt Hattie comes back in a flash and places a wet cloth on my head. The coolness soothes my throbbing temple.

"Does she have these often?" Aunt Hattie asks, as if I'm not in the room.

Walter shakes his head. "Only when she stresses out, Aunt Hattie. Angelina's been through a lot since our honeymoon ended. Did I tell you her brother in Seattle was missing? We found him, near the mountain pass, but he had quite a fall and wound up in the hospital. Plus, I think the funeral overwhelmed her more than she realized."

This time Aunt Hattie addresses me. "I'm so sorry, my dear girl. When you feel up to it come downstairs. I have some soup and cucumber sandwiches on the table. It's way past suppertime."

I stop digging my fingernails into Walter's arms for a moment. "Thank you, Aunt Hattie. I'll come down soon. I'll just wait until the queasiness passes."

Aunt Hattie gets the message. She comes over to me, pats my shoulder and leaves quietly. I hear her tiptoe down the stairs to the kitchen, no doubt to heat up the soup that is getting cold.

Walter puts his hand around my head, leans my body into his and kisses me on the cheek. "Was this a new one or a recurring dream, Angelina?"

"A new one."

"Do you want to talk about it?"

"Not now. I want to think about it. It's all mixed up. But somehow I think it has relevance to our case."

Our case. Seems like I'm taking ownership of the mess we've gotten into. Now that's a scary thought. I really don't want to go back to my dream or should I say, *nightmare.* I just want a normal life. *Why can't I be like Aunt Hattie? Own an art shop. Live near a pier. Have ladies drop in for tea...*

Walter speaks, as if reading my thoughts, "Sweetheart, just say the word and we can go home. Forget all about the governor. We don't have to do this anymore."

"No, my love. If we go home, I will never be free of this nightmare. It will haunt me and we'll regret running away from our chance to do some good. I know it, and you know it."

Walter leans down and kisses me on the lips, gently. "I know that I cherish you and I don't want to see you hurt."

"Yes, I know you do. You're terrific and I love you. You are my rock. Just give me some time. I think I can sort things out, as the pictures in my mind come into focus. In time maybe we can leave this horror show behind us and not regret anything. That is my hope." I sigh and return his kiss.

"Um, You taste wonderful, Angelina—a little salty but wonderful. And you know the one thing I don't regret is marrying you. My family, my only family, Aunt Hattie is crazy about you. She told me you remind her of herself when she was a young woman."

"You're kidding."

"No, honestly."

"Thanks, Walter. I take that as a huge compliment. I am feeling better. Let's go eat that delicious potato soup your aunt prepared for us. I'm starved."

"Potato soup, hum...that's my Tangie."

Walter pulls the covers off and helps me to my feet. He hands me my slippers, the slippers I kicked off two days ago and crumpled up against the wall, like arrows in a target.

"Your glass slippers, m'lady."

"Well, they're flannel, but they will serve the purpose." I lean over and kiss my handsome prince.

He smiles. "Pacific Northwest slippers. All the comforts of home." Then he takes me in his arms and carries me down the stairs to Aunt Hattie's supper feast.

Chapter Twenty-Four

"What do you know about Graham Gotthree, Aunt Hattie?" I chew on a celery stick stuffed with peanut butter after downing three cucumber sandwiches. Granted, the sandwiches are smaller than the size of a small deck of cards, so I am not over-indulging.

"Well, Tangie, I just met that young man today, as you did."

"Any feelings about him, one way or another?"

Aunt Hattie puts down her soupspoon. "He does seem a little stuffy, like he doesn't belong with the rest of the family. He also seems a little odd. But I noticed during the funeral and the dinner afterwards that he certainly knows his way around. My goodness, the funeral seems ages ago." Aunt Hattie sighs, wipes her lips with her napkin, and dabs at her brow. "This has been such a long day."

Walter stands up and pushes back his chair. "I bet you are exhausted, Aunt Hattie. Why don't you go upstairs and turn in for the night. Angelina and I can clear the dishes and clean up."

"You sure you two don't mind? All of a sudden, I'm very tired, like you were earlier. It just hit me."

I nod. "We understand, Aunt Hattie. Get some rest. We'll talk tomorrow."

Aunt Hattie pulls herself up from the table and looks at Walter and then me. "Thank you, dears. It certainly is good to have you both here in Newport with me. Stay here as long as you want. My home is your home." She starts walking towards the hall, turns and smiles, "I'll see you in the morning."

Walter smiles back. "Goodnight, Aunt Hattie. Remember, tomorrow, it's my turn to make breakfast."

"You'll get no argument from me. I can sleep in." Aunt Hattie chuckles as she grabs a cane from the corner of the room and uses it to make her way to the staircase leading upstairs.

She turns around one more time, whispering, "I only use this thing at night. I call it my balancing stick."

Walter resumes his spot at the kitchen table. We continue sipping tea like two old married folks. We grin at her and nod.

"You go, girl," I cheer. We can hear Aunt Hattie's laughter as she ascends the stairs.

We hear her bedroom door close. Walter takes my hand, wipes a few stray hairs off my brow and asks, "Why is Graham Gotthree on your mind, Tangie?"

I take a sip of my tea and put the cup down. "'Cause I ran into him during my walk with Pebbles. Pebbles nearly bit his hand off."

"Smart dog."

I smile at Walter and giggle. "I thought so too."

"What was Gotthree doing on the pier? Fishing?"

"Yeah. Fishing for me. He said he was out for a stroll. But a stroll is leisurely and he was all sweaty. I seriously think he was stalking me. He asked me out on a date."

"Jeez, Tangie…"

"Now don't get all mad and hot under the collar. I told him I'd meet him in a public place for lunch."

"What?"

"Don't worry. The worst that will happen is I'll probably throw up in the creep's lap. You're right about him and so is Aunt Hattie. He is strange. Next time I encounter him, promise me you will follow us, and keep me under surveillance at all times. I don't want to be alone with him."

"Most assuredly. I told you I don't trust the guy."

"I don't either. Say, what about our Steve? Did you call him? Is he coming to Newport?"

"Angelina, Sweetheart, I couldn't get a hold of him. He's on an undercover assignment. Barry couldn't or wouldn't tell me where he is or when he will be available."

I lift up my teacup and take another sip to fortify myself. "Oh, so he doesn't think what we are doing is important."

"We didn't tell Barry anything. Remember?"

I put my cup down. Walter refills it. I nod. "Oh, that's right, only Steve. You know, maybe Suzy will know where he is. Maybe she could get in touch with him."

"I doubt it, Love. If Barry won't tell me anything, I doubt Suzy knows anything. Steve keeps his business and pleasure separate, but you could give her a call if you wish."

"I can, but I have a feeling we are alone on this one, my sweet."

"Just you and me, Babe, at least until Steve finishes his assignment."

"Steve always seems to come to our aid at the last gunshot." I pout and pour the last of the cream in my second cup of tea. I add a teaspoon of sugar, take a sip and continue to groan. "Then he feels bad. Well, he can't get mad at us this time if we proceed without him."

Walter pours the last of the tea into his cup and sighs. "Angelina, my sweet, forget our Steve for the moment. We'll be okay for a few days on our own. When is your lunch date with this bad seed? You know I will cover your back. Come to think of it, it's a nice back."

I smile at Walter's last remark and moan as he massages my shoulders. "Don't know yet, but I like the way you talk." I take Walter's free hand and place it on my cheek and grin. "My love, you make this all a little easier. I'm thinking Graham will call here or maybe, like today, just run into me as I walk around town."

"Okay. We stick together like glue, but he doesn't know it."

I can tell by his frown and one raised eyebrow that my love is not at all pleased with our arrangement.

"You know, I can't let you out of my sight, Tang."

"Is that so bad?"

"It is, if I'm playing detective and have to be in disguise. That gets old. I'm not a big fan of make-up and hair pieces."

"Just do the minimum. Wear a wig. Put on some glasses."

"That I can do. I'll dig out some nerdy clothes from my trunk in the attic. I have an idea for a disguise. Seems it worked once before, when… oh, you'll see."

"You have extra clothes here?"

Walter grins. Well, yes. This used to be my second home when I went to Brown. I know my Aunt Hattie. She never throws anything away."

"And you are my boy scout—*always prepared.*"

"So tomorrow, you go for a walk. Start by strolling around Newport—plenty of quaint little shops around the waterfront, between here and the ocean. Tangie, leave Pebbles at home or you'll never get close to Graham. Plus, with me shadowing you, Pebbles will pick up my scent and spoil my cover."

"He likes your scent, as do I."

Walter smiles and kisses my nose. "I'll follow you at a distance."

"Not too distant. Remember I'm not crazy about doing this."

"I'll be within grabbing range."

"Good. That's my Watson." I let out a long sigh and yawn. "So tomorrow, Sweetie, we go hunting for Graham. Who knows? Some leads on this case may start to appear. We can hope. Who knows? Graham may take us somewhere or let something slip about someone or something. He might be privy to something about Eveline. I could question him about her."

"No, Tangie. That would be dangerous. It would be too obvious if you start pumping him for information. It might tip him off that we aren't just visitors. Just listen to him talk. Men love to talk, especially the obnoxious ones. Play like you're interested. You know, the flattering type."

"That isn't me. More like Suzy."

"You can act. You do that so well. Pretend you're Suzy."

"Curses. A woman trapped by her own talents."

"Think of the payoff. The sooner we have some answers, the sooner we can go home."

"Home..." I move my shoulders up and down. "I like the sound of that. I miss our house on Queen Anne, our castle in the clouds. I miss our kitty, Hildie. I miss the rain. And, I especially miss being with you whenever I want."

"Soon, my love." Walter gets up from the chair next to the fireplace, comes over to me and pulls me to my feet. "Soon," he repeats and crushes me in one of his special embraces. All the building fear that penetrates my body evaporates like the mist in the fog. I can feel my strength returning. I can do this caper and tomorrow will be better.

Chapter Twenty-Five

Rain. Stormy weather. You would think I'd be glad that this weather reminds me of home, but no. This is a gloomy rain, a nasty rain. Not a good sign. Not only do I have to walk around town for an opportunity to bump into Graham, I have to do it in the rain. That's all right. I'll pretend I'm in Seattle on a bad day. *Curses!* I forgot to call my mom last night. Oh well, I'll try her tonight. Right now I've got to figure out what to wear and what I'm going do. Strategize how to catch the worm.

I begin to think about more pleasant things, like last night. After we cleaned up the kitchen, Walter and I crawled up the stairs, tore our clothes off, fell into our guest room bed and collapsed in a dead sleep. No nightmares, no dreams, no "you've got that lovin' feelin'" jive, just exhaustion. We didn't even hear the thunderstorm that passed through Newport and left us with all this rain. But as always, it was lovely just to lie in bed together, engaged or unengaged. Right now I affirm that it's wonderful to be young and in love. Before getting dressed, I say a morning prayer of gratitude for my life and for Walter.

As I ponder whether to wear my new red and black wool short jacket and jeans, or my denim skirt and yellow elbow length sweater, I hear Walter calling my name from downstairs.

"Tangie, breakfast is served. Wear the red and black. It's sexy."

Great. Walter is now in the fashion business.

"Yes, dear," I giggle, imitating Peter Van Beek's sisters.

I lay myself down on Walter's side of our bed and hug his pillow. I am going nuts and I'm only twenty-seven, soon to be twenty-eight, but I can wait for that birthday. Getting too close to the big Three-0. Not looking forward to my first wrinkle and gray hair. I know there are products that help in those areas, but I go for the natural look. So does Walter. Ah, just thinking of Walter's natural body turns me on. I bury my head in his pillow. I can smell him. I close my eyes and imagine us lying naked on the beach in Fiji. Now that's a good dream or was, until Eveline entered into it. No rest for weary lovers until she is found out. Seems we have no choice but to go into detective mode and uncover the whole truth about her, her hit man and anyone else involved in this entire mess.

Breakfast with Walter, Aunt Hattie and Pebbles suits me fine. Walter makes his famous crepes with raspberries and Aunt Hattie eats four of them. She beats me. I don't know how she stays so thin. Must be the genes. Walter is on the lean side. Like Walter, Aunt Hattie loves to cook. Usually good cooks are on the plump side. There goes that stereotype. That gives me hope. I love to eat and Walter loves to cook. Good combo. Come to think of it, I love to cook but it is not a full-time habit. I'm just too busy chasing the bad guys. A person needs calm and peace to be domestic.

Walter hands me a glass of orange juice, freshly squeezed. "Okay, Tangie, when do you leave for your excursion around Newport?"

"Right after breakfast, I'll take Pebbles for a short walk, bring him home and then head out on my detecting caper."

"Don't take Pebbles too far. He might get suspicious. You know that pooch. He'll know something is up."

"What are you two planning?" Aunt Hattie inquires.

I take the last bite of my last crepe. "Oh, Aunt Hattie, you are sworn to secrecy. Walter and I are planning a cat and mouse game with Graham Gotthree."

"Now I understand your questions last night, Tangie. You think he has something to do with Peter Van Beek's..."

"Well, to tell the truth, I'm not sure. I think he knows something and I'm just going to do a little prying. For some reason, he likes me, so I may be successful. While I am on the hunt, Walter will follow me incognito."

"You two watch out. I don't want anything to happen to either of you. These days you can't trust anyone."

I lean over and hug Aunt Hattie. "Aunt Hattie, we'll be careful. Please, promise you won't say anything to anyone, especially to the sisters."

"Oh, I never tell them anything. They are lovely women but terrible gossips."

Walter rises to clear the table. "Thank you, Aunt Hattie."

"Oh, Walter, you leave those dishes right there. I'll take care of them. I've got all kinds of energy this morning. Tangie, go and take care of whatever you have to do. I have plenty of time to clean up. I'll also keep an eye on Pebbles for you. I'm taking the day off from the shop and plan to relax and do some reading. Don't even bother walking your darling pooch. I'll take Pebbles for a stroll later on. I can use the exercise after all those crepes."

"Are you sure you don't mind?"

"Tangie, just go. I am as anxious as you to get things moving. It's the least I can do."

I smile. "You're wonderful, Aunt Hattie. If by chance, that Graham fellow calls, tell him I'm walking around the waterfront, shopping."

"Did you give him my phone number?"

"Absolutely not, but I have a feeling he could get it if he wanted it badly enough."

"It's unlisted."

"I don't think that would stop him."

Aunt Hattie raises her eyebrows and gives me a look that signals panic. "You be careful, Tangie. Walter, you stay right behind her. Don't let her out of your sight."

Walter salutes her. "Aye, aye Captain. Remember to keep your phone line open in case I need to call you."

"My, this sounds serious."

"It could become that way," Walter answers. "I like to take precautions."

I put my hand on Walter's arm. "Did you find your disguise, my love?"

"Yes. Let's see if you recognize the dude."

Walter disappears into the hall. In two minutes he returns with bright red hair, brown horn-rimmed glasses and an Irish wool sports jacket.

"I've seen this guy before," I announce as I study his character. "Walter! You were at Anthony's Home Port in Seattle that evening last year—when I met with Santigo for the first time, over dinner. You devil! I never recognized you. What a fox!"

"That's why I thought this would be the perfect personage."

"You could be a Dubliner or a Classics professor at Brown. Great job!"

Walter answers me in an Irish brogue, "Well, I was a bit of a teacher in the ol' sod but not a professor. *Sure'n*, wouldn't you know it, lass. 'Tis true, I be a bit of a computer whiz in my spare time. *Be gorrah*, I may just fly out to see those Microsoft people in that place you call Seattle."

"Walter!" Aunt Hattie takes his arm and does a little jig with him. "I'm amazed! I'm your aunt and I don't know you!"

Walter leans over and kisses his aunt on the cheek. *"Sure'n* I must be thankin' ye, Aunt Hattie."

I interrupt their dancing with a whisper. "Walter." My voice and demeanor becomes solemn, clouds spoiling a sunny afternoon. "Something just occurred to me. What if Graham is hanging around the house, spying on us? What if he spots you leaving?"

Walter resumes speaking in his familiar voice, but his mood shifts to serious. "Way ahead of you, Tangie. Got it under control. There is a secret passageway through the boxwood hedge in the backyard. It leads out into an alley facing Mulberry Lane. Long ago I used it when the neighborhood kids and I played Hide n' Seek. They never found me."

My smile returned. "Even then you were mysterious, Walter."

Walter nods and kisses me on my forehead. "No, Sherlock. You're the mysterious one. You keep me guessing. But not to worry, I'll leave first, head out to Mulberry, then cut back to the next street that leads to the waterfront. When I see you heading down the hill, I will follow you at a safe distance. Now listen. This is very important. Under no circumstances are you to get into a vehicle with this dude. Got it?"

"Yes, Watson. If Graham wants to go somewhere, I will tell him that we can walk there, bike or jog, but no car. I am out for exercise as well as shopping. I have suddenly become a health nut."

"Thanks, Tangie. That's crucial. I could lose you if you got in a car."

"I don't want to get lost. Been there, done that. Although the last time I disappeared, you told me to stay *in* the car. And we know what happened when I didn't."

Walter hugs me gently and looks into my eyes. "Are we ready, Sweetheart? Have all your credit cards? Your cell phone?"

"Yes."

Walter turns to his aunt with a reminder. "Aunt Hattie, if necessary, Tangie will…" Walter then looks at me for a moment, pausing. "Tangie will call you and report her progress, where she is going and so forth in case I miss something or she loses me. You can call me and let me know where she is headed."

"I can do that, Walter."

"Now, this is very important. This may not happen, but I am telling you in case there is a problem. If there is, I will call the police. If someone is bothering you or comes to your door that you don't want here, tell me in code. Say, *I really wanted to go to my shop today, but my arthritis is acting up.* Can you do that?"

"I don't have arthritis, Walter. But I do have a bad back. I will say my back is acting up. If I lie, it will come out phony."

I smile at Walter's only living relative. "You're so good, Aunt Hattie. I hope this doesn't scare you too much."

"Not at all. I'm older than you, but I like adventure. I'm smart. I won't do anything stupid to block your progress. Good luck, my dears."

"Thanks, Aunt Hattie." Walter kisses her forehead. "We'll be seeing you. Remember, keep your phone line open."

Walter hugs her and then comes back to me and brushes a kiss on my lips. "Be careful, Angelina. Remember, I love you and I've got your back."

Walter opens the French door to the outside patio. I can see the rain tapering off. Perhaps the weather will clear up and the day will be ripe for sleuthing. Walter turns around and answers my prayers. "You can forget your umbrella. The sun is coming out."

In a flash, he turns and slips out the door like a ghost intent on doing some haunting. I experience an eerie feeling clear down to my toes. My hands and feet tingle. My shoulders shake. *Get a grip*, I tell myself.

Aunt Hattie gives me a look of panic, as if realizing that she or someone she loves could get hurt. She straightens up, leaves the table and goes into the hallway. When she comes back two seconds later, she places a metal lump in my hand. Pepper spray with a key chain attached.

"I don't want you going defenseless, my dear."

I take her hand, hug her thin frame and look into her eyes—eyes that match the steel-blue intensity of Walter's. "Thanks, Aunt Hattie. 'Never used this stuff before, but there's always a first time."

God help us. The three of us are setting in motion a series of events from which we cannot turn away, no matter what. For this reason, we will not change our minds about what we are doing. Just the thought of this movement toward possible disaster scares the bejeezus out of me.

Chapter Twenty-Six

My first stop after leaving the warmth of our present home turns out to be the doorway of the Crow's Nest. Somehow being near a familiar sign gives me comfort. I don't go inside the gallery, but look in the window and wave to Louisa. As usual, she is busy helping customers, this time a trio of tourists buying expensive souvenirs and studying the artwork. I am frozen in place not wanting to go anywhere else, except maybe running back to Aunt Hattie's for a cup of tea and comfort. I have to pry myself away from the window. I take a deep breath, wave goodbye to Louisa and continue to walk down the waterfront toward the docks. I force myself to find courage to face Graham. I can sense him prowling around somewhere. But right now I avoid that picture forming in my mind.

Next to the numerous "Boats for Hire" signs, I notice a small grey shack with a sign over the door that reads: "Bicycles for Rent by the hour". *Hum, that could be a good thing. I could cruise the waterfront. Get around without seeming to be looking for anyone, just a chick out for a spin along the docks.* I give the guy sitting on a barrel by the doorway a fifty. That includes a deposit, in case I bring the bike back late. I flip my purse into my backpack, hop on the ancient three-speed bike and speed off. Walter, I hope, will understand my motivation and rent a bike for himself. Chances are, he already has. This past week, he has been ten steps ahead of me.

I steer my bike towards the public beach located at the end of the shopping area and the waterfront park. As I approach the next block, I spot Graham Gotthree leaning against the storefront brick wall of a kite shop holding a dragon-shaped kite. Luckily, I'm wearing sunglasses to block the rising sun. Not wanting to be obvious, I pretend I don't see him. I steer my bike close to the curb of the sidewalk and whiz by, intend on coasting to the beach. As I pass him, I hear a yell and a hoot.

"Tangie! Hey, wait up. Woo, woo…"

I put on the breaks. Surprisingly, they work. I stop the rickety bike completely and turn around. Lifting my sunglasses off of my nose, I glare at him. "Graham, you sound like an owl."

"Hello to you, too, Mrs. Cunningham."

"Don't tell me you are going to fly a kite?"

"Why else would I be holding this paper dragon? It's windy enough after that storm last night. The beach is just two blocks away. Want to come?"

"I'm on my way to the beach. Okay, sounds like fun."

"Wait a minute." Graham hands me his kite, walks over to a van parked on the street, opens the back door and lifts out a ten-speed. Seems Mr. Gotthree comes prepared. Another boy scout—an evil boy scout. Graham looks to be about the same age as Walter, but he has a baby face. He could be older than he looks. I wonder if he ever crossed paths with Walter.

"Hey Graham, have you always lived in Rhode Island?"

"Why?"

"I was wondering if you ever met Walter before this week. He used to come to Newport when he was young. He went to college in Providence."

"No. I never met him before this week, nor his auntie."

"Hum, Aunt Hattie knows Peter Van Beek's family. Are you sure you never met her?"

"She doesn't look familiar. However I meet a lot of people working for the party and the governor. Why? Did she say she knows me?"

"No. In fact she didn't recognize you either. Strange. This is such a close-knit community."

"So it seems. However, while growing up, I always felt like an outsider. I moved here later, in my teens. Seems the cliques were already formed. I never really fit in. To New Englanders, I will forever more be a New Yorker."

"You don't say. Interesting. I don't hear an accent."

"Oh, I can put it on if I want, but I learned to ditch it when I got here. My English teacher forced me to go to speech class to get rid of it. I rebelled and told her what to do with her speech class."

"That's a cruel thing for a teacher to do, to single you out for your accent and make you feel bad."

"Yeah, well some people are just like that. Cruel. But I learned to play the game."

"I'm sorry, Graham. Should we get going?"

"Yeah. I'll lead. You follow."

"Sounds like a plan."

We ride our bikes down the winding road about three blocks. Not much traffic to worry about. Not many people head to the beach on a windy autumn day. I can picture the cars bumper to bumper in the summer with not much room for cyclists. As we near the beach, the wind gets stronger and I struggle to keep my bike erect. Graham rides in front of me, with his dragon kite fastened on his backpack. I think any minute the wind will sweep him up and he will take off like one of the monkeys in *The Wizard of Oz*. All he needs is a wicked "eek, eek, eek". I smile at the thought and then shudder. Graham turns around and notices, probably thinking I am interested in him. *God! Help me get through this afternoon.*

Graham pulls up in front of a sign that reads: "Newport Beach Number One".

"How many public beaches are there in Newport, Graham?"

"Oh, a few. This is Number One because it is the first one on the outskirts of town. You should come in the summer. Swimming is just about perfect then. Beach Two is the best. Great waves. Not too rough for body surfing but not much for board surfing."

"How do you know I don't surf?"

"I think of you more as a bathing beauty."

I groan inwardly, but play along with him. "I think I'd like to come here in the summer to swim. The water's freezing cold all year at our beaches back home. You need a wetsuit to surf in the ocean."

"So where do you swim?"

"Oh, we have lakes, rivers and indoor pools. Some places in the Puget Sound are bearable, but always chilly."

"I've never been to the Pacific Northwest."

"It's lovely. Like Rhode Island, but more rugged with mountain ranges, the Cascades and the Olympics. Camping is big out there, like it is in Maine. People are into nature."

"I'm not into camping."

"Everyone camps in the Northwest, at least once. I love nature and all that."

"All right then, you and I can take a nature walk on the beach."

As I follow Graham down the beach to the edge of the surf, I'm grateful to be wearing my black boots. Not in the mood for sandy toes. Too cold this fall morning to go barefoot. The sand is still damp from the rain. We stroll at a snail's pace. Graham releases the strings on his kite and lets the dragon soar in the breeze. Usually I feel very peaceful at the beach, smelling the salty breeze, as it whips my hair around my face, listening to the roar of the waves crashing at the shore. But every time I take a step and notice Graham's tan tennis shoes beside me, I shiver.

"You're chilled, Tangie. I've got some coffee in my van. We can hop on our bikes, peddle back and get some."

Now I don't want to go back to Graham's van, but I acquiesce. "Sure, let's head back. I'm freezing."

Graham pulls his kite from the wind's grasp, rolls up the strings and disassembles his dragon before leading the way. I follow like a faithful servant. The things I do for curiosity. I don't like playing the coy female, but that role seems to work with Graham.

We hop on our bikes in silence and peddle back into town. When we get to the van, Graham opens the passenger side and commands me in a soft voice, "Get in."

Remembering Walter's warning, I refuse. "No thanks. I'll wait here. I'm holding my bike." I am suddenly grateful I have an old bike with no kickstand. I know my excuse sounds feeble, but no way am I getting in his van.

"Have it your way," Graham answers, unperturbed. He walks around to the rear, opens the back door, deposits his kite and takes out a thermos. He returns, removes the top of the container, pours a cup of a steaming liquid and hands it to me.

"Thanks." I take a sip and gasp.

Now I've tasted bad coffee in my life, once or twice, but this is positively the worst coffee I've ever consumed. I try not to choke, but cannot help myself. I wind up spitting out any more liquid I might have consumed.

"I guess it's a little strong."

"Yeah, you might say that. Perhaps we could ride down the road a little and get some hot chocolate."

"No problem. You sure you don't want me to put your bike in the back? I could drive us around the town."

"No. I told Walter I would be biking along the waterfront. I don't want to tell him any lies when I get home. If I accidently run into you, well, that's okay. But if I drive around with you, now that would be a problem."

"I see. You are one smart cookie."

"Yeah. I think so."

"I've got a plan, Tangie. How about we head over to Bellevue Avenue and Memorial Drive? I'll show you the mansions of Newport. There is a scenic path that runs behind the magnificent homes, the Cliff Walk. It used to be private, but now it's public. I think you'll like it. We can get a beverage when we get near there. There are refreshment stands and shops nearby."

"Sounds inviting. I'd love it. Thanks, Graham."

"I aim to please."

I open my backpack and take out a windbreaker I brought, just in case. I put my arms in and zip it up, grateful for the protection from the wind.

Graham opens the passenger door to his van, tosses in his thermos and slams the door with a thud. He mounts his ten-speed and motions to me. "Follow me."

On the surface Graham, with a plaid black and tan scarf wrapped around his neck, looks perfectly innocent, even appealing. His straight blond hair blows in the breeze and he looks like a poster boy for bicycling. Underneath his charm, I sense a dark side, like when he talked about his teenage years. His anger rose to the surface. I'll have to be on guard. I put my hand in my coat pocket and finger the pepper spray, close by like a friend. One never knows.

We pedal through town and down the wide main road and pass through a residential area that consists of pleasant older homes. Some are shabby, some completely renovated, all fit into the New England land-scape. Saltboxes, colonials and Dutch colonials stand tall and of course, Cape Cods, which outnumber the rest. We turn a corner and in a flash, the neighborhood changes. We are no longer in a pleasant homespun community. Appearing before us are mansions and more mansions of monstrous proportions. It's like we're swimming through the ocean and encounter charming fishes of many shapes and sizes. Then we look up and we're immersed in the land of whales. Incredible. I can hardly believe single families once lived in these elegant castles by the sea.

I pump my pedals faster and catch up to Graham. "Okay, I think I am out of my element now."

"Relax, Tangie. No one lives here anymore. These homes belong to the town of Newport and the State of Rhode Island now. A few are part of the college here. They are open for tours and people rent them for weddings, proms, and just about anything."

"Yes, I am aware of that, but just for a moment, I was back in the era of *The Great Gatsby* and the Rockefellers. Are we going to stop soon?"

"Yes, at the Cliff Walk. It's just around the bend."

I follow Graham as he turns the corner and disappears. I spot him again as he rides alongside a gate and brings his bike to a quick halt.

He smiles at me. "End of our cruising. We will have to leave our bikes here and walk."

"Sounds like a plan."

"There's a sweet shop over there. I'll run in and get you some hot chocolate. You can watch the sea as you wait for me."

"Thanks, Graham."

As I watch Graham head around the corner, I almost feel sorry for him. Poor guy. He seems lonely. I am such a sucker for lonely people. But this is a scary lonely person. I whisper to myself, *Tangie, keep your mind on high alert. This guy is acting. So he's lonely. So he had a miserable childhood. Lots of people do. Don't slip into pity mode. He could be dangerous, very dangerous. You just don't know him. Be on guard.*

I lean my bike against a waiting grid for bikes and perch myself upon a stone wall that seems perfect for meditation. As I look to the east I can see the wide expanse of the ocean. I sigh and shrug my shoulders. On the walking path below my resting spot people are milling around and getting ready to walk along the cliff at the rear of the expansive homes. Sticking out in the crowd is a tall gentleman with a flash of red hair. He's wearing a green tweed sport coat. *Walter!* He's close. *How did he get in front of us?*

There is no end to his talents. I breathe a sigh of relief. This is my first spotting of him since I left Aunt Hattie's. *Okay. I'm ready to go home, Walter. I'm losing my nerve. I can pass on the Cliff Walk. I'd rather do it with my honey any way. I think I will ditch Graham.*

"Here you are, Tangie."

I look up. Graham holds a Styrofoam cup with steam coming out of the top.

"Thanks. That's very kind of you."

"Just a token. I can be kinder." He speaks in a crooning voice that reminds me of a crow. He sits down, puts his hand around my waist and kisses me on the cheek. I begin to think that married women turn him on, part of his little game. No commitment and some married women can be discreet.

I pause and look at Graham. I imagine the effect his show of affection has on Walter right about now. I hope my honey can stay in spy mode.

I sip the hot chocolate. It is definitely on the hot side and the taste is peculiar. After two sips I hand the cup to Graham. "Thanks, Graham, I've had enough. Sorry, I'm afraid it is not much better than your coffee." I stand up. "Let's go on the Cliff Walk now, before it gets too late."

This time I lead the way. I decide I can look around and figure things out. Graham, however, continues to play tour guide. His voice goes on and on, like an annoying tune on a merry-go-round.

"Over here we have the Marble House. Many movies have been filmed here. You referenced *The Great Gatsby*, and also *True Lies*."

"You know, Graham, I liked both of those films but I must admit, I haven't watched or read *Gatsby* since high school."

"We should read it together sometime—compare notes."

"Perhaps."

I begin to walk a little faster down the path. I can hear the surf and feel the sea air penetrating my senses. I pause to observe the salt water swirling around the rocks below. A rail protects walkers from falling over the cliff and into the crashing surf, but someone could mount the fence and jump over. Or a person could be pushed. That thought makes my stomach bounce up and down. No wonder some people are afraid of heights.

Graham looks around and not seeing any people nearby, grabs me around the waist and breathes down my neck. I try not to let on that I find him repulsive. I cannot stand the way he smells, like a moldy, sweaty shirt that has been worn for days. Exercise does nothing for him except make him stinky. I cannot stand his sickening sweet breath, nor his capped overly-white teeth. His only good feature perhaps would be his eyes, gold in color, distinctive. As he turns me around, he stares into my eyes, a vulture assessing his prey. His staring causes even his eyes to lose their charm. They become balls of cold fire piercing my body.

I can't help myself. I start shaking uncontrollably.

Graham notices my distaste and does not release his hold on me. His eyes continue to hold me in their grasp. "Who are you, Tangie? What do you want?"

I squirm and try to push him away, to get him to release me. "Nothing, nothing at all. I think this is a mistake. I just wanted to go shopping. I'm sorry I ran into you."

"I think you're lying." He twists me around and kisses me on the neck, apparently turned on by my deception and my refusal of his advances. He pins my arms around my back and presses his body into mine.

I gasp and attempt to push him away, but he moves me around once more, plants a sloppy kiss on my lips and tries to force my mouth open. When I can stand his serpent's tongue no longer, I kick him where "the sun don't shine". He must have had girls do that to him before, because again he is prepared. He catches my foot, before I can do any damage, and holds onto it. He leans my body over the cliff and whispers in my ear, "Girls who play dirty, usually get wet."

I deny my true motives and whisper back to him, "I'm not playing dirty. At first, I did want to get to know you better, before..."

His breath, strong and sickening sweet, makes me want to vomit. I feel the two sips of hot chocolate rising to the surface of my throat. I think any minute he will either slap me or throw me over the rocks and crush me like a broken clamshell. Shivering like a wet canary, I murmur, "Let me go. I don't like your games. I don't want this now. Leave me alone!"

I bite my tongue and do not shout, "You are a lunatic!" In the far recesses of my mind, I think that remark will send him over the top and for sure he will hurl me over the rail into the churning waves crashing stronger and stronger over the rocks. I buy myself a little time. "Graham, you don't understand. I'm lonely sometimes, like you. But I can't do this. Not now. Not this way. Please, let me go."

"I love it when dames beg." A sinister laugh pushes forth from his throat. It curdles the hot chocolate in my stomach and I start to gag.

When he says, "I love it when dames beg", an alarm goes off in my brain. I detect his New York accent. He really does know Steve, "Steve the Hit Man". I'm certain. No doubt the source of his twisted sense of humor. Somehow I've got to get to Walter.

"Walter, where are you?" I whisper silently, as Graham starts fondling my breasts, waist and thigh. I start screaming, not loud this time, as Graham has his mouth over mine. The world starts spinning, like when I sit in the dentist's chair, with the laughing gas turned on, defenseless and not caring. I fear blacking out any minute now. *Graham put something in the hot chocolate.* That rat. He put something in it. I'm sure, probably his favorite date-rape drug. Probably got it from his friend, Steve, "Steve the Murderer".

The mansion and then the water start spinning around and around in my limited consciousness. I find myself giving into sensations beyond my control. I lose all strength and become a defenseless toy, ready to be cast down into the sea. Someone is lifting me up and I cannot act, I cannot fight.

Somewhere in the distance, I hear an Irish brogue. I recognize Walter's voice, yelling in his fake Dublin accent, "What are you doing, you block! The Miss doesn't like you. Leave the lady be..."

I feel Graham releasing me and placing me on my feet once more, as he says, "Oh give it a rest, Bud. Mind your own business."

I begin to wonder, *"Bud?" Where did I hear that name before?* I know it is in my memory somewhere, but right now I can't think. I can hardly stand up.

I force myself to open my eyes and grasp the rail. I witness Walter grabbing Graham's collar, punching him in the face and barking orders at him. "Leave the Miss alone. Get out my sight, you beast, you bastard, before I call the constable."

Shuddering, I lean against the rail and stare at Walter, my hero, with his glowing red hair and horn-rimmed glasses all broken and twisted on his face.

Through the drug-induced fog that has taken over my body, I mumble, "Graham, I think you'd better leave for your own safety. Now."

"Tangie, you gonna let this stranger dictate to me?"

"Yes, and I think we don't need to see each other again."

What I really want to say is, *"Get the hell out of here or I am gonna let Walter throw you over the rocks"* but I don't. I force myself to keep whatever wits I still have about me.

Graham puts on a look of fake concern. "Are you going to be all right?"

"Yes. I'll let this helpful gentleman walk me to my bike."

Graham raises his eyebrows. "Are you sure you can ride?"

"No. But I can call a cab. You better leave now."

"I will call you."

"No don't. I don't think that is a good idea. Let's just leave it here."

"I'm sorry if I scared you. I hope you will be all right."

"Let that be the least of your worries. Just go."

Graham looks at Walter, then back at me. I cannot read Walter. Nor can Graham, it seems. Walter continues to do a good job of playing the concerned Irish tourist and not the ultra-jealous husband. I know he wants to thrash Graham's hard ass for good, but he exercises a magnificent amount of self-control, and plays his part as a Good Samaritan. He could get an Emmy. I am proud of him. I could kiss him on the spot but I refrain, as I too, have a role to play.

I say to my benevolent Irish stranger, with stressed hesitation in my voice, "Thank you, sir. Perhaps you could escort me to my bike and call me a cab. I am feeling a little faint."

The Irishman replies, "Sure'n, t'would be a pleasure to assist such a magnificent lady." He takes my arm. "I am at your service."

Graham studies me, and the tourist for a split-second and starts to say something. He hesitates, shakes his head and without a further word, turns his body around. He hikes back up the path to his ten-speed. The jerk does not look back, but just in case he does, I have a gesture all ready for him.

Chapter Twenty-Seven

When my Irish tourist and I get back to the entrance, we no longer see any sign of the creep. I grab the hand of my rescuer and whisper, "Walter, do you think Graham recognized you?"

"I don't think so, Angelina, but I am not taking any chances." Walter squeezes my hand. "Are you all right, Sweetheart?"

"Just a little shaky. I'm sure that Graham put some kind of date rape drug in the hot chocolate. He was out of my sight when he purchased the drink. That creep! He tried to have his way with me. One more minute, methinks, and I would be in his arms, headed to his van or off the cliff into the ocean. Take your pick. It's a good thing I didn't drink much of it. I wouldn't be able to walk right now."

"I'm sorry, Angelina. We shouldn't have done this. He's not worth risking your..."

"It's okay, Walter. I'll be okay. I just need a little time to rest."

"Sit on this bench for a moment to get your walking feet on. I'll call a cab. I need to stay in costume, just in case."

"You look just like a professor, my sweet. A nutty professor for sure, especially with your broken glasses."

Walter groans. "What was in that hot chocolate?"

"Like I know the answer. No doubt something he uses to loosen women up for action. Maybe if I drink some water, like about three gallons, I'll feel better. I'm not very lucid."

"I'll get you a bottle before we hop in the cab. I'm taking you right home."

I start chuckling, hearing myself snort, "To Seattle?"

181

Walter looks distressed. I love him when he's distressed. I begin to slur my words and then start singing. "Walter, take me home, country roads, to the place I belong in Seattle…The greenest green you ever seen, in Seattle…"

"No, Angelina. You know what I mean. Aunt Hattie's…"

Beginning to lose control of my senses I start cackling. "Thanks, Sweetie Pie. You know, you think of everything. I guess we're gonna stay in littl' ol' Newport for awhile. Nice place, Newport. Big houses. Water. Boats."

"Listen, Tangie, try to focus. After I take you to Aunt Hattie's, I'll come back to the waterfront, take the bikes back to the shed, stop at the Crow's Nest and change back into your Walter."

"I love my Walter. I miss him," I mumble, thinking somewhere in the recesses of my mind that I am a drunken fool, without any control over what I say or do. I start grabbing onto Walter and snuggle up to him, kissing him on the cheek.

"I love you too, Tangie, but please, listen."

"I'm listening. Oh, wait a minute. I need to lie down." I lean against his shoulder and burp, rather loudly.

"Oops! Musta been da hot chocolate…Good stuff!"

"Tangie, you've got to stay awake. Please, you've got to stay alert."

Walter stands up and I proceed to collapse on the bench. Walter pulls me to my feet and urges me to walk. "Come on Tangie, let's get our bikes. A little exercise will be good for you. When we get to the gate, I'll get you some coffee."

"But I already drank some really good hot chocolate."

"I know, Sweetheart, but coffee will be better for you. Trust me."

"I trust you, Walter, but you gotta help me. I can't seem to walk straight." I start giggling, swaying back and forth and then start singing, "Uh-oh, I gotta hold your hand…"

Walter holds me around my waist and escorts me back to the bicycles.

"I don't think I can ride a bike, right now, Sweetie."

"I know, Angelina. You just sit here. I'll get you some coffee." He removes my arm from around his neck and sits me down on the same stonewall I rested on earlier, waiting for Graham. I notice Walter ordering me a large coffee, without taking his eyes off me. He returns and hands me a steaming cup of black coffee. "Drink this, Tangie, all of it."

"Um, your coffee tastes sweet and strong at the same time just like you, my charming, lovable Walter. Got to remember that, lover. What would I do without my Honey Pie?"

Walter gives me a patient look of love, sits beside me and rubs my shoulders. I start giggling again non-stop until I see onlookers studying me. I start to answer their stares, "What is your problem?" but take another sip instead. Seems these tourists think laughing is a strange thing. I smile at a man and woman whose faces seem very large as they glance my way. They quickly look away and walk briskly down the trail to the Cliff Walk. "Good luck!" I shout. They pick up their pace and disappear. "No sense of humor, these Easterners."

Walter pulls out his cell phone, calls for a cab and relays the message to me. "They'll be here in fifteen minutes, Angelina. I think you will be able to walk by then."

"I hope so, my love."

I continue to sip my antidote until I get the hiccups. Walter tells me to take a few deep breaths and let them out slowly. I do as my sweetie orders. His remedy seems to work. But by then, my head begins to hurt even though I can see clearer than I could five minutes ago.

Walter starts massaging my neck. "Tangie, I'll discard my disguise at the Crow's Nest. I don't know how I'll get around Louisa, but I'll think of something."

"No phone booth there. Maybe you could ask to use the restroom in the back. Slip in there when she's busy with a customer, and come out as *Walter, My Hero.*"

"Yes, that's a good one. Thanks."

"No problemo. Sometimes I make perfect sense."

Suddenly the trees start spinning like tops and the cars on the street sound like giant foghorns. I hold my ears and cry. "Oh, Walter, I...I'm a...a mess." I begin hiccupping again and my entire body starts to ache. My feet feel like stone anchors. I can't move them or even wiggle them. "I don't think I can stand up."

"You will, Angelina. I'll help you. And I don't think you're a mess. You're wonderful and very brave. I'd love to hug you right now, but I have to play it cool on the surface. That bastard may be watching us. Please, love, take a few more deep breaths. That's good. Now let them out easy. That's my girl."

183

"I am your girl, aren't I?"

"Now and forever."

"I don't like that Graham guy. He's twisted."

"I know. One thing is for sure, when everything comes out in the open, I'm going to give him a piece of what he deserves."

"Me too! You know, I am feeling better now. More like my ol' self, except for the wobbly feet."

I take a few more deep breaths, let them out slowly and try to relax. Despite our efforts to restore my calm, a dark mood envelops my being. Tears start running down my cheeks as I murmur, "You know what I'm gonna do when I get home? Take a shower, then soak in the tub and wash away any remnants of Graham's greasy touch. You know his plan didn't go any farther than an unwanted kiss and his sloppy embrace, but he violated me. He drugged me! The scumbag! No way will I let this happen again. It's just not worth it. I hate the way I feel right now."

"Angelina, I'm sorry. Please, listen to me. I tried to get to you. I should have stopped him sooner. I tried. But a pair of mothers with their toddlers got in my way and I couldn't trample their children. I would have traumatized them." Walter hangs his head like a penitent child and closes his eyes. "I let you down."

I grasp his hand. "No, you didn't, Walter. I'm glad you watched out for the children. That's the kind of guy I married. Not to worry. You grabbed ol' Graham Cracker in the nick of time. You know he has a few bolts loose. I don't ever want to look in his eerie eyes again. I've seen enough."

A black and white cab pulls up by the roadside curb near the path in front of us. Walter motions to the driver and assists me to the cab and helps me into the backseat. He goes back for the bicycles, comes around to the driver's side and asks the cabbie if he could put them in the trunk. The driver pops the trunk and hands him two Bungie cords. Walter hands him a couple of Alexander Hamilton's and the cabbie shakes his hand."

We don't speak much during the ride. I manage to lose the hiccups and get my anxiety under control. Walter holds my hand and spells the words, "I love you" in my palm. I melt. I want to bury my head in his chest and wail like a baby, but I remain stoic, smile weakly at my lover and whisper, "Me too."

Seems that our intentions have limits imposed upon them. *Curses.* I just want all this to be over and us to be back on Queen Anne in our own little, well, not exactly little, Dutch colonial. I miss our life in the Pacific Northwest. Tonight, for sure, I will call my mother. I can use one of her long-distance hugs.

I close my eyes and rest against Walter's shoulder until I hear the brakes squeal and feel the taxi slow down and stop in front of Aunt Hattie's. Walter hops out the opened door, tells the cabbie to wait, helps me to my feet and leads me up the stairs. We stop at the top of the porch and resume our roles. I speak words of gratitude to my Good Samaritan. "You go ahead. Don't worry about me, sir. I'll be fine. Thank you for your kindness."

"Glad to be of assistance, Miss. Don't worry. I'll return your bike for you. You take care now. Watch out for those ruffians."

"I shall do that, Sir…uh…Professor. Thank you, again." I shake Walter's hand, continuing the charade, and watch as he descends the stairs and jumps into the cab. My heart doesn't want him to leave. Something tells me I will regret not stopping him and insisting he stay.

Before I ring the bell, I try Aunt Hattie's door and it opens. I hear chatting. Seems Aunt Hattie has company. *Good.* I'm glad she's not alone. I worry about her. "I'm home, Aunt Hattie," I announce and stroll into the kitchen.

Sitting at the breakfast nook, across from Walter's aunt, slumps Graham Gotthree, with a black eye starting to form. He has an ice pack on his cheek. I almost pee in my pants. *God!* I thought we got rid of him.

"You slime! What the hell do you think you are doing here?"

"Now, Tangie," Aunt Hattie tries to defuse the situation, or perhaps she herself feels threatened by Graham and is putting up a front. I don't know which, but I do know what it's like to deal with pond scum.

Aunt Hattie's voice trembles a little as she explains, "Graham just stopped by to chat for a bit. I gave him a bit of ice. Seems he tripped on a crack in the sidewalk in front of my house. He has been waiting for you. Walter called and asked if you were home yet. I didn't know what to tell him. He expected you an hour ago. He worries about you, you know."

"Yes, Aunt Hattie. He's a worrywart. Where is Walter?" I am thinking Aunt Hattie is trying to tell me something in code.

"Oh, he's doing a few errands for me. He should be home any minute. By the way, his friend, Steve called while you were both gone. Seems he might drop in for a visit."

"Steve? I haven't seen him in ages."

I look at Graham. He seems all ears by the way he moves his body half-way out of his seat. His eyes glow when he hears Steve's name mentioned. I must remember that. The name "Steve" sets him off.

"Would you like some tea, dear?" Aunt Hattie asks. "You look rather frazzled."

"Well, it's been an unusually trying afternoon. I'm surprised Graham didn't fill you in on that one."

"I'm sorry. At least it didn't rain. You didn't have a good time shopping?"

"No, I took a bike ride instead, among other things, like almost falling off a cliff."

"That's nice, dear. I'm glad you're home. The wind's kicking up again. It will probably start raining cats and dogs. They say a Nor'easter is on its way later this week. Time to batten down the hatches."

I love Aunt Hattie. She is so good at double talk. And she pretends not to hear my crack about the cliff. No doubt she is as panicked as I, and she doesn't know the entire story. I hope Graham didn't threaten her. I can see she's on to him. She knows he's about one click off and she has the smarts not to let him know. If he starts playing his power games with her, I might get in defense mode and clobber him.

"Aunt Hattie, could you please leave Graham and me alone for a bit? I would like to talk to him about something, something that..."

I don't have to finish. Aunt Hattie catches on.

"Of course, dear. You go right ahead. There is a pot of tea on the table. Help yourself. I have to go to the basement to check my laundry, anyway."

Before she opens the door to the basement, she gets a cup and saucer out of the cupboard and puts it on the table. She motions me to sit down. I smile at her and give her hand a squeeze. She returns my smile, releases my grip and ambles down the basement stairs. I notice she leaves the door ajar.

I put my hands on the table and remain standing, feeling a head taller than Graham. I repeat my earlier question. "What are you doing here, Graham? I don't appreciate you showing up at my doorstep. Plus, you ruined my day."

Now this statement rings true. The past afternoon ranks up there with one of my worst. Right next to that afternoon last winter at my old Ballard house, when I found Pebbles under my bed, with a bloody cloth in his mouth, after a break-in by a thug.

Graham becomes all sweetness and spice. "Calm down, Tangie. I came here to apologize. I know you think I was out of line."

"You got that right. I don't like your games. Frankly, you are not worth it. Find another playmate. I'm not the person you are looking for."

"Oh, I disagree. You are just what I am looking for. You see I love a challenge. You are the best I've had in a long time."

"Well, you don't have me, and I don't want you. So, I am asking you for the last time to leave, especially before Walter comes home. All I have to do is tell him one thing about what you did and you won't be able to walk out the door. You'll be limping and he'll be throwing you out on your a…"

"Yeah, yeah, I've heard that before, but not from you. By the way, who is this *Steve* fellow?"

For a moment I panic. I wish Aunt Hattie didn't mention Steve. No doubt she tried to help by frightening Graham, but he doesn't scare easily. A new person entering on the scene just heightens his curiosity.

"Steve is a body builder, in addition to being Walter's friend."

Well that is partly true. All policemen are body builders. Then a certain previous conversation in Fiji comes to my mind and I panic, remembering my confusion over the name "Steve". As I recall, I talked to this someone named "Steve" on our honeymoon and inferred to him that I have a friend named "Steve". Maybe Graham knows something about that conversation. Maybe "Steve the Murderer" blurted something out to Graham. Maybe Eveline's "Steve" caught on to my conversation. He would, if Eveline confronted him about the murder of Peter Van Beek, upon her return home from Fiji. Maybe she told her "Steve" she never got his phone call. If so, I'm toast.

Graham studies me while I wrestle with my thoughts. I can feel his eyes boring into my face and I begin to blush. Not a good thing. Dead giveaway. Blame it on the drug he slipped in my hot chocolate. My self-control is about shot. *God help me!* I hate that S.O.B. who is sitting across the table, staring at me.

187

"Tangie, I think you should consider accepting my apology. I rarely make them."

"That's supposed to make me feel special?"

"Oh, you're special all right. You're right up there with my first girl-friend."

"Yeah, and where is she?"

"Dead. You know, I never got over her until now."

"Great. And that is supposed to make me feel good."

"I never told anyone about her before."

"Graham, you are seriously in need of counseling."

"I've been there. Seems they can't help me, as I can't help myself."

"Or you don't want to."

"You got that right. I like myself just fine. It's the rest of the world that has a problem."

I can see that this conversation is going nowhere. I look at Graham and wonder when Walter is going to walk through the door. My arms turn to putty. Needles and pins prickle my legs down to my toes. I need to sit down, but I refuse to give up my position up at the head of the table. I force myself to stand tall for my own sanity. Call me a control freak, but right now, I can only think straight in an upright position.

Someone stomps on the welcome mat outside the front door. I hear Aunt Hattie's voice yelling from the front yard, telling someone to go in. *Please, let it be Walter.* I need my partner-in-crime detection. My options are beginning to get fuzzy. *Please, God! I can't think. I need help.* The door opens and closes. *Please, let it be Walter.* The footsteps continue down the hall, then the swinging door between the kitchen and the hallway moves, and in walks Steve—*my Steve.* I grin. Not Walter, but second best will do!

Leaving my post, my field of defense at the table, I twirl around and with tears in my eyes, I hug my favorite policeman.

"Gosh, Tangie, if I knew you missed me so much, I would have come sooner."

With my eyes rolling around in my head, my finger in front of my mouth and my back to Graham, I hush Steve then turn around and intro-duce him to Graham.

"Steve, this is Graham Gotthree. Graham is just leaving."

Graham gets up and walks over to Steve. "We were just talking about you."

"Good, I hope."

"You have a New York accent."

"Yes, I lived in the city before moving to…"

I interrupt before Steve can say too much. "Steve went to college with Walter. Brown, you know." They've been best buddies ever since. You know how it is."

"Yes, I do. It's a pleasure to meet you, Steve," Graham says in his crisp New England fake accent and extends his pale hand to Steve.

I notice Steve gives Graham a death-grip handshake. Good for Steve. He catches on quickly and knows how to send a guy a message: *Don't mess with Steve.*

Graham does not let on that his hand aches, but I know it does. I can tell by his heavy breathing and his attempt to be cool. He can't help rubbing the palm of his right hand when he thinks no one is paying attention to him.

Graham starts to chat in the mindless way he does, saying absolutely nothing coherent and finishes with, "See you around, Tangie. Steve, hope to run into you again sometime."

The guy never quits. I can't get him to leave and now Steve will be curious. Graham senses that. Apparently, in a rather blundering way, he has decided to set Steve up.

Steve takes the bait. "Say Graham," Steve asks in his interrogating voice, "What brings you here? Are you a friend of Walter?"

"Hardly. I came to see Tangie."

"She's quite a charmer."

"I would say that," Graham agrees in a high-pitched voice that he tries to lower after beginning to speak. He studies Steve for a second and continues in a lower octave, "You know, Steve, funny, I used to have a friend from the City. Also by the name of *Steve.*"

I knew it. I knew it! Then I groan inwardly. Things are not looking good.

"Oh really?" Steve perks up, showing interest. "Where from?"

"Oh, Manhattan." Graham tugs on his manicured fingernails. "We went to school together in the City. But we lost touch. He went his way; I went mine. We chose different paths. I feel sorry for the guy. He has a lot of anger issues. I hope some day he gets them under control."

Now look who's talking about issues. *Give me a break, Graham. You are just so in denial it isn't funny. Gag me with a spoon. Unfortunately for you, the hot chocolate didn't work.*

I hear the front door open, Aunt Hattie's voice greeting someone else, and again more footsteps leading to the kitchen. I am sure Aunt Hattie took the back entrance out of the cellar to come around to the front door and keep watch on Graham and me. Somehow that thought is a comfort to me. But if those extra footsteps aren't Walter's, I will for certain become unglued and fall apart piece by piece.

A tremendous sense of relief runs through my neck and shoulders as I see Walter brushing through the swinging door into the kitchen. I let out a slow deep breath, my heart's pitter-patter slows down a bit and calm takes over my body. *Yes. Okay.* I take a deep breath. I can continue playing this charade, for a little longer.

"Walter, honey, let me take your coat." I whisper sweet nothings in his ear as I kiss his cheek. "Look who popped in—your long-lost school chum, Steve. And wouldn't you know, Graham Gotthree dropped in for a visit."

Walter winks at me, then smiles at Steve. "Well, what do you know? Long time no see, Steve."

Walter hugs his best man and whispers something in his ear, something that only I detect. Graham continues to stare at me, as Walter questions Steve. "What have you been up to? I can see you are still working out. How is the security business these days?"

"Oh, business is good, Walter. I have some good people working with me. Makes my job easier."

Walter turns to Graham, the creep, and gives him a smile, abet fake, as he shakes his hand. "Hey, Graham, good to see you again. What brings you 'round?"

Now Walter is a better actor than I. I would give him an Oscar for his role as gracious host. I know he wants to beat Graham to a pulp. I see him wiping the sweat from Graham's handshake on his Dockers. I know that feeling. Revulsion.

Graham returns Walter's fake smile. "Hey, Walter, what do you know... it's a pleasure, but I am just about to leave. I've overstayed my welcome.

I've got some paperwork to do in my office before tomorrow morning. But seriously, I'll be in touch." Graham diverts his eyes back to me.

I groan in silence, *"Just go away. Go away."*

He continues chatting and I stop listening to him. I just can't take his mouth moving up and down like a catfish looking for a morsel. Then he pastes on his phony dapper smile, like he's warming up a crowd at a rally. He looks at us like we are totally interested in him. This guy has some serious issues. I think he needs reality therapy.

Graham snaps back into politician mode and floors all of us, by giving us a reason, whether true or fake, for his visit. "Before I go, I want to say, I only stopped by to invite you all to a reception for our new governor, Roberto Carboni. You can see the political scene up close in Rhode Island."

"I'm not much for politics, Graham." Walter struggles to get the words out of his throat. "Sorry."

During Walter's refusal, Aunt Hattie walks into the kitchen with Pebbles by her side. My pooch sits down next to her feet, as if also playing a role, that of the dutiful canine. Aunt Hattie pats Pebbles' head and smiles at the four of us. "Now you young ones may not want to go, but I would, for Peter Van Beek's sake. He would want us there. Walter, you and Tangie can escort me and perhaps, Steve can…"

"You are a dear, Aunt Hattie," Graham answers in a flash, to seal the deal. "Black tie. This Friday. And of course I can swing a ticket for you, Steve, if you would like to join us. The menu includes Prime Rib, just the right protein for body builders."

"Sure, why not? I like to eat. I'll still be around. Thanks, er…"

"Graham Gotthree. That's my name, like the cracker and 'got three'. Okay. I'll drop the tickets in the mail. Express. I'll be busy till then, so I'll catch you at the Governor's Mansion, this Friday."

"Thanks, Graham," Walter manages to spit out. "My aunt will enjoy it. May I walk you out?"

Graham looks at Pebbles, then me. "No thank you. You look tired. Stay here. Relax. I'll let myself out."

Aunt Hattie chirps, "Make sure you take an umbrella with you, young man. There are extra ones in the bottom of the hall tree. It's starting to pour."

"Oh, I like the rain. Reminds me of sailing." Graham smiles, turns and walks down the hall to the front door. Without another word he makes his way down the steps and disappears into the deluge battering the house.

Never before have I felt such relief for a visitor leaving. I let out a heavy sigh and pat Pebbles on the head, glad to see my pooch. His presence always reassures me. My dog is a link to the sane world after I emerge from the Looney Bin, this time with the likes of Graham Gotthree. What in the world possessed Walter and his aunt to accept his invitation? And Steve? You would think at least Steve would know better.

Aunt Hattie listens to make sure Graham exits. Pebbles lets out a low growl upon hearing footsteps. Walter keeps silent until the sound disappears. Then he gets up, walks down the hall to the front door, and notices the door is ajar. Walter starts to shut it but instead, comes face to face with Graham.

"I thought you left."

"Oh, it is teeming out here. Thought I would come back for that umbrella."

Walter reaches into the hall tree and takes out a striped bumbershoot and hands it to Graham without a word. Graham nods and marches down the steps. Walter waits until he is down the street before he shuts the door and locks it.

He comes back into the kitchen and says, "That brainless politician left the front door open." He sits down at the table beside Steve and lets out some steam. "What a jerk. I'd like to pound him into the pavement."

Aunt Hattie nods, then goes to her cupboard, takes out two more cups and pours everyone a new cup of tea from the kettle that has been whistling on the stove. Like the old woman who went to the cupboard, she calls to Pebbles and gives him a bone. Or should I say biscuit? Anyway, it seems she has a stockpile for visiting pooches.

I smile despite my building anxiety but then get a chilly picture in my mind. I visualize Graham in a sailboat, up to no good. Only he would like sailing in the rain. The creep probably uses his sailboat for his conquests, all his one-night stands. No one could bear to date him a second time. I shudder just thinking about all those young women suckered in by his flamboyant prep school looks and air of respectability. Innocent girls, traumatized by horrible memories of their "date from Hell" are forever scared, no longer innocent or trusting. One day the brute will get his just desserts and I want to be there when he does.

I pick up the Windsor chair near the hearth of the fireplace in the corner of the kitchen and place it at the head of the table near the window seat. I motion Aunt Hattie to sit down. I remove Graham's cup off the table, take it to the sink and pour some bleach into it. I scrub it hard, wash it with soap and place it in the dishwasher. After kicking my boots off by the hearth, I tiptoe back to the kitchen nook and squeeze myself in next to Walter, ready to talk business.

Chapter Twenty-Eight

Steve begins our conversation. "Okay, Walter, Tangie, perhaps one of you can tell me what's been going on the past few days."

Walter takes a sip from his cup and sets it down. "Sure. We've been on our own, Steve, as usual, handling something way out of our league. I don't want Angelina doing any more surveillance."

"Why not? She seems to have a gift for gab with this Graham fellow."

Sensing steam coming out of Walter's ears as well as mine, I explain, "You don't know it yet, Steve, but he's dangerous. He tried pushing me over a rail and down the rocks into the ocean during our Cliff Walk." I glance at Aunt Hattie, who sits there clasping her hands, with her mouth open. "Aunt Hattie, I'm sorry. I wish you hadn't accepted his invitation."

"Oh my! I apologize, dear. I had no idea of his real intentions. I know Graham is strange, but I didn't think dangerous. Silly me. I thought we could all do some sleuthing at the reception and I'd get to see Peter's sisters. I didn't know..."

"Aunt Hattie," Walter says in a soft tone, "This guy, Graham, is a threat to Angelina. I'm worried about her running into him again."

"Walter dear," Aunt Hattie answers with a tremble in her voice, "I am truly sorry, but I didn't know what happened. You didn't tell me."

I grasp Aunt Hattie's hand. "It's all right, Aunt Hattie. I didn't mean to upset you. It's just...we couldn't say anything earlier, with Graham in the room. We would have given our intentions away."

"What are your intentions?" Steve asks.

I take a sip of my tea. It tastes strong and sweet. "Steve, we want to discover out how, or if, Graham is connected to the murder of Peter Van Beek. I'm positive he is in some way. Either he has information, or he knows this guy, *Steve the Murderer,* the guy that did the dirty deed. What we need to find out is how Graham connects to Eveline Carboni and this other guy, Steve—*Steve the Murderer.* Only then can I fill in the blanks in my mind. You know, maybe going to the reception isn't such a bad idea after all. Perhaps we can figure all this out once and for all. Right now, all we have is speculation."

Walter takes my hand and squeezes it. "Tangie, Sweetheart, I don't want you taking any more chances with that serpent."

"If we go to the reception, I will not stray from you or Steve. I refuse to go it alone with Graham ever again. But I may get him to talk some more. I want to ask him about his friend, *Steve from New York City.* Like when he last saw him. He loves to talk and he opens up to me. I just know there's a connection between Graham, his Steve and Eveline. If I can make that connection, I can figure out a motive for the three of them and we can finally contact the local police."

Steve pours himself another cup of Earl Grey and adds two sugar cubes. Walter picks up a flask of whiskey that Aunt Hattie put on the table and pours a little into Steve's teacup.

Steve smiles. " You know me so well. So, you think it's time to let the locals in on all this?"

I nod. "Very soon." I pick up the flask and pour a little amber liquid into my cup as well. "And you, my dear Steve, are going to pave the way, starting tomorrow. You can introduce yourself to Newport's Finest."

"You don't think the police will think I'm nuts, Tangie?"

"Well, they probably will but that never stopped you before. Plus, we need to let them know you're here, that you are looking into things."

"Tangie, I don't think they'd like an outsider busting into their territory."

"You don't have to name names yet, or give details. Just inform them you are here on assignment. You're doing research."

"Now that I can do. That might work as long as I don't step on any toes. I'll call Barry Cardoso and let him smooth things out for me in advance."

Walter nods. "Probably would be a good time to call Barry in on this one. The guy's got connections."

Aunt Hattie looks at the three of us and sighs. "My goodness, I've certainly stirred a hornet's nest accepting that invitation."

Walter smiles. "You know, Aunt Hattie, if it weren't for you, I think we would have given up. God help us, we are going to need some prayers on this one."

"Time to call our friend, Don, the priest," I mumble. "We haven't talked to him since our wedding, and as you say, we need all the help we can get. Oh…and yes!" I jump up from my seat in the nook. "I've got to call my mom. I'm going to do that right now before another diversion sidetracks me. She gets worried if I don't call her at least semi-regularly."

I lean over the table and give Steve a hug.

"What's that for, Tangie? Not that I'm complaining or anything." Steve blushes as he smiles at me.

"Oh, just for being here. We can use another gun, figuratively speaking."

"That makes one, among the four of us," Walter says with a smirk.

"I've got a pistol in my underwear drawer," Aunt Hattie pipes up. "One never knows when a stranger tries to break in your home."

I smile. "Aunt Hattie, you can't bring that to a reception at the governor's mansion."

"Like they'd frisk an old woman."

Walter shakes his head. "They'll frisk anyone. Leave it at home, Aunt Hattie."

"Okay, I'll put it in my glove compartment. It seems like one of us has to be packing besides Steve."

Steve gives Aunt Hattie a fake stern look. "I hope it's registered."

"Of course, my boy. You don't think I would do anything illegal, do you?"

I lean over and hug Walter. "Thanks for being there for me today, Sweetheart. I'd be another notch on Graham's gat if it weren't for you."

"You're welcome." Walter smiles his most endearing smile at me as he takes the flask, pours some whiskey into his teacup and lifts it up. Here's to no more close encounters."

"Amen," chirps Aunt Hattie, as she takes the flask Walter hands to her and pours some liquid into her cup.

"You can count on that." I nod in agreement. We click our cups together. I blow kisses to my three partners-in-crime detecting as I rise from the table and depart into the living room to call my mother.

"Angelina! How have you been? What have you been up to, my dear?"

You might say my mom is excited when she hears my voice. I can almost see her jumping up and down, as I hear her speak to her only daughter.

"Turn down the television, Charles. I can't hear Tangie."

I raise my voice a bit. "Well, Mom, not too much. Just hanging out with Aunt Hattie and Walter."

"That's nice, dear. I hope you are having a restful vacation. How's the weather?"

"Oh, about the same as Seattle in the fall, windy, sunny, chilly and very scenic. Today I went on the Cliff Walk. I saw all the famous mansions in Newport."

"With Walter? That must have been exciting, Angelina."

"Yeah, Mom. He was there. It was very exciting. Nice place to visit. Wouldn't want to live in one of those houses; I'd get lost."

"When do you expect to be home, Tangie? The twins keep asking about you. Bryan and Andee are wondering what you and Walter are up to. We all miss you."

"I miss you too, Mom. Sorry, I don't know when we'll be heading back to Seattle. Walter is helping his aunt with a few things out here."

Things like trying to find the governor's murderer, but I can't tell my mother that. She'd never sleep at night.

"Mom, did you know that Aunt Hattie knew the governor out here?"

"Knew?"

"Yes. He passed away, so we escorted Aunt Hattie to the funeral."

"What a nice thing for you and Walter to do, Angelina. Seems I read in the Times about the governor of Rhode Island dying in a boating accident. Seems no one is safe from accidents, no matter who they are. You be careful out there. Don't take unnecessary chances."

"That's for sure. I won't. Mom, how are you, really? And Bryan? Is he doing better? How about Andee, Jason, Jeffrey and Charles?"

"Oh, you know. We keep busy—We're having a beautiful fall out here, so Charles and I are taking some lovely day trips. We just got back from Sequim. Bryan was released from the hospital and is walking around, with crutches. Not jogging around the neighborhood yet, but he enrolled at North Seattle Community College."

"Good for him."

"Yes, and Andee's busy sewing Halloween costumes for the boys."

"My favorite holiday, Halloween. I hope to get home in time to see Jason and Jeffrey all dressed up."

"Me too, dear. Oh, Charles and I are going to the opera tomorrow—*Macbeth.*"

"That's a good one for Halloween. Murder and mayhem."

"Well, we go for the music."

"I know, Mom. Just kidding. Now listen. I promise to call again soon. Sorry I've been so busy."

"You be careful, Angelina. Don't do anything foolish while you are out there."

"I won't, Mom. I love you."

"I love you too. Give Walter my best."

"I will. We both miss you. Talk to you soon." With tears forming in my eyes, I tap my i-Phone, let out a gasp and sit down on Aunt Hattie's favorite chair by the window. I glance outside the window and notice the trees bending in the wind. I shiver. As the sky darkens, I give into my fears and begin sobbing uncontrollably. In the far distance, I hear the sound of a bell echoing in the mist of the fog forming in my mind. Groaning with the wind, I heave my body and cry until there are no tears left.

I hate to lie to my mother. She suspects I am up to something, and in her usual fashion doesn't pry. She waits for me to tell her the details. Maybe she is in denial about what I do, so she doesn't worry so much. Perhaps it's better that I keep her in the dark. I miss being able to share this part of my life with her. She is such a good listener but I can't bring myself to burden her. She'd be frantic all the time and that is not good for her blood pressure. I know her too well. She is a wonderful, sensitive woman and I choose not to upset her.

I dab my eyes, dry my cheeks and take a long deep breath. It feels good to let everything out. I'm glad Marianna married Charles. He has the ability to take her mind off her children's problems. She can get anxious about us at any time. Seems like in our family there's always one crisis or another to stress her out.

I hear footsteps in the hall and then Walter's voice. "Tangie, why are you sitting here in the dark? Are you all right?"

"Yes, Sweetheart. I've just been thinking about my family. Everyone's fine. Bryan is getting better every day. Marianna sends you her best."

"I'm glad. How are you doing, really?"

I look up at Walter as he turns on a light. He notices my tear-stained face.

Walter kneels down next to me, takes me in his arms and starts kissing my eyelids, then my cheek and brushes my lips with his. "How can I help?"

"Just hold me for a minute. Everything that's happened this afternoon and missing my family at the same time is crashing down on me. I wish I could be in two places at once."

"Me too. Here and in bed. But first, we have to go out for dinner. Any requests?"

"Yes. Let's get out of Newport for awhile."

"That's easily done. How about Jamestown? Not too far, very scenic and a pleasant ride."

"We won't see anything. It's getting dark."

"Yes, *a dark and stormy night*." Walter chuckles. "I've always wanted to say that. Too bad the ferries aren't running."

I groan at Walter's joke as a clap of thunder shatters the quiet of the living room.

A look of concern returns to Walter's face. "Please, don't worry, Angelina. We'll take a pleasant ride. You'll like Jamestown. It's a great place for dinner. The bridges are lit up along the way. If you like it there, we can return later, in the daylight. Tonight you can use your imagination."

"Wherever we go, make sure they have a good wine list. I'm in a drinking mood."

Now I am not an alcoholic. Not driven to drink quite yet, but somehow drinking wine with my favorite men and Walter's favorite and only aunt, suddenly appeals to me.

"I know just the place." Walter grins and wrestles me up from sinking permanently into the overstuffed club chair.

Dinner turns out to be a great diversion from our plans to fight crime. The Bay View Inn has as much charm and history as its location in old Jamestown. We take turns telling corny jokes. We laugh and cry over our friendship and good times together, and we drink wine, lots of it, until the restaurant closes. I don't remember many specifics about the evening, or even what we ate, except it came from the sea, and that our bill displayed many zeroes. Walter fights with Steve over who will pay the bill. I smile blissfully, enjoying their affectionate bickering.

Steve winds up paying, saying it's his business expense. It's probably more like guilt money, Steve feeling bad because he wasn't here during a potentially dangerous situation. I'm just glad he showed up in Rhode Island. Walter and I are not isolated in this mess anymore. We have Aunt Hattie but she is getting a little frail, though neither she nor I would admit it. If confronted, I'm sure she would have no problem challenging someone to a shooting match with her handgun, her pepper spray or her shotgun. I know she has a shotgun. When I was doing some laundry, I saw it in her basement, hanging on the wall next to the furnace. Handy place to keep it, in case you encounter a criminal in the cellar.

I suspect our criminal is the white-collar variety with a painted face. Incognito. The last person one would suspect. Who'd expect a politician to be a criminal or his wife, or his confidante? I have the sensation of being close to knowing exactly what is happening or going to happen. But lately, when I get a vision, it disappears as quickly as it appears. More like a flash in a dream or a musing when I am not thinking about anything else. Maybe if I am patient, everything will come into focus. Until then, Walter and I will just have to muddle through like we've been doing. I know we are making some progress, thanks to Graham—the Creep—Gotthree. He keeps giving us information without realizing it, or perhaps he does realize it and takes pride in sharing his knowledge of dirty deeds committed by others.

When we return to Aunt Hattie's after our sojourn in Jamestown, Pebbles goes nuts leaping up and down around me. I leash him, ready to take him for his nightly walk. Walter takes my arm and whispers, "I'll take him, Tangie. I don't want you going out alone this late, especially tonight, after..."

Normally I would start an argument over this. I am not one to give up my independent ways, but I see a familiar flicker in Walter's eyes, fear and apprehension. That pushes my "be careful" button. Plus, I don't like to see my man scared for me, so I cave in.

"Okay, Walter, you win." I hand him Pebbles' leash and follow him as far as the doorway. "I'll fix a bed on the couch for Steve. You go on, Sweetie. Watch out. Goblins chase good guys too."

Walter grins and departs through the front door with Pebbles, whose eager paws rise above the floor. I swear that dog can fly. I'm convinced Pebbles' favorite person is Walter. But who am I to be jealous? He's my favorite person too.

I close the door and turn to Walter's aunt. "Aunt Hattie, do you have bedding for Steve?"

Aunt Hattie walks over to the window seat by the side window. "Right here in the cedar chest, my dear."

During our dinner at the Bay View Inn, Aunt Hattie kept to her limit of two glasses of wine, so she happens to be the more sober of the two women in the living room. She assists me in bringing the pillows and blankets to the sofa bed that we pull out together.

Steve walks into the living room, looking like he is ready to crash any minute. "Thank you, Aunt Hattie, for putting me up for the night."

He reminds me of a grateful hawk that finds a haven out of the cold on a winter's night. Like Aunt Hattie, Steve managed to stay sufficiently sober in the restaurant. Must be the policeman in him. Good cop. But I bet he's suffering from jet lag right about now.

Aunt Hattie fluffs two pillows and places them on the made-up bed. "Nonsense, my boy. You are family. You stay here as long as you want. Don't even think about checking into a hotel. I hope you will be comfortable. I just wish I still had another bedroom but my spare room has become my arts and craft room. The bed from there is stored in the basement. If you stay longer than a few days, we can drag it upstairs and I could pack away my crafts."

"Please, don't worry. I'm fine right here."

Steve gives Aunt Hattie one of his dazzling smiles, a smile that mesmerizes many girlfriends, particularly his latest, Suzy.

Steve yawns. "Matter of fact, I am used to crashing on Tangie and Walter's couch in their living room. Lately, it's become a habit."

I re-fluff the pillows and yawn. Must be contagious. "I'm sorry we keep pulling you away from your life, Steve."

"I needed a break. Plus, helping you is part of my life. I'm a cop. You know that."

"Yes, and you do it so well."

"Thanks. I appreciate you saying so, Tangie. That means a lot to me."

"What means a lot to you?" Walter strolls in through the front door with Pebbles at his side.

"Oh, Walter, I just told Steve how much we appreciate his help."

"Well, I haven't done anything yet," Steve mumbles.

I think Steve is more comfortable with criticism than with praise. Probably why Suzy likes him. She loves to complain. I know she adores him, but she is not one to ooh and ah over anyone or anything except perhaps the latest designer clothing. Deep down she has a good heart and I'm sure she appreciates him.

"Relax, good buddy." Walter grins. "You'll get your chance to help come Friday."

Friday. I used to love Fridays. Not anymore. After this Friday, I will be lucky to be alive. I just have this overwhelming fear that something terrible is going to happen. I recognize this fear. Wonder if Walter is experiencing the same feeling? He often outwits me in the "something's in the air" category. Seems I need to quiz him. Come to think of it, he didn't want to go to the reception either.

I start to shake uncontrollably. Walter notices. So does Aunt Hattie.

"Tangie, are you all right?" Walter grasps my hands to steady me.

Aunt Hattie has that same concerned look my mother gets when I start to freak out. "My dear, you look white as a ghost. Can I get you anything?"

"I'll be all right. I think I just drank too much wine, and I'm tired. I think I just need to lie down." I can feel my knees giving way and my body sinking to the floor.

The next thing I know, Walter is pressing a cold compress on my forehead and Steve is rubbing my ice-cold hands. Aunt Hattie tries to pour some warm tea through my closed lips and I struggle to open my eyes.

I force myself to sit up and speak. "Sorry. Did I faint? Maybe I'm having a delayed reaction to Graham's erratic behavior, and all the stress of the governor's funeral. I managed to put everything out of my mind this evening until now."

"Come on, Angelina." Walter takes me in his arms. "I'll carry you up to bed. You can get some sleep and you will feel better in the morning."

"Promise?"

My honey gives me a soft gentle kiss on my cheek. "I promise, my sweet Angelina."

"You get some rest dear," Aunt Hattie says in her soft, calm soothing voice. "Don't worry about fixing breakfast tomorrow. Steve and I will do the cooking."

I notice her winking at Steve.

Steve nods. He's the kind of guy that gets choked up at times like this. I think his inner kindness endears me to him. Now I know why Walter keeps him around as his best friend. He's the strong and silent type, the most awesome kind of good buddy.

"Steve is a keeper, Walter," I murmur, as Walter carries me up the stairs.

When we arrive at the top landing, Walter stops for a moment and kisses me softly. "So am I, Angelina."

"I know, my sweet."

"Listen, my love. I'll carry you to our *boudoir*. Then I'll come back later, after I talk with Steve. Will you be okay?"

"Sure, Sweetheart. I'm just very tired. Don't be too long. I need to talk to you before I nod off."

"Just rest for a while." Walter pulls the covers from the bed, lies me down and removes my clothing. He places a down blanket and handmade quilt over me. "Stay warm. Rest easy. I'll be back in a flash. Warm up the bed for me."

"I will, my sweet." I yawn and stretch out my arms as Walter leans down to kiss me goodnight, gently. Closing my eyes, I am once again a little girl just home from a night at the circus, exhausted and woozy from eating too much cotton candy. As I drift off, I think of the powerful love I feel for my husband and the upmost appreciation and gratitude I have for my family and good friends.

With no warning of impending doom, I slip into a deep slumber, peaceful at first but soon the serenity fades and then dissolves into nothingness. Then a sudden force hurls me into a nightmare of monstrous proportions. This time I cannot escape its grasp, nor stop its visions.

Chapter Twenty-Nine

"A beautiful evening to be on the water," Peter Van Beek whispers to himself. "Too much excitement at the capital." I need to take my *Mercedes,* my sailboat named after my beloved wife, out for an evening sail, away from all things political and personal. When I come back on Monday, I'll be a new man. I just know it."

The governor closes his laptop and puts it in his desk drawer, then locks the drawer and puts the key in his pocket. He picks up his cell phone and presses the number for the third party in his address book. No answer. He leaves a message on voicemail.

"Hey Buddy, Friday noon here. I'm in the office and leaving soon for Newport. Going to take an autumn sail before the weather changes. Keep things steady here in Providence. I'll be back Monday morning. Need to get away for a while. Have to think things over. Don't call me. I have some decisions to make this weekend."

The governor walks out of his inner office, nods to his secretary and strolls down the hall. He takes his sunglasses out of his top pocket and practically skips to the parking garage, like a kid let out of school early.

"Ah, I love the wind in my face," the governor murmurs as he crosses the Newport Bridge in his midnight blue Porsche Turbo. "Can't wait to get on the water. Four more hours of daylight until the sunset forces me back to the dock. That's enough time to sail to Jamestown and around Narragansett Bay, then back. I'll pick up a picnic supper at the dock, maybe a bottle of wine. Wish my wife, my love, my flesh and blood Mercedes, could be here with me at this moment. God, how I miss her."

Beating the rush hour traffic and only stopping for a take-out supper and wine, the governor reaches the dock with plenty of time for an evening sail. He waves to some fellow sailors on the dock and boards his vessel. He goes below and changes into the jeans and deck shoes he keeps on board. Then he comes on deck and checks the gas in the tank to make sure he has enough to motor in and out of the slip. As he casts off he looks at his watch. *Two o'clock.* He smiles and murmurs, "Plenty of time for an late afternoon sail." He doesn't need his windbreaker yet, but will once he casts the sails. A self-furling jib makes sailing solo a breeze. This is a luxury he installed after Mercedes died. His wife relished being his first mate since their first sail together, and always insisted on hoisting the jib while he managed the main sail. Now he does both. Whenever he unfurls the jib with just the touch of a finger, he feels his wife's palm guiding his every move.

With sails taut to the wind and the lines secure, the governor, keeping his foot on the steering wheel like a professional sailor, puts on his windbreaker and pours himself a glass of wine. He cuts a few pieces of President's French Brie and places the soft cheese on some thin-sliced French bread. He grabs some red grapes from his supper box and sighs. "Doesn't get any better than this, unless my love could be here to join me one last time. That would be perfect."

He passes the impressive mansion that was the childhood home of Jacqueline Kennedy Onassis. He looks at the edge of the bay, smiles at the miniature version of the home, the former first lady's playhouse, and waves to folks on the excursion boat cruising by. "Probably the last weekend for the tourists. Days like this are a treat in autumn. Soon I will have to dock you for the winter, my trusty *Mercedes*.

Later, after passing Newport Harbor and a few remaining fishing vessels left on the bay, the governor leans back and frowns, unable to forget politics on this beautiful evening. Thoughts about the lieutenant governor keep resurfacing. He murmurs aloud to no one but himself, "How can I tell Roberto his wife is up to no good? How can I tell him she's a liar and a cheat?" How can you tell a colleague that bit of information? It will upset him, but somebody's got to do it. Maybe I can do some damage control so the press won't have a field day. They'd love to crucify Carboni, knowing someday he'll be running for my office. But his wife, she's a piece of work. What did Roberto ever see in her?"

Upon reaching Jamestown, the governor's thoughts travel back to his late wife. He sighs and wipes the tears that fall down his cheeks, wishing he could speak directly with her; she could always take his mind off his work. He notices the sun slowly descending into the clouds forming in the early evening sky. He straightens his body. "Time to head back, *Mercedes*." He spins the wheel, bringing the yacht about. "Helm's a lee."

Just as the *Mercedes* comes about, Peter Van Beek hears the call.

"Governor! Oh Governor. Peter Van Beek! Help!"

A dinghy appears in the shadows, adrift in the choppy waters about 100 feet from the bank, out of reach of the marina on the west shore of Jamestown.

The governor squints then uses his binoculars to recognize a familiar face. He observes his assistant, distraught and frantic, waving both arms, trying to get his attention. To Peter he looks like a marshal directing an airplane.

Peter Van Beek waves back and yells, "Buddy, what in the world are you doing out here? In a dinghy no less?"

Buddy just keeps waving.

"Hold on, Buddy." The governor reels in the jib and lets the main sail luff allowing his sloop to drift toward the dinghy.

"What's going on, Buddy?" The governor yells. "I thought you stayed in Providence."

This time Buddy appears to hear him. "Guess I'm caught playing hooky. I'm in trouble. No oars. No power. May I come aboard?"

"Yes, of course. Let me hang out the ladder. I'll toss you a line.

"Thanks, boss. I owe you one."

Peter Van Beek locks the wheel and drops the ladder.

Buddy ties his dinghy and climbs aboard, shivering and grateful for the glass of wine the governor hands him. "Thanks, Governor. Sorry to be a bother. My friends played a trick on me and left me in the dinghy with no oars, daring me to get back to shore."

"Some friends. I'd hate to meet your enemies." Peter Van Beek gestures toward his seat. "Look in the sack. There's a sandwich if you're hungry. Here, take the wheel for a minute. I'll go below and get you a jacket and a blanket. You look a mess. How'd you get all wet?"

"You don't want to know."

The governor laughs and disappears below. Buddy laughs with him then focuses his eyes on the winch handle. He picks it up and feels its weight.

The governor pokes his head out the companion way and announces, "Here's a wool blanket for you, Buddy and another bottle of wine to warm you. I hope this jacket fits..."

He starts to smile at his guest, but then freezes, unable to move. Something strange, something distinctly evil appears in Buddy's eyes. Before the governor can react, Buddy lifts the winch handle high in the air. Then, with all his might, he strikes Peter Van Beek on his temple. He stops only to catch the governor before he falls backward into the cabin. The governor looks up in slow motion and glimpses Buddy's vacant eyes glistening in the setting sun. Peter Van Beek stares at Buddy, until his eyes too, become a blank stare. Buddy's fingers continue to wrap a rope around Peter Van Beek's neck and their vacant eyes remain locked together in a deadly bond.

Buddy breaks eye contact with his victim and smirks. "Thanks, Governor." He picks up the acrylic wine glass and refills it. "I need a drink. Yes, just the thing to take the chill off my bones on a brisk New England evening. Eternally grateful to you, my man."

Buddy pauses for a moment, looks around the bay and smiles, seeing no one in sight. "Now, let's see, what shall I do with you? Hum, for starters, I'll tighten this rope around your neck for insurance, like you are a package, only your drop box is the ocean. But first I'll set you down in the storage locker under the seat, for a while. Pardon me if I borrow your hat and sunglasses. That way, if anyone does spot me, they'll think that I am you." Buddy chuckles, takes another sip of wine and sits down. "I am so clever,

I surprise myself. Let's see, I have until Monday to decide what to do with your body. Not a problem, Governor, or should I say, *late* Governor. It will be so pleasant spending the weekend at your exclusive, private waterfront retreat. Ah, I could get used to this life."

Chapter Thirty

I jolt up in the bed, still half-asleep, sweating profusely and scream, "No! Not again! Please, someone help!"

"Tangie, what's the matter?"

Walter's voice echoes in the distance, as the sea, the sailboat and the face of Buddy fade from my memory. I try to go back to my nightmare, just for a moment to see Buddy's face, but my vision disappears. I open my eyes, which are moist with tears for Peter Van Beek. *Another one of my crying dreams*, I realize, pondering why there is so much violence, so much sadness in the world.

"Walter, you're here."

"Of course I'm here. And so are you."

"I was on a boat. Well, not me, but *Buddy* was, and the governor."

"Which governor?"

"The dead one, Peter Van Beek. He loved his wife, Mercedes. At least he is with her now."

"How were you there, Sweetheart?"

"I wasn't."

Walter looks into my eyes, frantic with fear, and understands.

"I saw it all, Walter. I dreamt about Peter Van Beek's death."

"Oh no." Walter wraps his arms around me and presses his cheek to mine. "Tangie, did you see what happened?"

"Walter, Buddy did it."

"*Buddy?* I thought you said that guy on the phone, the guy named Steve, did it."

213

"He did. But so did Buddy. I'm confused. Maybe that *Steve* and this *Buddy* are partners."

"Great, now we have two murderers."

"You haven't had any dreams, lately, have you, Walter?"

"Just one about me thrashing Graham. That was a good one."

"Ah, you have the good ones. I get the murderers." I start laughing and shaking at the same time. "I am going nuts."

"Angelina, who is this *Buddy* guy?"

"Darned if I know. I can't remember his face. I tried to go back—to see it—but I couldn't. You woke me up."

"All I did was kiss you."

"A wonderful kiss at that. You see what passion does to me. Messes up my psychic abilities."

"I'm sorry, Angelina. Here, have a sip of water."

I take a sip and then a deep breath. I'm okay, Walter. It's over. Don't ever be sorry for kissing me. Come here, my darling. Kiss me again—distract me.

Walter is great at taking direction. Not only does he kiss me, he unbuttons his shirt and takes off his jeans and unmentionables. He crawls into bed with me, encircles my naked body in a gentle embrace, and whispers, "I was planning on telling you what Steve and I discussed, but that can wait—enough drama for one night. I think it's time we forget about everything and just enjoy each other."

"I like that idea, immeasurably. Is our Steve comfortable on the couch?"

"Yes. He's sound asleep, with his Magnum under his pillow, playing watchdog, along with Pebbles. Aunt Hattie is snoozing in her room down the hall, probably with her pistol under her pillow. Just you and I are awake."

I smile despite my angst. "You know how to make a woman forget the bad guys, my sweet."

"Let's see, Angelina, *How do I love you? Let me count the ways.*"

"A kiss is worth a thousand words."

"Ah*, you are so beautiful...*"

"*To me...*"

And the rest is private. You know how we private detectives are. We keep our personal snooping to ourselves.

Chapter Thirty-One

The next morning, a delicious scent drifts into our bedroom. I sit up as the smell of sausage and bacon, French toast with cinnamon and coffee, wonderful coffee beckons.

My sleeping prince smiles at me with his eyes closed. I kiss him on his cheek and feel the stubble of a beard. I smile back at Walter, slip out of bed without disturbing him and don my robe and slippers. Then I tiptoe down the stairs to breakfast.

Steve the Cop stands before Aunt Hattie's stove like a conductor directing a symphony, waving his spatula in time to Aaron Copland's *American Suite*. I love a man who cooks with classical music in the background. Steve looks like he has a passion for music as well as cooking. Who would have thought? Lucky Suzy, but she better watch her waistline. A girl could gain a few pounds on the breakfasts he orchestrates.

Aunt Hattie plays first violin, setting the table and pouring the coffee. Not my usual espresso, but it smells wonderful, sweet and nutty.

I wonder what time it is? How long did Walter and I sleep? I glance at an antique clock on the wall by the kitchen nook. Twelve o'clock noon!

"Aunt Hattie! Why didn't you wake us?"

"Oh, Tangie, you and Walter need your rest. The two of you looked exhausted last night."

Steve chuckles, and stops his hovering over the stove for a moment. "We haven't been up that long ourselves. Just three or four hours."

"Now I feel bad."

To tell the truth, I really didn't. Last night turned out to be rather dreamy, the latter part for sure. I smile, thinking of Walter and me and our passionate nature. By now, it's no surprise to Steve and Aunt Hattie.

"Sit down, Tangie." Aunt Hattie speaks in her authoritative voice that one cannot refuse. "Eat. You need nourishment; you didn't eat much last night."

"No, but I drank a lot of wine. That I remember."

"Well, you needed to unwind. You've had a rough week, my dear. I know this entire situation is getting to you."

"You've got that right. Let's create a new rule. No shoptalk while eating breakfast."

Steve nods. "Tangie, you are a woman after my own heart,"

I scoot into the far side of the breakfast nook. "Now, Steve, I think Suzy has your heart just about sewn to hers."

"She does and one of these days she's gonna appreciate my breakfasts."

"She will, once she gets off her diet month."

Suzy is always going on and off a diet. She diets for a month at a time and then eats for two months. It's always feast or famine with her. She has the body of a fashion model and the looks to go with it, perfect teeth, evenly-set baby blue eyes that Steve calls bedroom eyes and hair that is naturally straight, but not naturally blonde. She's still the perfect package for just about any male and in this case, she's Steve's package—the one he will fight to keep. I pity any fellow who tries to break them up. The guy will be toast.

Steve sighs. "I never know which month she's eating. She drives me crazy sometimes. However, just thinking of her makes me...Oh, I almost forgot! I've got to call her before she goes to work."

As our Steve takes off his "I Love to Cook" apron and rushes to the next room, I think to myself, "Work?" Now I know for a fact, Suzy doesn't work. Sometimes she volunteers at the library and the Seattle Art Museum, but I don't think she ever drew a paycheck. Must ask Steve about that.

I look at the bowl of fruit cut up like flowers in the center of the table. "Aunt Hattie, how did Steve have time to do all this?"

"Oh, our Steve is a wonder in the kitchen. He insisted on going out and getting thick-sliced French bread and Maine maple syrup. He insisted on cutting up all this fruit. Our breakfast protein is Canadian strip bacon. Seems it's your favorite."

"That it is. Fletcher's is my favorite." I pick up a slice, break it in pieces and plop it in my mouth. "Um, I think I died and went to heaven. I love breakfast. Thanks for letting Steve take control. I didn't realize what a good cook he is. He usually defers to Walter in the kitchen."

"You know, dear, things are so different than they used to be. My generation delighted in typecasting people. Men rarely spent time in the kitchen, unless they were professional chefs. Your generation is lucky; everyone is self-sufficient and independent." Aunt Hattie leans back in her chair and closes her eyes as if remembering something. "Maybe, if things were different back then, I might have married. But I didn't want to give up my independence. I thought it would interrupt my *joie d'vivre*."

"I'm sorry, Aunt Hattie. Are you referring to a special man in your life?"

"There was someone I cared about a lot but I couldn't stand his mother. I figured, if I didn't like his mother, sooner or later, it would come between us, so I let him go."

"That's so sad."

"It was, at first. But I've had a good life. Yet I sometimes wonder, if I put my pride aside, I might not have been alone all these years. Independence came at a price in those days. You are more fortunate than I."

"I don't know about being more fortunate, Aunt Hattie. You are a very special person. I do know that Walter is a wonderful husband. I feel blessed in that department."

"He is my favorite nephew."

"And your only nephew."

"It seems that way. I wish you could have met his grandfather. Walter reminds me of my father. I miss him terribly."

"I still miss my father. He died when I was seven. A long time ago."

"Sometimes you never get over a loss. You just get used to it and go on."

"I am glad we are family, Aunt Hattie." I lean over and hug her.

"Me too, dear. Now let's eat Steve's breakfast delight, before it gets cold. Pass me the syrup, please."

I smile and chuckle, "Of course. You're right. If we wait for Steve to get back, or Walter to get up, we'll be old ladies!" As if on cue, we reach for the plate of mile-high thick French toast, sprinkled with powdered sugar.

Aunt Hattie grins. "No doubt, Tangie, this is going to be a high-energy day."

Steve never does come back into the kitchen to eat breakfast. I hear his footsteps creaking up the stairs, still "uh-huh-ing" into his phone, listening to Suzy as he lands on each step. Walter remains in Snoozeville, so Aunt Hattie and I relax, joke and share stories about our precious Walter at various stages of his life. One particular story gets me going in uncontrollable fits of laughter. As I stand up to clear the table, I almost drop the plates on the way to the dishwasher. Aunt Hattie cackles as she helps me clear off the table and load the rest of the dishes.

Walter strolls into the kitchen, freshly showered and dressed, looking like an ad in *Gentleman's Quarterly*. "What's up, you two?"

I can't help myself. I whistle.

Aunt Hattie smiles at me. I know that look. Things have changed. Girls never used to whistle at their men.

Walter grins, leans down and plants a kiss on each of us, smelling divinely like Hawaiian soap. "What have you been up to, ladies?"

"Well, we've been up a while, but unlike you, we haven't dressed for the day. We shared some scrumptious stories about you and ate a wonderful breakfast, prepared by none other than our Steve."

"Hum, stories. Aunt Hattie, hopefully not the one about the toad."

Aunt Hattie grins. "No I left that one out."

"Thank goodness." Walter picks up a piece of bacon from the stovetop and crunches it. "Not bad. Next time Steve stays with us in Seattle, he cooks. Where is our fearless officer of the law?"

"Suzy. Need I say more?"

"Are they together again?"

"I think so. If they were fighting, he'd be off the phone by now."

"Are you going to get dressed?"

"Well, yeah, but I thought you like me in my robe."

"I do, Angelina, but…"

I love making Walter uncomfortable. Seems our banter embarrasses him in front of Aunt Hattie. I don't know why it does. She is very cool about life. He should know that, but I can take a hint.

"Aunt Hattie and I enjoyed breakfast together this morning—just two girls hanging out."

"Glad to hear that. Are you feeling better, my love?" Walter stands next to me and massages my shoulders.

"Never felt better, thanks to you." I give Walter my Cheshire cat and continue. "If shopping is in our plans today, I will feel even better. Seems I need an evening dress."

I turn to Walter's aunt. "How about you, Aunt Hattie?"

"Oh Tangie, I've been around long enough to have plenty of evening dresses in my closet. You go ahead and get ready. I'll finish the dishes and keep Walter company as he finishes devouring his breakfast." She winks at me. "Steve will probably stay home with me this afternoon. He has some other phone calls to make when his girlfriend lets him hang up."

Seems like Aunt Hattie and Steve did a bit of chatting while Walter and I slumbered this morning. Both early risers, I surmise. Not my forte. I'm still not used to Eastern Standard Time. Neither is Walter, I suspect. Actually we are both night owls and the time change is killing us.

I smile. "Aunt Hattie, thank you. You are wonderful."

I give my honey a kiss on the cheek. "Sweetheart, I'll be ready in about fifteen minutes. Just need to shower and wash my hair."

"I'll be timing you." Walter smiles, sits down and chomps on another piece of bacon.

I push the swinging door, walk down the hallway and run up the stairs, almost colliding with "our Steve", as we now refer to him, at least until the other Steve, "Steve the Murderer", surfaces and is put away for good.

"Tangie! Jeez. Watch out. I almost knocked you down the stairs. Then what would I tell Walter?"

"Tell him I almost knocked *you* down the stairs. That would be the truth. Sorry, Steve. I'm in a hurry. I didn't see you. Did you sleep all right? How's Suzy?"

"I slept fine. Suzy's good. She misses me."

"Who wouldn't miss you? You're a tall, dark and handsome hunk of a man. Surely she knows what a catch you are. You know girls drool over your beautiful brown eyes, your broad shoulders, your black curly hair, cut short so a girl can run her fingers through it."

"Cut it out, Tangie; you're making me blush."

I giggle, pat his shoulder and then get serious. "Things are better now with you two?"

"More than better. I think I'm in love, for real this time."

"Congratulations. Hey, what's this about a job?"

"Oh, Suzy had a job but they fired her last night. She couldn't type. If you are a secretary, it's a job requirement. She didn't know that."

"Sounds like Suzy. Why did she want the job in the first place? She doesn't need it."

"Beats me. She says she'll tell me when I get back. She told me to say "hi". She wants to get together for lunch when you get back. She misses you."

"Thanks, Steve. I will. You be good and have fun this afternoon with Aunt Hattie."

"Hey, she's a cool lady."

"I know that. Did you call Barry?"

"Cardoso? Not yet. But I'm gonna after I eat."

"You didn't eat? You'd better get downstairs. Everything's cold by now. Be grateful for the microwave."

"Yeah, the twenty-first century."

"They've been here since the twentieth."

"Yeah, I know that and I'm starved. See you later," Steve mutters. He leaps two steps at a time down the stairs, passing me.

I hope Walter left him some French toast. I bet the bacon's gone. Well, there's always coffee.

Chapter Thirty-Two

I find an evening gown in the first department store we visit in Providence. That would be Nordstrom's. I love that the first one ever was in Seattle and it's my hometown store. And yes, they know how to treat their customers— like family.

After we leave downtown and head towards the highway, I beg Walter to make a stop at the Christmas Tree Shop in Warwick. Seems these specialty stores are everywhere in New England, but nowhere in the Northwest. Like everything else, that will change. There'll probably be one in Seattle someday. For now, I'll be content to shop in New England for their great deals.

We stroll into the shop, which is all decked out for the Halloween holiday. Orange and purple lights twinkle everywhere and ghosts fly from the ceiling. I can't wait to go down every isle. The place begs shoppers to buy neat stuff in huge quantities that they don't really need but "have to have". But before I get all psyched to shop, I grab Walter's arm, suddenly all concerned about him. "Hey Honey, I just thought of something. Don't you need a tux? Should we stop by a men's store when we're done here, so you can rent one? Or do you want to buy one?"

"I've got two stored in the attic at Aunt Hattie's. I used to go to lots of affairs when I lived out here. People are so formal here on the East Coast. Everyone dresses up. Not like the Northwest at all. I've got them tucked away. One for our Steve and one for me."

"Just when I figure you out, you surprise me. What guy has two tuxes just waiting for him at his aunt's home? Just in case? You're like some

221

spy who has disguises hidden all over the place to be used on a moment's notice." I smile at him and plant a kiss on his cheek. "You're definitely my kind of guy and I love you."

"Look at it this way, Angelina. We have more time to spend in this cornucopia of collectible treasures or junk. Take your pick."

I laugh and push the cart. "Walter. I love this store. Do we need anything?"

"No."

"But the prices are great!" I pick up a teapot and notice the label glued to the bottom: Made in Poland. The intricate floral-mosaic design fascinates me. This is hand-painted stoneware at such a cheap price. I remember seeing a similar pattern at Pike Place Market for five times the amount on this label. I show it to Walter. "I love this, Walter. Who says everything is more expensive on the East Coast?"

Walter smiles. "Let's take a stroll around the place. I'm sure you'll find something else you can't live without."

I place the teapot in our cart and smile.

We leave the Christmas Tree Shop with five bags of merchandise. Most of our purchases include presents, which I will have to mail home, but heck, I did get a lot of Christmas shopping done early and some great Halloween decorations for our home on Queen Anne. Makes me even more determined to get to Seattle before one of my favorite holidays bites the dust.

"Want to stop for lunch, Angelina?"

"Sure! I'm starved. Shopping always makes me hungry."

"I'd love to take you to Aunt Carrie's down by Point Judith. They have the best clam cakes and chowder, but they're closed for the season. For now, let's take a drive along the Narragansett Bay and stop in Wickford for lunch. It's a great little antique shopping town. It will remind you of that quaint waterfront town, not far from the tulip fields—north of Seattle— you remember, La Conner. Seems you loved it when we stayed in a bed and breakfast there. I think you'll like Wickford too."

"Sounds wonderful. If it's anything like La Conner, I will love it. You know, my love, today is intoxicating, just the two of us. I'm so grateful for this time together with no distractions."

"Oui, ma chère, ma femme." Walter reaches for my hand and brings it up to his lips.

I feel a tingle up and down my spine. I know we are married but when I spend time with Walter and we are hanging out together, it always feels like a first date.

We get in a little traffic tie-up before entering Wickford. Walter looks at me while we wait for a broken-down truck to be towed away. "Angelina, I wish we didn't have to go to that reception."

"Me too. Why don't we just bag it and go home to Seattle?"

"Because we have to finish what we started."

"Why?"

"Wishing and doing are two separate things. I wish never to leave your side, Angelina, but I do. Sweetheart, you know I will always return to you."

"Walter, is this a farewell speech? What is going on in your mind?"

"Just that I love you."

The traffic opens and Walter puts his foot on the gas pedal and focuses on driving once more. I look at him with tears in my eyes, knowing something happened. He knows something he isn't sharing.

"Walter, I love you too, and I don't want to lose you, ever. What did you and Steve talk about last night? Does your mood have anything to do with that conversation? Tell me."

"I will Tangie, over lunch. It's hard to talk about serious stuff when I'm driving, or when I'm hungry."

I tend to agree with Walter, but I know he's stalling and deliberately being vague. I'm on to him.

We arrive in Wickford, a bucolic haven by the bay, in the late afternoon; Walter parks in the community parking lot and we hop out. While Walter strolls across the street to a seafood take-out restaurant, I head to the little girls' room nearby. We agree to meet on a bench by the nearest dock overlooking the waterfront. As my task consumes little of my time, I arrive ahead of Walter, sit down and take in the view. I survey the seagulls as they chatter and fly overhead, the sailing vessels tied to the docks and the large Cape Cod cottages that dot the shoreline. I study the shops to my left and notice many of them to be antique or collectible shops, just as Walter promised. My mother would like it here. Maybe the two of us will take a trip here some time, just us girls, to visit Aunt Hattie. Maybe I could find a little treasure for her today as a remembrance. She's been on my mind a lot.

I breathe in the sea air and enjoy the sun and its warmth caressing my body. I get a feeling of the calm before the storm, but I am hell bent to enjoy this peacefulness. Come Friday the storm will catch us, but that can wait. Not everything in life is gloom and doom.

I hear footsteps. Walter's footsteps, a soothing sound. I look to my left and there stands my love. I hop up to help unburden him of his three bags of steaming seafood and two mugs of hot tea.

"Walter! Who gives ceramic mugs with takeout?"

"Oh, Finn's Seafood has a promotion going on. I got you Barry's Irish tea with lemon and sugar added. Is that okay?"

"Great! Thanks, Sweetie. I drank my share of coffee today."

"And some shrimp and clam cakes."

"I'm in heaven."

"Well, for a little while at least. At least they smell as good as the ones at Aunt Carrie's."

I lean my head against Walter's shoulder as he joins me on the bench. We content ourselves with munching on crispy treats from the sea and feeling the sea breeze as it gently caresses our shoulders. I can stay like this forever. A street musician strolls by and starts playing his guitar. Shortly afterwards, his colleague joins in playing the violin. The guitarist hands Walter an advertisement. The two of them and their band will be presenting a concert at the community center at the end of the park.

Walter takes two Lincolns out of his pocket and gives them to the violinist. "Good luck."

The violinist nods and hands me a rose.

Before they continue serenading us, the guitarist smiles and says, "Thanks, sir. Please, come if you can."

I don't think I ever heard anyone other than some foolish waiter call Walter "sir" before. Guess we must be looking like an old married couple, after one month.

I kiss Walter on the cheek, lean against him and close my eyes. We sit in peace, listening to the sound of the music, the seagulls and the foghorns in the distance. I don't want Walter to talk shop and he knows that. His plans and Steve's ideas can wait. I want to enjoy this moment of "splendor in the grass, glory in the flower" and sweet music in the afternoon.

As the musicians stop playing and stroll along the waterfront, I look up and murmur to Walter, "Why do good things have to end? Life can be so beautiful. Then it switches and we don't even notice the change until it is too late."

"Oh we notice all right. We just don't want to admit it. It's too painful to accept."

"Walter, are we going to be all right?"

"I think so, Angelina."

"But you aren't sure."

"No. But we can't avoid these conflicts. They'll just get bigger and drown us."

"So we carry on."

"In a manner of speaking."

"So what did you and Steve talk about?"

Walter looks at me as I open my eyes wide. I look deeply into his eyes. I see his pain and that old familiar fear he gets when he sees something awful.

"What are you planning?"

"A trap for Graham. He is going to tell us what we want to know, one way or another."

"Is that wise? He could hurt you."

"I'm bigger than he is. So is our Steve."

"But he also has a friend named Steve, *Steve the Murderer.* This Steve is evil."

"We don't know for sure that *this Steve* is Graham's friend. But I'm going to find out."

"Great. Not! What do I do while you are out risking your life?"

225

"You stay put at the reception. Our Steve will watch you and Aunt Hattie. I will try to get Graham to have a drink with me or take a stroll around town or something."

That "something" has me a little worried. I think Walter is deliberately being vague, again. I start to quiz him. "Where is this reception, anyway?"

"Darned if I know. The tickets should be in the mail today. We'll check when we get home and finalize our plans. I think if I can get Graham alone, he will talk. With you there, I get nervous. You see, I am afraid he might hurt you. Then I lose focus."

"But you're not afraid he might hurt you."

"I didn't say that."

I begin to get panic-stricken. The love of my life is sitting next to me telling me he is taking a chance with his life and our life together.

"He's not worth it, Walter."

"I know, but other people are involved. The police out here aren't cooperating. Plus, they'll think we're daft. Heck, we don't live here. We're outsiders. They won't believe anything until they have proof. I intend to get some proof or at least a motive. I think I can get the motive and part of the story from Graham. He knows something. We both understand that to be a fact, but no one else realizes this except Aunt Hattie and our Steve."

"All right, Walter. We'll do it. But our Steve and I are going to be your back up. Carry your phone and call us if a problem occurs. I think I'll call Barry and bug him big time. He's got to help us. This is getting bigger than we can handle."

"Wait a bit. I think Steve is calling Barry as we speak. He'll come through for us."

"I hope so."

"Let's head home. Don't feed the seagulls. They'll drive the rest of the tourists crazy."

"I'm from Seattle, Walter. Like I would feed the seagulls! I know what those creatures are capable of doing to a person with a French fry."

Looking around, I don't notice many tourists. All the people strolling around seem like locals to me, but maybe Walter sees things differently. Just the same, like I said, I don't want to encourage the seagulls.

Sometimes they act like flying rats, and there are enough rats flying around Rhode Island at the moment.

When we get home from our diversion excursion, I see the sun losing it grip on this part of the earth. Aunt Hattie notices us, and waves from her lighted perch by the front window. She holds up four tickets and rolls her eyes.

When we walk in the front door, I ask, "From Graham?"

"Special messenger delivery. He must really want us to come."

"Great. Now all we need is a limo to make a good impression on the guy," Walter groans, in his most sarcastic tone.

"Walter, we've got to think of this as a lead. We're on our way."

"Yeah, Tangie. On our way to Graham's tangled web of deceit."

"What tangled web of deceit?" Our Steve enters the living room. He wears a blue running suit and a terry cloth sweatband. He looks as if he just came in from a jog or working out. He must have sneaked in the back door. The guy has discipline, I'll hand him that.

"Oh, Steve," Aunt Hattie answers, "We've just got the tickets. We are going to the reception to figure out this web thing."

Aunt Hattie makes it sound like we plan to go to a sporting event. In a way, she's right. A hunting party and the victor takes all. Only in this case, we don't know whom the hunter and the hunted are, just tips to follow.

"Good news, guys." Steve announces. "Not to worry. I finally got in touch with Barry. He'll be coming on Saturday. That is the earliest he can get away."

I sigh. "Good. I'm grateful he's coming. I'll feel safer in numbers."

Walter pats his friend on the back. "That is good news, Steve. This calls for a celebration. Tangie, I'll help you take your packages upstairs, and then we we'll go out for a drink. Steve, you remember the pub down the street, don't you? I've been wanting to go there with you and Angelina."

"I could always use a brew, or two. Give me a few minutes to shower and get dressed."

"What about dinner?" My stomach starts growling, as if on cue.

"Tangie, we just ate, a lot of..."

"Seems like light years ago. And what about Aunt Hattie?"

Aunt Hattie interrupts, finishing my thoughts. "Now listen, Angelina. I am perfectly capable of taking care of myself. I do it all the time. You young folks need a night out, away from politics and all this gloom and doom. And I need some rest. Go. Have some fun. Besides, Steve and I just ate some lobster rolls."

"Lobster rolls? You're holding out on us, Aunt Hattie." Walter has a grin plastered all over his face, like a little kid remembering he didn't have spun cotton candy at the carnival yet.

"Oh no, dear, I'm not." Aunt Hattie squeezes his adorable cheeks, like I love to do. "There's plenty of lobster salad left. You can have some later. Perhaps a midnight snack."

"Now you're talking, dear, sweet, Auntie." Walter smiles and hugs his aunt.

Gosh he is smooth.

I echo Walter's enthusiasm and match his grin. "You are a dear, Aunt Hattie."

"I know," Aunt Hattie chuckles, then winks at me. "I have a few things to do before the big event on Friday, so you three go ahead and celebrate, or whatever you call it. I'll be fine and I'll keep an eye on Pebbles for you. He and I have become quite good friends. I will certainly miss him when you go back to Seattle."

Walter gives Aunt Hattie one of his famous bear hugs. Steve smiles at the two of them and I blow them all a kiss as I race upstairs with my packages.

Chapter Thirty-Three

One can describe Maxwell's Pub, a few blocks past Brick Alley Road, on the main drag, as loud and quaint. It is situated near the wharf off Ocean Drive above a clothing and collectible shop. As we walk up the steep stairs that lead to the second-story bar, I hear creaking and feel boards bending. I hope our walkway doesn't come crashing down before we get to the top. Rock music from the Seventies blasts inside the joint.

I look at Walter. "Live music. That's a plus."

A bouncer stands by the entrance and looks ready to hurl us down the rickety stairs.

I whisper, "We must remember to make nice with him."

Walter smiles and hands "Mr. Hulk", the doorman, a twenty. In turn, Mr. Hulk allows the three of us to pass through the door that resembles a wooden plank, probably used in a past life by victims forced to march overboard at sea.

Our Steve chooses three stools by the bar, but I insist we sit at a table. The only one open happens to be near a window overlooking the lights flickering across the harbor. I smile and snuggle into a seat by the window, claiming my turf. The pulsing vibrations of the band crank out the sounds to one of my favorite Seventies' tunes. I love oldies. The band does a decent job. Probably why Walter likes this place. I lean back and listen to the musicians as they capture the festive mood and echo their notes out to the crowd. For a weeknight, there are lots of patrons hanging out here.

After the band wraps up a favorite classic, the lead singer announces they'll be taking a break. In the lull that fills the air, I hear the chatter circulating around a pool table in the far corner of the room next to one of the windows. A voice sounds familiar, but I cannot make it out. I crank my head a bit and think I recognize the woman shooting pool with a dark-haired young man with tinted glasses.

Steve sits across from me. Walter sits down next to me, on my right. A young woman, with extreme make-up comes from behind the bar and asks what our pleasure will be.

"Our pleasure will be three lagers." Walter puts a fifty on the table.

I blink a few times and mumble, "And peanuts and popcorn or whatever snacks you serve."

The barmaid ignores me but smiles at Walter, noticing his clean, rugged appearance. My honey sits comfortably dressed in his blue button-down shirt, leather jacket and designer jeans. She glances at me as if I'm a caterpillar. Any minute now I think she will squash me. The reason she doesn't smile in my direction is an easy one to figure out. The best good-looking hunks around are keeping me company. What can I say? I'm working. Part of the job assignment.

Our Steve grins with his pearly whites, stretches his arms over his head and reveals his broad shoulders. "Thank you, Miss."

That seems to please her, because she shoots a toothy grin back at him, turns her body, moves her hips and retreats to get our drinks and hopefully my snacks.

I don't usually drink beer or ale, but this seems like the kind of place to partake of that particular beverage or get clobbered.

Finally! I recognize that familiar voice, the laugh and then the growl. Yes, I'd recognize that growl anywhere. Eveline. Here, in the bar. I poke Walter and nod to him to look towards the pool table. Then I put my lips by his ear and pretend to whisper sweet nothings in his ear. "Look! Eveline over there, talking to that dark-haired stranger."

Walter gives me a look of understanding, then leans over and whispers to our buddy, "Steve, you're closer. Listen to the older dame behind you. Tell us exactly what she is saying and what her companion is saying. Be discreet."

Our Steve whispers back, "Consider it done, good buddy."

The barmaid arrives all cheery with our beers just as Steve takes out his little black book that resembles an address book. I know it is his memory keeper. He writes stuff down that he doesn't want to forget. Our server smiles at Steve. She must think he is getting ready to ask for her phone number. He grins back at her and to my surprise, does ask for her name and phone number. Good cover on his part. At least, I hope that what it is. She leans over, whispers something in his ear, and places his drink down. She leans across him to give Walter his brew, and as an after thought, she slams mine down, spilling half of it on my sweater.

"Oh, I'm terribly sorry," she coos. "I'll get a towel."

"No problem. I'll just use this napkin here on the table."

I pick up the tiny piece of soft paper and wipe the foam off my favorite cashmere, smiling at Miss Airhead. Sometimes, sweetness kills. She shrugs her shoulders and leaves to fill up my peanut bowl.

When she returns a minute later with peanuts and pretzels, Walter gestures to her to come closer then places a bill in her free hand. She snuggles up close to him as he whispers, "Say Miss—the couple over by the pool table—do you know who they are? Do they come in here often?"

Our server looks at him for a split second and studies his face. She leans down exposing ample breasts to my beloved. I feel myself getting steamy. Walter grabs my hand under the table to reassure me he can handle her proclivities. I should be so lucky. Now I have a taste of what he feels like when guys pay attention to me.

Our server smiles as Walter places another bill in her apron pocket. "Yeah, I know them. They've been here a few times. Seems to me the dame's a little old for the guy. Anyway, he's a creep. Don't know whatever she sees in him, unless she just prefers younger men and doesn't care who they are. But who am I to judge? The creep's a good tipper and the lady's a bitch."

"You ever hear them talk?"

"I don't eavesdrop on people's conversation."

Now I know that to be a lie, but I am not about to interrupt the progress Walter is making, grilling her for information. I keep my lips sealed.

Walter places a twenty in her bosom. "I know, Miss. I just want to know if you heard anything strange when you weren't listening."

I am not thrilled about where Walter places his money, but I understand his intentions. Good thing I'm not the jealous type. *Hah!*

The mistress of the bar becomes all smiles. She enjoys this game and whispers in Walter's ear. I can't hear her exact words, but Walter nods and places another twenty in her bosom after she finishes whispering more tidbits in his ear.

I am tempted to groan out loud or gag but doing so will not help our mission to discover the down and dirty on Eveline. So I exert necessary self-control, divert my attention from this hussy lunging at my man, and check out the bar surroundings, particularly Eveline and her companion. I study the femme fatale and her boy toy having a heated conversation behind the pool table. I can't make out what they are saying. Eveline looks distressed and the younger man looks peeved. Maybe she is breaking up with him. Maybe he is breaking up with her. It's obvious she is up to no good. She's a married woman, meeting a much younger man, a creep, in a bar. So she cheats on her "respectable" husband. It's been done before, but what a piece of work. I see the mystery man putting his arms around her. She relaxes a bit. Then I see her pushing him away.

As our barmaid finishes spilling all her insights onto Walter, I notice Eveline's dark-haired young man run out of the poolroom toward the door. I hear him say out loud, "This time you pay the bill." His voice resonates in a low tremble, as if echoing a person in authority. At least someone is telling Eveline off.

As I watch in my most discreet way, I notice as Eveline collapses on a chair near the pool table and then lets out a sob. She straightens her body, dabs her mascara-streaked cheeks with a cocktail napkin, and as if gaining strength, grabs her purse, gets up and walks over to the bar. I watch as she opens up her wallet, takes out a few large bills and places them on the counter. The bartender takes one look at her tear-stained face and the bills, and places a tall glass on the counter. "Lady, you look like you need a strong drink." She nods and sits down on a stool. She eyes the Scotch he generously pours for her, picks up the glass and salutes him. She chugs the drink, closes her purse, and stumbles off her stool. Her ankles bend as she walks toward the door and she holds onto the bar for support.

"Wait!" the bartender barks at her. "You shouldn't be driving. I'll call you a cab."

Eveline turns around and throws him a dagger stare. "Don't bother. I have a driver." She exits and leaves the door wide open. Everyone in the bar can hear her yelling at Mr. Hulk, "Get your filthy hands off me. I'm perfectly capable of walking down these half-assed stairs by myself!"

I glance at Steve and Walter, who join in listening to Eveline's tantrum. Steve laughs. "Never a dull moment at Maxwell's."

I whisper to Walter, "That's our Eveline."

As I look up, I notice our well-endowed barmaid, still standing by Walter's side. Apparently, she surmises Eveline's distress and smiles a toothy grin. Seems this hussy is pleased with another hussy's misery and thrilled at her own good fortune. She's a lot richer after her confidences to Walter. She winks at Steve and leans over our table. This time her bosom crowds me out, as she whispers to Steve, "Later." She wafts over to another table near the bar. I can hear her giggling with the two men who inhabit that spot. No doubt she is convinced her lucky charm is working tonight.

We sit around the table, finish our beers and listen to the band's return to the Seventies. Steve orders us another round and Walter, not to be undone, orders another. So it goes until the band announces the last song for the evening. Steve joins Walter in crooning, "*Sing…a song, piano man…*" slightly off-key.

"Great band," I announce. "Walter, now I know why you like this place."

"Yes, my sweet, they play all kinds of music and I'm partial to the Seventies' Rock. Great pianist. Do you know the composer of that song used to dock his boat here at Newport?"

"Really? No, you didn't tell me."

"Yes, indeed-y he did. Not too far from Aunt Hattie's ol' yacht. Probably why they're playing his music. Hey! Friday is Jazz Night. Darn. Sorry, my sweet one. We'll miss that one. We'll be at that poofy reception."

"I don't want to go to that reception either."

"Sorry, Tang, I forgot. No shop talk, just fun." Walter takes my hand and kisses it, rather sloppily.

I think my lover is succumbing to the drink of Ninkasi. No wonder I prefer the drink of Dionysus.

Steve appears to have a shot of lucidity and asks, "Hey guys, don't you want to know what Eveline said to Lover Boy?"

"Yes!" I answer. Please, Steve! I'm dying here. Tell us."

"Not here—Hush, hush—but it's juicy. You'll like it."

Walter pushes back his chair and stands. "Let's drink up." He holds his beer glass in the air, then clinks it to ours.

I smile at my love and his best friend. "No matter what, I am glad we three are together."

"Like the Three Musketeers," Steve laughs and then burps rather loudly. "All we need are capes."

"A cape I can do, but I refuse to grow a mustache." I laugh and chug my last glass.

Walter laughs and pinches me in the derriere. "My love, you couldn't grow one if you wanted to."

"Uh oh," Steve groans. "We gotta get outta here. I see the barmaid approaching. She's got her apron off. And she's after me!"

Walter lets out a hoot as Steve jumps up rather unsteadily. He places his hand on Steve's shoulder. "You better hurry, Steve—Go with Tangie and leave. I'll take care of the bill. I'll be right behind you. Don't' worry. I'll tell Miss Eager Lips that you were called away suddenly—that you had to go to work."

"Like she'll believe that."

"I have a way with words...hiccup."

Now Walter is a gentleman and a scholar, but tonight, he is a drunken sailor. Remember how that song goes, "What can you do with a drunken sailor, early in the morning?" Not much.

Chapter Thirty-Four

Steve and I wait for Walter across the street from Maxwell's Tavern under a streetlight in front of the marina. The marina runs the entire length of the old section of town on Ocean Drive. I don't see a single soul out strolling. Steve sits down on a nearby bench while I survey the lights twinkling from the boats moored by the docks. I listen to the sound of the water lapping against the posts as if in rhythm with the music that I hear in my head, the music of the night. A few minutes later, Walter joins us, laughing like a banshee in the shadows as he hurries to meet us under the streetlight.

I slip my arm under his. "Okay, tell us. What's so funny, Captain Walt?"

"Steve, you won't believe it. The barmaid's name is Suzy. And she begged me to tell you not to forget her."

"Well, I may forget her face, but never her..."

"That's enough, guys. Remember me, Tangie? I'm here. And sweet Steve, don't forget about your main squeeze. Lest you forget, I am a good friend of Suzy from Seattle."

"Oh c...come on, Tangie." Steve hiccups. "You wouldn't, would you? We were only trying to get information on..."

"Sure. But I wonder, would your Suzy would see it that way?"

Steve attempts to rise from the park bench and then sits down. "N..n... no, she wouldn't. You know that. You wouldn't, would you, Tangie? I mean t...tell her?

"Relax, Steve, your secret is safe with me."

"And me," Walter chirps.

"Th...that's good. Yu...you really know ha...how to sc...scare a guy, Ta...Ta...Tangie."

I could kick the two of them—they drive me nuts—but I laugh along with them, enjoying their comic relief. Walter helps Steve to his feet. Then with arms linked, we stroll along the waterfront, enjoying the night air and each other's company. As we inch our way up the hill to Aunt Hattie's home, I stop in my tracks and listen in the dark.

"Sh...guys. I think I hear someone in the bushes."

"Ta...Ta...Ta...Tangie, it's not Halloween, yet. But da...da...don't worry. You're safe with us. The witch, I mean, *the bitch*, left before us." Steve laughs while still hiccupping.

"Wait a minute, Steve," Walter whispers. "I hear it too."

"Meow."

A mangy black cat comes meandering out from under the bush, and walks across our path. I study the pathetic thing and think of my ol' neighbor's cat, Spike. "The poor little kitty looks like a stray."

It hisses at me before running down the street.

"Yeah," Steve answers. "A s...s...s...stray black cat from Salem, Ma... Ma...Massachusetts. Looking to h...h...hitch a ride from a bitch, I mean a witch, with a b...b...broomstick."

"Good one, Steve," Walter chuckles. "We should point the cat in Eveline's direction."

"Great idea, Walter." Steve starts snorting. "Here kitty, kitty."

I groan. "One too many lagers for you guys. Come on. I'll race you home and I know I'll win."

"Tangie! Come back, come back," Walter croons.

I turn around and glance at my two drunks as they carouse under the streetlight halfway up Brick Alley Road. I can picture Walter and Steve letting loose in their college days, getting drunk on a Friday night, and hanging out at Aunt Hattie's home rather than going back to the dorm. Some things never change, like friendship, camaraderie and love—and they are certainly better than death and taxes. As I run up the hill, I can hear Walter and Steve harmonizing in ultra loud brotherly voices,

"Makin' love to my lager and beer," and doing their upmost best to fracture a favorite tune of mine.

Back at home in the wee hours of the morning, Steve, Walter and I sit around the nook in Aunt Hattie's kitchen, eating lobster rolls that I assembled for the three of us. Don't know if I did it right, but heck, I'm from the Pacific Northwest. I brew some of Aunt Hattie's hazelnut coffee to go with the tasty seafood treats, and cut up some orange slices, figuring it would be a good idea to feast while we share the events of the evening.

I begin quizzing my inebriated friends. "Okay, does anyone remember anything about Eveline and her stranger?"

All I hear is munching and sighing.

I try again. "Steve, did you write anything interesting in your little black book?"

No luck.

I turn to my beloved. "Walter, my sweet…how about Suzy Q.? Did she tell you anything worth repeating?"

"Ouch, Steve. Tangie really knows how to swing her weapons, *n'est-il pas aussi?*"

Steve shrugs his shoulders, laughs uncontrollably and does not let up until I stand up and stare at him. I wonder if he sees the steam coming out of my ears. I sigh. He's hopeless.

I turn my attention to my drunken sailor. "Walter, come on. I want to know! Tell me."

Steve resumes laughing. "Walter, Tangie wants something from us. You go first. I'll finish the job."

Walter looks at Steve and then me. His eyes are glassed over. Seems he drank a lot more than either Steve or me, but at least he makes an attempt to answer my question. "Okay, I'll tell you, Sweetheart, but let me think a minute. This girl with the big breasts leans over and says…"

Walter closes his eyes. "Hey, Steve, what did that formidable female say?"

Steve looks up from his coffee that until now remains untouched. "I d...d...don't know, good buddy. She talked to you. She whispered sweet na...na...nothings in your ear."

"Oh, yeah, that's right. She told me about that couple. Eveline and what's his name, Scott. No, not Scott, but Steve. That's it! *Steve.* She came there...to Maxwell's with Scott, I mean, *Steve.* Wait, yes, she meets him there, every Wednesday night about eight o'clock for about a month. Then, nadda, nothing, until tonight."

"*Steve?*" I look at Walter and feel my blood pressure rising. "*Steve?!* As in *Steve the Murderer?*"

"She didn't say *Steve the Murderer*, but yep, I think that's the one, Sweetheart."

"Why didn't we follow him? Or check out his car?"

"Seems he already left, as I remember. Or did he leave? Yes! He left! What could we do? Send out a search party? Yep, that's it, Steve. We shudda sent out a search party. Call in the crusaders."

I groan and look at my two drunks. I never saw Walter this drunk before. Our Steve either, matter of fact. So here I sit with two worthless drunks who have information that could seal this case and neither one seems the least bit interested. It's gonna be a long night. I lift the coffee pot and poured each of them a second helping of fresh, hot piping cup of coffee. Black. No sugar.

"Drink up, maties," I order. "Tomorrow is gonna be a killer."

"Gosh, that's strong stuff, Tangie, and ha...ha...hot!" Steve yelps, as his takes a swig and slams his cup down, missing the saucer and spilling some coffee on Aunt Hattie's tablecloth. "Oh...o...oops."

I pick up a napkin and dab at the coffee stain. "Steve," I plead with as much patience as I can muster, overlooking his foible. "Please, I need you to tell me what you wrote in your book."

Steve reaches in his pocket and fumbles for his little black book. "Here it is! S...s...see for yourself."

I open it, study it and sigh. I hand it back to him. "It's in code, Steve. I can't make any sense of it."

"Oops, I forgot. Pa...pa...pa...police code, top-secret stuff you know. Sh...Wh...wa...what if it got in the wrong hands?"

"Please, Steve. Tell us."

"Maybe tomorrow. I da...da...do...don't feel so good."

Steve slides out from under the nook and leans against the wall. I help him walk around the corner to the downstairs' bathroom, lead him in and shut the door. I don't stay to hear the retching sounds that will follow. I return to the kitchen, wipe up the spilled coffee off the table and dab the linen tablecloth with some cold water and soap. When Steve comes out of the bathroom, he smiles. "I feel better." He burps, saturating the air with the smell of pungent stale ale.

I turn my head away from him. "Glad that's over."

"Yup. And now I will make my final announcement: I am going to bed."

I shake my head as he waltzes, doing a two-step, into the living room and collapses on the sofa bed Aunt Hattie prepared for him. He stretches across the couch in a diagonal fashion, and doesn't even crawl under the covers. Seems our informer is dead to the world. I pick up a quilt draped on the nearby chair, shake it out and place it over him. Steve rolls over and begins snoring, one more unpleasant side effect of over-indulgence. There will be no getting any information out of him tonight. At least we have the next morning and afternoon free. Not much time left before tomorrow night's reception and the meeting of our suspects. I've waited this long; a few more hours won't matter, one way or another.

Ambling back into the kitchen, I sit down and finish my coffee and lobster roll. It seems a long time since lunch. The peanuts and pretzels in the bar didn't do much for me. I munch on my lobster roll while listening to Walter's heavy breathing. While I was guiding Steve to the living room, Walter outstretched himself on the window seat bench like a pretzel. I'd love to coax him upstairs to our bed, but he's just a tad bit too bulky for me to transport. I smile, despite my urge to shake him, and wake him from his drunken stupor. I take a final swig of my coffee, stand up and tiptoe back into the living room. I grab a throw pillow and an extra afghan folded on the rocking chair by the front window, carry both into the kitchen to cover up Captain Walt. Placing the pillow under his head, I lean down and kiss his cheek. I remove his shoes and tuck the afghan around his body, hoping he'll be warm enough. As if on autopilot, I clear the dishes from the table, rinse them and load the dishwasher. Remembering at the last minute to shut the coffee pot off, I sigh, shut off the lights and walk silently up the stairs. It's been awhile since I slept alone, but sometimes the dice do not rule in your favor.

Chapter Thirty-Five

Awakening with the sun, I get dressed and take Pebbles for a run by the waterfront, returning before anyone else makes an appearance. Pebbles comes in the kitchen all panting and tired, so I fill his water bowl and give him some kibbles and canned chicken, his favorite breakfast. He lets out a "ruff" and licks my hand. I pet him, promising him some bacon for treats for later, and think it's good to be appreciated. My canine friend chomps on his food, burps and then lies down on a pillow near the fireplace. Love these old houses with working fireplaces in the kitchen. This one happens to be fire-ready, so I pick up a match from the counter, strike it and light the paper and kindling. Pebbles barks momentarily. He hates matches but settles down when I scold him. I guess he's too tired to put up a fight. I dig out my portable espresso maker from its storage place in Aunt Hattie's pantry and brew one perfect cup of cappuccino complete with foamed milk. I take a sip. "Ah, it's been a while."

I carry my cup into the living room, past a sleeping and snoring Steve lying face up on the sofa bed, and sit on Aunt Hattie's rocker, the one she perches on while watching the goings-on outside. I can see a few leaves beginning to fall off the trees as the wind blows. In a few weeks all their beautiful colors will be memories. I focus on a black furry object moving in the breeze. It comes closer to Aunt Hattie's front lawn and I recognize the black cat we stumbled upon last night. He looks like he can use a good meal. I put my cup down, return to the kitchen and pour some milk in an old chipped cup and add some of Pebbles' kibbles. I carry the breakfast to the front door and turn the handle. I tiptoe out on the porch, down the stairs and place the kitty's meal next to a bush by the picket fence. What can I say? I feed the homeless.

I return to the living room and resume my spot at Aunt Hattie's look-out station". Sure enough, the little black hissy kitty comes up to the dish and starts munching the treats. Don't know if Aunt Hattie wants a cat roaming around her home, but what can you do?

I sit and watch as the mangy cat eats its morsels and suddenly I feel as forlorn as the little kitty. I decide to call my good friend, and former fiancé, Father Don, and ask for his prayers, and maybe a little advice. I take another sip of my coffee brew, place the cup on a coaster decorated with an anchor and take my phone out of my pocket. Scrolling down to Father Don's name, I press "Padre". Funny. He used to be my main squeeze and now I call him Padre. It's a good thing I don't know everything that can happen to me. I'd go nuts.

Don picks up on the third ring. "Hi Angelina. How are you? How's the old married couple?"

"Oh Don, I'm only twenty-seven and Walter's younger than me."

"He is? I never knew that. He seems older."

"That's 'cause I still act like a kid. Actually, we're fine. Yes, as a couple, we are just awesome. Fiji is beautiful. We loved it. I'd like to go back someday."

"Yes, I've heard it has that effect on people. Like Hawaii, but different. More remote."

"Yes, but sometimes the world finds you even there."

"What's going on, Angelina?"

"Well, I'm in Rhode Island. Newport, actually."

"With Walter?"

"Of course. Remember Aunt Hattie? From the wedding?"

"Oh yes. She's Walter's aunt and she lives in Newport."

"Right. We're visiting her at her home."

"So soon after your honeymoon?"

I detect a questioning tone in Father Don's voice. He senses I chose to leave something out of our conversation.

"Padre, all is fine with Walter and me, and I hope with you also."

"That's a relief. All is well here in Santiago. It's beautiful this time of the year. All the flowers are in bloom. And our students are wonderful. But tell me, Angelina, have you gotten into some kind of trouble?"

"Yes, well sort of. Not me, but someone, and I cannot talk about it."

"Does Walter know?"

"Yes. And he can't talk about it either."

"So you need my prayers."

"Yes, Padre. I'm close to desperate. I'm worried. Not about myself, but about Walter. And Steve. You do remember Steve?"

At the mention of his name, Steve stirs on the couch, then rolls over on his stomach and places a pillow over his head.

I decide to finish my phone conversation in the kitchen. I pick up my coffee cup, walk into the hallway and head to the breakfast nook.

There is a moment of silence before Don answers my question. "Your Steve…he's the best man, the cop, and the one Suzy was hanging all over at the reception. Is that right?"

"That's the one. He's here helping us."

"Okay, Angelina. I'll keep you all in my prayers. I'll have the nuns pray for you as well. Promise me you will not take any unnecessary chances. And please, call me when you have this all straightened out, so I won't worry. Well, I will worry, until you call. On second thought, call me whenever you want. You don't have to wait until things are resolved. Just know I am here for you."

I sit down at the kitchen table and sigh. "Thanks, Don. That means a lot to me. I'm glad we got to see each other again, this summer. Thanks for extending your leave for our wedding. I know it wasn't easy to do."

"*Au Contraire*, I think the mission and school managed quite well without me. I'm sorry you had to postpone your wedding until September, but really, that was fine with me. I'm just glad your injury has finally healed. You are such a trouper, Tangie."

Subconsciously, I rub my shoulder. "Thanks, Don. I love you—always have, always will. You are my forever friend, my spiritual guide. And thanks again, Padre, for praying for us all. I will pray for you, the sisters, and your students."

"*Pax Domini sit semper vobiscum.*"

"Et cum spiritu tuo."

"Call me."

"I promise."

I end the call with tears in my eyes. I chant to myself, "All will be well. Father Don is praying for us. The nuns are praying for us. Please, Lord, grant us peace. *Dona nobis pacem.*"

I stare at Felix the Cat keeping time on the wall next to the stove and become mesmerized at the tail going back and forth. Now I know where the clock on our own kitchen wall back in Seattle, came from. Aunt Hattie. Perhaps she is a cat lover after all. Maybe the mangy cat will find a home here. "Hum, seven o'clock." Seems to me it will be at least two hours until anyone joins me in the kitchen. I might as well tidy up the place from last evening and take a turn at making breakfast.

Seems not much tidying up is needed, so I dig Aunt Hattie's waffle iron out of the bottom cupboard and decide to whip up some blueberry Belgium waffles. I rummage through the refrigerator and pull out a pint of blueberries, a pound of thick sliced bacon and a carton of eggs. I discover some fresh strawberries hidden in the potato bin, slice them up, then swirl the whip cream. With the blueberry waffles, we'll have a red, white and blue breakfast. I pour fresh-squeezed orange juice into jelly glasses and brew some hazelnut coffee for everyone. That blend seems to be Aunt Hattie's favorite.

Like clockwork, with the aroma of waffles steaming in the iron and bacon frying, my family, one by one, shows up for the morning feast.

Aunt Hattie takes first place. She comes in fully dressed, in a green velour exercise suit and tennis shoes. Her hair looks freshly washed and styled. "Hello, my dear." She gives me a kiss on the cheek. "Thank you for preparing breakfast. I know the reception tonight will be a late night affair so I slept in a wee bit. After all, I need to get my beauty sleep."

I nod and smile as I take the waffles out of the iron. "You look great this morning, Aunt Hattie."

"Thank you, dear. I took an extra-long shower, washed my hair and styled it. Seems I'm ready for this evening's event. My dress is laid out and I just need to match my shoes and purse. Perhaps you could help me with those, Tangie?"

"I'd love to, Aunt Hattie. You know, I love fashion."

"It's obvious, dear. You dress with such style. You have a knack for wearing just the right thing."

"Why, thank you, Aunt Hattie. Coming from you that is high praise."

Steve shuffles into the kitchen. "I am afraid, you won't have high praise for me." "I feel like I've been hit by a tank."

I smile at him. "That bad, huh?"

Steve nods and put his hand on his head, as if to hold it up.

"Sorry, Steve. I thought by now you'd be feeling better."

Steve eyes the table with my gourmet breakfast spread out before him and his mood seems to lighten up. "Well, nothing that a few aspirins and your delicious breakfast won't cure. It smells wonderful. I'm gonna take a quick shower. I'll be back in time to devour those waffles. I'm starved."

"You do that, Steve." I hand him a cup of coffee and three aspirins. "Here. Take these with you. You'll need them."

"You know me so well."

I laugh, enjoying our banter. "What are friends for? Now go. Get out of here and come back soon."

Steve stumbles into the hall and bumps into Walter who seems in a hurry to get to the waffles.

"Honey, I'm home." Walter grins as he strolls into the kitchen, smelling fresh from his shower and dressed in jeans and his favorite Eddie Bauer blue flannel shirt.

"Glad you made it upstairs last night." I smile and hug him tightly.

"Yes. Me too. Sleeping in the nook has its drawbacks. You weren't there."

"What time did you come to bed? I was zonked out."

Walter brushes my lips with his. "About five a.m., I think. It was dark, but the birds were singing. Um, you smell like maple syrup, Tangie. Good enough to eat."

"You can eat my waffles and have some strawberries and cream…and coffee of course. Are you sure you are back to normal? Whatever normal is."

"Couldn't be better. Norm is my middle name. Good morning, Aunt Hattie." Walter strolls over to his aunt, places a kiss on her cheek and sits down next her.

Walter puts two Belgium waffles on his plate, butters them and douses them with Vermont maple syrup. "What happened to Steve? He didn't say much after plowing into me."

"He's still waking up. He doesn't have your strong recuperative powers."

"Gosh, he's getting soft. He used to drink me under the table."

With a hint of a smile, Aunt Hattie whispers, "I take it you all had a good time at Maxwell's."

I answer for all of us. "Yes. Very informative, that is, if we ever get the complete information from these two night owls."

"Whoo are you calling a night owl?" Steve strolls back into the kitchen with an empty cup. He shows it to me and I fill it for him.

"Thanks, Tangie."

"You're welcome. I hope you two birds are prepared to do some unveiling of the tantalizing tidbits you unearthed last night."

Walter crunches on a slice of bacon and groans. "After breakfast. I promise. Remember our rule: No shoptalk while eating your delicious breakfast. Afterwards, I'm sure Steve will reveal all his secrets written in that little black book."

"Yes indeed. I promise." Steve begins stuffing food into his mouth like he just crossed the desert and hadn't eaten in days. "Right after my waffles and my third cup of coffee."

Aunt Hattie smiles, clasps her hands and shakes them like a prize-fighter's coach. "Oh good. I love a juicy story."

Walter returns her smile. "These aren't stories, Aunt Hattie. They're facts, ma'am. Nothing but the facts."

I grin. "Walter, you're beginning to sound like Joe Friday."

"Well, it is *TGIF*, Tangie."

My grin turns to a groan. "Just eat, Walter. Have some bacon." I pass the plate of perfectly fried, lean thick bacon to him and then to Steve. "You, too, Fearless Fosdick."

"Yum," Walter smiles at me. "Who taught you to cook?"

"First, my mom. She taught me take-out. My grandmother taught me Hungarian. Bryan taught me to barbecue, but you instructed me on the art of gourmet cooking. Now finish your waffles so you can tell me the rest your tale. All you told me last night was that Eveline and her *gigolo*—also named *Steve*—meet together every Wednesday at the tavern, until recently. Then they didn't meet again until Thursday, which was last night."

"Eveline and *Steve*, huh. I told you that?"

"You did. Last night when we got home."

Our Steve stops eating for a moment. "Hey, Walter, that's a very important detail."

"Funny, Steve. I don't remember. I do, however, remember putting bills in Suzy's bosom." Walter chomps on two more strips of bacon and starts forking the strawberries I place on his plate.

Aunt Hattie has her mouth open like a fish not ready to take the bait, as if she wants to say something, but then changes her mind. Probably thinking silence works best sometimes. I know that feeling. I just don't practice it.

I poke Walter. "You would remember that detail. Do you recall anything else?"

"Well, I remember that the barmaid, Suzy, informed me that Eveline and *Steve* always acted lovey-dovey until last night. That night their mood changed. She told me they were always hot and heavy, couldn't keep their hands off each other before that."

Our Steve rises from the table, having ravenously consumed three waffles and five slices of bacon. He picks up the plates as we finish them and insists on cleaning up all the dishes, except for the coffee cups, which I top off with a third round of freshly brewed coffee. This last pot I made from Camano Island Roasters, which I always stash in my suitcase for emergencies. Even Steve is crazy about the stuff. Our Steve starts the dishwasher, like a pro. Seems our Suzy has him trained. Suzy hates housework, but loves cleanliness.

Steve returns to the kitchen nook, reaches into his pants pocket and takes out his little black book. He sips his coffee, looks at the waiting faces of Aunt Hattie, Walter and me, and begins deciphering his code. He squints for a moment, and runs his fingers up and down the pages. He looks up and stares at me. "Tangie, I took this down exactly as they spoke. I will read it as the conversation I heard. It will be easier that way. Please, wait until I finish before you ask questions. I don't want to become distracted and mess up my code."

"I can do that. I'll take notes." I get up from my perch and grab a notebook and pen from the desk in the corner of the kitchen. Aunt Hattie is a very organized person, with all the necessary tools nearby.

Our Steve studies his notes for a moment, scratches his head, and begins his narrative of the conversation between Eveline and her Steve.

Eveline says, "I'm glad you could meet me here. I need to clear some things up between us."

" I thought you called me because you couldn't keep your hands off me."

"That was before."

"Before what?"

"You know, the governor."

"Oh, the Gov'ner. I thought you'd be pleased."

"Not that way. That was all talk. I never meant for any of this to happen."

"Oh really? What exactly did you expect to happen?

"Not this. I thought maybe impeachment."

"Impeachment? Are you kiddin'? The guy's reputation is lily white. The guy was too good for this game."

"Oh, so it's all just a game to you?"

"Yeah, isn't it to you? Isn't that why you meet me? Part of the game? And this is the part of the game when you break up with me, isn't it?"

"Yes. I never want to see you again. But don't worry. Your secret is safe with me. I have too much to lose by talking. But I will not be a party to your schemes."

"You already are part of them whether you like it or not. You are in this as deep as I am, and so is your husband."

"Roberto? He knows nothing."

"No? Don't be so sure...and for sure, he will, if you don't keep your mouth shut."

"So what do I do?"

"Nothing. Absolutely nothing. Play the first lady. Party. Be happy."

"I can't. My nerves are shot."

"Too bad. I kind of liked our rendezvous on Wednesdays."

"Today is Thursday," Eveline sulks. "I'm only here because you said it was important for us to meet. God knows I'm busy. Tomorrow is the reception."

"So you go and act like nothing has happened. You're a good actress. You can pull it off."

Eveline takes a swig of her drink and then polishes off the remaining liquor. She motions the barmaid for another and her eyes start to tear.

"Oh come on, Eveline," the gigolo speaks, "We've had a good ride. Good times. I don't kiss and tell. Your affair is safe with me, but it is time for payback. I will be in touch for that."

"Payback? What do you mean payback? I never wanted any of this to happen. I am sorry I hooked up with you in the first place. You are a creep with a capital 'C'. What was I thinking?"

"You weren't thinking. I did all the thinking and I'm tired of it, and you. So if this is goodbye, I would suggest you don't contact me anymore for personal services. But, you do owe me, big time, and I expect to collect. Starting now."

Eveline stares at her gigolo and starts to open her mouth to protest but the gigolo puts his hand over her mouth and says, "This time, you pay for the drinks," and storms out of the joint.

Steve puts down his book and sighs. "Well, that's about the gist of it. I think you know the rest of the story. That's all I wrote down."

I nod at our Steve, stare into his penetrating chocolate eyes, and recognize what girls admire about him—his intensity, his focus. It's a turn on, even more than his good looks. "Wow! I'm impressed. What great notes. Perfect recall."

Walter watches as I stare at our Steve and catches my admiration for his good buddy on his radar. I can sense a sudden rush of jealousy rising up in him as an undercurrent swirling in the sea. Hard to spot, but you know it's there. He does a good job of covering it up as he stares at his best friend and says, "Thanks good buddy. Yes, I agree, great notes. I see why they keep you on the force in Seattle. That's quite a conversation, but nothing to incriminate anyone, unless you know the background, like we do. We need more proof. I intend to get it at the reception, or afterwards...but soon."

Feeling a deepening cloud of depression forming around me, I frown, half knowing the answer to my question. "How are you going to do that?"

"When we are at the reception, I'm going to track Graham down, corner him and find a way to shake him down. He's the link between Eveline and that other Steve guy. I'm sure."

"Have you ever heard of them hanging out together?" Our Steve asks.

Walter shakes his head. "No, but as we all know Graham has some Steve guy as a friend. And, although Graham tries to hide it, he's got a New York accent."

Walter looks at me as I nod back at him. He continues, "Just like Eveline's Steve. There's a connection. When we find that link, everything will fall into place."

I study my honey, not knowing whether to be pleased with his deductions or frightened because of the imminent danger this looming situation presents to us. "You're positive about this, aren't you, Walter?"

"Yes, I'm sure. We'll finally have some proof to bring to the cops and the Feds."

Steve gets up and stretches his arms. "So you want to put our plan into motion tonight?"

Walter nods at Steve. "Yes. I'll corner Graham. Then make plans to meet up with him on a social basis, after the reception. I'll grill him, man to man, just as you and I planned."

I slouch in my seat. "Where does this leave me?"

"Tangie, you already know what Graham is capable of doing. I want you to stay in the background. Steve will hang out with you and Aunt Hattie and keep you out of harm's way. You have a knack for getting into trouble. You know that; I know that. We don't want any repeats of last spring."

"What about you? Who will be keeping you out of danger?"

"I'm bigger than Graham. And stronger."

"Yes, you are my love." I put my head on his shoulder and caress his arm. "But he plays dirty. You've got to promise me you'll be careful. No unnecessary chances."

"I plan to come home to you, like I always do."

"You better swear."

"I swear."

Somehow, his words do not bring comfort, but the hug he gives me helps a bit. Aunt Hattie has that nervous look on her face. Her eyes dart back and forth, and her brow wrinkles in a frown. I know that look. I've seen it on my mother's face when she senses something or someone threatening a member of our family.

Steve sits down at the table, with his arms bent and his chin on his grasped hands like the famous statue, *The Thinker*. His thoughts run deep and I cannot read them.

Three stoic individuals—these are the three people I trust with my life. But as much as I try, I cannot shake the fear rising within me, not for myself, but for Walter, Steve and Aunt Hattie.

Chapter Thirty-Six

At the waiting line to get into the Governor's mansion, the security guards frisk everyone for weapons. Good thing Aunt Hattie didn't pack her piece. While we stand around, I look around at all the guests. I don't recognize any of the politicians, as they are all local to the state of Rhode Island. Aunt Hattie does; she points out various senators and representatives to us. Like Walter, Aunt Hattie wears many hats.

When she spots Jenny and Clarissa ahead of us in the line, she calls their names and waves to them. They motion for us to join them. To the annoyance of those ahead of us in line, we do, inching our way up to the front of the reception waiting line. In my present mood, I don't feel any guilt doing so. Aunt Hattie begins chatting immediately with Jenny and Clarissa, telling them what we have been doing, but leaves out all the detective stuff. She knows just the right things to say. She introduces the sisters to Steve. He bows and shakes their hands like he hangs around politicians and their family members all the time. For all I know, he does. Steve, like Walter, is somewhat of a private person. Come to think of it, I can see Steve running for District Attorney some day. He just needs to finish his law degree. Walter told me he majored in pre-law at Brown and then, after graduation went directly into police work, while attending night classes at the U-Dub. Not many Brown graduates in police work. If Suzy gets wind of Steve's talents, I'm sure she'll put pressure on him to climb the ladder. Suzy loves prestige, and power intoxicates her.

As we approach the new governor, Roberto Carboni, and his first lady, Eveline, my palms start sweating and my heart begins palpitating at a high rate. Walter takes my hands and rubs them with his. He senses my hesitation.

"Just act natural," he whispers. "Like you are meeting them for the first time." He squeezes my hand, kisses my cheek and continues, "Remember, you never met the governor and try to forget anything you know about his wife."

I look into Walter's eyes and feel an overwhelming urge to bolt out of the posh reception. Too late—Before I can take two steps backward, I feel a warm, strong hand embracing mine. Robert Carboni stands before me, stares into my eyes, and welcomes me into the governor's mansion with his words and his overly firm handshake. "Thank you for coming. Any friend of Peter Van Beek's is a friend of mine. And, my dear, your beauty graces the governor's mansion." He studies Walter for a moment then looks back at me, asking, "Who is this chap?"

"Thank you, Governor Carboni." I regain my calm, rub my hand on my dress, trying to get some feeling back into it, and straighten the sides of my purple haze evening gown. I stare into Roberto Carboni's piercing hazel eyes, sensing he takes everything in, that he doesn't miss much. I notice his perfectly sculptured teeth as he smiles down at me. At six-foot-four, he towers over most of the people at the reception. His salt and pepper hair give him a distinguished air and his confident manner seems unforced and relaxed. When I briefly held onto his hand, I sensed his aura of power and decisiveness. He is someone who likes to get the job done and there is something else that I can't quite make out. His eyes are distracting. They feast on me as if I could be dessert. What is it about politicians? Every one I've met so far makes me feel uncomfortable. I decide to stifle that feeling for the time being. "You are very gracious, Governor. This is my husband, Walter, Walter Cunningham."

Roberto Carboni takes Walter's hand. I witness the firm grasp each of them displays upon contact—two confident men, sizing each other up. Walter will not be intimidated by Roberto's death grip.

"Oh yes, Walter." Roberto releases his grasp on Walter and displays his large toothy grin. "I recognize you. You are Hattie's nephew. I've heard of you—all good—including Brown graduate, sailor and musician. You went off to Seattle as I recall."

"Yes, Governor. I live there with my beautiful wife." Walter takes my hand and kisses it, undoing the damage Roberto did with his death grip on me. "We are visiting Aunt Hattie in Newport; we extended our visit for a few days to be her escorts to Peter Van Beek's funeral. It's been a great loss for her."

"I am sure your Aunt Hattie appreciates your being here with her. She and Peter were great friends. It's kind of you to do so. Thank you. Are you by any chance working at Microsoft?"

"No sir. Not my career choice. I stick to music." Walter grabs Steve by the arm and introduces him to the governor. "Governor, this is my friend, Steve. He's also from Seattle and also a Brown graduate. He's visiting with us, and tonight *he's* Aunt Hattie's escort."

Governor Carboni extends his hand to our Steve. "Nice to meet you, Steve. What line of work are you in?"

Steve knows that lying to this governor could cause problems but he answers with a straight face, "Oh, I work in securities."

"Ah, a money man. Hard work in these economic times."

"Well, so far it still pays the bills."

Roberto Carboni turns and places his hand on his wife's arm. "Dear, let me introduce you to a few of Peter Van Beek's friends. This is Walter Cunningham and his wife. I sorry dear, I didn't get your name."

"You can call me Tangie."

"Now isn't that cute," Eveline replies and smiles a fake acknowledgement of my presence. Then she seems to study me a little closer. "You look awfully familiar. Tell me, have we met before?"

"Walter and I attended Peter Van Beek's funeral and reception. Maybe you saw me there." My heart starts ticking in overdrive.

"Must be that. Anyway, welcome."

I can feel her intense stare sizing me up like I am bait for her hook.

Walter intervenes, saving me from Eveline's scrutiny. "This is Steve, a friend of ours."

Eveline brightens considerably when she feasts her eyes on "Steve the Hunk". She takes his hand, leans into him and whispers in his ear, loud enough for me to hear. "You are some piece of work, mister." She smiles, steps back and releases her grip on him. "Seems like I've seen you before, too."

"Oh, I get around." Steve smiles a dazzling smile, showing his dimples, fabulous teeth and his steamy brown eyes, which ooze his strong sex appeal. I sometimes call him Taurus the Bull. Steve, when he wants to be, can be irresistible to females. He knows how to turn on the charm. And Eveline, forever a cat on the prowl, warms up to his animal magnetism.

"Roberto, I think we should place Aunt Hattie and her group at our table. They are delightful."

I wonder if she would feel this way if she had a clue about our knowledge of her clandestine activities and her love interests. I don't really want to sit at her table. In fact, I don't want to be here at all. But I do want to see this whole mess out to the finish line; so here we are and an opportunity has fallen into our laps. I think perhaps we should take it.

Walter seals the deal. "Thank you, that's super. If it's no trouble, we'll have to include Peter's sisters, Jenny and Clarissa. They are like family to Aunt Hattie."

"Consider it done," Roberto Carboni answers in his commanding tone. "It will be a family affair. We'll just move the senators to an adjoining table with Graham as their host."

"Oh thank you, Governor." I smile, grateful that Graham will be somewhere else. "Walter, we should move along and let the others greet the new governor and his first lady."

"Yes, Angelina, my sweet." He turns to the governor. "We'll see you again after cocktails, Governor Carboni."

"My pleasure, my boy. And please, call me Roberto."

Walter nods. "*Roberto*, it is." He shakes the governor's hand once more, but not as aggressively as before. The governor also seems to have lightened his grip.

I smile my ingénue smile. I can be cute when it counts. Perhaps dodging Eveline's conversation will be less difficult than enduring Graham's ogling.

Our little ensemble leaves the reception line and strolls into the ballroom where small tables are arranged in little groupings hugging the windows. Walter leads us. He and Steve assist Aunt Hattie and the Van Beek sisters to chairs. Glowing votive candles and fresh flowers adorn the tables. The overpowering scent of lilies rekindles my memory of Peter Van Beek's funeral. Our party occupies two of the tables.

Walter helps me to my seat, kisses my cheek and whispers in my ear, "I have a not-so-good feeling about the governor. Watch what you say, Angelina."

I look in his eyes and see that fear, that fear that is not going away. I nod. "I understand, Walter. Love you too."

At the same time that Steve informs us he will step over to the bar and get some drinks, a waiter, dressed in tails and white gloves, comes by and offers us champagne.

"Thank you, my man." Walter smiles at the waiter. "You are an answer to our prayers."

The waiter, standing stiff as a matchstick, sets a few glasses of bubbly in front of the ladies and places a glass of champagne in Walter's hand and one in Steve's. Then he moves on to another group. Our escorts stand near us like sentinels. I admire how they stand tall, propped against the fresco wall next to a humongous potted plant with an overgrown fern sticking out. Walter and Steve, dressed to the nines in their matching tuxedoes, look like an ad for *Esquire Magazine*. I sigh. Aunt Hattie and I should be commended for our good taste. Another waiter appears and places another glass of bubbly in front of me. I lift my glass to clink Aunt Hattie's, take a sip of the wonderful champagne and smile. Maybe this evening won't be a total disaster.

Walter leans down behind me and whispers, "I'm going to cruise around for awhile, my sweet. I'll be on the prowl for Graham. I can't seem to locate him in the crowd."

I nod. "If and when you find him, don't point me out to him. I don't care if I ever see the creep again."

Walter nods and walks slowly away. As if on cue, Steve follows, weaving his way around the tables and sipping his champagne, as his eyes feast on young ladies waltzing about the room during the cocktail hour. I notice how their eyes inevitably focus on him. Girls seem to sense available virile men. Walter is every bit of a hunk as Steve, but he might as well be wearing a sign saying: "I'm taken." He has that contented cat appearance, as if he just consumed a feast and wants no more. Steve, even though he has "Suzy in Seattle", emits his radar to women that says: "I'm available." If he ever does get married, his wife will have her hands full. Women do all sorts of things to get him to notice them. Poor Suzy. She attracts men in the exact way. Now she is serious about a man who has that same effect on women. Perhaps our Steve and our Suzy happen to be a good match after all. Each understands that whole business of attract-ability. Steve takes these things in stride. Walter gets jealous. I too, on occasion, turn into that green-eyed monster.

I started tapping my evening purse on the table. Nerves, I guess. Aunt Hattie looks at me like I have a tick. I smile at her and stop tapping. The Van Beek sisters sip their champagne and smile at me. I raise my glass and smile, then chug the entire glass of champagne and wave to a waiter for a refill.

Clarissa grins and starts chatting. "Tangie, it is so good to see you and Walter again. Remember, you still owe us a visit. We are having our annual brunch on Sunday in our conservatory. I do hope you could join us."

Jenny nods and echoes her sister sentiments. "We are having just a few friends, nothing fancy. We like to celebrate the beginning of fall with a brunch. Makes saying goodbye to summer a little easier."

"How sweet. That sounds delightful, Jenny, Clarissa. I think we can make it. I'll check with Walter."

Jenny smiles. "You do that, dear. Just let us know."

"Yes," Clarissa chimes in. "We'd like to get to know the two of you better."

Aunt Hattie sends me a look that reads: "One does not stand up these ladies." Then she vocalizes, "Yes, Tangie, the sisters stir up such a wonderful brunch every fall. Not to be missed. It can be your last hurrah before you return home."

I smile broadly and nod. We continue to chat amicably, discussing the weather, the leaves that are beginning to change colors and the delicious *hors d'ouerves* the waiters keep bringing us. I begin to focus on the crowd that flows into the ballroom, noting singles and couples, but no children. No doubt, strictly a grown-up affair. Maybe the governor will throw a luncheon for families later on with children as invited guests. Maybe he'll have a Halloween party. I can imagine the costume Eveline would wear.

Without intending to, I spot Graham before Walter does. From my seat at the table, I notice him standing on a raised area in the hallway, leaning against a small sign that reads: "Private Restrooms, This Way."

Walter waltzes back to my side and I nudge him. He leans down as I tug on his arm and listens intently to me as I whisper, "Over there, up the stairs by the doorway in the hall. Graham. "

Walter kisses me on the cheek, squeezes my shoulder gently and whispers back, "Gotcha. Thanks, Sweetie."

I watch as my soul mate disappears into the crowd and resurfaces by the stairs in front of Graham. He clinks glasses with him and I can see him talking energetically with Mr. Creep. Walter is so good at acting cool and playing nonchalant. He can get anyone to do anything, especially if he wants something bad enough. I know he wants this meeting with Graham as much as I want this whole thing to be over.

I notice Walter taking a pen out of his side pocket, and a business card from his back pocket. He leans against the wall and starts to write, just as my body begins to twitch. Sitting and making small talk with the sisters and Aunt Hattie is not something I can do right now. I excuse myself, pick up my purse and trot over to the vicinity of the little girls' room that happens to be near the spot Walter and Graham are conversing.

I eye Walter as I put my hand on the door and pull the handle.

"Don't be long, Tangie," Walter murmurs. "Dinner is starting in five minutes. We don't want to keep the governor waiting."

"Now Walter, you know it takes me longer than that to comb my hair." I smile and close the door.

I imagine Graham doing his heavy panting thing, as he had his eyes on my boobs the whole time I paused in the doorway. I look down at my chest, and then in the mirror. "Hum, seems I am busting out of this dress," I say to no one in particular. I pull my dress up at the top and dust my high-heeled purple sling-backs with a tissue. Seems during my entrance in here, I collided with a puddle, some spilled champagne or something worse. I shudder to think about that "something else" and make my way into one of the three empty stalls. I look up at the window above the first stall and noticed it is ajar. Great. No way I am going to use the ladies room with some voyeur staring at me. I climb up on the toilet seat, reach the window and close it just as I hear the door slam, and then slam again. I think to myself, "I hope Graham is not charging in here, with Walter following him." I freeze for a moment and decide to listen to the conversation before I make my whereabouts known.

"Now you've gone and done it, Eveline."

"Oh Roberto, give me a break. You are such a fool."

Uh, oh. The governor and his wife are in here, chatting and me in the stall. How do I get out gracefully? I hold my breath.

"Roberto, why are you following me? This is the ladies room."

"I have a guy posted outside. No one is coming in until we have this settled."

"Have what settled?"

"You and that fellow. I had you followed."

"What fellow?"

"That guy from Long Island. The one you meet every Wednesday, and now it seems, on Thursdays."

Oh my God, The governor's men have been to Maxwell's and spying, like us. Rats! I hope *we* weren't recognized.

"What do you know about him?" Eveline pleads.

"Just that you've been seeing him. You know that is not a smart thing to do."

"Yes, I agree. But Ste...He is...was a distraction. He's history."

"And what about you and your drinking? You said you were giving that up too."

"Oh, Roberto, when are you going to give up trying to reform me? I try. God knows I try. It doesn't work."

"You don't try hard enough. You are getting to be a liability. Do you want me to resign at the end of the term? Seems I have no choice. You need someone to take care of you. You are liable to..."

"Liable to do what?"

"Hurt yourself, or someone."

Listen, Roberto. You can't quit. He's crazy..."

"Who's crazy?"

"Him. *Steve.* Roberto, you can't quit. He is liable to..."

"Eveline, please. Let me help you. I'll pay to send you to the Betty Ford Center. Just say the word and I will resign. I'll stay near you."

"Roberto, you just don't understand. You can't resign. You have to stay on as governor."

"Why? I don't know if I am fond of the job. My family's always been about politics. I don't know if I enjoy being governor. My father pressured me to get into public service, but he's gone. I can do what I want now. And I want to take care of you."

"Oh Roberto, can't you see, I'm not worth it. I can't help what I do. You are too good for me."

"Eveline, don't cry. It will be all right. Look, you don't have to go out there now. I can have Graham drive you home. Things will be better tomorrow. You'll see, no more pressure, no more politics."

"But you don't know. You don't know what I know. This is a dangerous business, an ugly business."

"Then we will get out of it together. I love you, Eveline."

"I know, Roberto. I wish I could love you more. I don't deserve you."

"Eveline, please don't say anymore in your condition. I'll have Graham drive you to our private residence. This is not the place for you right now."

"I hate that creep."

"So do I, but he's good for a few things. Get some sleep. I'll tell everyone you have a migraine."

"You are too good for me, Roberto."

"I know. For now, just go with Graham."

"All right. Make my apologies."

"I will. I love you. And you will love me when all this is over. "

"What will be over?"

"You'll see."

I hear the door shut, no slamming this time. I hear Eveline sobbing, then water rushing out of the faucet and someone turning off the water. The sound of towels being ripped out of the holder unnerves me. A door opens up and I hear Graham's voice, soothing and tender, but in my mind, evil.

"Eveline, the boss wants me to take you home."

"Yes, the boss. Some boss. More like a quitter."

"Oh, you underestimate him. He's more ambitious than you give him credit."

"Yes, I give him credit for the way I feel, lousy."

"Let me take you home."

"Why not? Let's go."

I hear the door shut but wait for a minute or two before I climb down from my perch.

I start mulling over what just happened. Graham saw me come in here. I wonder if he knows I am still here. Probably does, but what do I care? He's a creep. Besides, he's taking Eveline home. I will be rid of the two of them. The evening may turn out all right after all.

Chapter Thirty-Seven

After using the little girls' room for what it is intended, I stop by the self-serve bar and pick up another glass of champagne. I tiptoe into the darkened dining room, now lit only with candles and wait for my eyes to adjust. I look around the dim-lit room and search for my honey and the rest of my party. Silly me. I must be losing it. All I really need to do is find the massive head table, which is conveniently at the front of the room near a picture window that looks out into the garden. The garden is lit up with twinkling lights, like a scene from *A Midsummer Night's Dream*, a fairy world. Should be easy to find. I notice Walter standing up, waving to me and pointing to my seat. I hold my breath, sucking in my stomach to keep my skin-tight dress smooth, and saunter over to the table, pretending I walk around like this everyday.

I sit down, lean over to Walter and whisper, "Please, do not mention to anyone where I've been. I'll tell you why later."

Walter nods and pours me another glass of champagne. He pulls me close and kisses me gently, but with a sudden urgency he cannot hide. "I love you, Angelina."

"I love you too, Walter." I kiss him back. "Let's get out of here."

"No can do. We have to eat, dance, and make nice with the politicians. Then we can go home and…"

"Promise?"

"Have I ever been known to break a promise?"

"On occasion, but only when you can't help it."

"Yes, you're right, my love." Walter brushes my lips with his. "Remember that. And you know, Angelina, I have a feeling that in a few days all this will be over."

"Just a feeling?"

Walter nods and embraces me, practically squeezing out all my breath. "Anyone hurt?" I whisper. Tears start streaming down my face. I can hardly breathe and my fear begins to climb to panic level.

"Don't have a feeling on that one, love."

"Now where is a psychic when you need one?" Making an attempt to be funny doesn't work. My sense of humor deserts me. I still feel the sadness growing inside me; I can't shake that sinking feeling.

Walter kisses my eyelids. "I'm looking at her, right now and I am in love."

"Hey you two lovebirds," Roberto Carboni exclaims from the head of the table, "I heard you recently came back from your honeymoon. Seems like you are still on it."

"Yes sir, Governor. Sorry." Walter straightens his tie and then grins. "You know, the lady just can't keep her hands off me."

"I can see that. You are one lucky man."

"I know."

I groan inside, thinking of the governor and his distasteful wife. He may think he understands her, but she is poison in a pretty package. I'm sure he knows what she is, deep down. But then again, for all I know, he's no prize either.

As if on cue, Roberto Carboni rises from his seat. "Friends, I have an announcement. As you may have noticed, my wife is absent from the table. She is feeling ill and won't be joining us."

"That is a pity." I shake my head, showing fake concern. "So sorry to hear that."

Carboni frowns. "Seems she's has another one of her migraines."

I perceive a fake note of sympathy and I begin to think he isn't such a good actor. Probably why he isn't such a good politician.

"They can be deadly," Aunt Hattie joins in.

"What could be deadly?" My mind drifts from one unrelated topic to another.

"Migraines." Aunt Hattie clarifies her statement.

"How do you handle them?" Roberto asks Aunt Hattie.

"I gave up the man I loved. Poof! They went away."

"Well, that's an unusual ending to a love story," Roberto answers, tugging at his collar, looking uncomfortable.

"Yes, but I never had another one once I decided marrying him was not for me."

Clarissa clears her throat, fingers the expensive pearls around her neck, and as if thinking of something important, blurts out, "Roberto."

"Yes, Clarissa?"

"I just want to tell you I am glad you are doing so well with this transition into the governor's office. I know it is not an easy job. Peter was good at it, but it was never easy for him."

"Funny," Roberto purrs and turns on his charm. "He seemed so natural at it. I thought he and this job were suited for one another."

"Yes, but he often confided in me how stressful it was and he hated that the job took time away from his family. He said that was the worst part of being a public servant. My brother was a hard worker, but he paid a price."

"You are so right, Clarissa," Jenny interjects. "Our brother missed a lot of his children's activities when they were growing up. His beloved wife, Mercedes, Clarissa and I tried to fill in when he was at political events, but I know it bothered him to be away from home so often. If it weren't for his sailing, he'd be…"

Alive, I think. *He died on his sailboat.*

Roberto nods. "Well, my only comfort in losing him is that he is in a better place, a place we can all hope to go to sometime."

"But not too soon," I add, as Walter squeezes my hand.

"You are so right, my charming Tangie." Roberto stands up and winks at me. "I propose a toast, to life, and to living it to the fullest." The governor clinks my glass and peers at me with a leering stare. My discomfort level switches to high gear.

Maybe there's a reason Eveline sleeps around. A look of alarm creeps over my face, no matter how much I try to hide it behind a smile. Walter notices. He squeezes my hand, kisses it, then whispers in my ear, "I'm with you, my love. Please, don't let your guard down on anything. But try not to worry too much about Evaline or the governor."

"Amen to that." I hear Steve responding to the governor's toast. I think he picks up on the governor's penchant for being a ladies' man. Steve, as a ladies' man himself, senses guys on the prowl. Our Steve clicks his glass to mine, then Walter's glass, that by now is empty. Seems Walter chugged his after the governor's beady eyes feasted on my neckline.

The three of us click glasses with Aunt Hattie, Clarissa and Jenny, who quietly sip their champagne. Walter picks up a bottle and refills his glass.

Roberto raises his glass once more and smiles at those gathered around his table. "I hope you all have a marvelous evening."

After that opening exchange, things loosen up a bit, and the reception transforms itself into a festive party. The band begins playing quiet jazz during the first hour then switches to pop music as the evening passes into night. The lead vocalist's voice soars in perfect pitch and the band plays on, without a break. The governor roars rakishly when Steve and Walter share some politically incorrect jokes with him. Seems to me, Eveline's absence doesn't bother him in the slightest. The waiters, dressed in tuxedos themselves, serve a delicious seven-course meal, highlighted by filet mignon and lobster and ending with an assortment of decadent desserts. We devour everything put before us, as if it is our last supper, and I choose raspberry chocolate cheesecake for my closing number. Eating first class always excites my palate. I have no shame. If I did this on a regular basis, I'd probably weigh 200 pounds. I have no resistance. Aunt Hattie, Jenny and Clarissa chat among themselves and chew their food politely as if they are accustomed to dining like queens. They don't feel the need to eat everything in sight. Walter, Steve and I restaurant hop a lot, and enjoy the good life on occasion, but we don't live in the lap of luxury. This lifestyle takes getting used to, as does listening to a full-piece band playing nonstop while dining.

Steve gets up from his seat. "Let's dance." He pulls out my chair, grabs my hand and leads me on to the dance floor. Before we disappear into the crowd, he shouts as an after thought, "You don't mind, Walter, good buddy?"

"Not at all, Steve," Walter laughs. "After all, you are my best man."

On the dance floor, only a handful of people are shaking to the beat of the *bossa nova*. Steve and I struggle somewhat, making up dance steps as we go along. We laugh and carry on until the governor approaches and taps Steve on the shoulder. Roberto takes my hand as the band switches to a slow dance.

"You don't mind if I cut in, young man?"

"Certainly not, Governor." Steve releases my hand to Roberto's. "But don't keep her long. Her husband's in line over there." Steve points to Walter leaning against one of the speakers by the band, studying the three of us.

The governor smiles and squeezes my hand. "She'll wear me out before too long." He twirls me around the dance floor in perfect step to the music. Seems the governor's been to Arthur Murray's.

I feel like a trading card after this exchange, but I persevere and the two of us continue moving in sync to the music. The governor continues to have a firm grasp on my hand and waist. Seems Governor Roberto Carboni excels at the waltz and he can talk and dance at the same time.

He looks in my eyes and becomes the Quiz Master. "So, Tangie, how do you like our state?"

I smile, hiding my angst. "It's reminds me of home, governor. Water everywhere, landscape in full of color and it's inviting. Your homes display a certain history and elegance not visible in the Pacific Northwest. We are a bit more rustic, but then again we do have our *purple mountains majesty*. I miss them."

"Well put, my dear. I've been to your fair city a number of times. Quite hilly, you know, for being near the coast. Reminds me of San Francisco."

"It does get steep around downtown Seattle. When were you there, Roberto?"

"I went to a conference in Seattle a couple of years ago. Evelina and I took a road trip across the country back then. We saw the *Wild West* on the way. Not so wild anymore."

"Oh, I think it can get wild just about anywhere, if the wrong people start running things. Fortunately, today people don't accept bad behavior."

"You are so right, my dear, and very insightful."

He spins me around as the band stops playing the waltz, but he keeps his grip on me. He takes my hand and raises it to his lips.

I sense a warm presence nearby—not the governor.

"Tangie, how about if you give your husband a dance, before the night is over?" Walter asks, through clenched teeth. He forces a smile and pats the governor on the shoulder, saving me from any more conversation with Rhode Island's Head of State.

"Forgive me, my dear." Roberto Carboni releases my hand and places it in Walter's palm, but not before lifting it to his lips once more. Suddenly I feel the same aversion to the governor that I have for Graham; they're two of a kind.

Carboni stares into my eyes, lingers for a moment, then replies, "You young people have a good time. I must attend to the rest of the guests." He smiles his pearly whites, then leaves in somewhat of a huff, off to chat with a senator no doubt.

"Well, that was fun, Walter. Glad you cut in."

"I don't think he likes me. He enjoys you too much. I don't trust him."

"You know, Walter, you are on to something. I think he enjoys having his wife stuffed away so he can party solo."

"Listen," Walter whispers in my ear as he kisses it. "They are playing our song."

I listen while the band switches to a familiar oldie from our hot and heavy courtship. The lead singer croons, "My love is your love...don't need anyone but you..."

We dance until the music stops, keeping our feet moving throughout the song and the three that follow. I lean my head on Walter's chest and feel a sense of foreboding in the pit of my stomach. I close my eyes and whisper, "Don't leave me, Walter."

"I'm not going to do that. Not ever. But I do have to do something before we go home tonight."

"Walter, what is more important than our dancing together?

"Nothing is more important than dancing with you," he murmurs as he pulls me closer to him and kisses me on my neck.

I feel chills going up and down my spine, as the old tune echoes, "Baby, I'm yours, forever..."

"Then why are you leaving me? Why are you going off somewhere?" I sigh, having a hard time keeping my voice soft and inaudible to others. My longing for him increases tri-fold after our dancing cheek to cheek. "What is more important right now than this?" I lean up and kiss him hard on the mouth.

Walter pulls me over to a dark corner of the room and kisses me back, holding me in a bear hug, squeezing the wind out of me. After this moment of bliss, he releases me. "I have to meet Graham."

"Oh, come on, Walter. He isn't even here. I haven't seen him all night."

"He's over by the doorway. Look." He pulls me out of the darkness and urges me to focus on the dim light flooding the room. I squint and sure enough Graham appears. He looks a little disheveled with his hair all messed up, rather than plastered down like in its usual fashion, and his red bow tie is askew. Looks like another woman jilted him. Smart cookie. Got out while she could. I watch as Graham finishes chatting with the governor. Carboni takes Graham's hand and shakes it, probably thanking Graham for disposing of his wife, after her "headache". The governor turns and walks out abruptly. Graham leans against the wall eyeing the small group of people on the dance floor and catches me staring at him. He smiles and blows a kiss. I groan and turn to Walter.

"Look, Walter, I just can't deal with Graham right now."

My heart starts to beat in double time. Graham's slimy smile reinforces the anger that begins to develop in the back of my throat and I can hardly breath. Walter takes my hands in his, puts them up to his lips and kisses my palms.

"Please, Tangie, don't worry so much."

"Walter," I whisper. "Are you crazy? You can't meet him tonight. I have a really bad feeling about all this. Things have changed. I just don't know how, but something's very wrong. Besides, don't you remember what happened to Peter Van Beek?"

"Tangie, please, take a deep breath. Calm down. Graham and Peter Van Beek are two different stories with different endings, different players. Listen, my Sweet. I'm certain Graham knows something that will complete our puzzle and I think tonight he is willing to share that puzzle piece. Call it a hunch on my part. I've got to snatch the opportunity. I've got a feeling he's mad at someone and he wants to chat with me about it tonight, on his sailboat.

"Walter, can't you put this off until tomorrow? When it's daylight? Barry Cardoso will be here then. He, our Steve and I could follow you. I have a strange feeling about you meeting Graham all alone tonight, on the water. It's dark, cold. No one will see you or hear you. To me, it's wrong, all wrong. Graham is sinister. I don't trust him. You know that. Look what he tried to do to me in broad daylight."

"Tangie, please. Stay focused. Remember why we came here, and remember who got us into all of this."

"Oh, great! So now you are laying guilt on me, as well as fear. You are no help at all."

Sobs begin pouring out of my throat like gurgles in a rushing stream.

"Angelina, please..." Walter takes me back in his arms and whispers softly in my ear. "Please, try to understand. I'm telling you now, why I'm doing this...I want to help you."

"So now, Walter, my love, I am asking you *not* to do this. For my sake, do not meet Graham."

"Tangie, I promise, I won't be gone long. We'll sail close to the shore and talk, man to man."

"Oh, Walter, you aren't hearing what I am saying. Graham is not a man. He's a worm."

"So I have nothing to fear from worms."

"Did you ever read *Dune*, that book about worms? Worms are not small creatures in that book. They devour anyone in their path, including innocent bystanders."

"No, but I saw the movie. Very strange flick, but that was fiction, science fiction at that."

I cling to my love, refusing to let him go. "Please, Walter, all of my signals are on high alert. This is not a good thing. Stay away from Graham."

"I'll be all right." Walter asserts. He pries my fingers and hands from around his neck one by one. My arms continue to grasp him like those of a giant squid. Tears form in my eyes, blinding me as they mingle with my mascara. Through my tears I can see the beginning of a vision: Walter, in the water, drowning, searching for a place to escape. Walter, in trouble, and then the vision disappears as I loosen my grasp on him.

Walter shakes himself free and grabs both my hands in his, like a policeman getting ready to make an arrest. Sometimes he can be the most irritating guy on the planet. He speaks to me in what I perceive as a condescending tone, like a parent would talk to a child. I am convinced he does this to infuriate me. His plan works. He pisses me off, big time.

"Steve will take you and Aunt Hattie home. Trust me, Angelina. Remember, we planned to do this. I'm just acting on our plan. I'll meet you at the house. Don't wait up. Get some rest."

"Like that's gonna happen." I spit out the words as my passion turns to full blown anger. Walter, you are forgetting who I am and what I can see. You have to believe me. I don't want to lose you, ever, and you don't understand."

Walter caresses both my hands and kisses them. "Angelina, you are wrong. I do understand, and I love you. Please, trust me. I have to do this, even if I don't want to."

My love, my only love, takes me in his arms, embraces me and kisses me hard on the lips. The band resumes playing a simple love song, slow, soft, melodious. I feel my anger melting and sadness and fear commanding their place in my heart.

Walter releases me and walks away, leaving me on the dance floor alone. Tears form in my eyes and my vision blurs. I cannot see my beloved. His body begins to fade from my sight as he approaches the door and blends in with the shadows. But I can make out Graham following close behind him. Graham, looking like a troll, Graham, the cretin, patting my Walter on the back and laughing. I will never forget that laugh, high-pitched, out of control, crazy. And in my mind, I see Walter, my love, sinking beneath the water, with his hand outstretched, calling my name, "Help me, Tangie. Help me…"

I feel a hand grasp mine and I jump about a foot in the air before I see Steve—our Steve, Steve the Cop, our true and trusted friend. He leads me away from the dance floor and presents me with a handkerchief from his jacket pocket. As we get back to our table, I take the handkerchief with gratitude, and dab my eyes. So what if I have mascara streaming down my cheeks and I look like a forlorn raccoon. I blow my nose and try to hold back a sob. Steve pulls out a chair for me and I collapse into it, shaking the table as I do so. I try not to look at my dinner companions staring at me. I want to put my head down on the table and cry my eyes out. Not to do so takes all my inner strength. Steve sits down next to me, puts his arm around my shoulder and whispers, "Walter will be okay, Tangie. He's smart."

"Please, Steve, you know that doesn't count when everything is going wrong. And this is wrong. I can feel it. I can see it, even if I don't have anything tangible to tell you. I don't know what to do."

I can sense another person standing above me. Please, not the governor again. I close my eyes, willing him to go away.

"You two have a lover's spat?" Roberto Carboni voice booms. I can visualize a smile on his face. At this moment, I hate the guy. Another worm.

I look at him with a straight face. "No, he just left me to go sailing."

"Oh is that all? Well, you know how we sailors are. When the mood strikes us, we have to get on the water."

"Yes, I guess you're right, Governor."

I decide to pull myself together. I don't want him to catch on to my angst. With a calm in my voice I do not feel in my body, I say softly, "I forget sometimes how much sailing means to Walter."

"Yes, my dear, but now I must leave you. Stay as long as you wish, but I have a meeting at this late hour. I am sure you are in good hands with your buddy, Steve."

"Yes, Governor. Thank you." No appreciation is apparent in my voice. His departure leaves me with a sense of relief. If I never see this governor again, it will be too soon. I watch as he strides across the room and meets three men, also dressed in tuxedos, by the doorway. He starts to walk out of the ballroom with them. These three goons are probably his hired thugs. Seems Graham is not the only creep running around here. As I stare at them, one of the three men turns around and catches my gaze. I recognize him as Eveline's bodyguard, whom I last saw in Fiji. He escorted the governor's wife home and was on the same plane with Walter and me. I wonder if he recognizes me? I feel a chill run up and down my spine, my neck hurts and my palms turn sweaty. I can't take any more complications. I start rubbing my hands up and down my arms to warm up. My body is turning to ice and I sense a fog moving in. Cold, damp chilling cold is blowing in my face and all around me.

Aunt Hattie studies me, then leans over and taps me on the shoulder. "Tangie, are you all right?"

"Not really, Aunt Hattie. I'm worried about Walter." I let out a sob.

"Oh, dear, me." Jenny Van Beek notices my distress and gets my attention with her overly loud voice. "Now Tangie, don't you go worrying about your Walter. When I went to the little girls' room, I heard Buddy tell the governor he was taking your sweet husband sailing with him tonight. Nothing to fear, dear. I am sure Buddy, like our dear sweet Peter, is an excellent sailor."

"Buddy?" My ears pick up the sound of the name and my tears stop. My body switches into high alert.

"You know—*Graham*. Peter always called him *Buddy*. I think he could never remember his given name or perhaps he called him that because Graham became such an asset in his last campaign."

"Buddy, an asset. Yeah, some asset." I nod in stunned silence and sit immobile for a few minutes. I look at Jenny, and then Steve with my eyes wide open. "Buddy is not a nice man."

"Well, my dear, I know Graham can be a bit overbearing at times, but he tries to be pleasant." Jenny went on defending the slime, not having a clue of his true nature. "I didn't realize he affects you this way, Tangie."

I snap out of my frozen state of shock, stand up and zoom into red alert mode. I look at Steve with panic plastered all over my face and motion to the door. "I'm sorry, Jenny, Clarissa, if I've upset you, but we have to go."

"Oh dear," Aunt Hattie exclaims. "Seems I have forgotten something here."

"Aunt Hattie, listen. It's very important. We have to leave, *now*. We have to follow Walter and Graham."

I watch Aunt Hattie's face as she begins to focus and remember my stories from the past week, and my dream about Governor Van Beek and "Buddy". She whispers, "Graham. He's the one, isn't he? He's Buddy. Tangie, we have to follow them before it's too late."

"Yes, Aunt Hattie, we do. I don't know how, but we have to."

"I have a racing sailboat," Aunt Hattie answers.

"You do?"

Yes. And it has a motor for backup."

I can hear her proud voice taking over; her ability to help invigorates her. "Steve, can you sail it for us? We'll be your crew."

"I can do that, Aunt Hattie, but let's try to catch them before they get on the water."

Clarissa looks puzzled. "Whatever is going on, Tangie? Hattie, can we help?"

I cannot help myself. I blurt out, "Buddy knows something about Peter Van Beek's death and Walter is questioning him. I don't think my husband is safe out there in the dark with him. Something might happen this late at night. We have to talk to Graham tonight. Help us, Clarissa. Do you have any idea where Buddy's boat is moored?"

Clarissa stares at me like she has been hit with a stun gun. Add her to the list of persons frozen in fear. Not a place she wishes to be. I can only imagine the thought waves I transmit to her psyche. I feel sorry for my outburst, but I can't help myself.

Clarissa remains dumbfounded. She sits at her seat wringing her hands and mutters like a penitent child, "I'm sorry. I'm so sorry."

Like a contestant on Jeopardy, Jenny leaps into our conversation with the answer. "I know! Peter told me when he took us sailing one afternoon this summer. He pointed Graham's sailboat out to me. It's moored not far from Peter's waterfront home in Newport, not too far from the pleasure cruisers in that marina and not too far from your shop, Hattie. Graham used to brag about his craft to Peter, telling him he inherited it from a famous politician. He calls it *The Reckoning*, I think. Yes, *The Reckoning*, and it's moored at Gray's Landing."

Aunt Hattie nods. "I know the place. It's just down the wharf, not too far from where my boat is moored. Please, Jenny, Clarissa, keep this between us for now. If you don't hear from us the next day, call the police." Aunt Hattie rises. "Come, Tangie, Steve. We don't have any time to waste."

She hugs the Van Beek sisters in haste before we depart. "Thank you, Jenny. Thank you, Clarissa. If all goes well, we'll see you at your brunch on Sunday."

Always the lady, Aunt Hattie makes apologies to the rest of the people at the table for our leaving in such a hasty manner. As we depart, I notice the two sisters with their mouths open, as if catching flies. I surmise they are wondering what in the world we plan to do. I wonder myself, but one thing I know for sure, we have to find Graham's yacht. Walter's life depends upon us doing just that.

Chapter Thirty-Eight

After we exit the governor's mansion and hop into our limo, Aunt Hattie grabs my arm and in a whisper asks for clarification. *"Buddy* is the killer in your dream, isn't he?"

I nod and take her hand. She squeezes mine back to reassure me.

"Walter is smart, Tangie. You know that, don't you?"

I shake my head up and down, unable to speak.

Steve gives our driver directions to Gray's Landing as relayed from Aunt Hattie.

We sit in silence for fifteen minutes. I begin to feel as if I'm going to scream. I break the unnatural quiet. "Can't our chauffeur drive any faster? Steve, why don't you drive?"

"Be patient. I know it's hard. One more bridge and we'll be there. The traffic is light. Heck, if we're lucky, we'll meet up with Graham and Walter before they cast off."

I feel my panic level rising. "That would be too easy. Nothing works easy for us. I just hope we find Walter before Graham..."

Aunt Hattie interrupts my panic attack. "Now, Tangie, quit thinking that way. You've got to be positive."

"I am positive, Aunt Hattie. I am positive that Graham, *Buddy*, is going to hurt Walter. We have to stop him...stop him before..."

I close my eyes and will the images I am seeing out of my mind. I cannot think or act if I continue to see Graham in my subconscious, choking Walter, and Walter trying to come up for air in the ice-cold water. We have to get to them before it is too late. We have to.

The limo comes to a screeching halt. I jump out first. Steve follows me and last, Aunt Hattie. We look around Gray's Landing. No sign of *The Reckoning* or any boat out in open water. Steve takes a flashlight out of his pocket and together we race down the dock toward the moored sailboats. We find an empty slip with just a rowboat tied to the dock. Steve shines his flashlight on the registration number and picks up his cell phone. He makes one call and talks to someone on the other end. I hear him saying, "Uh huh, yeah...Thanks..."

Steve looks at me and I see the concern on his face. "My friend at the DMV was able to get me the info on the skiff. This is where Graham docks his boat."

My body becomes weak and I cannot breathe. I kneel down on the dock. "We missed them. He's gone. Walter's gone."

Aunt Hattie grabs my shoulders and shakes me. "Tangie, we missed them on land, but we can catch them at sea."

Through the fog forming in my soul, I look at her and see her spirit shining and lifting me up. I'm puzzled by her cheerfulness.

"My racer is five minutes north. We can follow them."

"Follow them where?" Steve asks.

Aunt Hattie's positive nature and her determination to sail out to sea renew my hope. Suddenly I feel energized. "Let's get back in the limo and race to Aunt Hattie's boat, Steve. We're wasting time."

We pile back into the limo and tell our chauffeur to drive to the next landing, *pronto*. We hop out again. This time we all race to Aunt Hattie's boat with Aunt Hattie taking the lead. She doesn't have high heels on, like me. But neither does Steve, and she is beating him.

I look back and notice Steve handing the limo driver some bills and hear him telling the man to wait for us. I signal Steve as I am jogging to catch up to Aunt Hattie. "Hurry up!" I yell, as I stumble in my high heels. He takes off down the dock after us and passes me as I pause to take off my shoes so I can move faster.

Aunt Hattie's sailboat is clean and cared for despite the lack of use. It is painted a bright red, with white trim; the sails remain rolled up and covered in white duck. The motor, black and shiny looks freshly polished and ready to go. Probably has a full tank of gas.

"I have a mate who keeps my boat in good repair. You never know when you might want to take an evening sail," Aunt Hattie announces, as if on cue. She climbs aboard, starts the engine and asks Steve to untie the mooring lines. I hop in before he unties the last line. Steve tosses the line on the dock, lets it go and leaps into the boat like a Daddy Long Legs spider.

Steve praises Aunt Hattie. "You got that engine running in no time. Great. We'll need it to work so we can motor out of the harbor."

"Of course. I keep fuel in reserve. You might have to pump it, but it always starts."

I catch Steve saying a few prayers under his breath as he takes the tiller from Aunt Hattie.

I smile and think of Father Don saying, "Prayers are always better than curses."

Aunt Hattie catches my smile and hands me a pair of socks and then some rubber boots. "You might need these, dear. It gets cold at night on the water.

We motor at a snail's pace out of the harbor. I blow the foghorn just in case other boats need warning of our presence. I always wanted to do that. Never thought I would under these frantic circumstances.

I look up at the sky. "Good thing we have a full moon. At least we can see a few feet ahead. Steve, Aunt Hattie, what do you think we should do? Should we stay near the shore or go into the open waters?"

Steve puts on a watch cap that Aunt Hattie hands him and looks at the white caps forming. "The water's a little rough. My guess is Graham would go where he is familiar at night. He probably wouldn't stray far from shore. He doesn't think anyone is following him. That's in our favor. "

Aunt Hattie taps me on the shoulder. "Tangie, any feelers on what direction to head? North or south?"

I look at Aunt Hattie with tears forming in my eyes and shake my head. I close my eyes, searching for something in my subconscious. Nothing.

Just darkness. Then, very slowly, I visualize a faint picture with dim light streaming out of it. I can make out a house coming into view—the governor's house on the shore, all lit up. Peter Van Beek's home, the one Walter and I saw on our afternoon cruise.

"Aunt Hattie, do you know how to get to Peter Van Beek's home from here? Could you point us into that direction?"

"Yes, I can do that. I know where Peter lives, *lived*. Steve, head south. Don't even bother with the sails. We can motor there. It's not far and it will be safer at night, not raising the sails."

I flop down on a damp cushion, next to Steve who commands the tiller and steers the boat. I listen to the waves lapping against the sides of the sailboat and close my eyes.

Again I see nothing, just darkness, only darkness. *Then the fighting in the dark begins. I hear the sounds of a struggle. I see a dark shadow pushing Walter overboard and laughing as he kicks him in the face. Walter is grabbing the shadow's foot, trying to drag the creep with him into the freezing water. Walter, without a life jacket, is hit, and then thrown in. He ducks under the water, escapes from the attacker's view, and begins swimming below the white caps. He tries to get away. He tries to...*

I open my eyes. I can't see anymore. "Help him, God! Help him!"

I begin to scream, "Steve, hurry, please! "We don't have much time left."

"Tangie, I hear you. Our craft is moving as fast as it can by motor. Like Aunt Hattie said, it's just too dangerous to put the sails up now. The current and the wind are unpredictable. We'll get there, Tangie. Have faith."

The wind picks up as we continue to head south, towards Peter Van Beek's house situated not too far from Newport Harbor. I look at the lights along the shore. They twinkle in the distance and their presence comforts me, unlike the whitecaps that continually rock the boat. They continue to hammer at the hull and increase my anxiety. Steve coaxes the craft with a steady hand and follows the path close to the shoreline. Thank God for his calm and cool disposition.

"Not too much further," Aunt Hattie announces. "We should be near Peter Van Beek's home soon. I think it is around the bend, past that little lighthouse."

I look at the light beam in the distance. It shines from what appears to be the smallest lighthouse around here. But it does the trick. We can see our way as we move along and we avoid crashing into the rocks that surround us. We inch our way in the dark, searching for Graham's boat.

I feel an alarm in the pit of my stomach. A kneading feeling not caused from seasickness. I close my eyes. *I can see Walter, Walter hanging onto a buoy. I hear bells…bells ringing and then a clanging sound. I see Walter hanging on, ice cold, no life jacket. His head is bleeding; his eyes are closing.* "Hang on, Walter! Hang on! Don't go to sleep! We're coming. I can *see* you!"

Then I whisper to him, only him, willing him to hear me, praying that he will hold on and not lose consciousness.

Steve continues to steer the boat as I mutter to myself. I open my eyes to see Aunt Hattie pointing to a house on the shore. "That's it. That's Peter's home. It's all lit up."

"Does anyone live there now?" Steve asks.

Aunt Hattie shakes her head. "I don't know. Maybe his children are there."

"Walter is close by, Aunt Hattie." I feel myself breathing hard, almost hyperventilating. "I can feel his presence. Is there a buoy around here somewhere? Perhaps a guide for boaters?"

Steve looks at me. "Should I cut the motor?"

"Just for a minute. I need to listen for bells."

"Bells?"

"Yes, Steve. This is what I know: Walter is hanging on to a buoy, and there is a bell attached to it. I can hear it in my head. Listen. If you hear it too, we will be near him."

"Tangie, my dear," Aunt Hattie takes my hand and squeezes it. "There is a buoy by that little lighthouse. It has a clacker attached to it. I heard the sound as we passed it."

I give Aunt Hattie a hug. "That must be it. Can you turn around, Steve?"

"Sure, but I have to turn the motor on again."

"Yes, do so, but when you get back to that miniature lighthouse, cut the motor again."

"Well, here goes."

This time, we travel against the current and the wind. Moving the watercraft becomes twice as difficult in these dark, murky waters. The white caps leap into the racing yacht and the craft lists, displacing us all over to the starboard side.

"Hold on, everyone," Steve shouts as he gains back his footing and grabs the till. "We are almost there. I can make out the lighthouse."

"Can you cut the motor?" I plead.

"I can, but it will be rough going. The boat will take on water. The waves are choppy."

Aunt Hattie goes to a storage box and takes out three life jackets. "Go ahead, Steve, do it. Here, you two. Put these on. Attach your life jacket to one of the clips on the lifelines on the sides of the boat."

Aunt Hattie demonstrates her safety precautions as she puts on a life jacket over her fur coat and attaches it to one of the lifelines.

I follow her example, donning a life jacket over my velvet evening jacket and hooking it to a nearby line.

Steve puts on the life jacket but remains unhooked. "I need to be free to move, Aunt Hattie. I may spot Walter and will need to get him. Tangie, I'm cutting the motor. Let's look for that buoy and listen for the ringing of bells."

Steve takes out his flashlight and shines it on the choppy water as we all listen for the ringing of bells. To think Walter's life depends on a little bell.

"I hear something," Aunt Hattie whispers.

"I hear it too!" I shout above the wind. "Bells, and the clacker. Walter! Can you hear us?"

Steve shouts back, "Tangie, keep calling him. I'll look around for the buoy."

He continues to flash his light around the waters as our boat drifts towards the lighthouse. I open my eyes wide and pray to see something, anything.

"Steve, over there! Start the motor. I see it! The buoy! And something or someone's on it."

Steve tries to start the motor, but it won't turn over. Flooded, probably by the same white caps that continue to send their spray onto the boat.

Steve stands up and takes off his life jacket. "One of us has to swim to that buoy. It's only about 300 yards. I think I can do it."

"I have a life raft below deck," Aunt Hattie informs us. Leave your life jacket on, Steve, and hook yourself up for the moment. We don't want to lose you. I'll go get the raft and you can blow it up. It has a pull cord. While I'm down below, drop anchor so we don't crash into the rocks."

Steve ties his life jacket and lifts the anchor. "Will do, but time is of the essence."

"Aunt Hattie, I'll come help you. Despite the tears in my eyes, I attempt a smile and follow her below deck to help get the needed supplies.

It doesn't take long to locate the raft and a towline. We drag them above deck and I bring the raft to Steve. He pulls the cord. Aunt Hattie hands him the towline. He fastens it to the boat and then to the raft.

"I think this line will be long enough, Tangie. If I have to, I'll jump off the raft to get Walter and put us both back in the raft. That is, if he is there…"

"He's there. He's got to be there. Hurry, Steve, he doesn't have much time left. The creep, I'm sure, dumped him overboard without a life jacket."

Aunt Hattie kisses Steve on the cheek. "That's for good luck. Be careful, my boy. Come back with your friend, my dear sweet nephew…"

"My husband." I let out a sob.

Steve kicks off his shoes, gives me a kiss on my forehead and hands me the flashlight. Then he jumps into the life raft and starts paddling towards the buoy.

We watch as Steve pushes the raft along the waves as if he is riding a surfboard. Then he disappears out of our sight. I shine the flashlight on the water in search of the distant raft. I can hear the sound of bells faintly in the distance, but the evening fog envelops us. Soon, there is nothing but darkness.

Chapter Thirty-Nine

As the fog creeps slowly over the night like a silent predator, it encompasses us, giving us a feeling of helplessness and despair. Our sight of anything, including the light beam from the miniscule lighthouse, becomes nonexistent. Minutes pass, then a half-hour, as the fog increases around us, a banshee holding us captive. We cannot see or hear any trace of Steve or Walter. Aunt Hattie puts her arm around me and I bury my head in her embrace. "We've lost them both," I cry.

"No. Have courage my dear. They are strong men. You brought us this far. They will be all right. We didn't come all this way to lose Walter. My boat isn't called *Salvation* for nothing.

In the mist of my despair, I laugh at Aunt Hattie's grit and determination. "*Salvation*? Really? My God, you are made of steel, Aunt Hattie. I hope some of it rubs off on me. You're right, as usual. Perhaps we could pray a bit, while we wait…"

"That always seems to help."

Aunt Hattie and I sit on deck for what seems eternity, whispering silent prayers. Then, in the near distance, I hear someone shouting.

"Tangie, I've got him! He's unconscious, but he's breathing—be prepared to help us aboard."

I shine the flashlight in the direction where I hear the distant voice. The fog shows some mercy and clears a bit around us. I spot the yellow raft riding up and down the waves, a rubber duck out for a midnight swim. "I hear you, Steve!"

I smile through my tears as I lean over the edge and pull on the line. Aunt Hattie fastens the line to a lead attached to the side of the sailboat, secures the winch and starts turning it.

"This will make things a little easier, Tangie."

My smile turns to a grin. "Thanks, Aunt Hattie. You think of everything. Let me help you."

"Sure, Tangie. Here, you take over. I need to get some blankets."

"Aye, aye, Captain."

I continue turning the winch, exhausting myself. Despite the fact that my body is now an iceberg, sweat pours down my brow and my legs start quivering. Turning a winch is not an easy task on the cold sea, in a rocking boat in the middle of the night. But using the winch makes it possible for me to move the small raft toward the sailboat amid the choppy waters. I take pride in my work, as I know I am making progress. I refuse to give up. I continue to turn the winch with all my might, and say a few prayers to keep my arms working. Between turning the winch and struggling as the boat rocks in the choppy waves, I shine the light on the water, looking for Steve and Walter. I can make out Steve's profile as he swims in the frigid water and paddles along side the raft.

Aunt Hattie returns with the blankets and puts them by the tiller. Then she goes over to the side bench on deck that doubles as a storage bin. She pulls out a small ladder and places it on the outer side of the boat for Steve and Walter to use when they reach the sailboat.

"This will make it easier for us to get the boys into the boat."

"That's great, Aunt Hattie. For our boys." Between my turning the winch and staring out to sea, I smile, thinking...*these are grown men, not boys*. Nevertheless, Aunt Hattie's comments do their trick. They keep me going amid the turbulence surrounding us. I watch as Steve makes it to the boat, grasps onto the ladder and steadies the life raft. I stop pulling on the winch and help him. I notice his breathing is labored. He lifts Walter out of the raft and forces his friend's limp body onto the ladder. Aunt Hattie and I pull on Walter until we lose our footing and fall backwards, but my beloved comes with us and lands in the cockpit on top of us, dead weight, a ton of bricks upon our bodies. I never loved a ton of bricks so much in my life, as I do at this moment. Walter smells like a slimy sea creature and feels so cold, so limp. I put my face next to his. I can detect his breath upon me. My heart rejoices. I kiss his cheek. "Walter! You've come back to me."

Steve crawls up the side of the boat, grasping onto the ladder and heaves himself on the floor of the deck, next to us. He lies there for a bit, gasping for air and shivering. Aunt Hattie squirms out of the pile of bricks that is Walter, stands up and places a blanket over Steve, then Walter, then me. She wraps the fourth blanket around herself and with a sigh, collapses on the captain's seat next to the tiller.

Steve coaxes the blanket around him, shivers uncontrollably, and pulls himself upright. "Ladies, I think it is about time we light up some flares."

Chapter Forty

Aunt Hattie speaks to the Coast Guard on my satellite phone as Steve sets off one flare and then another. They inform us they should reach us in a half hour or less. We try to stay warm, but the night air is frigid and we are soaking wet under our blankets. I hold Walter's head in my lap as we sit on the floor of the cockpit. Aunt Hattie hands me a flask of whiskey, which I attempt to pour into Walter's mouth. After three tries, I am successful. Walter's mouth sputters and he opens his glassy eyes just as the first Coast Guard cadet boards our vessel.

I hug my beloved as tight as I. "Walter, you're safe! You're home with us."

"Tangie, I…" Walter begins coughing and shivering, but manages to whisper, "I'm safe, but don't know about home. Where are we? I'm so cold. A warm bath would be nice right about now."

"Soon, soon." I hug him again and kiss his cold cheek. "You're safe, my love."

The Coast Guard sailor speaks up, "Ma'am, is this gentleman in need of assistance?"

Walter can barely sit up, but he shakes his head. "No."

I interrupt. "Yes, sir. He does need assistance. Do you have some dry clothes? Can you warm him up on your ship?"

"We do and we can. He can board our ship with me."

"I don't want to leave you, Tangie."

I have never heard Walter sound fragile, but his voice breaks my heart.

"Would it be all right if I come along, Cadet? I'm his wife."

"Sure. Under the circumstances, I think that will be fine. Are the other two okay to stay in the sailboat as we tow it to the marina?"

Steve speaks up. "I will be all right, here, if you bring me a ch..ch.. change of clothing. How about you, Aunt Hattie?"

"I think as captain of this vessel, I will stay aboard. I am warm enough. And I've got some sweats below I can put on. Plus, I've got my fur coat. But perhaps you could bring me some nice warm wool socks. My feet are soaking wet."

I smile at Aunt Hattie. "You are awesome, Aunt Hattie. Thank you."

Aunt Hattie smiles at me then kisses Walter on the cheek. "You get warm, my dear nephew. Steve and I will see you at home, in Newport. Hurry back."

A second Coast Guard cadet comes aboard and hands a pile of clothing to Steve. He hands Aunt Hattie some socks and two more blankets, just in case. Then, the two cadets turn their attention to Walter and carry him onto their long boat, and then on to their adjoining ship. I follow behind the three of them.

"We'll see you at the dock, Aunt Hattie," I yell as I board the Coast Guard vessel. "Get warm, Steve." I don't know if they can hear me, but I feel better after communicating with them.

The two cadets lead Walter and me to a guest cabin on their ship. Other cadets leave their posts to rig Aunt Hattie's sailboat for towing. Because Walter cannot walk by himself, the two strong men hold his arms and carry him swiftly into the quarters.

"Miss, he needs to shower, get dry and put on some warm clothes. You can wait here."

"I'm his wife. I can help."

The cadet places a bundle on the nearby cot. "Sure, Ma'am, that would be fine, but he may fall. We will help him in the shower. You can spread these clothes out for him, and help dress him."

"I can do that."

I busy myself with the clothing. They consist of standard military issue underwear, socks, sneakers, a fleece jacket and warm-up pants, appropriately named. After about ten minutes, the two men return with Walter in their arms but I can see that he is supporting himself on his own feet. My heart begins to race. He is returning to me. I help both cadets towel dry

Walter and dress him. He's so weak, like a patient in a hospital recovering from surgery.

In my usual fashion, I keep talking to calm my nerves. "You will be okay, Walter. No one will hurt you here. Aren't these cadets great? By the way, gentlemen, what are your names? Mine is Tangie and this is my husband, Walter. Mr. and Mrs. Cunningham. Thank you both so much, and the entire crew."

The two cadets, standing about six feet two, close in height to Walter, smile down at me. Walter sits comfortably on the bed, dressed in his new sweats, which smell fresh and warm. I swear the cadets heated them in the microwave. Probably did.

The first cadet grins and hands me a fleece jacket, as I too am soaked from the splashing of the waves. "Please to meet you both. We are Cadet Mason and Cadet Granger, at your service."

I peel off my velvet evening top and slip into the warm fleece jacket, feeling instant comfort. "Thank you both so much. I can't tell you how much we appreciate what you have done for us."

Cadet Granger is a little more formal, all business. "Just doing our job, Ma'am. The Coast Guard should be near your marina, before too long. We can help you to your car, when we get there. I understand you have a driver waiting for you."

Walter straightens his frame and mumbles, "We will and thanks again for your a...a...assistance. He clears his voice and takes a drink of hot chocolate offered by Cadet Mason. "Yikes, Tangie! I wonder who is going pay the limo guy?" This time his voice does not tremble. His sense of humor is coming back.

I smile, kiss him on his lips and give him a tight hug. "Who cares? The tab, whatever it is, is worth it. You are worth it."

My Walter has come back to me and for now, that is all that matters. *Deo Gracias!*

Chapter Forty-One

Walter refuses to go to the hospital. Aunt Hattie and Steve request the limo driver to head that way anyway.

Walter succumbs to being seen by a doctor in the emergency room and promptly checks himself out. He smiles at all of us. "The doctor told me I can walk and talk, and that is enough for him and me."

I shrug my shoulders, take his hand and follow him out the automatic door. Aunt Hattie, follows in her sweat pants, boots and her mink coat, along with Steve, who manages to look dapper in his Coast Guard apparel. I still have my evening gown on, and trudge along wearing Aunt Hattie's boots and a Coast Guard jacket. None of us speak any words, overcome by exhaustion. We crawl back into the limo, parked near the emergency entrance, and sit in silence for the ride home. We arrive at Aunt Hattie's before sunrise, bid *adieu* to the limo driver, who finally introduces himself as Sam. Steve hands him a few more big bucks.

Sam smiles. "Glad you are all well. Call me again, anytime, if you need my services."

I grin and nod. "Sorry we kept you up all night." I take Walter's arm and he leans on me a bit for support. He is still unsteady as we walk into the house.

Steve takes Aunt Hattie's arm and leads her into the living room. "Why don't you go to bed, Aunt Hattie?" I'll tuck in Tangie and Walter then make up my bed down here. Seems I am the only one with the least bit of energy left."

"You sure you don't mind, Steve? My years are catching up with me."
Aunt Hattie yawns, starts up the stairs and hangs tightly onto the rail. "I
think I can make it up to my room in one piece, before I collapse. Everyone,
sleep in tomorrow."

"We'll do that. Good night, Aunt Hattie." Steve smiles and blows her
a kiss. He finds his bedding in the window seat, places it on the pulled-out
couch, then turns his gaze on Walter, who stands leaning against the banis-
ter in the hallway. "Do you two need help getting upstairs?"

"No, we're fine, Steve." I answer and I give him a short hug. I think
we can manage. Thank you, for everything. Good night." I yawn, take
Walter's hand and lead him up the stairs to our bedroom. I open the door,
go over to the bed and pull down the covers. Walter lies down in his sweats
and collapses in a fetal position. He knows how close he came to dying.
Tears start to form in my eyes and exhaustion replaces panic, grief and then
relief. I peel off my evening dress and put on a flannel nightshirt that waits
on the side chair. I crawl under the covers next to my beloved and snuggle
my body alongside his. As I lay beside him, gratitude fills my heart. I
know how close I came to losing him. Putting my head on Walter's chest,
I listen to his heartbeat. It's steady beat is mesmerizing and calming. My
eyelids become heavy and I drift into a deep sleep. Where my thoughts
and dreams will takes me I don't know. Because I am so exhausted, I don't
care. Walter is alive and I don't think about anything else. However, the
pieces of this nightmare are coming into place and as usual, they come alive
in my dreams.

Chapter Forty-Two

Evaline casts an evil eye at Rosa Maria, the live-in maid. "What are you looking at?"

"Nothing, Senora." Rosa excuses herself and leaves to go to her room at the end of the hallway. She winces, even thought she is used to the grating tone of her mistress' voice. She closes the door to her bedroom and tries to block out the yelling that will surely follow.

Evaline struts into her husband's home office ranting and raving in a voice that, as expected, carries all the way down the hall. "Roberto, I'm your wife, damn you! If I want to see you, I will see you, with or without an appointment, even if it is the middle of the night! Your secretary can go to hell! Who hired her anyway? The nerve of her! Telling me I can't see you now." She slams the door behind her and stands facing her husband.

Roberto places his phone on the receiver and stands up behind his desk. "For Pete's sake, Evaline, lower your voice. You will wake up the rest of the staff. I can hear you loud and clear. Why are you so upset? What's happened?"

"What's happened? What's happened? Wouldn't you like to know? Wouldn't I like to know? All I know is I never see you anymore. You don't even act like a husband. If I knew it was going to be like this, I never would have…"

"Never would have what?"

"Never mind. It doesn't matter."

"Evelina, maybe you need to take another trip. That always seems to relax you."

"I don't need another trip. I need my husband."

"I'm sorry, Eveline. This job is so overwhelming. It's a lot more complicated than I envisioned, with all the decisions, all the responsibilities. It's taken me awhile to get used to everything that needs to be done. Peter Van Beek made the job look easy. He was a natural. I'm beginning to think I'm not cut out for politics. I think I'll finish this term and then retire from public office."

"Retire? Are you crazy? After all I've done for you! You can't quit! I have great plans for you!"

"Eveline, please, try to understand. Those are your plans, not mine."

"I thought they were our plans. You're making me crazy. I thought you loved politics."

"I do. I did. It's natural that I am interested. My family has always been involved, but I am not cut out for public office. Being governor has made me realize that. It's an eye-opener. I don't have time for anything else, and I don't want to live like this. I thought you'd be glad. We could spend more time together."

"What makes you think I would want to spend time with a has-been?"

"Eveline, I don't think I know you anymore. You aren't acting like the woman I knew. You've changed."

"That's because I'm not acting. This is the real me. Yes, I'm ambitious. I thought the same of you. But you're nothing but a wimp, a patsy, a dimwit."

"Eveline, I may know my limits in politics. That doesn't make me a dimwit. It makes me honest, but not what I can say about you. I'm shocked. I can only say you aren't the same person I married. I don't know you anymore."

"Oh, Roberto, you are such a fool. To think of the things I have done for you..."

"I never asked you for anything. I don't need your money. I get along just fine on a limited budget. I am not a *kept* man."

"You never complained about my money before."

"I just put up with all the glamour and glitz because I thought you needed all that. I don't. And I don't need you any more. I don't love you anymore. I don't want your *help* as you put it. I don't need it. Maybe you could hook some other *putz*, as you would say, to be your *yes* man. I'm through."

"Robert, you're crazy."

"Yes, crazy to have ever thought I loved you. Right now, I have to doubt my sanity on that one. Seems to me you took advantage of my grief and my availability, after my wife died. You are just one evil broad who thinks only of herself. So, I give you permission to be yourself. Go your merry way. Spoil yourself silly. I will contact my lawyer in the morning. Don't bother to come back to our private residence. I'll send your personal things to you tomorrow, special delivery. Being governor comes with some clout."

Governor Carboni tosses a set of car keys at Eveline as he glares at her with lightning in his eyes. He raises the volume in his voice. "Here, take the BMW. I never liked it anyway. It's parked in the governor's space. Find yourself a room in the Four Seasons. I'll put you up for a month. After that, you're on your own. You've got your own money. Use it. See you in court. Don't come here again."

"I can put myself up, and I will." Eveline glares at her husband, murder in her eyes.

He notices the hateful glint directed at him and his voice quivers. "God, you're a monster."

"Yeah, one of your making. So, that is the way you want to play?"

Carboni nods.

Eveline tosses her head to one side. "Good. I can do much worse you know. I built you up. I can tear you down. Just watch me."

"Now if I really wanted to be in public office, I would care. But I don't. So pull out all your claws. Go to town on me. I don't give a damn. I'm going to sail off into the sunset and spend my time enjoying myself. I don't plan to be another Peter Van Beek. He lowers his voice. "Just stay away from me, or else…"

"Is that a threat?"

"No. It's a promise," Roberto whispers and reaches for the phone.

Evaline grabs the keys to the BMW. "You'll be sorry you double-crossed me. I don't forgive my enemies. I say, to hell with anyone who disappoints me. You, Governor Carboni, are a huge disappointment. I'll see you in court. You are the one who will be sorry."

Governor Carboni puts the phone down, comes from behind his desk, goes over to the door and grasps the handle. "I'll hold the door for you,

Eveline, so you don't slam it on your way out. Keep clear of the house staff. I don't want anyone getting upset because of you."

"Humpf, your house staff. You'd never have a staff if it weren't for me. You are such a simpleton. Go to hell."

"You first," Roberto snarls at his departing wife. "Good-bye, Eveline. You should be very happy, with only yourself as company. That's all you need."

Eveline struts out the door in the same fashion she came in, cursing and swearing at the top of her lungs—so much for following her husband's requests.

Roberto Carboni observes Eveline as she weaves down the hall hurling curses at him. Members of his staff pop their heads out of their doors and stare at her as she continues shouting and cursing at anyone who dares to look in her direction.

After Eveline leaves the governor's retreat house, a young aide, wearing his bathrobe and slippers, walks over to Roberto's study. He peeks in and looks at the governor sitting at his desk. "Perhaps I should call security, sir?"

"Don't bother, I already have. Nothing in this job is easy, least of all Eveline."

Eveline finds herself at her husband's parking spot and wonders how she got to the back of the estate. She can't remember walking there and mumbles to herself, "I can't remember the past five minutes, I am so upset. I hate Roberto. He will get his. And I can do it."

"Get what?"

Eveline looks over to the other side of the BMW and sees Graham leaning against it. "Buddy! What are you doing here? Quit hanging on my car."

Buddy points to the sign posted above the car. "I thought this car belongs to the governor."

"It was his car. I gave it to him. Now it's mine. He gave it back to me."

"Oh, trouble in paradise, I see."

"Yes. You see good."

"No, I never see good. I see bad."

"Buddy, you are a tease."

"Tell you what, Eveline. You look upset. Want me to take you somewhere? You can talk to me."

"I can't talk to anyone. No one would understand."

"You don't know until you try me."

"You are a baby."

"I'm not so young, and I'm not so innocent. I'm ambitious. You're ambitious too. Together we can go places."

"I've been there, done that, Buddy. I'm through. It's not worth it. Nothing's worth anything anymore."

"Come on, Eveline. You don't believe that. You are just feeling sorry for yourself. Come on, I'll take you for a ride."

"I don't want to go for a ride. I'm going to the Four Seasons."

Buddy grins. "That's even better. I'll drive." Buddy pries the keys out of Eveline's hand and winks at her. "That's a good girl. Let Buddy take care of you for a while. Not to worry."

Eveline shrugs. "Go for it, Buddy. But I warn you, I'm not good company right now."

"I told you. I'm not looking for good company."

Eveline stares at Buddy and sees what she surmises to be a glint of passion in his eyes. It appears Eveline is so far gone in her self-delusion, she cannot not see the signs flashing in front of her eyes. She'll have to find out the hard way, like everyone else.

"Buddy, have it your way. You drive. It will be good to have someone else take charge for a change."

Chapter Forty-Three

I sit up, totally alert. What is going on? I look over at Walter, sleeping beside me and I sigh. Thank goodness. I am only dreaming. Why can't I get Eveline out of my mind? I try to think good thoughts, far away from Evaline and Roberto Carboni. I think of being home in Seattle, sitting in front of our fireplace, and then Walter and I in Fiji, frolicking on our honeymoon, before Eveline entered our lives. Reclining once more, I put my arm around Walter, who is sleeping peacefully, breathing evenly, in and out. I listen to his breathing and soon I feel myself falling back to sleep. Calm or distressed, I don't know. I am just oh, so tired…

Chapter Forty-Four

Eveline looks out the window as Buddy drives through the early morning weekend traffic in Providence. People are coming out of bars, heading to restaurants for a late evening/early morning breakfast. She mutters to herself and begins cursing. "At this rate, we'll be here until next evening and sleeping on the sidewalk. Where do all these people come from?"

Buddy rolls down his window to let some air in the car. "Did you say something, Eveline?"

"Just talking to myself. Buddy, why don't we pull over and chat for a while. I hate sitting in traffic."

"No place to pull over. Hey, there's an all-night car wash. I can wash the car for you and we can sit outside after it's done and chat. They wouldn't chase us away if we're waiting for the car to dry out. Plus, we won't have to worry about finding a parking space this time of night in a safe spot."

"Go for it, Buddy. I told you to lead the way. I'm tired of making all the decisions around here."

"Good girl. I'll take over."

Buddy pulls into the X-Rated Car Wash and grins. "You've got to love that name."

Eveline laughs for the first time that evening. "Seems you know how to chose the greatest places."

"Hey, Eveline, ever do it in a car wash?"

"Do what?"

Buddy smiles at her and Eveline sees the same fire in his eyes that she saw earlier. This time, however she gets chills. *Maybe I am taking too many chances*, she thinks to herself.

"Come on, it'll be fun. Hop in the back seat. I'll join you later, after I pay the guy. Don't worry. No one will see us."

"You naughty boy. I have the feeling you've done this before."

"You'll never know." Buddy smiles and starts panting and sweating uncontrollably, a warning signal Eveline doesn't seem to notice, or chooses to ignore. She leans over and puts her arms around Buddy. She unfastens his crimson bow tie and places it around her neck. Giggling like a schoolgirl on her first date, she flops into the back seat as Buddy pulls up to the attendant and hands him a fifty.

Buddy smiles. "Hey dude, give me the deluxe car wash. X-rated, and keep the change."

"Right on, sir. Thank you. Takes about fifteen minutes for the deluxe."

"Just enough time," Buddy mumbles.

"What's that, sir?"

"Oh, that will be fine. Just fine." Buddy looks at the attendant's nametag. "Thanks, Fred." He winks at him, shells over another ten and steers the BMW up to the entrance of the car wash. He turns to grin at Eveline in the back seat and puts the car in neutral.

The attendant looks at the bills in his hand. Best tip he ever got. "Tonight would be a good night to get loaded. Get a jump start on Saturday night, right after work."

The cleaning brushes start moving and then the soap and water. Buddy crawls into the back seat with anticipation of climaxing his desire. When he gets there he doesn't waste any time. First he kisses Eveline to disarm her. Then he expertly pins her hands behind her back, with his right arm.

"I love a man who plays rough," she whispers.

"I'm glad," Buddy whispers back. "That will make things so much easier."

His eyes swell with fire but when Eveline's gaze penetrates them, she does not see passion. She sees murder. Calculated, cold murder. She feels Buddy's sweaty body leaning into hers and feels him wrapping the cold, expensive silk tie around her neck, tighter and tighter. She becomes light-headed. She cannot scream. If she could, no one would hear her anyway. She starts to cry, but even that seems a hopeless waste of time. She starts

302

to fight, kicking, biting and trying to wriggle herself out of Buddy's grasp. She can't move her legs, as Buddy leans harder against her, pinning her legs to the back seat as he pulls harder and harder on the tie around her neck. Her voice comes back and she screams, just as the water begins to pound on the roof of the vehicle. She can see the car windows covered with soapsuds and can feel the pounding of the brushes against the top of the car. "No one can hear me!" she whispers. "No one can hear me!" She tries to shout, "Help! Help!"

"You are such a fool, Eveline. Of course no one can hear you, except maybe Steve, and even he doesn't care."

Another familiar voice enters the conversation. "Yes. You're right, Graham, I don't care. Evaline, my pet, this time, you pay."

Evaline can hear two distinct voices talking to her at once, but only one person is in the car with her and then she knows, *she knows*, and it is too late, *too late*. No one can help her anymore.

Fred, the attendant, stands in his booth, and waits for the next car to pull up to the entrance. He notices the fancy BMW, with the generous tipper in the driver's seat, making a sharp left turn, out of the carwash. He sees the same older woman that came in with the younger man now leaning against the back seat window, asleep. "How anyone can snooze in a car wash is beyond my understanding," he mumbles as he scratches his shoulder. "I guess it takes all kinds to make up this world." He means his words for no one in particular, as he makes change for his next customer.

Chapter Forty-Five

"Angelina...Honey, are you all right?"

I hear a voice, Walter's voice, calling me. I must go to him. "Walter, my love. Are you all right?"

"I'm fine, Angel...It's *you*. You are having another bad dream. You're all sweaty. You were thrashing around. Do you remember anything?"

I feel him pulling me up. "Yes, Walter, but I'm so tired. I'm exhausted. I cannot talk about it right now. I have to lie down. Please, let me." I close my eyes and slip back into the dream...

Chapter Forty-Six

I see that The Four Seasons Hotel—the honeymoon suite—the one Walter and I made love in, on our wonderful night together, is the next stop. It seems "Steve" is taking Evaline there. The concierge merely glances up and thinks Eveline is asleep, or drunk when "Steve" and Eveline enter the elevator. "Steve" is carrying Eveline's limp body and is now opening the door to the hotel suite. He is arranging her body on the bed. He is taking a liquor bottle out of the bar, pouring it down her mouth and spilling it on her clothing. Then, he is covering her up. He goes into the bathroom and washes his face, with a cloth, but is careful not to remove any makeup, particularly his mustache. Graham wants to remain "Steve" until he is out of the hotel. He looks in the mirror, smiles and says, "Well done, Buddy." Then he walks into the living area, wipes off the key card and throws it on the coffee table. He leaves the suite, heads toward the elevator, and remembers to look directly into the surveillance camera hanging on the wall. After he passes it, he laughs and pushes the elevator button.

Chapter Forty-Seven

I wake up briefly, during the night, remembering very little of the dream. Exhausted, I fall back to sleep. Walter and I remain entwined in each other's arms, as a deep slumber keeps us zonked out, practically comatose into the late morning. In the deep recesses of my mind I hear a bell. At first I think we are still on the water, in the sailboat. I panic, sit up suddenly, alert. I feel the softness of our bed and sigh. I hear the bell again. I shake Walter. "Walter, honey, I hear a bell. Someone's at the door."

Walter sits up in bed. "What?"

He looks like the walking dead, pale, with his hair all messed up. He's as groggy as a drugged patient in a hospital ward.

"I'm sorry, Walter. I shouldn't have disturbed you."

He stretches and shakes his head around. "That's all right. I'm feeling okay now. I think. How about you? That was some dream you had."

"Dream? Funny, I don't quite remember having a dream..."

"It was a screamer. Woke me."

"I'm sorry, honey."

"Don't be. What's the problem, Sweetheart?"

"The doorbell."

"I don't hear anything."

"Come to think of it, neither do I, but I did."

"Maybe we should get up."

"Are you sure you feel all right, Walter?"

"Not great, but I'll feel better after a shower and some breakfast."

"How about if we go out for brunch? It's probably late now. I think Steve and Aunt Hattie are still sleeping, if the doorbell didn't wake them up."

"Steve probably got the door, Tangie. He is sleeping in the living room."

"Walter, I think I know who rang the bell. Must be Barry."

"Barry?"

"Yes, Barry. We forgot to pick him up at the airport this morning."

"How did we forget to pick up the boss?"

"Remember last night?"

"Oh yes, my midnight swim."

"Yes, your near death experience." I lean into my honey and hug him tight. "You promised me you'd never leave me."

"And I didn't. I'm here aren't I?"

"Yes, by the grace of God. Please, Walter, don't do that to me again. I can't take much more. You, my love, are not a cat with nine lives."

"I think I used up two of them last night. But you found me, my love. I need to show you my gratitude, Angelina."

Walter encircles my waist and pulls me down, next to him and starts kissing my ear.

I sigh, but resist, reluctantly. "Cut that out. We have to get up."

"Why?"

I just love Walter's persistence and I begin to cave, but alarms in my head begin to go off. "Honey, I think we should get up and see Barry. We have to talk to him." Walter stares at me with such passion in his eyes, I can kick myself. I sigh and think, *"Where are my priorities?"*

I give my honey a kiss. "I love you so much, Sweetheart. There's no rush. Barry can wait." Walter kisses my neck as he lifts my nightshirt over my head and caresses my naked body. I moan and kiss his waiting lips. Like my love, I cannot stand to have clothes separating us. I slip off his Coast Guard attire. He pulls up the covers over our heads, as if trying to protect us from the world outside. I gasp, Walter sighs, as we become one flesh, one body. Yes, Barry can wait. Heaven cannot.

Chapter Forty-Eight

It is after twelve noon when Walter and I, freshly showered and dressed, finally creak down the stairs. Barry, Steve and Aunt Hattie are chatting and drinking coffee in the living room.

Aunt Hattie smiles at our entrance. "Oh, hi dears. Steve has introduced me to your Barry and we've been chatting up a storm, but we haven't eaten yet. We thought we'd wait for you."

"Hi Barry. Glad to see you."

"Yes, Barry." Walter shakes his hand. " Welcome to Newport. Glad you were able to get away to help us with this dilemma. Sorry we forgot to pick you up this morning, but I am sure Steve explained…"

I smile at Aunt Hattie. "Shall we go out for breakfast? Walter and I are all ready and dressed to go, for a change. I don't think anyone wants to cook."

"That would be great, dear. You are right, after last night."

Barry's antennae come out. "Last night? What happened last night?"

"Oh, you know how it is, Barry," I mutter. "Just one adventure after another. I thought Steve told you."

"No, he hasn't." Barry gives Steve a quick glance. "Steve hasn't shared anything with me."

Walter nods. "Probably waiting for Tangie and me to get up. We'll fill you in over breakfast." As Steve gets up from his chair, Walter goes over to him, gives him a hug and whispers in his ear, "Thanks for the ride in the raft last night, Steve. You are the Best Man ever."

"Anytime, good buddy. Anytime you need a lift, I'm here."

I join Walter and hug Steve. "Thanks, Steve. We owe you, big time. Aunt Hattie and I could not have gotten to Walter without you."

"Come on guys, tell me." Barry shuffles from one foot to another and takes off his glasses.

Aunt Hattie smiles. "These children have to eat first. Let's get our things together and go out for breakfast...ah brunch."

"Yes, Aunt Hattie, suddenly I'm starved. I'll just go upstairs and put some makeup on."

"I just need to get my shoes and coat." Walter announces. "Be right back."

I hear Steve say to Barry as we amble up the stairs, "Let's sit down in the living room, Barry. Relax. With those two, you never know how long it will take. Sometimes a minute turns into an hour."

I think I hear Barry chuckle for the first time, ever.

We don't keep Barry waiting long. Unbeknownst to him and Steve, we already had our dessert.

Hunger drives us forward and to the Bridge Diner. I love diners. Seems the East Coast has the monopoly on the best of them. They serve fantastic breakfasts all day long. Good thing since it is afternoon by the time we walk through the revolving door.

We each order something different for breakfast and share our plates. That way, we have a variety of tastes to begin our new day. The waitress gives us a look that says, "You folks are weird," but what the heck. That is how we do things in the Pacific Northwest. Aunt Hattie delights in our share fest and gets giddy. She too, seems to be coming back to life. I think yesterday and last night taxed her energy. I never saw her as tired as she was early this morning, when we finally got home. I understand. I get really silly when I don't get enough sleep, and last night we really piled on the excitement.

One thing I like about this diner is they serve espresso. It's hard to find really good espresso on the East Coast, except perhaps in New York City. Walter must be privy to this knowledge as he chose the place. Seems he and Steve used to hang out here in their college days, after an exhausting night of carousing.

We sit in a large corner booth that can seat eight people. It is somewhat private, well as private as diners can be. People come and go, but no one seems to pay attention to us. Mostly families with kids and college students fill this place on a Saturday afternoon.

After we stuff ourselves silly, we chat peacefully about Newport and Seattle, not bringing up any unpleasant topics. Barry decides to get in detective mode and makes eye contact with each of us. "So, Walter, Steve, Tangie, Aunt Hattie, is there anything you want to tell me? Perhaps you could begin by letting me know why I am here and how I can help you."

Steve begins, then Walter, then me. Then Aunt Hattie tells her part in the whole scenario. We begin our story in Fiji and end where we come home exhausted, after Walter takes his midnight swim, after being tossed off Graham's sailboat.

Walter stares at me and takes my hand. "Tangie, you are right. There is a connection between Graham and *Steve the Murderer*. His pal, *Hit Man Steve,* is the one who threw me off the boat."

"What?" I open my mouth and it takes a while for more words to come out. "But Walter, Graham is Buddy."

"What?"

"You know, Buddy, in my dream."

"Okay, Tangie, I think I understand you, but all I know is, Graham went down below to get us some wine, and out comes his buddy, *Steve.* And *he* throws me off the boat."

"So, either they are in cahoots together, or Graham is toast too."

Our Steve shakes his head. "Something is really wrong here. Barry, you have more clout than me. Could you call the Newport Police and see if they picked up anyone by the name of Graham Gotthree or anyone else, resembling him, last night, or early this morning?"

Barry doesn't ask any questions. He picks up his cell, calls a few numbers, reaches the local police station and asks them the right questions. I can hear his reply: "Yes, uh. No. Oh, yes. Thank you. I'll be in touch."

"Well, Barry, any news?" I look at him and nod my head like a beagle puppy, waiting for him to speak.

"The harbor police picked up Graham, not too far from where you found Walter. Graham told the police he radioed for help. Says he doesn't know what happened. Says he is concerned about his passenger. That would be you, Walter, who disappeared."

I roll my eyes. "I bet..."

Barry studies me, then Walter. "They said this Graham fellow didn't want any medical attention. He got a tow to his dock and took off, refusing to say anymore. He asked the police to call him if they found you, Walter."

Our Steve gets up and grabs the bill. "Seems this Graham guy covers his tracks. I think we should head back to Aunt Hattie's. If I know anything about anyone, I think this Graham fellow will show up on her doorstep and we need to be ready for him."

"Oh, great! Just who I want to see." I stare at Walter. "Do you think this is a good idea?"

"Sure, Tangie. Steve has good police sense. And Barry will be with us if things get out of hand."

Barry stands up, takes off his glasses, blows on them and cleans them on his shirt. "You know, Tangie, I think we should give Theo Lee a call, give him a heads-up. He happens to be working on a case nearby at the moment. He will help us if we need him. We don't have to get involved, just the three of us..." Barry clears his throat, looks at Aunt Hattie and continues, "Just the four of us."

"Oh, dear," Aunt Hattie mumbles. "I think I need a nap. I don't think I could face that young man again without thrashing him."

I smile at Walter's aunt. "Me, too, Aunt Hattie. Only when we get home, I'm gonna take a bath. I need to get the seaweed out of my hair."

When we open the door, Pebbles greets all of us and jumps all around me like a spinning top. "I think the sweet little pooch needs a walk. Wait to talk shop until I return from my walk with Pebbles. We'll be back in a flash."

Upon my return with Pebbles, my partners and I work out a plan. Barry, our Steve and Walter will wait in the living room for Graham to appear. We all agree with our Steve that Graham will be in curious mode and will not be able to stay away. If for some reason Graham doesn't show up, Walter will call him and read him the riot act for abandoning him at sea. That will get him over in a hurry. Aunt Hattie and I will hang out upstairs with Pebbles, out of harm's way. But if things get out of hand, we are to call the police. Easy enough directions to follow, we can do that. No problem. But I can't help thinking that the best laid plans usually go wrong somewhere.

After our team meeting, Aunt Hattie immediately excuses herself, saying she has to go to the cellar for something before heading upstairs for her nap. I know what she is after in the cellar. Her shotgun. She doesn't fool me and I don't think she fools Walter. We don't mention this to Steve or Barry. Better they don't know. After all, this is her home and she has a right to protect herself.

I give Walter a kiss and wave to Barry and Steve. "I am off to soak in bubbles for a bit. I hope Graham doesn't show up for a while, so I can relax." Walter grins at me, probably picturing me in the tub. I wink at him and grin back. Before I head upstairs, I whisper in his ear, "Later, my love..."

I recline in the porcelain-soaking tub and stare at the waterfowl marching across the wallpaper border above me. I watch the flying creatures staring back at me as I smile and relax. Aunt Hattie has a sense of humor. Pebbles lies down on the rug adjacent to the oversized tub and begins to lick the water droplets collecting on the porcelain. I lean over and pat his head. Picking up the pale yellow sponge floating in the water, I grin at its duck shape, squeeze it, and let the soapy water flow over my neck. My smile freezes. I sit up, on full alert. Suddenly, I remember. I remember my dream from last night. Horrible! It's all coming back to me. I see Graham, squeezing Eveline's neck. Hard, sharp, no mercy. Alas, the poor bird doesn't have a chance. And who would know? No witnesses to the crime. Graham is so smug. I close my eyes and sink my entire body under the water and analyze my vision.

I must admit that was some crazy dream, but parts of it are real, very real. But how can I turn my supposition, my insight and my dream into fact? How can I nail the creep?

I bring my head above the water and peer out the bay window, noticing the light filtering into the oversized bathroom. I study the garden, like an artist looking for a scene to paint. The golden leaves on the birch tree unleash themselves from the limbs of the tree and fly away in the wind like the fragments of my scattered dream. I see the sun peek out from behind a cloud and then go back behind it, perhaps for good. The room darkens. I take a match from the table beside the soaking tub, light an aromatic candle, breathe in and close my eyes. The scent of lemon-lime permeates the room and I sink deeper into the bubbly water. I turn on the pulsating jets and try to relax.

The vibrations of the water flowing over my back and shoulders soothe my aching muscles and I focus on what I want to remember. Yes, it's coming back to me, but I don't like what I see. *Horrible.*

Chapter Forty-Nine

I close my eyes and try with all my will not to get upset or lose my concentration, but it is not easy. I don't want to remember. I try because I must, because I know "the truth will set me free…"

I lie back, submerge my entire body underwater and hold my breath. I see Graham, grabbing Evaline and strangling her with a tie, a red tie. I hear his laughter, then his voice changing to that of an animal, to that of *Steve—Steve the Murderer*. I push my head out of the water and breathe deeply. Graham is *Buddy*. Graham is *Steve*. Graham is the murderer! *Oh, no!* And the tie, the tie around Evaline's throat is his. I remember seeing him wearing it last night, *that red tie* accenting his tuxedo, both at the reception and in my dream. That tie, not his hands, is the murder weapon! If we can find the tie, we've got the connection, and we'll nail the S.O.B.

I turn off the jets, stand up and reach for the over-sized Turkish towel. I dry my eyes, momentarily place the towel on a nearby wooden chair and climb out of the tub. My feet feel cold on the marble floor as I wrap the towel, rough from drying in the sun, around me. Pebbles gets up, shakes his fur and licks the water off my calf.

"Okay, Pebbles, I'll get you a drink. I can take a hint." I reach down under the sink, find a bowl, fill it and place it on the floor under the window for Pebbles to lap up. Looking out the window, I notice the sun totally disappearing behind a cloud and a storm developing in the distance. Dark clouds form rapidly and then, thunder. I remove my wet towel, grab my tangerine robe hanging on the hook behind the door and wrap it around me tightly. Slipping into my matching slippers, I blow out the candle. As I rush out the door, I squint as lightning flashes through the hall window. I hold my breath and head towards the stairs to alert the others.

I practically collide with Aunt Hattie in the upstairs hallway. True to my predictions, she has her shotgun in one arm and her other hand on a pistol in her apron pocket. I can't help but smile at her appearance as a pioneer woman from the *Wild West*. "Aunt Hattie, what's going on?"

Aunt Hattie whispers "Shush." She leans down, pets Pebbles, and flashes me a look of distress. My smile evaporates. Her eyebrows are raised, and her brow is all wrinkled. "Be very quiet and hold Pebbles tight. That Graham fellow is downstairs, in my house. Listen carefully. Walter, Steve and your boss, Barry, are questioning Graham as we speak. We best stay up here."

I think about correcting her about Barry being my boss, but come to think of it, he did deputize me earlier this year. Maybe that's still in effect. I put my arm around her shoulder and whisper, "Aunt Hattie, I have to speak with them. I have to tell them..."

"What? You surely don't want to talk to them in Graham's presence?"

"Well then, you and I must call the police, the local police. Let's hurry before he gets away. He's probably giving Steve, Walter and Barry a load of crap."

"Tangie, I think Walter can see through Graham."

"Yes, he can, but he doesn't know about this connection. I have the connection."

"Which is?"

"Graham is *Steve*. Graham is *Buddy*. *Graham* murdered Peter Van Beek. He murdered Evaline as well. I'm positive now. I put it all together. We can't wait any longer. Call the police. It's urgent. We cannot wait."

"Peter? Eveline? When?

"Yes, both of them. I saw it in my last dream: the entire dream just resurfaced in my memory. Trust me, please. *I know*, and now, I can prove it.

Aunt Hattie hands me her shotgun and collapses on a bench in the hallway. "Tangie, I am too old for this. We have a murderer in my home! What do you want me to do?"

I hand the shotgun back to her, take Pebbles' leash lying on the bench and latch it to my furry friend. "You need to go into your bedroom and call the police. I think they might listen to you. You have lived here for a long time. You know a lot of people. Ask the police to search Graham's home for a red tie and a fake, but good quality theatrical mustache. Have them send a couple of officers here so we have some backup. We don't have much time. Things have a way of going to hell in a hurry when Graham's around. I am beginning to think he has a support system, or something else is going on. I don't know what, but we can't wait to call the police any longer."

Aunt Hattie rises from the bench with her shotgun. She takes a pistol out of her apron pocket and hands it to me. "You take this dear. It's loaded. Do you know how to use it?"

I nod.

"Good. Stay by the landing and listen." She pauses for a moment, then goes to a small table on the landing, opens the drawer and pulls out a canister of some kind. "Here, take this bear spray. It works as far as thirty feet and is powerful. Use this first."

I look at her in astonishment.

"Give me Pebbles' leash. I'll take care of him so he doesn't bark. And now I'll go to my bedroom and call the police. Don't let anything happen to you."

"I won't. I promise." I give her a hug and watch as she leads Pebbles with one hand and holds her shotgun with the other. She shoos him into the bedroom and shuts the door.

I turn my attention to the conversation going on downstairs. I tiptoe to the landing, hold my breath and strain my ears while I try to make out the words. I hear Barry and Steve grilling Graham. I close my eyes and imagine Walter trying to figure out what else there is to know about Graham's involvement. Steve keeps asking Graham about his "Steve" friend. Graham tells him that he is no friend of "Steve" any longer. He says they were friends in high school, but no more.

Our Steve informs Graham he checked his high school's records and "his friend, Steve", does not exist. Graham replies, "Well maybe his legal name is not *Steve*, but that is what he went by in high school."

"Smug," I whisper to myself. "The jerk has an answer for everything."

I don't think they will get anything out of Graham. He's too slick, but also, he's too confident, as if he knows something they don't know.

In the dark at the top of the stairs, I wait. It seems like hours since Aunt Hattie and I conversed in the hallway, but I'm guessing only a few minutes passed. I begin to get nervous. The pistol in my hand gets heavy. It's an iron weight that I would like to throw down, but I dare not move or let go of the gat. My body freezes when I hear the sound of someone bursting through the front door. A second later, someone rushes in from the rear of the house. I cannot breathe. I am a useless statue, stone cold. Voices, angry, loud voices shout. They order Walter, Barry and Steve to lie on the floor and not move. Then Graham singles out Walter. "Where's Tangie? Where's your pesky Aunt Hattie?"

I hear Walter's voice responding to his demands. "Tangie's shopping. Aunt Hattie's visiting friends."

Graham does not believe him. I hear a thud and then Graham shouting orders to one of the intruders. "Look upstairs."

I panic. With my right hand, I feel for the bear spray in my robe pocket, while grasping the pistol in my other hand, and wait. As an after thought, I check to see that the gun is cocked. I put my finger on the trigger and hope I don't have to fire the pistol. I take a stand on the landing and hope for the best.

I hear Walter's voice. "Leave Tangie out of this, Graham. You're wasting your time. Tangie's safe, away from you. She's not here, I tell you, you basta...don't!"

I hear Walter struggle to finish his sentence, then someone being struck hard. A noise drifts up the stairs that sounds like moaning. I whisper in silence, "These men are beating Walter to death." Tears stream down my face and I get mad, really mad. Anger replaces fear. I switch the pistol to my left hand and lift the bear spray out of my pocket.

I hear the footsteps before I see anyone. It is pitch dark on the landing and stairs, so I wait patiently until I can picture who is climbing the stairs. The lightning flashes through a window on the lower stairs for a brief second, and I recognize Evaline's bodyguard, the same bodyguard from Fiji, only now he is looking for Aunt Hattie and me. I lift the bear spray, push the button and immobilize him. I watch as he grasps at his face, drops his over-sized gun, and stumbles down the stairs.

Another man immediately runs up towards me as the lightning flashes again. I recognize him as one of the thugs talking to Roberto Carboni at the governor's reception last night. Perhaps they planned this all along—coming to the house, getting rid of us. I want to close my eyes and block it all out. Instead, I use the remaining bear spray to stop the thug from getting any closer. He grabs at his face with one arm and stumbles, then suddenly stands up, lifts his gun and points it in my direction. I toss the used-up canister at him and lift my 25-caliber weapon. With both my arms raised and without hesitation, I fire the weapon. One shot, at his arm. He drops the gun, and then picks it up with his other hand. Somehow he continues toward me. I shoot again. Finally he falls, and tumbles in slow motion down the stairs.

I exhale, relieved, but still on guard. Another figure appears at the landing. I smell sweat and cologne. *Graham.* He doesn't come up the stairs. I can make out his profile in the shadows, as he studies the two thugs lying crumpled on the stairs. He puts his hand into his jacket pocket. I raise my gun once more.

He speaks on his cell phone. "Boss, we have a problem. I need a cleaning crew quick, and more men to help me…Yes, two men down. No, I cannot do this alone. I need help. Send me your personal bodyguard then. You owe me."

I hear a sharp clunk as Graham throws his phone on the wooden floor.

He stands guard at the downstairs landing. His voice, his sickening high-pitched voice speaks and all I can do is shudder when he calls to me.

"Tangie, I know you are up there. Must say, you are a good shot. I think we need to talk."

I don't answer him. I play mute.

He lowers his voice, taunting me. "If you don't come down, I will put a bullet in your husband's head. I give you three minutes to think it over. Come down or lover boy is dead."

I stay in the shadows, panic-stricken. I take another deep breath, exhale then tiptoe over to Aunt Hattie's bedroom and open the door. Aunt Hattie stands perfectly still with her shotgun in her arm. "Aunt Hattie, stay here by the phone. I have to go downstairs or Graham will shoot Walter. Stay on guard, but be calm. The police should be here soon. Have faith. I'll be praying for us the whole time. You do the same."

Aunt Hattie puts her twelve-gauge on the bed and hugs me. "Go, help him if you must. I love you, child. Be careful. Please. Try to think of something. Good luck."

I nod, and try to fight the tears that run down my face. I pat Pebbles on the head and scratch behind his ears. He licks my hand and lays his head down on the bed. I feel like I am heading off to war. I pick up the shotgun and place it back in Aunt Hattie's arms. "Take care, Aunt Hattie. Be strong. Stay quiet. They don't know you are here. I love you, too."

I walk out the bedroom door with a heavy heart. I have no plan, no hope and no wish for anything except to be with Walter. I descend the stairs to face Graham.

Chapter Fifty

In the dark, I crawl carefully over the two fallen men, one of whom I shot at point blank range. Both are breathing, one just barely. Sighing, I close my eyes for a moment and hold onto the rail. At the bottom of the stairs, Graham notices my reaction, but not the condition of the men.

He smiles. "Of course you know you will be arrested for murder. Shooting an aide to the governor, or should I say, two aides, is deemed a capital offense. With a little cooperation on your part, I can get you off." He snaps his fingers. "I can make this all go away."

I stare at Graham. "Get me off? Are you crazy? Who do you think you are? Are you now judge and jury? I acted in self-defense. And how do you know they are dead? Why are you here? What do you want?"

"Tangie, Tangie, Tangie, so many questions. I do believe you never shot anyone before. It gets easier. Why do you have to be so nosy? You are such a beautiful girl. You should be having fun, not causing all this trouble."

"Me? What have I done?"

"I see double homicide. The media will see it that way, unless you plead insanity. That sometimes works. We can make a deal."

"The only insane person around here is you, Graham. Where's Walter? What have you done to him?"

"I'll ignore the first part. Come this way; I'll show you."

I feel Graham's sweaty hand as he takes Aunt Hattie's pistol from my possession. He places it in his pocket then pauses to retrieve his cell phone. He grabs my arm and leads me into the living room. My body trembles as

323

he points to Walter lying on the floor, next to the window seat. He kicks his body and lifts his head up momentarily, so I can see his face. "There's your lover boy, your Irish professor, your husband, where he belongs, facedown. Some hero. Ha! Your other two goons are in the closet, sleeping peacefully, two peas in a pod. No, I didn't murder them. I'm not as trigger-happy as you at the moment. I just frisked them, and drugged them of course. You remember that drug, don't you? Oh, that's right, you spit it out, too smart for me. Anyway, your friends were giving us some trouble, so we had to disarm them. We removed their ID's—two of Seattle's finest. Do you always travel with cops?"

I ignore Graham, kneel down next to Walter, hug him gently and feel his pulse. It's irregular and faint. "What did you give him?"

"Oh, just a few punches, plus an injection to calm him down. He'll be out for hours, but by then, you and he...Ha, I haven't decided what to do with you yet. But Walter, I know. He will feed the fishes."

"Graham, you won't get away with any of this."

"Oh yes I will. I have all the cards. You have nothing."

"I do have something. I have knowledge of you."

"Big deal. Is that all?"

"Yes. And for your information, at this very moment the police are searching your place."

"Oh, really? Says who?"

"Says me."

"I seriously doubt that, Angelina."

"Don't discount my abilities. I can visualize the police finding a red tie, your red tie, and that winch from Peter Van Beek's yacht. You have them hidden under your bed, under the floorboards."

"What are you talking about?"

"You know, Graham, or should I say, *Buddy*, or *Steve*? You like to save the murder weapons. They make you feel powerful. You like to look at them, touch them and re-live the experience."

"Tangie, I don't know what you are talking about, and neither do you."

"Oh yeah? What do you think I was doing upstairs?"

Graham studies my robe. "From the looks of it, with your wet hair and all, I'd say, taking a bath."

I cinch the tie on my robe tighter. "That's just a cover. I've got you hook, line and sinker."

"I seriously doubt it. I have friends, powerful friends."

"Roberto Carboni?"

"For starters."

"You mean there's more?"

"There's always more. Surprised? You think I am in this alone?" He grabs my wrist and displays a twisted smile. "Bitch, you're nothing but a…"

I cannot stand him, his sweaty palms or his overwhelming cologne one minute more. I knee him where the sun does not shine. Graham collapses on the floor and starts moaning. I lean down and remove Aunt Hattie's pistol from his jacket and return it to the pocket of my robe. As I stand up, I notice an ebony sculpture of a raven displayed on the nearby mantle. As an afterthought, I pick up the *objet d'art* and clunk Graham over the head with it. In a somewhat dazed state, I recite, "…Quoth the Raven 'Nevermore'…"

After placing the statue, none the worse for wear, back on the mantle, I take the pistol out of my pocket and keep it pointed it at Graham just in case he decides to move. Moving cautiously to the side table next to the Queen Anne chair, I pick up Aunt Hattie's landline phone and dial the direct line to the FBI. "Hello. This is Tangie, ah…Angelina Seraphina… Cunningham. I need to speak with Agent Theo Lee. It's urgent."

Chapter Fifty-One

My foot falls asleep, so I start tapping it, while continuing to wrap my robe tighter around my waist. Not an easy task with a gun in one hand and a corded phone in the other. I look around the room, at Graham, and then Walter, and wonder how things have gone so terribly wrong.

A voice comes on the line. "Tangie? Is that you? Theo speaking. How can I help?"

I recognize the voice as belonging to the agent who helped us in Idaho last spring—with the Sargento case, at the Neo-Nazi camp, Camp Adairwolf.

"Theo? Yes. Tangie here. So you remember me, and the Adolphus Sargento case? Right now, I am in Newport, Rhode Island and I must be quick. I don't know if the police or the governor's thugs will get here first. But, Theo, I have to tell you this: the new governor, Roberto Carboni, is dirty, and he's after me. The police should have shown up an hour ago, and they're still not here. Something's terribly wrong. I need help. I need backup. Walter, Barry and Steve are down. Still alive, but they've been drugged. They can't help me. Please send someone ASAP. I can't hold on much longer."

Before Theo can answer me, I hear another voice, in the room with me.

"Put the phone down."

I recognize the voice of Carboni's personal bodyguard, the tall dude. I only encountered him once before, but I remember his gravelly voice. I shudder and do as he says. I put the phone down, but I place the receiver on the table, behind an arrangement of lilies in a vase, not totally on the cradle of the phone. Perhaps the dude won't notice. Then, taking the gun out of my pocket, I turn around and face my captor.

"Drop your pistol, Tangie. I'm a trained assassin for Pete's sake. I can shoot you before you get off a shot."

I believe him. I drop the gun.

He looks at the floor. "Looks like Graham didn't do so well."

"Looks that way."

"Listen, Babe. It doesn't have to be this way for you. The governor likes you. He will make allowances."

"Like he made allowances for his wife?"

"What do you know about her?"

"I know a lot of things. If you bring the governor here, I can tell him a thing or two."

"How about I take you to him?"

"Come on, I know he's right outside, in his limo. Call him. What harm could that do? There's no one here but me. Everyone else is, how do you say, *neutralized*."

The bodyguard looks at me, pauses for a moment and takes out his cell. "Governor, I think you should come in. Yes, it's safe—just the strawberry-blonde. What a mess this place is. She tells me she has information for you, about Graham and your wife. You might want to hear what she has to say, before I...

Yes, sir, Graham's here. He's lying on the floor. Don't know if he's alive. He really screwed things up here. Uh huh, okay. Gotcha. Will do."

"So he's coming in?"

"Maybe, maybe not. Depends on you. What you have to say to him."

"Call him back. Tell him I know about Evaline—that she's dead. Tell him I know details. Tell him..."

"Enough. I'll call."

Roberto Carboni enters through the back door. Alone. Angry. Armed. "Jefferson, for cryin' out loud, can't you do a job by yourself? Do I have to hold your hand?"

I study the governor. His face is red and twisted like a snake has crawled out of his skin. His handsome demeanor is gone. I whisper to myself, "If I make this guy any angrier, he's liable to explode."

Carboni turns and focuses on me. He leans into my body, so close I can smell his breath mints.

For whom would he want to have sweet breath? Evaline? The public? I can't help but think he is one politician whose pedestal is crumbling.

Jefferson shrugs his shoulders. "Governor…Sir…Hum…Tangie has information about Eveline, er, Mrs. Carboni. I don't know where she got her knowledge of the situation. I don't know who she told about it."

Carboni starts breathing in my face. I feel like I'm going to choke. He pulls my hair then grabs both my arms and pins them behind my back. "Tell me what you know."

"Can I please sit down and get comfortable? I think better when I am comfortable."

Jefferson rolls his eyes. "See what I mean, Boss…I mean, Governor."

Carboni glares at Jefferson. "Close the curtains." Then he slowly releases my arms and barks, "Sit."

I sit down on Aunt Hattie's rocking chair by the window.

"Not by the window. Over here by the fireplace."

I comply and move over to the Queen Anne chair. Thoughts of our Queen Anne chairs alongside the fireplace in our Seattle home come to mind and I start to cry—the last thing I want to do. I know I have to stay strong and not lose my composure. I begin with a voice I don't recognize as my own, but at least it is a voice, and it becomes louder as I go along. I stop crying and feel stronger, more in control of the situation. A strength I didn't know I had takes over.

"Governor Carboni, it seems you have gone through a lot of trouble to get rid of people and inflict harm on others. Why?"

"Shut up. I'll ask the questions."

He then twists my arm so tight I feel the pain rushing to my head.

I nod and try not to pass out.

He lessens his grip. "What do you know?"

I take a deep breath and whisper, "What do you want to know?"

"Quit playing games with me. I don't have all day. I am a busy man." Again, he tightens his grip. Again the pain becomes unbearable.

"I know that, Governor. Please release your arm. You're hurting me. I just don't know where to start. You make it hard for me to think."

Carboni releases my arm and I can breathe again.

"Start at the beginning."

"Well it all began with Steve."

"*Steve?*"

"You mean you don't know about Steve, *Steve the Murderer?* I gesture with my foot to Graham, who lies moaning on the floor beneath my chair. I am tempted to kick him in the side. "Here lies *Steve the Murderer*. Also known as *Buddy*. I am sure you know about *Buddy*."

The governor nods his head. "Tell me about this *Steve*."

"Steve romanced your wife."

"Oh, so that schmuck was Steve?"

"Yep. Alias, Graham."

"So that's how he did it. He didn't tell me."

"You should keep better tabs on your help."

"I don't need your advice." The governor snarls at me, this time like a wild beast that is getting ready to attack. The next moment, his voice becomes softer, more persuasive. "You know, Tangie, if I didn't have to get rid of you, I could use you on my team. You are as sharp as they come. Pity."

"You may want to keep me around. I know things. Lots of things."

"What else?"

"Can I hold your hand?"

Roberto studies me for a moment and then looks at Jefferson. "Watch her. Warn me if anything is out of sorts. Or shoot her if she gets crazy."

Roberto gives me his hand. I study the lines of his palm. I reach for his other hand and do the same to the other one. I drop his left hand and concentrate on his right. I caress it and put it to my face despite being repulsed by his touch. "You are not a nice man, Roberto. You are the cause of your first wife's death. You are as guilty as if you did it yourself. You ordered Graham/Buddy/Steve to kill Peter Van Beek, then your second wife, Eveline."

"How do you know these things?"

"*I know*. I know that you can only make love to prostitutes or women you dishonor in some way before taking them to your bed. I know that your children know nothing of your secret life. You kept them safe, in boarding school, away from your fantasy world. Their mother knew, and she died because of her knowledge of you. *She will get in the way of my plans*, you thought. I can see clearly that you didn't hire anyone to commit that murder. You did it yourself. Pills, to slow her heart. She just faded away. You excelled at playing the grieving husband. Poor Evaline didn't have a clue."

"You tell me you know these things. How? You haven't given me any proof. You don't know what you are talking about."

"Oh but I do. I can see them. Ask yourself if I am telling the truth. I have friends who believe in me. And they will not look kindly on my disappearance. So what are you going to do about it? Hide out in the governor's mansion, or your private retreat, while your wife lies dead in the Four Seasons Hotel? Perhaps the hotel staff has found her body by now, or the police. Remember, you were the last one seen with her."

"I was not. Buddy was. There are surveillance cameras at the Four Seasons. He told me he…"

"Yes, but those cameras only recorded *Steve*. You are forgetting Buddy/ Graham/Steve works for you. Or did." I point my toe at Graham. "He doesn't look so helpful now."

The governor grabs both my arms and shakes me. "Enough already. I've heard enough. Tell me. Who sent you here, to Rhode Island?"

"No one sent me. I came here looking for your wife, your second wife, Eveline. Or should I say, Evelina? She ticked me off in Fiji."

"I knew it! She told me she recognized you and I didn't believe her. My one mistake."

"Perhaps you acted too hastily in getting rid of her. Second thoughts?"

"It had to be done. Just like my getting rid of you, has to be done."

"Right now?"

"No, my sweet. You have an hour before Jefferson dumps you in the bay. He'll wait until dark."

"*Night's cloak* to hide his dirty deed?"

"Something like that. It's been a pleasure chatting. You are charming as ever. But as you know, what must be will be. All's well does not always end well. Now, if you don't mind, I'll excuse myself and leave you in Jefferson's strong arms. He will take care of you and the others. Have a good swim, Angelina. Sorry it's raining outside. If you are lucky, it won't be lightning when you all go out to sea.

He leans over to Jefferson, and whispers, "Take her upstairs. Drug her, and take the husband with you. Make it look like a murder-suicide. Then drag those cops out of the closet. Take them out the back way to the van. Shove them in and dump them in the bay. Remember to weigh them down so they don't float. I'll go look for the aunt. She's the only one missing. My guess is she's with the Van Beek sisters. Don't call me until tomorrow, when it's all over."

Roberto Carboni leaves the same way he came in, by the backdoor. I hear the sound of thunder rumbling as he closes the door. Through the front bay window, through the Irish lace curtains, a flash of lightning illuminates Jefferson's face, demonic, coming toward me. Any good omen I longed for earlier disappears from my thoughts. Again, fear—cold, hard fear—takes over.

Chapter Fifty-Two

My eyes start to flutter and I feel warmth encompass my body, beginning in my fingertips and leading to my heart muscle. I realize one person can save us from Roberto's henchman. Aunt Hattie, hiding upstairs with her shotgun. In a moment Jefferson will force me upstairs. He plans to throw me on the bed, put a pillow next to my head and shoot me. Then, he'll drag Walter's body up the stairs and shoot him, lying next to me. Or perhaps he will make me drag Walter's body with him.

"Hey you! Tangie! Get over here." Jefferson waves a very long gun at me. I recognize it as a Magnum, capable of doing a lot of harm. I shudder as Jefferson lifts Walter's upper torso up with one arm. "Help me with your lover boy."

I do as I am told. I pick up Walter's feet and follow Jefferson, who hooks his arm under Walter's back and wedges it between Walter's shoulder and neck. The two of us struggle up the stairs, Jefferson leading, but walking backwards with his gun pointed at me. He has a clear visual of me, but not of Aunt Hattie, as she stands at the top of the stairs, as I hope and pray she will be. I dare not look up and give her away, but I sense her presence. Creepy people sense stuff like that too. I try not to reveal my rising hope. Each step up the stairs seems like an eternity. I pray in silence, "Please, Pebbles, don't bark; don't give yourself away. Aunt Hattie, I am praying for you. Holy Mary, Mother of God…"

"Boom!"

One gunshot.

Jefferson loses his grip on Walter and slumps over with a groan and a whimper. He lies limp near the top of the stairs. Walter starts falling. I catch my love before he tumbles down the stairs. I grasp at his feet and then his shoulders. I shake him, trying to revive him, but cannot do so. I cry, "How can he not hear what is going on? Murder...mayhem...and he's out cold. Oh God!"

Looking up, I see Aunt Hattie is standing over us with the twelve-gauge over her shoulder. She sighs. "What in the devil is taking the police so long?"

"I've been thinking the same thing, Aunt Hattie. After going down-stairs and knocking out Graham, I called Theo Lee from the FBI. Still, we haven't had backup from the police, the FBI or anyone."

"Oh dear, what do we do now, Tangie?"

"I have to think, Aunt Hattie. I called Theo before things got really bad. I left the receiver off its holder, when this Jefferson guy came in. I don't know how much Theo heard, or if he caught on to what is going on. I hope he's on his way."

Aunt Hattie sets the shotgun on the landing against the floral wallpa-per in the upstairs hall, wallpaper that seems out of place in this carnival of crime. She clutches the railing, sidesteps over Jefferson's body and walks down to the middle of the stairs to be with me. She hugs me so hard I can't breathe. "Don't worry, Tangie. We're alive. Walter's alive. These thugs didn't get us."

I hug her back, take a deep breath and exhale. I leave her beside Walter and climb up the few stairs to her extension phone in the hallway and pick it up. Dead. I wonder if it is from the storm or if someone cut the wires. My body stiffens like a rail, on alert once more. I notice Walter's dear sweet aunt looking ready to keel over. Her head starts moving back and forth and she begins moaning.

I whisper, "Please, Aunt Hattie, hold on."

I go to the landing, pick up the twelve-gauge and walk down to the spot occupied by Walter and her. I look her straight in the eyes, put my free arm on her shoulder and say, "You've been so brave, Aunt Hattie. Try to hang on a little longer."

She sighs. "I'm out of energy, Tangie. Help me. I don't think I can move anymore."

I smooth her frazzled hair and pat her cheek. "You will be okay. You are one of the strongest people I know. Really."

She maintains eye contact with me and nods. "I'll try. I really will." She stands up slowly and says, "I think I can go on now. I just needed to sit a bit."

I hand her the gun. "Your shotgun—take it. It's not over yet. Roberto Carboni is on the loose. He's headed over to the Van Beeks' home. We must alert Clarissa and Jenny. We can't give up. And it's urgent we find someone to help us."

"Yes, Tangie, whatever you say. I can do this." She brushes aside her hair and attempts a firm posture.

I speak to her in a steady voice. "Steve and Barry are tied up in the downstairs hall closet, drugged like Walter. They need medical attention."

Aunt Hattie shakes her head, trying to stay lucid.

I put my arm around her. "I know it's hard, Aunt Hattie. Try to stay alert. Do you have a cell phone? Call 911. Ask them to send an ambulance right away."

"Tangie, I…"

"Maybe the medics will be quicker than the cops. I've come to the conclusion that Roberto Carboni alerted the police. He must have informed them that any call from this house would be a false alarm. He could have done that, you know. It fits his profile. No doubt he had your house phone bugged."

"Tangie, I don't have a cell phone. You must have one I could use. Don't you?"

"Yes, of course. It's downstairs, in the kitchen. At least, I hope it's still there. But who would look in the breadbasket? That's where I put it when we came home from brunch. Don't ask me why. Sometimes I do weird things and don't know why."

Aunt Hattie nods in understanding and pats my shoulder. "You did great, Angelina."

With gratitude and words unspoken, I extend my arms, she puts the gun aside and we hug each, like surviving soldiers after a fierce battle.

"Time to take care of our wounded, Aunt Hattie."

We traipse down the stairs together, carrying Walter's body, trying not to drop him as we inch our way into the foyer. Considering his muscular frame and his height, over six feet, this is not an easy feat. Somehow we carry him into the parlor and place him on the couch. I cover his shoulders with an afghan that is draped on the back of the sofa, kiss his unresponsive lips, and smooth down his hair. I go into the kitchen with Aunt Hattie to get some cold washcloths and make some strong coffee. Perhaps that will do the trick. It worked for me when I was drugged. Aunt Hattie finds my cell phone and calls the Newport First Aid Squad.

After I get the coffee going, I walk to the foyer and check the coat closet. Sure enough, squeezed between Aunt Hattie's old furs, winter coats and mothballs stand Barry and Steve. They are propped upright and wedged between all the clothing in the tiny closet, tied with plastic cords, and secured with duct tape over their mouths. I can see their eyes flickering, trying to focus. Their bodies, unsteady, start to fall on me. Reluctantly, I have to shut the door, so they don't tumble down and crash to the floor. I don't want to hurt them.

I lean against the closed door and shout. "Sorry, Steve! Sorry, Barry. I need help to get you out of the closet safely. "

Aunt Hattie comes into the hallway. "The medics should be here in a few minutes. They're quick. They can help us with Steve and Barry."

"Look on the bright side, Aunt Hattie. Our men are alive. You know it's strange. I haven't heard Pebbles bark, not even once."

"Tangie, I keep a few sedatives in my bedside table for emergencies. I broke one into tiny pieces and gave one piece to him. Perhaps you should check on him."

"Yes, of course. Poor dog. I'll run up the stairs and get him."

I race up the stairs, careful not to disturb the bodies strewn all over. I find Pebbles lying on Aunt Hattie's bed perfectly content. I hug him. "Good dog! You know when to be quiet." I scoop him into my arms, tip-toe back down the stairs and avoid looking at Carboni's thugs lying there.

Aunt Hattie meets me at the bottom. "Tangie, I'm worried about the Van Beek sisters. If the governor is headed over there, don't you think we should do something?"

We walk into the parlor and I place Pebbles on the rocking chair by the window, pet his head, and look at Aunt Hattie. "How long do you think it will take Carboni to get there?"

Aunt Hattie frowns. "He's probably there already."

"We have to call the sisters. Tell them not to answer the door and..."

Aunt Hattie picks up my cell and taps a few numbers. "Hello, Jenny. This is Hattie and this is important. Do you have any visitors?"

I show Aunt Hattie how to put the phone on speaker so we can both hear.

I hear Jenny sighing on her end of the phone. "Hattie. I am so glad you called. Clarissa and I always retire to our bedrooms for our usual nap, before we watch the evening news, and just as I am about to nod off, the doorbell rings. It keeps ringing. I don't want to answer it in my robe, nor does Clarissa."

"Good. Don't answer it under any circumstances. It is Roberto Carboni and he is responsible for...I'll tell you later. He is looking for me. He thinks that I'm there with you."

"He's looking for you? Why?"

"It's a long story, but he pieced together what we all know about him, and it's not good. Now he wants to get rid of me and he's on a rampage. He doesn't care who he harms. You are not safe in your own home at this very moment. Tangie and I are trying to alert the police, but..."

"Oh dear! What should Clarissa and I do?"

"Do you have a place to hide in your house?"

I hear Jenny cackle. "Oh, yes! We do. We have a hidden staircase by the fireplace. No one knows about it but us. This is an old home, like yours, from before the Civil War. It used to be part of the Underground Railroad."

"Good. Get Clarissa. Turn off all the lights. Use a flashlight and go there."

"That won't be a problem, dear. All the lights are already out. At least we still have phone service."

"Yes. Good. Take a cordless phone with you and stay hidden until help arrives. Don't come out until you hear my code: *Follow the Drinking Gourd*. Then you will know it is safe. Silence the ringer. Just watch for incoming calls."

"We can do all that. I will bring the new cell phone. Clarissa and I bought it for emergencies. This seems to be one."

"Yes it is. You are doing just fine. If all goes well, Tangie or I will call you soon or come over. Stay safe until then. Don't turn on any lights. Oh, and give me your cell phone number, so I can call you back."

"Yes, Hattie. Here it is: It is the same as our home phone except for the last digit. That is now three. I'll alert Clarissa. We'll go to our hide-out, just as we did when we were little. Good thing we stay in shape. It's a tight fit."

"Yes. That's a great plan. Talk to you soon."

"You too, Hattie. And for God's sake, be careful."

I smile at Aunt Hattie as she taps the phone and hands it to me. "You are a rock. You know that?"

"It's just an act, Tangie. I'm scared to death. Look what we have done! I've never shot another person in my life."

"Neither have I. But I can't think about that now. I'll go crazy. I'm going to take this coffee into the living room and try to get Walter to drink some. Maybe it will revive him. Let's keep the curtains shut, and the lights dim. At least we have power."

Aunt Hattie leans down and picks up a roll of duct tape from the floor. "I think I'll go tie up those three attackers lying on the stairs. Two of them might be moving around soon. We don't need them coming after us again."

Chapter Fifty-Three

I hear the sirens as I return to the living room with the coffee. After placing the pot and cups on the coffee table, I peek through the window curtains and see the ambulance stopping and two men dressed in blue uniforms, getting out. They head our way with a stretcher. I sigh, grateful that help is finally here. However, the next moment, I shudder, hoping these saviors in blue are not evil men in disguise. I motion to Aunt Hattie as she returns to the living room with an empty roll of duct tape and a smile on her face.

"Well, I have those felons secured. They won't bother us again. It seems like the bear spray did the job on the first one, but he's beginning to move a bit. The others...I can't say..."

I nod, then gesture to her. "Aunt Hattie, come look out the window."

She joins me and opens the curtain. "Well, at least somebody has finally made an appearance."

"Do you recognize the medics?"

"Well, one of them is the son of a friend of mine—that's Billy Majore. The other one looks familiar. Yes, I believe he's a neighbor of Louisa. I've met them both, briefly, and I'm pretty sure we can trust them."

"Well, if we ever needed some men worthy of trust, it would be now." I close the curtains and rush to the front door, unaware of how I am dressed, clad only in my bathrobe.

"Gentlemen, come in. My name is Tangie Seraphina, and this is my aunt, Hattie Cunningham. She owns this house and there's been a break-in. Three men attacked us. One of them tried to kidnap me, two tried to shoot me. Two policemen from Seattle tried to help us, but they are now in the hall closet. They're tied up, beaten and drugged by the assailants. We tried to rescue them, but we couldn't get them out of the closet. We need your help so they don't fall over. My husband is lying on the couch, unresponsive. I brought him some coffee. Seems he's been beaten and drugged also. But I think what he really needs is medical attention. I don't know what to do."

A blank stare answers me.

Aunt Hattie looks at the medics and shakes the hand of one of them. "So, Billy, good to see you again. How is your mom? Your colleague, here...what is his name? I've forgotten it."

"This is Sam Welding, ma'am. We are here to help you, but, Holy Sh...!

Aunt Hattie takes Billy's arm and speaks in a soothing voice, trying not to sound alarmed. "Billy, we can explain this. As Tangie said, we had intruders. They didn't fare so well."

Billy glances up the stairs and then peaks into the living room. He notices all three bodies sprawled out, two of them moaning, one lifeless. "I think we are going to need another ambulance."

I nod. "And I think the coroner for one of them. Could you please tell them to come in the back way and not use sirens? We may still be in danger until the FBI gets here."

Sam looks bewildered but doesn't say a word or question me. He scratches his head, nods to me and picks up a cell phone. I hear him as he orders an additional first aid truck and tells whoever answers the phone that it is urgent. "No sirens, please. Just come and pull around the back of the residence."

"Sam, we did call the police, and the FBI, but neither responded to our calls. I don't know what's keeping them. I do think the FBI is on the way, even though my conversation with them was cut off by one of the thugs, but I am sure the police haven't got a clue what's going on."

"I will call the police for you and find out, ma'am."

"Thanks, Sam. Maybe they will listen to you."

Billy follows me into the living room and kneels beside Walter, who lies on the couch, still unresponsive. I notice Pebbles, sitting next to Walter, guarding him and licking his hand. I pick up my faithful pooch and place him on the club chair to give the medic more room. Billy leans over, places his head on Walter's chest and listens to his heart. He takes Walter's pulse, puts on his stethoscope and listens again to his heartbeat. He looks at me and frowns. "Ma'am, we need to transport your husband to the hospital. I don't know what drugs you say he ingested, but he needs more than coffee to revive him. His heart rate is very low."

My panic level borders on terror. It soars way beyond my attempt to keep calm. I try not to lose my composure, but I can feel the room spinning and my own heartbeat slowing down. I step over Graham's body and collapse in the Queen Anne Chair by the hearth. Any fire burning there earlier is out.

As I struggle to pull myself together, I feel an arm grab my leg.

"Ah! Help!" I scream the shriek of a banshee. Aunt Hattie witnesses Graham's revival. She rushes for her shotgun and hits Graham's face with the butt of the gun.

The two medics look at her in astonishment.

"I'm sorry, boys, but that degenerate has angered me for the last time. The police better come soon and take him away, or I will use the other end of the shotgun if he pisses me off again."

Sam's eyes widen and he does his best to reassure Aunt Hattie. "Ma'am, I just talked to the Newport Police Department. This time, the police are on their way. Seems someone called them and cancelled your 911 call, claiming it was a false alarm. Apparently some official, high up, requested them to do so."

This time, I roll my eyes. "Roberto Carboni."

Billy turns momentarily from assisting Walter, to question me. "The governor?"

"None other. I must warn you guys to stay clear of that fellow. I don't think he will be governor after tonight. Right now, he is breaking into the home of friends of Aunt Hattie, the late governor's sisters. I pray the police or FBI catch him this time. I think the Van Beek sisters have a silent alarm. At least I hope so."

"They do, dear." Aunt Hattie smiles and pats my shoulder to reassure me.

I lean back in the chair and smile back at her. She gives me such hope. And I hope the images I am visualizing in my subconscious mind are real: *Carboni toast. FBI agents and police surround the Van Beek's house and arrive on the scene just in time to prevent another crime.* And the headlines: *Carboni Caught in the Act—Sweet Justice.*

I sit up, focused and alert once more. "Billy, will it be all right if I ride in the ambulance with Walter?"

"I don't think that will be a problem. Sure, ah..."

"Tangie. Call me Tangie."

Aunt Hattie nods at me. "You do that dear. I will stay here with Barry and Steve and wait for the second ambulance."

I look at Billy and Sam. "Guys, I think one of you should stay until the police come. We have bodies on the stairs, and Graham here, and we need to explain what happened."

Aunt Hattie takes my hand and urges me on. "Tangie, you've done enough for one night. You go with your husband. I'll explain things to the police, and tie up Graham before they get here. If you stay here any longer, they'll detain you, and you need to be with Walter. They can question you later. Go...go with Walter. I'll stay with Steve and Barry and Pebbles. Don't worry. I'll wait for the second ambulance. If necessary, the medics can transport Steve and Barry without me. They're grown men— cops, medics—they are used to this sort of thing. I'll stay and talk to the Newport police, whenever they get here."

I hug my fearless defender. "Thank you for your strength, Aunt Hattie. I love you."

"I love your too, dear. Now you get off that chair and go with Walter. He needs you."

I smile for the second time that evening. Then I hug Pebbles, hand his leash to Aunt Hattie and follow the medics out the door. Sam helps Billy put Walter in the back of the ambulance and I hop in with Walter.

Billy hands me a blanket. "Stay with the patient, Tangie. I'll assist Sam in getting your colleagues out of the closet safely, and then I will be back, pronto."

I brush Walter's hair with my hand and press my cheek to his. He feels cold and clammy, comatose. I drape the blanket over him. There is nothing else I can do, except cry and pray. I begin to chant, "Please, God, let him be all right. Please let him be all right. Please..."

Billy returns before I finish my prayer. I look up in a daze. Before he closes the rear door, he says, "Sam and I pulled your friends out of the closet. They are a little shaky, but lucid. Sam is attending to them now. I don't think you need to worry about them. I'll return to help Sam, after I transport Walter and you to Newport Hospital.

Coming out of my stupor, I nod, feeling relief in his words. Billy gets in the driver's seat and takes off, speeding down the narrow cobblestone street en route to 11 Friendship Street. I remember the address. We were just there last night. At my request, he does not put on the siren until we get out of Aunt Hattie's neighborhood.

Chapter Fifty-Four

When we arrive at the emergency room, I inform the doctor on duty that Walter ingested a high dose of some date rape drug. "I know, Doctor, because the culprit who injected it into him alluded to that fact. This lowlife, Graham, gave Walter the same drug he slipped into my hot cocoa, earlier in the week."

The doctor listens patiently as I continue. "I spit it out, before it could get totally into my system, so I didn't suffer any long-term effects of the drug. Walter apparently has. Doctor, that Graham is not a nice person. He told me he planned to shoot Walter in the head. That's when I…"

The doctor looks at me with wide eyes. "Seems like you've had a busy evening, Miss."

"You don't know the half of it, but I am too tired to talk about it."

I collapse on a chair next to Walter's bed and hold my beloved's hand while the doctor examines him.

I watch as the orderlies wheel Walter out of the ER with IV's attached to his arm and tubes inserted into his mouth and nose.

I glance at the doctor's nametag, which reads: "Dr. Carey". He speaks to me in a voice that is soft and reassuring. "Your husband is being moved to a private room. You may follow and stay with him. The next five hours are crucial. Walter is young and he is strong. He should recover. We are pumping fluids into his body to counter-act the drugs that are slowing down his vitals. I don't want to give you false hope, but I think he will pull through. Just my feeling."

I stand up and give the emergency doctor a kiss on the cheek. "Thank you, Dr. Carey, for my husband's life." I shake his hand and follow the orderlies into the elevator, still wearing my tangerine bathrobe and slippers and not caring a fig how I look.

As I sit in Walter's private room, staring at the tubes and IV's attached to his body, I have a flashback to my stay in the hospital last spring, and again, more recent, this past fall. Now I know how my family must have felt. It is worse than being the patient, being the family member, waiting for your loved one to turn the corner and get well. It doesn't happen right away. And now it seems we are in for a long night. Well, at least I am dressed for the occasion.

A nurse enters. "Ma'am, would you like a cot to lie down upon while you wait?"

"Yes, that would be lovely. I can lie next to Walter and hold his hand." I stifle a yawn. "I can hardly keep my eyes open."

I brush the hair off his face and smile at him. He has such a distinguished profile, rugged, yet handsome. He could be a model but I would never tell him that. He's not into looking good. Not on his list of things that are important. He's just a natural charmer. Deep. Thoughtful. Loving. I sigh, "Oh, how I miss him being awake." But I am patient, and oh, so tired.

I nod to the nurse when she returns wheeling the cot. I crawl in as soon as she opens it, not even thanking her for her efforts. I close my eyes and slip into a deep slumber.

The door creaks open.

I open my eyes wide. Engaged, ready. I think Roberto's men are attacking me again. I scream.

The light switch goes on, and there stands Theo Lee, chief FBI agent.

"Easy, Tangie. Everything is all right." He walks over and takes my hand. "You are safe. So is Walter."

I stare at him, tears streaming down my face. "What took you so long?"

"I had to take care of a few things at the Van Beek residence and then at Aunt Hattie's. I'll only stay a few minutes. I know how tired you are."

"Yeah, I've been busy. Doing your job. I am not a cop and I am not an FBI agent."

Theo smiles. "You could have fooled the lot of us. Tangie, you know you should have called us sooner. You didn't give us much notice."

"Like what would I tell you? *Oh, I have a feeling about this guy and…*"

"But Tangie, we *know* you. We could have helped sooner. It takes us time to get organized and out in the field. You wanted us here in minutes. When we got to your aunt's residence, Steve and Barry were being carried into the ambulance, then to the hospital to be checked. I have good news to report. They are conscious, not as heavily drugged as Walter. But the thugs hit them over their heads and tied them up. Both Steve and Barry have mild concussions, but aren't doing badly, all things considered."

"What about the van, in the back of the house?"

"The police confiscated it. The driver was asleep with earphones on, listening to some really weird music. How he could sleep through everything going on still amazes me. He put up no resistance. I think we can use him as a witness."

"Well that's a relief. He was a loose end."

"He's all tied up now. Remember Tangie, next time, call us sooner."

"I hope there won't be a next time."

"Me too, for your sake, but you have a way of…"

"I know, getting involved in stuff I should stay out of."

"Actually, I was going to say, I am grateful for all you have accomplished this evening, with very little help. Next time call us early. We will trust you. Believe me. And we will help. Just ask." Theo takes my chin in his hand and looks directly in my eyes. "Tangie, you and Aunt Hattie saved lives tonight—Walter, Steve and Barry—and quite possibly the Van Beek sisters. They're all still here because of you."

I am not good at receiving compliments and I blush and get a little tongue-tied. Tha…Thanks, Theo. "I…I'm so relieved Steve and Barry are recovering from their injuries—but Walter…Walter still has not come to—he is not yet conscious." I wipe my tears off my face with the sleeve of my robe. "But the doctor gives me hope."

Theo nods. "I know it's hard right now, Tangie. He'll be okay. Just wait."

I squeeze Theo's arm. "What about Aunt Hattie? Where is she?"

"She's at her home, talking with the police. She said to tell you she'll be at the hospital soon, and that she'll ask Louisa to watch Pebbles."

"That's Aunt Hattie—so thoughtful. And Jenny and Clarissa—what about the Van Beek sisters?"

"Well, we, my agents and I, and the police went to their home. We heard Carboni's plan on the phone line you left open, until the storm cut off the power. The first thing we did was to rush over to the Van Beek's home. We caught Roberto Carboni in the act of breaking into the sisters' home. We couldn't locate the Van Beek sisters. The police are holding the governor on breaking and entering, and more charges are pending. We will need your testimony, as well as Walter's, Barry's and Steve's. This is one time the governor's hotshot lawyer won't be able to get him off. We plan to file federal kidnapping charges against him. And soon, he will be charged with murder."

"Thanks, Theo. There is a lot more for me to tell you, and it is not all dreams or conjecture. I have proof. Funny how crooks talk when they think they have something in the bag. Or in my case, they felt certain of my demise."

"I'm sorry you had to go through this, Tangie."

I swing my legs around the side of the cot, yawn and invite Theo to sit down. "Yeah. Me too. Did you know I shot a man? I never did that before and hope to never again. Horrible. I'm sorry, but it was self-defense. I had no choice. Carboni's thugs were coming after Aunt Hattie and me. I'm sure they meant to kill us. They're the ones that beat up Walter. They planned to kill him as soon as they found me. That really made me mad, really mad."

"Aunt Hattie filled me in."

"What about Graham?"

"Graham?"

"Graham, the head henchman, assistant to Roberto Carboni and former corrupt aide to Peter Van Beek. He is the one who set the governor up for *an accident*. Add *Murderer* to his resume. He also threw Walter off his sailboat the evening before. And this past evening, he is the one who drugged Walter. I am the one who hit Graham, the creep, over the head, with a little help from the raven statue. Aunt Hattie also popped him once on the head, with the butt of her shotgun, when he grabbed my leg."

"Oh, that's the guy with the head injury."

"Yes, that guy. The jerk just wouldn't give up. I hate his guts but I hope I didn't kill him. I don't need his death on my conscience. A part of me knows I shouldn't feel guilty. I can prove that Graham is responsible for the deaths of two people, Peter Van Beek and Eveline—Roberto Carboni's wife."

Don't worry, Tangie. He has a fractured skull, but the doctors think he'll recover and be able to face trial."

"That makes me feel better. He more or less confessed two murders to me when I confronted him. You need to get a search warrant, go to his apartment, look under his bed. Check under the floorboards. I'm sure you'll find the murder weapons. For the governor's murder, you'll discover a winch from Peter Van Beek's yacht. From the other murder, you'll find a red tie, Graham's tie, used to strangle Eveline Carboni. I have a feeling when you find those items, Graham will sing."

Theo nods. "I'll let my staff and the police know. We'll also check for DNA."

"Oh, one more thing, Theo. Roberto Carboni confessed to murder in a round about way. He ordered the killings."

"Yes, we heard his bragging about that on the phone. Great evidence, thanks to you, Tangie. We recorded that and all of Carboni's threats to you from the phone you left off the hook."

"Thank God you heard all that. So you heard all that scary stuff before the power went out?"

Theo nods and shakes my hand. "Smart move, Tangie. We got it all. The phone service went off after he left you."

"That's a relief. Thanks, Theo."

"No, Tangie, the thanks go entirely to you."

"You know, Theo, sometimes I feel numb. Sometimes the stress of being responsible for another person's life or death comes crashing down on me. I don't know how to react."

Theo squeezes my hand, gently, reassuring me. "I know the shooting is hard on you. You weren't mentally prepared for this to happen. I have some more news."

"Good, I hope."

"Well, this Graham fellow is in the prison hospital, not here. The police did not want to bring him to Newport General. He will be kept locked up."

"Good. Let him stay there." I take a deep breath and let it out slowly. "Theo, you know I have more information about the murder of Evaline Carboni at the Four Seasons Hotel, and the murder of Peter Van Beek on his sailboat, but I am so tired. I can't keep my eyes open. Can we talk later?"

"Yes, Mrs. Cunningham." Theo smiles and stands up and pulls the covers over me as I crawl back into my cocoon. "You've given us plenty to work on, so later will be fine. I have some phone calls to make, but I will be just outside. For now, you rest. I will be nearby, keeping watch." Theo smiles down at me. When you want to talk some more, I will be here. And Tangie…"

I yawn. "What?"

"You did what you had to do to protect your family. So did Aunt Hattie. No one is judging your actions. No one will. Self-defense. For now, everything that happened is being kept under wraps, confidential, until the facts are sorted out. You won't be going to the news media, will you?"

"Fat chance of that. Even though I would love to see Carboni's smug face plastered all over the news channels, I don't like publicity. Not my cup of tea. Last thing I need in my life is to be known as a psychic. In some circles that spells *kook*. Like in *crazy*. I will keep my mouth shut. How are you going to keep this quiet?"

"We're working on it. Damage control. We don't want you or Aunt Hattie in any more danger, and we'll try to keep your names out of everything. We want to be sure there is no one out there, who will be a threat to you. And if you do have to testify, you will be protected. We can keep your identity hidden. This is now a federal case; we are in charge. We'll talk some more, later. Get some rest. When Walter is awake, we'll have a meeting."

I nod and stifle another yawn. "One thing, Theo, please. Would you call Aunt Hattie? Remind her she needs to call the Van Beek sisters and give them the code so they can come out of hiding. They are in a secret location in their house and are probably still there. In all the excitement, she might have forgotten to call them. Tell her what I told you, exactly, and make sure you tell her all is clear at the Van Beek's house."

Theo smiles at me, and nods. Then he opens the door and is gone.

A sudden urge possesses me to leave my cot and go to Walter's bedside. Despite my exhaustion, I sit beside him amongst all the tubes. He looks so peaceful, like he is having a sweet dream in a far-away place. I brush the hair out of his face and kiss his forehead. "When you are awake my love, we will talk."

I kiss his lips. They are warm now, but still not responsive. Tears form in my eyes. I fight them back at first, then crawl into my cot, snuggle into my pillow and let the tears fall where they may as I drift off into a dreamless sleep.

Chapter Fifty-Five

I wake with a start and hear a constant beep. Opening my eyes, I look up at the ceiling. White. Plain. I see a hospital bed next to me and remember I am in Walter's room and breathe a sign of relief. I notice Aunt Hattie stretched out in a chair, like a slumped-over stuffed animal with her eyes closed and her feet resting on a footstool. She brings back a memory of my mother, who sat by my bedside for ten days last spring, when the doctors put me into a medically induced coma. I say a prayer of thanksgiving for Walter's courageous aunt and smile in gratitude. I rise from my cot, careful not to disturb Walter or Aunt Hattie, wrap my robe tight around my waist and go over to the window and look outside. Daylight is dawning. It's sunny with a little haze forming over the buildings outside. I begin to hum a familiar tune in my head, "Morning has broken…like the first dew drop, Eden saw play…"

I return to Walter's bedside, press my cheek upon his and brush his lips with mine. His body stirs. My smile broadens. It feels so good to see him move. I scoot my body next to him on the bed, careful not to disturb the tubes and IV. I lean my head down onto his pillow so I can be close to him and close my eyes.

When I open my eyes a second time, it is late morning. Aunt Hattie is gone and Walter and I are alone, together. One of his arms is resting on mine and he is breathing evenly. I sit up slowly and kiss him gently. This time, Walter responds. I feel his body returning to me and tears begin to flow. I press my cheek to his and whisper, "Oh, Walter, you've come back to me."

He murmurs, "I never left you, Tangie."

"You almost did. I've been frantic. Worried sick, my love."

"What day is it?"

"I think it is Sunday, my love."

"We missed church."

"We miss it a lot. Maybe we can start going again. I feel the need to say a prayer. Like really pray. I am so grateful we are here together after everything that has happened. I don't have the words to say what I feel. I am just so happy you are alive."

Walter looks deep into my eyes and a smile appears on his face. He nods, and a tear runs down his face. Others follow. He too, is overcome by emotion. He whispers, hoarsely, "Me too. Are you all right, my love? What about Aunt Hattie, Steve and Barry?"

"Aunt Hattie came here and stayed all night. She's an early riser. Probably went to get breakfast, or to Louisa's to check on Pebbles. Steve and Barry are a bit beat up, but otherwise fine."

"I feel like I've been run over by a truck. I cannot lift my head."

"You're getting better. It just takes time. Rest, Sweetheart." I kiss his forehead, his cheeks and his lips, slowly and softly.

Walter closes his eyes and smiles. "I love you, Angelina."

"And I love you. Rest. I'll be right here with you."

I put my head down on half of Walter's pillow but do not return to sleep. My mind starts racing. I breathe a sigh of relief over Walter's return to the living and recite a silent prayer that he will be his old self soon. I think about the past night's events, and wonder if I will ever be the same. Faced with my own mortality and my place in the universe, I start to shake. "Oh no." I whisper to myself. "I don't want to be this way. I want to be strong. I want to be brave." I feel myself falling away, out of touch with the real world. The night's occurrences are too much for me. I begin my deep breathing, meditating on my blessings, and gratitude for living. That helps raise me up and pull me back to where I want to be. I affirm to myself, "When I get home, I will call Father Don. He will know what to say to me. He said he would always be there if I ever need him. And I am so in need of spiritual guidance right now." I sit there sobbing for quite a while. Then the door opens. In walk two answers to my prayers.

Steve and Barry, looking a little like prizefighters after a knock out but otherwise cheery and robust, stroll over to Walter's bedside and grin at me. They take turns kissing my tear-stained cheeks.

"Well hello, Ms. Seraphina, er, Mrs. Cunningham," Barry begins. "Thank you…"

Steve smiles at me. "Hi Tang. Thanks for rescuing us from our midnight swim with the fishes.

"Yes," Barry continues. "We could hear your intervention and your prevention of our demise from our closet cell."

I dab at my eyes with my sleeve and can't help but smile at their chipper comments and glowing faces. "I'm sorry I left you in there, guys. I couldn't lift you out. You would have fallen over. I didn't want you to fall on the floor, or against something, hit your head and get hurt."

"Sure, sure." Barry smiles at me. "You just wanted all the glory to yourself, kid."

"Barry, you know I don't like this kind of glory. Too much gore involved."

Steve takes my hand and pats it. "You don't really like being a cop, do you, Tangie."

"You got that one right, Steve. There is no way I could operate at this level on a regular basis. I need calm in my life. Serenity. Peace. I cannot stand the seedy side of life, no matter what class of people we are talking about."

"There are creeps everywhere. They come in high and low places. Seems you found that out."

"Yes, Steve, I did. So, are you checked out of the hospital?"

"Yeah. They released Barry and me this morning."

Barry lifts up his arms. "We thought you and Walter would enjoy these."

"Cappuccinos! Thanks, Barry! Might be just the thing to wake up lover boy, here."

I pat Walter gently, lean down and kiss his forehead. "He's doing much better. He overdosed on that drug Graham injected into him. There was a ton of it in his bloodstream. It was touch and go for awhile."

I wiped the last of my tears off my face with my sleeve. "If anything ever happened to him, I don't...I can't imagine what I would do."

Steve leans down and hugs me. "I know, Tangie. I know how close you two are. Everything will be all right. You'll see."

"Now look who's psychic." Then I laugh for the first time in days. It feels good. "Thanks for the cappuccinos, guys." I take a sip and move slightly to get off the bed. I feel an arm grab my waist.

"Oh no, you don't, Sweetheart. I've got you captive."

"Walter! You're awake! You're joking! You must be back with us!"

"I told you I'm back. And now, I'm hungry."

Walter eyes Barry and Steve. "Hi guys. What's going on?"

"Well, we're waiting for Theo to show up, and then we'll have a meeting."

I look at Steve and Barry. "Wait a minute, you two. Do you know where Aunt Hattie is?"

Barry nods. "As a matter of fact, we do. She came into our room early this morning to check on us, just as the doctor was releasing us. Seems she is going to that brunch the Van Beek sisters put on every year."

"The Van Beek sisters are having their brunch?"

"Yes. They had everything ordered and the caterer showed up on time because they forgot to cancel it. Even though they were somewhat frantic, the sisters decided to go ahead and have their brunch. Aunt Hattie went over to help and give them some support."

I sigh. "That lady is a rock."

Walter nods. "That she is."

I kiss Walter on the cheek. "Now I know where you get your strength of character, Walter."

"Ah, my love. It seems, you and Aunt Hattie are the rocks. You rescued us, got us out of the clutches of those nasty politicians and their hit men."

Steve nods and shakes Walter's hand. "That they did. Good to have you back, good buddy."

Barry steps toward Walter, and mirrors Steve, shaking Walter's hand. "Welcome back, Walter. What an ordeal, but glad you're intact. We'll fill you in on the details when Agent Lee comes in."

Steve nods. "Yeah, good buddy. He should be here any minute. I think he went to get some breakfast."

Walter perks up. "Speaking of breakfast, what do we have to do to get a meal around here?"

"Oh, " Barry points. "Just push that button over there. They deliver."

I look at Walter and grin. "Our favorite, hospital food. What do you think, Walter? Can you eat? Can you sit up?"

"Yes, on both counts. Eating with you anywhere, anytime is a feast."

"I love it when you talk smooth."

"I know. Come here." Walter pulls me towards him and plants a warm, inviting kiss on my mouth, as Barry and Steve stroll over to the window and look out. I don't know if they are embarrassed or just want to give us some privacy. They continue to stare out the window until our meal arrives, wheeled in on a cart by none other than Agent Theo Lee of the FBI.

"Hi Tangie. Good to see you up and looking alive again, Walter."

Walter extends his arm to Theo and shakes his hand. "Nice to see you too, Theo. What's up?"

"Well, I talked to your doctor. He can release you shortly, as soon as they take out the IV's and check your vitals. I thought you, Tangie, and these guys..." Theo nods to Barry and Steve. "I thought perhaps we could all attend the Van Beek's brunch. This hospital food doesn't look so good."

Theo picks up the lid on the breakfast tray. "Name your preference: Oatmeal and applesauce, or *Brunch at the Van Beeks*, which I shall dub, *Spoiling the Slimy Governor's Term in Office*."

"What?" My eyes open wide and I can get nothing else out of my mind.

"Here's the latest twist in the tale. While you all were snoozing, Aunt Hattie and I hatched a plan. We talked the Van Beek sisters into letting the governor come to the brunch. Obviously he hasn't heard from Jefferson yet, and doesn't know that you are all alive. I will stand guard. You will all show up alive. Tangie, I will play the FBI recording we made of his conversation with you. All of his goons are neutralized, so it will just be Carboni. His personal chauffeur will be in the limo a safe distance away, under police guard. Undercover police will be surrounding the house. Safe. The governor doesn't wear a gun. He has others do his dirty work for him. And those others now are either dead or in jail."

"Theo, I don't trust Carboni. Remember, I've seen his dirty deeds. He might have a couple of goons, or guns stashed away somewhere."

"Tangie, we've got it all arranged. It will be all right. We can deal with anything out of kilter. We are in control of the situation."

I need reassurance. "Are you sure he won't be carrying a weapon?"

"Not absolutely, but I'll have someone posted close to him at all times when he arrives. I don't think he will try anything with a household of his supporters."

"You don't know this guy, Theo. He's so dirty, pigeons won't go near him."

Walter smiles. "Tangie, I'm glad to see you are back to your old jovial self."

Barry takes off his glasses, cleans them with a handkerchief from his pocket and reiterates, "Theo, don't you think you should let Walter know what has happened, while he was sleeping?"

"Sure Barry, but I have a feeling Walter senses the gist of it." Theo comes over to Walter and pats his back. "Glad to have you back with the living, Walter. I'll fill you in on the details while we drive to the brunch. Just know for now, that you have a very brave wife, and your aunt is a treasure."

"I've always known that." Walter leans over and kisses me. "Thanks, Angelina, my love. I know I'm here, alive, because of you."

"And Aunt Hattie." I smile at my love, feeling totally energized.

Theo smiles at the two of us as he picks up the bedside phone. I hear him ask the doctor to come to Walter's room A.S.A.P. and check him out.

Some people have clout. Theo happens to be one of them. Dr. Carey appears in minutes with a nurse. He orders the tubes and IV's removed, then shakes all of our hands, smiles at us and bids us adieu. Then, he leaves in a flash to make his rounds. As luck would have it, we are ready to leave in no time at all.

I look at the four men remaining in the room, each showering me with love and attention. I feel warmth surrounding me, like angels flying over-head. I know, somehow, I will get through all of this. The guilt, the sorrow of taking another person's life, and the horror of the past evening will find their place in the past and not haunt my present. I am blessed.

Chapter Fifty-Six

Theo informs Walter of the events of yesterday afternoon and evening while we ride in a stretch limo to the Van Beeks' residence. Seems the Van Beeks insisted we use their transportation service. Theo climaxes his story by telling us he made a plea deal with Governor Carboni. "You see, Carboni posted bail. I had the police convince Carboni he would not charged with breaking and entering, if he will just apologize to the sisters. He thinks he is in the clear, safe. Carboni does not know of everything the FBI has on him. I want to keep him in the dark and play the tape in front of his constituents. That way, we can be assured of Roberto Carboni's cooperation when we file the more serious charges against him. Charges, like conspiracy, kidnapping and murder. If there are any others in this conspiracy, Carboni will rat on them. I am positive of that."

I grin. "Rather sneaky, but oh so clever, Theo."

Theo smiles. "I think so, Tangie."

"I am a little worried about the *others* in this conspiracy. Graham alluded to more people, higher up, involved in this mess."

"Tangie, you don't have to worry anymore. The FBI is taking over. We will protect you. If there are any more supporters of Carboni and his criminal tactics, we will hunt them down and we will find them."

Walter looks thoughtful and then his face lights up, his color returning. "Don't you think Carboni might have a coronary when he sees Tangie and me? He thinks his only known offense is prowling around the Van Beek's home. He assumes we are dead."

"Yes, dear colleagues. He's convinced he can worm his way out of the breaking and entering charges." Theo scratches his head. "Yes, at the moment Governor Carboni is thinking, *no problemo*. He will soon find out how wrong he is."

I can hardly contain myself as we drive to the Van Beek's home. Theo's scheme is right up my alley. I love this kind of closure. I live for it.

As we pull up in front of the picturesque estate, a classic seacoast mansion bordering Newport Harbor, I admire how it is landscaped to perfection. Boxwood trimmed, roses still blooming, mums and pumpkins decorating the walkway to the front door. Our driver stops the limo by the main entrance.

Theo gets out, picks up his cell and calls his assistant who is waiting for orders with Carboni in tow. "We are at the Van Beek's estate. You can escort the governor here now."

I smile as Theo helps me out of the limo. Walter is next. He is a little shaky but able to walk on his own two feet without assistance. Steve and Barry follow. Theo tells the driver to park nearby, unobserved, and await instructions.

I look at my men in arms. "So, who's hungry?"

Walter smiles. "I don't remember the last time I ate."

Barry pats him on the shoulder. "You lead, Walter. You know the way."

Walter strolls up the entry stairs and up to the front door, with me on his arm, like it is the most natural thing in the world. Good thing Aunt Hattie brought some clothes for me to the hospital last night, or I'd still be wearing that tangerine robe. She thinks of everything, kind of like Walter with a feminine touch. She arranged Pebbles' care and the dear soul helped with this brunch. I must get a special gift for her before we leave for Seattle. And today, I must remember to bring Pebbles some leftovers.

I am not surprised when Aunt Hattie spots us, runs over and embraces Walter, me, then Steve. She shakes Barry and Theo's hands and grins. "I can't believe you all came. I was hoping you would, but I wasn't sure. Walter, are you sure you are up to this?"

"Now Aunt Hattie, you know I bounce back quickly, like the lost sheep in the flock coming back."

"You're no lost sheep. You are my favorite nephew. And you, Tangie, are a treasure. Come here."

Aunt Hattie hugs me tight as I whisper in her ear, "Thanks for the clothes."

"Somehow I thought you would need them."

I grin at her and spot the Van Beek sisters tottering toward us.

I shake their white-gloved hands. "Clarissa, Jenny, so good to see you again. I hope you are well, after all the excitement."

Clarissa nods. "Oh, yes. It will take more than a break-in to stop us."

Jenny smiles and gives Walter a hug. "We heard, dear Walter, that you were in the hospital. Come sit down, near this end table. We'll bring you some food and refreshment right now. It's all spread out in our conservatory, but I don't think you can wait until we all go in there. Don't argue."

Walter doesn't argue. He smiles and strolls over to the Lazy Boy club chair near the fireplace and sits down. The chair reminds me of the oversized one in our living room in Seattle. I sigh. He motions me to join him.

I oblige, squeeze next to him, and whisper as I put my head on his shoulder, "I wish we were in our chair back home."

He squeezes my waist, saying, "Soon, Tangie, soon," and kisses my ear.

Steve and Barry stand guard near us and Theo remains near the door. We smile at each other as the Van Beek sisters hurry off to get Walter some food. At that moment they remind me of twin versions of my grandmother.

Walter sits in our chair, scoops Eggs Benedict into his mouth and bites on a croissant in between scoops. I sip some of his coffee, while sitting next to him, and munch on one of his mini-sweet rolls, filled with cinnamon and sugar. I close my eyes and for a moment I forget we are still embroiled in the world of crime. There is a sudden hush in the room. I hear the front door open. That calm, so precious and fleeting, deserts me.

Footsteps stride in the hallway, and a voice booms, "Thank you, ladies for inviting me. I am sorry I gave you a scare last night. It was urgent I get in touch with you. I discovered some information about your brother, God rest his soul, and it could not wait."

Jenny replies, "Oh don't worry, Robert. Everything is taken care of. Won't you please come into the living room and make yourself comfortable? Some old friends of ours are here."

Clarissa adds, "I'm sure you will be surprised to see them."

I take a final sip of my coffee and put the cup down before Roberto Carboni reaches the living room. Walter sits up straight. Theo and his assistant stand by the fireplace and Steve and Barry stand on either side of the doorway from the hall to the living room. Two uniformed policemen enter the living room through the dining room entrance and post themselves at that escape route.

Roberto Carboni enters and immediately turns a whiter shade of pale. Ghostly. Sensing gloom and doom coming, his eyes dart from Walter to Aunt Hattie and then to me. I can hear a noticeable gasp from his throat. He stares at me. "You! You, you did this..."

"Did what, Roberto? You must admit, I tried to warn you."

Roberto Carboni continues to stare at me. His face becomes twisted and turns a shade of purple, so deep I can hardly make out his features. Theo senses a need to divert Carboni's attention from me and begins to play the recorded conversation of Roberto and me from the previous night. At this moment the invited guests at the brunch gasp and groan. Horrified, each person in attendance struggles to find a chair or a wall to lean against.

Clarissa stands at the doorway and holds onto the doorsill in shock. A nearby policeman notices her distress and steadies her. She nods to him and whispers, "I'm okay." Then she shouts at the governor, "How could you, Roberto? My brother loved you. And your wife! What kind of husband are you? How could you do that? What kind of monster are you?"

Jenny stands straight, holds her ground and says with an eerie calm, "If I had a gun right now, I would use it. It would be worth prison to see you dead. You are nothing but scum. You bastard!" She looks at the uniformed policemen posted by the dining room entrance. "Please, take him away. Get him out of our home. I...we can't stand to look at him a moment longer."

Roberto shrugs, knowing for certain his time of reckoning has come. He diverts his eyes from the sisters and starts to walk to the policemen posted at the doorway. "You can take me away. Please don't handcuff me."

One of the policemen grabs him when he takes his first step. "Not on your life, buster. You will be treated and processed like any other felon. Put your hands behind your back and don't give me a struggle."

The other policeman pats the governor down like a common criminal. But my thinking on the matter is, he is not common at all, but base, evil, malevolent—the worst kind of criminal. The policeman finds a gun strapped to Carboni's calf, hidden by his trousers. The worm. I could have guessed that would be there. The policeman removes it, hands the gun to Theo, and proceeds to read the governor his rights.

I feel no sorrow at this moment, only relief. Relief that Walter, Aunt Hattie, Steve, Barry, the Van Beek sisters and I are still alive and intact. I cannot say the same thing for Carboni and his gang of thugs. The ones still living will spend the rest of their lifetime in some remote prison, counting the hours and meditating on their crimes. Not a fun way to spend your life, but then again, they all made their choices to become monsters, or to follow monsters. Monsters are not born. They develop over time. They choose to do dirty deeds. No one forces another human being to commit murder. No one forces another human being to become so self-absorbed and without conscience that their dirty deeds become more important than the life of another person. People like Carboni can justify any evil they do without a blink of the eye.

I meditate on the past twenty-four hours. Thoughts come into my head and will not go away. I am responsible for the taking of a life in self-defense. I know my deeds will haunt me. But I know I am not a monster. Yes, I will have nightmares for a time and relive the horror until my mind can deal with the entire ordeal. I will need to put it in its proper place. But I will get over it. I *will* get over it. I have Walter and Father Don, Steve, Barry and Theo to help me. Don't know about my mom. I don't want to burden her nor my brother. God, how I miss them right now. It seems ages since I saw them. I will not be able to hide this caper from them, but I don't know how to tell them.

Walter takes my hand and squeezes it. I lean against his body and feel a wonderful calm, a calm that comes from having an enormous overwhelming weight lifted off of me and thrown into the abyss. I can breathe again. Carboni is led out of the Van Beeks' living room, into the foyer and out the front door. The loud sound of the door shutting permeates the room.

Looking up at Walter, I study his face and his curly black hair that keeps falling in his face. *I love him so much.* As he kisses me on the cheek, I melt into him. "Walter, how soon can we go home?" Then I burst into tears and collapse in his arms.

Epilogue

We stay at the Van Beek's home with Aunt Hattie until multiple cleaning crews restore her house to normal. Well, as normal as it can be after the dead and injured bodies on her stairs are removed and remnants of their sojourn are gone. One crewmember even tries to fix the raven statue, but I am afraid that sculpture is permanently bent.

In a few days, after we return her home, Aunt Hattie tells me she likes the raven statue better that way—says it now looks like the old bird is ready to take off in flight. "Quoth the Raven 'Nevermore'," she recites and chuckles, "Thanks to you, Tangie, I have a new appreciation for Edgar Allen Poe."

I laugh with her despite my trepidation about leaving her alone in Newport. But she insists we return to the Pacific Northwest. "You two have your own lives. Your home is in Seattle. Go. Enjoy yourselves. I am sure you will be back to see your old aunt in no time."

"Aunt Hattie, for the last time, you are not old and we love you. Why don't you come out and spend Christmas with us, or come with us now— for Halloween and Thanksgiving?"

Aunt Hattie shakes her head and smiles. "I will be fine. I've got lots to keep me busy. And, I am giving you orders: You are not to worry about me."

Tears fall down my cheeks as I kiss her goodbye. "Please tell Louisa that I love her art and especially the paintings Walter purchased. She is quite talented, and such a fine helper for you. I know we are leaving you in good hands. And give our love and thanks to the Van Beek sisters, again."

Walter hugs his aunt. "We'll be back if we are needed for any hearing or trial that may come up, but my guess is Carboni will take that plea deal with the Feds. No doubt he's thinking that will keep his name out of the news, minimize the damage to his reputation, and spare the wrath of his children. Probably not save his reputation, but maybe he'll save the taxpayers some money for a change."

"My dear nephew, I don't care what he does as long as he never gets out of prison."

I give her another hug. "Please Aunt Hattie, think about joining us in the Northwest for Christmas. Walter and I have lots of room."

"Maybe, but I have a feeling you'll be back here after Christmas. So I'll wait for you two to return."

Walter wipes a tear from his eye as he hugs his aunt for the last time. "Our taxi's here. We'll miss you, Aunt Hattie. Please take care of yourself. Be good. Say goodbye to Jenny and Clarissa for us."

"I will dears, and thank you. Thank you for setting things right."

"We could not have done it without you, Aunt Hattie." I feel my eyes once more welling with tears.

Walter taps me on my shoulder and whispers in my ear.

My face brightens up. "Oh, yes! Aunt Hattie, I, we, wanted to get you something special, as a memory of us and Pebbles, and here she is!" Walter picks up a package, with an open lid. I pull a little Westie out of the box like I am doing the ol' magician hat trick. However, I use two hands and cradle the puppy in my arms like a precious jewel. "I hope you don't mind a furry beast inhabiting your home on a permanent basis."

Aunt Hattie's eyes tear up, as I hand her the little fur ball. "Mind? Of course not! I was wondering how I was going to get over missing Pebbles, and here is this wonderful present to help me." Her eyes light up as she hugs the snow-white bundle and her smile turns into a grin. "Bless you child. She's special. I will love her and keep her beside me, just as you do your little pooch."

Walter grins back at her. "Do you know what you will call her, Aunt Hattie?"

"Haven't got a clue, but when I do, you will be the first to know!"

I pet the rambunctious puppy and hug Aunt Hattie one last time, before leashing Pebbles and walking to the waiting taxi. Walter lingers a bit to say his final farewell to his aunt. I look at them together and my heart melts. She is Walter's only family member and they live on opposite coasts. I watch as the little Westie licks Walter's face, and then Aunt Hattie's. Walter gives his aunt one last hug, then joins me at the taxi. We jump in the back seat with Pebbles in tow and wave goodbye. "Love you! We'll call from Seattle."

I keep my eyes on her, our dear, sweet, unbelievably brave Aunt Hattie, as the driver pulls his cab away. That vision of Aunt Hattie, with the snow-white puppy licking her cheek, as she stands tall and waves at us, will be etched in my memory. I notice the red scarf draped around her shoulders matches the maple leaves falling from the trees and covering the ground. Fall has finally come to Newport. As we leave its streets, which are lit up with colors of crimson, orange and yellow, I turn to Walter and say, "Sometimes sadness and joy come together and it is hard to tell them apart, kind of like autumn."

Walter smiles and kisses my forehead. "Tangie, the philosopher. I love you, Sweetheart."

With my honey's arm around me, I sigh and relax in the backseat for the short ride to Providence International Airport, just as his cell rings.

"Un huh. Yes. Sounds great. When? New Year's Eve? Fantastic! Tangie will love it! I can tell you that for sure. Talk to you soon. Yes, when we get home. *Adios*, Bento, *Gracias.*"

"Okay, Walter. Who's Bento? And what will Tangie love?"

"I have a surprise for you, my lovely Angelina."

"Yes, but who is Bento?"

"Bento is one of my musician buddies. He plays a killer sax. He's been playing in Europe with his band—well, a jazz combo really—and he needs a pianist." Walter smiles. "And a flutist."

"Oh, no. I see that look in your eyes. You aren't going to get me to play the flute. I stink. I am happy for you. Play the piano, but leave me out of it. I'm just a college flute player. I'm not a pro like you."

"Tangie, honey. You're good. I've heard you play. You may not know it, but you are great. Relax. They only need a flute player for two pieces and since you'll be there with me, you can do that electric flute thing you do so well."

"That was in college."

369

"But this is in Paris, on New Year's."

"Paris? On New Year's?"

"Yes! We can spend your favorite holidays, Halloween, Thanksgiving and Christmas in Seattle. After that, we can stop for a short visit, after Christmas, with Aunt Hattie, before flying to France for our gig. We'll celebrate New Year's Eve at the Eiffel Tower, before joining Bento. You and I could use a break from all of this...this trauma. We could have a second honeymoon."

"Oh, Walter."

"So, you'll do it?"

"Yes! Of course I'll do it. Playing in Paris! Wow! But I'll have to practice. Big time."

"So will I. We'll practice together. We've got two months. And Angelina..."

"Yes, my love..."

"In Paris, we won't always be playing with Bento's combo. We'll have time to enjoy each other. We'll experience the city and all its treasures. We'll go on tours to the countryside, with no interruptions from anyone."

"Can you promise me that?"

"I can try."

"Oh Walter!" I grab my lover around his broad shoulders and hug him, tightly. If I weren't in the taxi, I'd be jumping up and down. The driver glances back at me to see if I am all right, as I rock the taxi. I smile at him and nod that all is well. Then I focus on Walter. "Paris! I love Paris. With you, it will be heaven. Oh my goodness! Yes! We'll enjoy two months home in Seattle, with Mom, Charles, Bryan, Andee and the twins. Then we'll fly back to see Aunt Hattie en route to Paris, the City of Lights. What could possibly go wrong this time?"

"Not a thing, my love. Not a thing."

"Promise?"

"I said so."

I notice Walter has his fingers crossed behind his back. Well, I know I can't have everything. Peace of mind has not always come my way. But *Paris*! Paris, France. I'm ready, willing and eager—to heck with the odds. We'll sort things out as they come. Come wind, come fire, come storm, I am not afraid and I will be the mistress of my destiny. I lean over and give

Walter an extra-special kiss. We do not break our embrace until the taxi stops in front of the airport, and by then any fear I have of the unknown is gone, or safely buried in a far corner of my mind where it will stay for a long time.

Made in the USA
Las Vegas, NV
03 June 2022

49747602R00213